NELLIE'S WAR

When the Fire Brigade find sixteen-year-old Vicky Hobson's shoe in the rubble of the bombed Barratts Orphanage, it seemed she was the only fatality. But Vicky had stumbled from the rubble, dazed and unable to remember her name. She is taken in by 'Toff' Hecht and his gang of runaway teenage evacuees, but when tragedy strikes, she moves on, finding a job as a waitress. Eventually, she is given a glimpse into the world of the music hall in her new life as a theatrical seamstress, but even though she is happy with her new life, she still thinks of 'Toff'.

NELLIE'S WAR

NELLIE'S WAR

by

Victor Pemberton

Magna Large Print Books
Long Preston, North Yorkshire,
England.

British Library Cataloguing in Publication Data.

Pemberton, Victor
  Nellie's war.

A catalogue record for this book is
available from the British Library

ISBN 0-7505-1371-3

First published in Great Britain by Headline Book Publishing, 1998

Cover illustration © Gordon Crabb by arrangement with Headline
Book Publishing Ltd.

The right of Victor Pemberton to be identified as the author
of this work has been asserted by him in accordance with the
Copyright, Designs and Patents Act, 1988

Published in Large Print 1999 by arrangement with Headline Book
Publishing Ltd.

Magna Large Print is an imprint of
Library Magna Books Ltd.
Printed and bound in Great Britain by
T.J. International Ltd., Cornwall, PL28 8RW.

Author's note:

Some of the specific theatre performances mentioned in this book are fictional, but are true to the spirit of the time.

For Peter and Josephine, my dear friends.

Dedicated to that great little dancing duo, Les Street and Jose, and all the wonderful troupers of the British Music Hall, who kept a smile on our faces during those dark days of the Second World War.

Chapter 1

Thick black smoke spluttered up from the wreckage of the old Victorian building and was gradually swallowed by the brooding mist of a dark November night. The ferocious glow of endless fires cast sinister dancing shadows across the surface of the huge mound of red bricks and masonry, and the crackling sound of burning timbers competed with the frantic clanging of ambulance and fire-engine bells and the constant overhead roar of enemy planes discharging their deadly cargo of high-explosive bombs. Soon the place would be crawling with people from the emergency services, desperately searching the debris for any survivors. But this 'incident' was just one of many in the surrounding area that night, and it would have to wait its turn for attention.

It was several minutes before the first sign of life appeared—tiny pink fingertips, pushing their way through several layers of cement dust, desperately searching for an escape. Finally, the fingers forged enough passage for a hand. It was a small hand, connected to a thin, white, delicate arm, streaked with bleeding scratches. But it was an obstinate hand, for it suddenly tensed and formed into a clenched fist which pushed and shoved until it had cleared a way for a shoulder, then the other shoulder, and

9

finally the head itself. It was a young head, with a face covered in white dust, and straggly, mousey-coloured hair that was gritty with chips of red brick and broken glass. It was only when the raw fingertips managed to clear the eyes of thick white dust that the outline of a face began to emerge. It was a girl, a teenager of about fifteen or sixteen, whose eyes were brown and oval-shaped, and glistening with the reflection of the fires raging around her.

After a hard struggle, she managed to release herself from the rubble she was pinned beneath. But when she tried to move her right foot, she found it obstinately wedged between a shattered chest of drawers and a pile of bricks. It took supreme effort to free herself completely, and when she finally did, she was engulfed by a burning pain from a long gash in her left leg, from which blood was seeping through the white dust that covered it. Using her elbows for support, she eased herself up, and, once she was confident enough to move, she gradually began to pick her way cautiously across the rubble. But when she tried to stand upright, it was with great difficulty, for not only was her injured leg stiff and painful, but she discovered that she had lost her shoes.

A few minutes later, the whole place was flooded with bright white lights, and Alsatian tracker dogs were sniffing out the rubble for any signs of human life. By the time the emergency services arrived, the teenage survivor was already making her way along a wide main road. She had to tread carefully in order to avoid the broken glass from shattered shop windows all along the street. It wasn't easy, for she was in a daze, not knowing who or where she was, or what had happened to her. All around, people were rushing past, desperate to get to the devastation of the latest bomb blast, unaware of the small teenage girl who had just pulled herself out of the debris. Sirens wailed, ambulance bells clanged, anti-aircraft shells exploded in the dark sky above, and in between all this was the sound of anxious voices calling out the names of friends, relatives or neighbours who might be buried beneath the wreckage. The year was 1940. And this was the ugly face of war.

Several hours later, the teenage girl was still wandering the streets aimlessly. The constant barrage of anti-aircraft guns had gradually come to a halt, and the air was once again relatively silent. But it was still pitch dark, and her flimsy cotton dress was no protection against the biting cold. She couldn't feel the cold, however, perhaps because she was too dazed, or because the pain from the gash in her leg was distracting her from any discomfort. Her mind was unable to take anything in; she had not even noticed that she had found her way into a narrow, unlit back street that had seemingly been untouched by the night's air raid. After a while she found herself at the bottom of a small flight of stone steps. Her ice-cold feet were unable to walk any further, so she started to climb the steps, with difficulty, one at a time. At the top, a large arch-shaped door was partly open. It was quite heavy to move and she had to use all the little strength she had left to squeeze herself inside.

She found herself in a strange, unfamiliar place. It was like a large, narrow hall, with high stone walls and stained-glass windows, and carved stone faces and coloured pictures. At the front of the hall to one side was a tall statue of a woman with what seemed like a scarf over her head. Her eyes looked almost real. Two tall candles burning brightly nearby cast eerie shadows on the high ceiling above. Rows and rows of long wooden benches led into the gloom. This place was unlike anything the girl had ever seen before. Exhausted, she stretched out on one of the benches. It was only a few moments before her eyes closed, and in her sleep she saw so much. Young people of her own age, laughing, chasing each other mischievously in a playground. She could even see herself ...

Toff had never robbed a church before. The idea had always given him an uncomfortable feeling, especially as he was brought up in the Jewish faith which condemned stealing as a major sin. But he had heard rumours that the doors of St Mary Magdalene's Roman Catholic Church in Bedale Street were never locked, and that there were always a few coins lying in the collection plate just by the main door. So his mind was made up. Funds were getting low. This was no time for a guilty conscience.

'But what 'appens if we get nicked?' asked

Nutty who, at fourteen, was the youngest of this gang of vacs, or evacuees, who had returned to live on the streets of London in preference to the safety of country homes belonging to unfriendly strangers. 'The cops'll frow the book at us for doin' over a church.'

'We're not doing over a church,' replied Toff. He was already quite tall for his sixteen years and, unlike the others, spoke with no trace of East End Cockney, which was why they called him Toff. 'In any case, we've never been nicked before, and we're not going to be this time either.'

The others agreed. There were only eight of them in all, and they'd had a busy night doing over people's houses during one of the fiercest air raids of the Blitz so far.

Toff blew out the candle, leaving only the flickering light from the embers of a dying fire. There was nothing left in what was once the back parlour of Dicks' Hardware Shop, for an oil bomb two weeks before had virtually gutted the place, leaving only a charred table, a few chairs, and the remains of a floral patterned sofa. 'Anyway, we don't all have to go to the church,' Toff said, tying a heavy woollen scarf over his head and round his neck. 'Rats and Bonkers, you can come with me. The rest of you can carry on doing Dalston.'

Nutty, for one, looked relieved. During air raids, he much preferred doing 'safe' houses, where he was quite sure the occupants were taking cover in an outside shelter.

Rats and Bonkers were uneasy. Since joining

the gang, they had become something of a double act. They were both aged fifteen and not only thought alike, they had so many similar features that some people thought they were brothers, which they weren't. They both wore nicked men's overcoats that were far too big for them, but they didn't at all mind how weird they looked; at least the coats kept them warm during their nightly winter forays into other people's homes.

'Is it really worf doin' a church?' asked Bonkers, who was an inch taller than his other half and wore a battered old RAF cap halfway down his forehead. 'I mean, they don't get much in them collection plates.'

'A quid at the most,' added Rats, whose trilby covered his ears.

Toff tensed. 'A quid is a quid!' he snapped. 'We've got hardly nothing left in the kitty, and if we don't do something about it pretty soon, we're going to have to spend every night looking for grub.'

'But what about the Clapton Road vacs?' called Shortso from the doorway; he got his nickname because of his short back-and-sides haircut.

'What about them?' Toff growled without bothering to look at Shortso.

'I hear they work the Bedale Road area,' said Nutty, whose voice was squeaky and several octaves higher than the others'. 'If we muscle in on their territory, there'll be trouble.'

Toff swung round to address all the shadowy faces surrounding him. 'Look, if there's trouble,

14

we'll give as good as we get!' He pushed his way to the door. 'If anyone wants to come with me,' he said as he went, 'they can come. The rest of you can please yourselves.'

For a moment, no one moved. Rats and Bonkers were the first to follow. Although they didn't fancy the idea of a punch-up with the Clapton Road vacs, they knew only too well that without Toff they hadn't a chance in hell of surviving life out on the streets.

From the outside, St Mary Magdalene's Church wasn't a very imposing building. It was built around the turn of the century to establish a Roman Catholic presence in this part of the East End and had had to rely mainly on public contributions to keep it in good repair. The war had already taken its toll on the place; the exterior red bricks and stucco were pitted with holes and abrasions from a bomb blast at a nearby secret ammunitions factory. But St Mary Magdalene's had retained its dignity, and prided itself on never locking its doors; anyone, rich or poor, could take spiritual respite from the nightly air raids.

By the time Toff, Rats, and Bonkers reached the seedy back street, all hell had broken loose again overhead and the sky was vibrating to a barrage of ack-ack fire. The three of them eased their way silently through the half-open church door without touching it.

Toff signalled to his companions not to speak until they had checked the place out, so for a while they stood in silence in the shadows

15

watching the light from the two huge flickering candles cast eerie shadows across the tall stone walls right up to the eaves of the plain arched ceiling.

'The collection plate's over there,' Toff whispered, indicating the font. 'See what you can find. I'll have a quick look to see if there's anything we can flog.'

Rats and Bonkers were both wearing old army boots, so their efforts to tiptoe quietly to the collection plate were not entirely successful.

Toff used the torch he had taken from someone's bicycle to make his way cautiously down the central aisle. There wasn't too much life left in the battery but there was enough to pick out the seemingly endless rows of stark wooden pews on each side as he went. When he finally reached the two wide steps which led up to the area in front of the altar, he paused for a moment, taking in the strange objects and tall candles that were picked out in the fading beam of his torchlight. He felt strange standing here, almost as though he was smaller in size than he actually was. It was the same feeling that he had had before the war, when he was a small boy standing with his father before the holy tabernacle in the synagogue, with its altar of incense and golden candlestick. As his torchlight picked out the plain, simple cross on the wall behind the altar, he felt uneasy, for if he were to steal from this holy place, it would be like stealing from his father's own place of worship. He quickly moved on until he reached the statue of the Madonna, beneath which were two lit candles and various scraps of paper which he discovered were notes left by worshippers. 'Dear Mother Mary,' read one, 'please protect my family against the bombs.' 'Dear Mother Mary,' read another, 'please end the war.' Toff could read no more. He turned off the torch.

'There's nuffink 'ere!' came a strangulated whisper from behind.

Toff turned, to find Rats making his way up the aisle.

'A tanner and two farvins,' he complained. 'It weren't worf the effort.'

'Sixpence is better than nothing at all,' Toff replied, holding out one hand. 'It'll buy us a couple of loaves and some milk.'

Rats reluctantly dropped the sixpence into the palm of Toff's hand.

'Toff!'

Toff and Rats turned with a start. Bonkers was rushing up the aisle towards them, the steel tips of his boots echoing on the stone floors as he came.

'There's someone 'ere!' he spluttered, his voice only just audible. 'Up the back!'

Toff immediately put a finger to his mouth, warning the other two to keep quiet. Then he slowly moved along one of the pews to the far aisle, keeping in the shadows as much as possible. Rats and Bonkers followed him. When they reached the back of the church, Bonkers pointed silently in the direction from which he had heard the movement. In one swift action, Toff turned on his bicycle torch and shone the beam along the last but one pew from the back. As he did so, there was a groaning sound. Bonkers gasped.

The beam from Toffs torch quickly passed along the pew until it picked out the tattered figure of a young teenage girl, curled up and fast asleep.

'It's a gel!' squealed Rats, suddenly scared by the echo his own voice was making.

Toff edged his way along the pew until his torch beam finally rested on the face of the girl. He was shocked by her appearance, the cuts on her face and arms, and the white dust and small pieces of rubble still embedded in her hair. But the real shock was when his torch beam found the long gash in her leg, which was oozing blood, and her feet which were also cut and bleeding.

'Blimey!' was all Bonkers could say as he and Rats peered at the girl from the pew just in front.

'Is she dead?' asked Rats nervously.

'Take the torch,' instructed Toff, handing the torch to Rats who directed the beam straight at the girl's face.

Toff bent down and gently prodded her shoulder with his hand. 'Are you all right, miss?' he asked softly. 'Miss?'

There was no response from the girl.

'She *is* dead!' gulped Rats.

Toff tried again. 'Miss?' he called, carefully using one finger to clear away some of the girl's dust-filled hair from her eyes. 'Miss? Are you all r—?'

The girl's eyes suddenly sprang open, and with a startled yell she sat bolt upright.

Rats and Bonkers immediately ducked for cover.

Toff grabbed hold of her shoulders and held on to them. 'It's all right! It's all right. I won't hurt you.'

By now the girl was almost hysterical, and struggling to get up. 'Leave me alone!' she yelled over and over again, her voice echoing up to the high ceiling.

'What's happened to you?' Toff said, trying to restrain her. 'You're bleeding all over.'

'Leave me alone! Leave me alone!'

'You're injured,' yelled Toff as he struggled to hold on to her. 'You're badly injured. You need help!'

Suddenly the girl slumped into his arms.

Rats and Bonkers were horrified. 'Crikey,' gulped Rats. 'She's dead!'

'She's not dead,' snapped Toff. 'Get round here quick. Give me a hand.'

The two boys climbed over the pew and helped Toff lower the girl gently back on to the bench.

'Rats,' Toff said urgently. 'Give me your scarf, and one of your bootlaces. You too, Bonkers.'

'What?' protested Rats.

'What for?' squealed Bonkers indignantly.

'Don't ask questions! Just do it!'

Rats and Bonkers took off their long woollen scarves and reluctantly handed them over to Toff. Then they sat down and began the arduous task of untying a lace from one each

19

of their boots. Toff propped the bicycle torch on the pew in front of the bench where the girl was lying. He took out a handkerchief from his trouser pocket, which he used to wrap round the gash on the girl's injured leg. Then he took off his own cotton scarf and wrapped that round the wound as well.

'What are we doin' all this for?' complained Bonkers miserably as he held out his bootlace. 'She oughta be in a 'ospital or somefin'.'

Toff was now carefully wrapping one of the girl's badly lacerated feet in Rats' scarf. 'She's not going to a hospital. She's coming back with us.'

'What?' gasped Rats. 'Yer can't do that.'

'Why not?'

''Cos she's a gel,' replied Rats as he finished untying his own bootlace. 'We don't 'ave no gels wiv us.'

'Anyway, 'ow we gonna move 'er?' added Bonkers. 'Look at 'er. She's out fer the count.'

'We'll use the pram, the big one,' said Toff, who was now wrapping the girl's other foot in Bonkers' scarf.

'Yer don't mean the one we use fer carryin' the goods around?' asked Rats indignantly. 'We'll never get her in there!'

'Stop griping, Rats!' snapped Toff. He used the two boys' bootlaces to tie the scarves round the girl's bloody feet. 'Both of you get back to the shop and bring that pram here as fast as you can. It'll be daylight in another couple of hours. We've got to get her back before the All Clear.'

Rats and Bonkers knew better than to try to argue with Toff. Although he hadn't been brought up on the streets like they had, he was still the boss of the outfit, and it was his brains that were keeping them and all the others from starving. So they did as they were told and hurried out of the church.

After they had gone, Toff took off his duffel coat and covered the girl with it. He picked up his torch and directed the beam straight on to her face. He was intrigued to know who this mysterious creature was, and how she had received her terrible injuries. As he bent down to take a closer look at her soft but badly drawn and scratched face, he told himself he ought to do what Bonkers had suggested, and just take her to the nearest hospital to be looked after by those who knew how. But no. There was something about that face, the expression, the high cheek bones, and the almost white complexion and full lips, something quite sensual and hypnotic.

He couldn't let her go. Not now.

It was a dazzling white light. Her eyes couldn't really cope with it, not for a few moments anyway. But gradually she felt adventurous enough to open them again, and when she did, it wasn't too difficult to see the paraffin lamp suspended from a piece of wire dangling from the ceiling just above her. When she tried to sit up, a sharp pain shot across her neck and down her spine. She felt as though she had been dragged through a hedge backwards;

21

her entire body seemed to be a mass of bruises. And when she put her fingers up to her face, the cuts and scratches there seemed to be wide open. Her injured leg and both her feet were burning hot, as though she was lying on a bed of hot ashes. Only then did she realise that she was in fact lying on something quite different—a rather smelly mattress laid out on the stone floor of a totally bare room. For a moment, she panicked. She had no idea what had happened to her, where she was, or where she came from.

'How are you feeling?'

The male voice came from the other side of the room, but when she turned to look, all she could see was a shadowy figure in the corner.

'Who are yer?' she asked tentatively, her throat parched from the amount of dust she had swallowed beneath the debris of the bomb blast. 'W—where am I?'

The figure slowly came across to her. 'My name's Martin. But nobody calls me that round here.' As he leaned down towards her, the bright paraffin light picked out the strong features of a good-looking teenage boy. 'They call me Toff,' he said with a wry smile. 'Apparently I talk posh.' He drew a little closer, so that his face seemed almost larger than life. 'How about you?' he asked. 'What's your name?'

The girl didn't reply. Her mind was confused, and all she could do was look at him.

'What's your name?' Toff asked again. 'Aren't you going to tell me?'

'Dunno.'

'Don't know your own name?'

She shook her head.

'Where d'you come from?'

Again, she shook her head.

'Don't you know what happened to you?'

The girl was becoming irritated. 'Why all the questions?' she snapped.

Toff wasn't offended. He was only too aware that she was still suffering from shock. 'You've had a bad time,' he said. 'When we found you, we thought you were going to die. Anyway, you're going to be all right. I managed to patch up your leg and feet.'

The girl immediately threw back the eiderdown and duffel coat that covered her. Her right leg and both feet were swathed in bandages. The smell of disinfectant was overpowering. 'What have you done to me?' she wailed. 'I can't move my legs!'

Toff tried to calm her. 'There's nothing to worry about,' he said reassuringly. 'I cleaned up the gash on your leg with some disinfectant. Your feet too. They were in a terrible state. I remember how my father used to clean up wounds. He's a doctor in casualty at the Royal Northern.'

The girl looked devastated. 'What happened to me?'

Toff knelt beside her. 'That's what we'd all like to know. Don't you remember anything? Anything at all?'

She shook her head slowly. 'I don't remember nuffin'.'

'Not even your name?'

Again, the girl shook her head.

Toff gave her a huge, comforting smile. 'Then we'll have to give you one, won't we? Until you get your memory back, that is.' He bent his head down lower to try to get her to look at him. 'OK?'

She looked up, and found herself staring straight into Toff's eyes. They were dark eyes, almost as dark as his jet-black hair. And, if he hadn't spoken in such a posh voice, she would have been convinced that he was a foreigner.

'Where did you find me?' she asked.

'In Saint Mary Magdalene's,' Toff replied, getting to his feet.

The girl looked puzzled.

'The Catholic church in Bedale Street,' explained Toff. 'You must have gone in there to shelter from the air raid.' He looked at her. 'Unless you went there to pray.'

'Is that why *you* were there? To pray?'

Toff went to the paraffin lamp, raised the glass, turned down the wick, and blew out the flame. 'I don't pray any more. I used to, when my father took me to the synagogue. But not any more.'

Daylight was filtering through an old blanket hanging across what was once the back door. Toff went across and drew it to one side. Dull morning light indicated the start of a new day. For a moment, Toff just stood there, looking out solemnly at the grey November mist and the ruins of what had once been a row of shops. Then he reached under his pullover and retrieved a half-smoked cigarette from the top pocket of his shirt.

'Are you old enough to smoke?' he asked.

The girl thought about this for a moment, then answered, 'I dunno.'

In the dim light, Toff turned to smile at her. 'You really have got a lot of catching up to do, haven't you?' He found a match in his trouser pocket, struck it against the cement pointing between the bricks on the wall, and lit his cigarette.

The smell of cigarette smoke drifted towards her. 'How did you get me here?' she asked.

Toff leaned his head against the wall and inhaled deeply. 'We had our own transport,' he said loftily.

The large baby's pram, covered with a pink eiderdown and pushed by three teenage boys through the streets of Dalston only a couple of hours ago, would have raised more than a few eyebrows if anybody had been about to see them. As it was, most people were taking cover from an air raid.

'You'll find out a lot about us, when you get to know us,' Toff said, taking one last puff of his cigarette before throwing it on to the stone floor and grinding his heel on it. Then he turned and made his way back to the girl, exhaling a spiral of smoke as he came. 'It's beginning to get light. I'd get some sleep if I were you. When you wake up, we'll see if we can get you some breakfast.'

The girl did in fact feel drowsy enough to lay her head back on the embroidered cushion.

25

Toff stood over her. 'You've got nothing to worry about now. I don't care what the others say. We're going to take care of you even if you are a girl.'

When she closed her eyes, Toff turned away. From the open doorway he said, 'How about Nellie? That was my gran's name. Nellie Esther Rabinovitz. Yes. Sounds good. Anyway, if it was good enough for my gran, it should be good enough for you. What d'you think?'

She didn't hear him. Nellie was already fast asleep.

Chapter 2

It was one of those mornings when the sun was absolutely determined to poke through the clouds. As it was November, it was quite a struggle, for the clouds were in reality dirty grey banks of fog, caused mainly by the endless coal fires belching up thick black smoke from chimneys all over North London. Fires caused by the previous night's air raid, one of the worst of the war so far, added to the smoke; a trail of havoc and destruction stretched from one side of the capital to the other.

Of all the worst hit targets of the night, none distressed the local community more than the bombing of Barratts' Orphanage in the Islington part of New North Road. Founded in 1902 by the late Louisa Barratt and her husband,

Clarence, the Victorian building had originally been the site of the Islington Workhouse, a hellhole of a place that had been closed down at the turn of the century because it was infested with rats and cockroaches. When Louisa and Clarence took over, they cleaned up the place with their own hands, converted the old building into living quarters for children, and opened their doors to any abandoned child or homeless waif the authorities decided to send to them. When the place was full, more than forty children of varying ages were given food, board, and loving care and attention there. When Louisa died in 1936, her husband decided he could no longer cope with the stress and strain of running the orphanage on his own, so he handed it over to a much younger woman, Ethel Ackroyd, from Yorkshire, who immediately embraced the young boarders in her charge as her own family. Both staff and orphans adored her, for she treated everyone the same, with absolutely no favourites—with one possible exception.

The destruction of Barratts' Orphanage by a high-explosive bomb was a tragedy. By the grace of God no one was killed; at the time of the explosion, all the staff and boarders were sheltering in the vaults beneath the old workhouse building—all, that is, except one.

'If she's under that rubble,' warned Fire Brigade Officer Mick Jenkins, 'she wouldn't have stood a chance.' He and his men had been working all night searching for even the faintest sign of life beneath the debris, but now grim reality had to be faced. 'She's gone, I'm afraid.'

Ethel Ackroyd looked as though all the blood had drained from her body. 'Don't give up. Please don't give up,' she said, her tired pale blue eyes pleading. 'We can't just abandon Vicky. She's got so much to live for.'

The group of orphanage staff with Ethel lowered their heads sadly. They knew how guilty she was feeling, but it was unjustified guilt. Vicky Hobson was a rebel. If she had got herself killed, then it was her own fault.

Ethel pulled up the collar of her camelhair overcoat and tried to wrap it closer round her neck. Although she appeared tough, it was well known that she was very emotional, and when anything happened to one of her flock, she felt as though her insides had been torn apart. 'I should never have gone down that shelter knowing she wasn't there,' she said, her Yorkshire accent now only very slight after years of living and working in London. 'Oh, why wouldn't she ever do what she was told? Where was she when the air raid started? She must have heard the siren.'

Before her were the ruins of the old Barratts' building, the timber beams still smouldering from the fire that had raged through it. It was a truly tragic sight, with the remains of toys and teddy bears and articles of children's clothing scattered everywhere. The scene was now calmer than the previous night but there was an air of deep despondency among the rescue workers, a mixture of frustration and anger that an

28

orphanage could be the victim of such wanton, mindless destruction. It was a miracle that there was apparently only one fatality. If the staff had not herded the youngsters into the shelter as quickly as they had, it would have been a very different story.

'It's no use hanging around here now, dearie,' said grim-faced Mrs Hare, the orphanage cook. She put her arm round Ethel's waist as they watched the weary rescue workers clambering over what was left of the old building. 'It's all over now. We can't bring back what's gone for ever.'

Well-intentioned though it was meant, Mrs Hare's remark irritated Ethel. 'You're wrong, Mrs Hare,' she replied firmly, climbing up on to a lump of masonry. 'This is not the end of Barratts'. It'll take more than Hitler to destroy a lifetime's work.'

Mrs Hare brushed away a tear. The kindly, plump old woman had always been a mother figure to the children, and she found it hard to come to terms with the fact that 'the family' had been broken up in such a way. 'I can't bear the thought that we'll never see young Vicky again,' she sniffed, dabbing her eyes with her tear-drenched ball of handkerchief. 'She was a handful all right, even though she was only an 'alf-pint. But I'll miss 'er. Oh yes. I'll miss that real stubborn streak, that's fer sure.'

Ethel refused to give in to her own feelings of total emptiness. Despite being the rebel of the orphanage, Vicky Hobson, or 'Half-Pint' as she was known because of her below-average height for her sixteen years, was Ethel's favourite. The girl had character, guts and determination, which had helped her to survive her life as an orphan. As she stood there, Ethel could see the girl in front of her, with her mousey-brown hair, oval-shaped eyes, and sallow complexion. But behind that frail look was a steel-like obstinacy that reminded Ethel of what she used to be like when she was that age back home in rural Yorkshire. 'We don't give up till we know, Mrs Hare,' she said, her face grim and determined as her eyes scanned the remains of the orphanage. 'As far as I'm concerned, Vicky's still alive until they find—until they find her.'

A few minutes later, a large crane appeared on the back of a lorry to start the arduous task of removing pile after pile of bricks and rubble. If Half-Pint was buried beneath the remains of the orphanage, the determined emergency workers would find her. So it was a depressing moment when, several hours later, they unearthed something of significance from the beneath the rubble of what had once been the girl's dormitory.

It was one of Half-Pint's shoes.

Nellie had no intention of lying flat on her back on a smelly, flea-infested mattress all day, shut up in the grubby, bombed-out remains of Dicks' Hardware Shop. She wasn't dying, she kept saying to herself, she wasn't ill, so why should she take orders from this toffee-nosed knuckle-head with the plum in his mouth? But when she threw back the pink eiderdown and tried to stand up, it was a different story. Despite the fact that her feet were swathed in bandages and smelt like a hospital, they hurt like mad. And the gash on her leg was throbbing, and the scratches on her face were smarting. If only she could remember what had happened last night. How had she reached that church? She must have got caught in an air raid, but where? And who was she? What was her real name, and where did she come from?

Daylight was now streaming into the dark room through the partially covered doorway. The fire in the grate had been allowed to go out and the room was freezing. Nellie picked up the eiderdown and wrapped it round her shoulders. The rough floor hurt her feet and she found it difficult to walk. Then she noticed that a large pair of women's warm indoor slippers had been left beside her mattress, so she carefully put them on. They fitted comfortably over her bandaged feet and she managed to shuffle towards the doorway.

Outside, Nellie found a scene of devastation. She had been brought to a bomb site. Four or five shops had been reduced to rubble, and the surrounding area of old terraced houses and a pub was pitted with blast damage, the windows boarded up with crude pieces of wood. She stared in horror at it all, shivering with cold.

'Feeling better?'

Nellie turned with a start to find Toff and a sea of cold red faces staring at her. 'What you lot gawpin' at?' she squawked, quick as a flash.

31

Toff grinned. 'Yes,' he said, 'you *are* better. We were very concerned about you.' He made a few steps towards her.

'Don't you come near me!' snapped Nellie, nearly tripping over her eiderdown as she backed away. 'Who are you lot?' She eyed them all up suspiciously. 'Why ain't you all in yer own 'omes?'

There was complete silence from the group. As well as Toff, Nutty, Shortso, Rats and Bonkers, there were several other teenage boys, all wearing a weird assortment of winter clothes that were either too big or too small for them.

'We don't have homes, Nell,' said Toff, who looked positively normal compared to his companions.

'Not since we got kicked out,' squealed Nutty, who was barely visible behind some of the taller boys.

Nellie was curious. 'What d'yer mean, kicked out?'

Toff looked around his pals then back to Nellie again. 'We're all evacuees. Nell,' he explained. 'Most of us were sent away from our homes as soon as war broke out. It was supposed to be for our own protection, because of the Blitz.'

'Ter get rid of us, more like!' yelled Shortso, digging his hands angrily into the pockets of his raincoat.

'The fact is,' continued Toff, 'none of us wanted to go. Well, not us lot anyway. They bunged us into all sorts of places out in the country, places like Hertfordshire, Surrey,

Wales, Somerset—everywhere.'

'Yeah!' piped Nutty. 'And wiv people we'd never met in our lives.'

'People who'd clack yer 'round the ear'ole if yer even opened yer mouf!' This from one of the boys at the back.

The others responded with a disapproving chorus of, 'Yeah!'

'Mind you,' said Toff, 'some were lucky. They found themselves a real cushy number, in far better homes than they'd come from. But not us,' he said.

Nellie looked at the faces in front of her, all of them young but disillusioned with life as they had lived it so far. 'So why don't yer just go back 'ome to yer mums and dads an' 'ave it out wiv 'em?' she asked.

'Because they wouldn't listen to us!' came the reply from a tall, thin boy of about fourteen, who looked as if he was in need of a decent meal.

'Once parents have made up their minds that what they're doing is good for their kids,' said Toff, in sadness rather than in anger, 'nothing will change them. That's how it was with my mother and father. They know best, and nothing in the whole wide world will ever change them.'

'S'pose they *are* right?' Nellie was now so cold she pulled the eiderdown right up over her head. 'S'pose they *did* send yer away fer yer own good?'

'It isn't true, Nell,' replied Toff, who had crossed his arms and put his hands under them to keep warm. 'Sending us off to live with other people was just an excuse to get us out of the way. Not for everyone, mind. But it was with us.' He twisted his head to look at his companions. 'That's how we came to meet up. That's why we decided to stick together.' He turned back to Nellie. 'That's the reason we live the way we do. We can't go home because they'd send us right back to where we came from.'

One or two of the boys decided they'd hung around long enough and wandered off. Nellie watched them go in bewilderment.

'Yer mean you're livin' out rough like this, in the streets?' she asked.

Toff smiled. 'It's not so bad, once you get used to it.'

'In this sorta wevver? 'Ow'd yer keep warm? 'Ow'd yer get grub?'

'We nick it,' said Rats. 'Durin' the air raids.'

'When they've all gone down the shelter,' added Bonkers.

Nellie was horrified and took a step back. 'You *nick* from people's 'ouses?'

'Only food and clothes,' said Toff quickly, trying to sound reassuring. 'We only take money as a last resort.'

'But that's breakin' the law!' Nellie's eyes were bulging with disapproval. 'Wot 'appens if the rozzers catch up wiv yer?'

The boys laughed. 'Rozzers can't catch us!' yelled Shortso who was perched on top of a pile of bricks. 'We're too clever by 'alf!'

Nellie's eyes scanned the bleak scene around her. Pile upon pile of rubble everywhere. Across the road, two drunken men came out of the pub; clearly its boarded-up windows were no hindrance to trade. As the door opened briefly, the sound of someone tinkling on a tinny piano inside was audible. The pianist had no ear for music, for it was a tuneless sound, but at least it lifted the gloomy, atmosphere; it was like an act of defiance in the unrelenting grind of war.

'So does this mean yer'll never go 'ome?' Nellie asked, her nose now red and numb with cold.

'We'll go 'ome when the war's over,' said Shortso. 'When they can't send us away no more.'

'Livin' in the country ain't like livin' round 'ere,' squeaked Nutty forlornly. 'It's too quiet.'

The others agreed.

Nellie was beginning to feel the strain of the extraordinary situation she found herself in. What was she doing with this wild bunch who were willing to forsake the comfort of their own homes to live rough in the streets of North London? Her head was thumping with pain and confusion. She wished she could remember who she was and where she came from.

'If you want, you can join us,' Toff said suddenly.

There was a gasp from some of the boys behind him.

'No!' protested Rats.

'She's a gel!' complained Bonkers.

'Yer remember wot we said, Toff,' grumbled Shortso. 'No gels!'

Toff paused briefly before turning to face the group. 'Listen, you lot,' he said calmly. 'Nell went through a hell of a time last night. Just look at her. She might have died if we hadn't got to her when we did.'

'No gels, Toff!' yelled one of the boys. 'Yer promised!'

Toff refused to be intimidated. 'It doesn't matter whether she's a girl or a bloke. What sort of people d'you think we are if we let her go off and live out rough on the streets? If Nell needs our help, we're going to give it. It's our duty to look after her.'

This angered Nellie. ''Ang on a mo!' she said. 'Who said anyfin' about me needin' anyone ter look after me?' In her anger, she threw the eiderdown from her shoulders to the ground. She was dressed in nothing more than the thin, tattered cotton frock she had been wearing when she clambered out of the ruins of the orphanage. 'I know 'ow ter take of meself, see! I got me own family ter go to, me own mum an' dad ter look after me. If you fink I'm goin' ter knock around the streets wiv the likes of you lot, yer've got anuvver fink comin'! Oh no. Me? I'm goin' straight back ter me own 'ome!'

She turned and started to climb over the rubble towards the street.

Toff watched her for a moment, then called, 'What home is that, Nell?'

Nellie came to an abrupt halt. She turned

slowly and gazed helplessly at the young faces staring at her.

Ethel Ackroyd spent the day with her staff, caring for the youngsters in her charge, trying to help them come to terms with the traumatic events of the night before. Thanks to the intervention of Islington Borough Council, Barratts' Orphanage had been given temporary accommodation in a local school which had been closed since the start of the Blitz. But there was no heating in the old building, and it was left to the voluntary services to provide food, clothes, and beds for the indefinite stay. The children were still in a state of shock after being rescued from their underground shelter, but most of them adapted pretty well to their new surroundings. At least they were all alive—except one.

'The last time I checked the top-floor dormitory,' said Martha Driscoll, who taught sewing and dress making to some of the older girls in the orphanage, 'Vicky was listening to *Variety Bandbox* on the wireless. She was the only one there. The others were downstairs playing table tennis.'

'What time was that?' asked Ethel, who hadn't touched the piping hot tomato soup that she and the rest of the staff were eating at a makeshift dinner table.

'Must have been soon after eight,' replied Martha. Her eyes were red and sore from crying. 'I blame myself,' she said, after trying unsuccessfully to swallow a mouthful of soup. 'If only I'd gone up to the dormitory as soon as

I heard that siren, Vicky would still be alive.'

'Don't talk like that, please, Martha,' said Ethel firmly. 'Vicky's not dead until we know—officially.'

'I think the chances are not good, Miss Ackroyd,' said Arthur Driscoll, Martha's husband, who helped out with sports and handicraft activities for the boys at Barratts'. 'I mean, let's face it, we've spent most of the day out there on the site but they still haven't found her.'

'They found her shoe,' replied Ethel, whose eyes were firmly fixed on the youngsters eating at tables around the bare old school hall.

Arthur exchanged a grim look with his wife. Only a few hours before, the chief fire officer at the scene had told him that there was not a chance in hell of finding Vicky alive. And even if they did, there would be very little left of her, for the dormitory on the top floor of the building would have taken the full brunt of the explosion. Arthur twisted the end of his thick moustache, trying to fight his own feelings of guilt about Vicky Hobson, for in his heart of hearts he knew that he had never liked her. Many a time he had heard the girl giving lip to his wife, and he had often wanted to give her a piece of his mind. Vicky was a real firecracker with a mind of her own. If anyone was going to get into trouble, it was inevitable that it should be her. And at a time like this—especially at a time like this—he felt nothing but a deep sense of guilt for even thinking of such things.

'It's so unfair,' said Martha, trying to keep her voice low in the sombre, unnatural atmosphere of children eating in virtual silence. 'Vicky wasn't a beautiful child, but she had such character. It's amazing when you think that she was barely five feet tall.' Once again she dabbed her eyes with her handkerchief. 'I remember once, when she was in knitting class, she asked me what it was like being married. I thought it was such an odd question from a girl who was no more than fifteen at the time. But she wanted to know. She really wanted to know. I don't think Vicky was ever a child. She was always a woman.'

The conversation was too maudlin for Ethel. 'If you'll excuse me,' she said, rising from the table, 'I must get some fresh air.'

By the time Ethel reached the bombed orphanage, the watery sun had already set, and the nightly November mist was undulating eerily around the narrow North London back streets. A small group of local manual workers had taken over from the emergency services at the bomb site. Ethel stared at the pitiful heap of personal belongings and children's toys that had been retrieved from the rubble. She had come here still clinging to a vestige of hope that the one missing youngster in her charge had been found alive, but the look on everyone's faces soon told her otherwise. Despite an all-day search, no trace had been found of Vicky Hobson. As mist and darkness descended on the sombre pile of bricks and stones, the search was abandoned until the next morning.

After the last workers had gone, Ethel climbed

up a flight of stone steps which had miraculously survived intact. They had led from the courtyard at the back of the orphanage up to one of the first-floor classrooms. As she stood on the top step, she sought solace in memories of the much-loved institution which only a few hours before had been her domain, her world, her kingdom. She could hear the sound of her children's voices, lining up for morning roll call or hurrying into the dining room for their midday meal. She could hear the little ones reciting the alphabet and multiplication tables, laughing, singing, and playing in the back courtyard. She could hear the babies crying in the nursery, those poor little unwanted creatures left abandoned on the orphanage doorstep by wayward mothers and uncaring fathers. Her mind was echoing to the sounds from her past. But no sound registered more than that of Vicky Hobson.

Standing alone on those steps in the dark, a tall but slight figure silhouetted against the final light of day, Ethel recalled the time when Vicky was first brought to Barratts'. It was sixteen or so years ago, soon after her father had been killed accidentally in a fall from scaffolding on a building site, and her mother, bereft and unable to cope, had thrown herself into the path of a train at Stepney Green Underground Station. Even then, Vicky had shown a determined, free-willed spirit. Like so many of the other young orphans at Barratts', she had grown up never knowing the love of real parents and, despite the efforts of so many, she had always been determined to live life her own way.

'*When I leave this place, I ain't never goin' ter come back.*' Ethel could hear Vicky's voice ringing in her mind as clearly as though she was standing in front of her right now. And she could see her face, pallid but defiant, lips curled and stiff, eyes staring straight through her—those wonderful brown, perfectly shaped eyes. '*I'm sick of bein' shut up in a prison. I'm sick of people lookin' down at me.*'

Ethel turned the words over and over in her mind. Why was the child so concerned about how small she was? Why did she think that such things were important? What Vicky lacked in height she made up for in personality. She was the most vivacious child Ethel had ever known, and when she wanted to, Vicky had the ability to make so many people laugh. Oh, how she yearned to see that face and to hear that defiant voice again. She refused to believe that the child had just vanished into thin air. She refused to believe that somewhere beneath those ruins Vicky Hobson wasn't mischievously hiding, just waiting to be found, waiting to get on with her life and make something of herself. And if she wasn't beneath the ruins, where was she?

Ethel pulled up the collar of her coat, adjusted her headscarf, and dug her hands deep into her pockets. And as she stood there, she vowed that, whatever happened, she would never allow Vicky to leave her. If that extraordinary girl was still alive, then Ethel Ackroyd would make it her mission in life to find her.

Suddenly the air was pierced by the wailing sound of the air-raid warning siren. Another night of horror was about to begin.

Chapter 3

It took Nellie several weeks before she plucked up enough courage to do her first 'job'. By then the swelling in her lacerated feet had subsided and, thanks to Toff's expert medical attention, learnt from his father, the gash in her leg had healed. In fact, Nellie had a lot to be grateful for. Toff had been wonderful to her, dressing her wounds, getting her warm clothes to wear and hot food to eat. Most admirable of all was the way he protected her from the boys in the gang. Since Nellie still had no idea who she was or where she came from, she had decided to take the plunge and join them. But being part of a street gang was one thing, breaking into someone's house in the middle of an air raid was something quite different.

'You don't have to do it if you don't want to,' said Toff reassuringly. 'This is really a boy's job. I know that.'

Nellie took umbrage at this. She was already dressed for the night's work, tucked up in a warm, newly stolen coat, with woollen gloves and a knitted hat. 'What d'yer mean, a boy's job?' she scowled indignantly. 'Yer fink I'm made of jelly or somefin'?'

'That's not what I'm saying, Nell.' Toff offered her a cup of tea that he had just stewed up in an old aluminium kettle over a makeshift fire indoors. 'I just don't want you to think we're forcing you to do something.'

Nellie grabbed the chipped cup. 'Let me be the judge of that, mate!'

Toff shrugged his shoulders and smiled.

When she saw his smile, Nellie suddenly felt guilty. The fact was that although she was getting a bit fed up with this boy looking after her like an old nanny, every time he looked at her, she was beginning to feel a bit funny inside. So she did her best to make sure that whenever he did smile at her, she averted her gaze.

Nellie warmed her hands round the cup and blew on the hot tea. 'Just tell me wot I'm s'posed ter do.'

Toff finished pouring a cup of tea for himself, then put a teaspoonful of dried milk into it. 'You don't have to do anything until we hear the siren,' he said. 'Then we'll take you down to this place near Highbury.'

Nellie was beginning to get nervous. ''Ighbury? Where's that?'

Toff looked at her. 'Don't you remember anything about anywhere?' he asked.

Nellie thought hard for a moment, then slowly shook her head.

Toff took his cup and crouched down on Nellie's mattress which had been laid on the floor just in front of the fire. For a moment he said nothing and just sipped his tea, staring into the flames of burning timber taken from the bombed buildings outside. The room was cosier since Nellie had first arrived; it was full of loot and supplies of food taken from people's houses during the nightly air raids. In one corner, tins of spam, dried eggs, packets of tea, and bottles of Camp coffee were stuffed untidily into wooden fruit boxes; warm coats, hats, and several pairs of shoes were stacked in a neat pile along one wall, together with several blankets and pillows. There was also a prize possession: a paraffin stove. Unfortunately it contained no paraffin.

'One of the boys has been watching this house we found,' Toff said. 'Two old women live there. I think they must be sisters or something. Anyway, they go down Highbury Tube every night at five on the dot. People shelter down there during the air raid. They never come back till the morning, till the all clear.'

Nellie now felt easy enough in Toff's company to join him in front of the fire.

'It's a nice house,' Toff continued. 'Three or four storeys high. In a terrace.' He turned to look at Nellie. 'They must be well-stacked.'

Nellie became aware that her heart was beating faster than normal. 'What do I 'ave ter do?' she said, the flickering flames of the fire reflected in her eyes.

Toff smiled. 'Nothing to it, really,' he said reassuringly. 'We'll get you in there. Just make your way to the kitchen, grab some food—fresh stuff if you can—then get the hell out of the place.' As they knelt there, Toff could almost hear Nellie's heart thumping. 'You really don't have to do it, Nell,' he said softly, sympathetically. 'It's not expected.'

Nellie looked up at him, but when her eyes met his, she quickly averted her gaze. 'I'm not scared or nuffin',' she said. 'It's just that I don't like the idea of takin' fings that don't belong ter me.'

Toff smiled again, then raised her chin so that she had to look at him. 'Sounds like you've been brought up the right way,' he said.

Nellie did a puzzled double take, and suddenly felt a cold chill down her spine.

And then came the wail of the air-raid siren.

Dolly and Mabel Gresham were late for the shelter that night. This was unlike them, for every day, immediately after they had had their afternoon nap and tea, they always made early preparations for their nightly trip to the shelter. It took them about ten minutes to walk from their house in Highbury New Park to the Tube station, for Mabel suffered from bad rheumatism in one of her thighs and their progress was slow, especially as they carried a deck chair each, together with a blanket and a flask of hot cocoa.

The tall, elegant, Edwardian house had been in the Gresham family for many years, and after their parents died, Dolly and Mabel, who had never married, lived there alone together. People in the neighbourhood knew very little about them for they kept themselves to themselves and never asked for help, even when some of their windows were blown in by a bomb which landed in a road close by. The house was a gem, with large rooms and a spacious kitchen and hall, and a long back garden where the sisters spent much of their time pruning and weeding during the summer months.

When the sisters came out through the front door and locked up, the air-raid siren had already sounded but enemy planes had not yet begun buzzing overhead. The sun had set and blackout curtains were firmly drawn. The wide tree-lined street was very dark, concealing Nellie, Toff, Shortso, and Nuts while they waited in silence until the two elderly sisters were well on their way to the Tube station.

'Go after them, Shortso,' whispered Toff, emerging from behind a tall elm tree. 'Whatever you do, don't let them out of your sight. If they change their mind and come back, get back here soon as you can.'

Shortso didn't have to be told twice. He hurried off into the darkness after the sisters.

'Wait out here, Nuts,' Toff instructed. 'We're going round the back. If there's any sign of anyone at all, you know what to do.'

Nuts didn't answer. He was well used to the routine.

'This way, Nell,' said Toff, gently pinching Nellie's arm and leading her off.

Nellie felt quite sick as she followed him across the street. It was pitch dark, and all she could see was a dim outline of the terrace. She could hear distant voices singing Christmas carols, and it made her realise just how close

46

Christmas was. How she wished she was sitting in some nice warm room sharing it with just about anybody other than this wild bunch of vacs.

Toff avoided the front door and led Nellie to an iron gate which gave access to the back garden. Once they had got that far, Toff decided it was safe enough to use his torch. But he played safe and kept the bright beam partially covered with one hand. 'There,' he whispered, directing the beam on to the upper part of a back window. 'The old girls always leave that window open. There's not much room to get in, but if you can get your head and shoulders through, I reckon you can make it. Now you know why we wanted you for this job.'

Nellie looked up at the small space she was expected to crawl through. 'I'll never get through that,' she protested, forgetting to whisper. Toff clamped his hand over her mouth to keep her quiet.

'There's nothing of you, Nell,' he whispered. 'You'll get through easy. I wish I was your size,' he added to spare her feelings.

Nellie didn't notice. She was feeling far too queasy about the whole thing.

'Here, take the torch,' Toff continued, giving it to her. 'I'll give you a bunk up. When you get inside, make your way down to the street door and let me in. OK?'

'I'll try,' was all Nellie could reply. Although her heart was racing, a sense of excitement was building in her. She watched Toff quietly roll an old water tub under the open window and carefully tip out the rainwater it contained. He turned it upside down and helped Nellie climb on to it. 'Wot 'appens if someone comes while I'm in there?' she asked anxiously.

'You'll have plenty of time,' whispered Toff. 'Nuts is on lookout. He'll give us a signal.'

Not at all reassured, Nellie turned off the torch, put it into her topcoat pocket, and with surprisingly little effort climbed up to the small open window. But even with her height and build, it was a struggle to squeeze through.

She dropped quietly on to the floor inside and froze, too nervous to turn on the torch. She could make nothing out in the darkness and had no idea what part of the house she was in. When she did finally turn on the torch, the beam picked out a single bed, a chair, and a washbasin on a pedestal table. The bedroom was small and cramped but to Nellie it seemed the height of luxury, and for a few seconds she looked all around her, and even tried lying down briefly on the bed to feel how comfortable it was. Then she made her way to the door.

It opened on to what was obviously the main hall. A number of doors led off it, but she had no way of telling which one would take her to the kitchen. She began to shake all over as realisation hit her that she was actually standing in the middle of somebody else's house without their knowledge or permission. And what a house it was, so unlike anything she had experienced before, or if she had, she just couldn't remember it. It was all so different from the life she was living now, a cast-off in the streets in the company of a wild bunch of mixed-up teenage boys. She spent so long shining her torch around the elegant hallway, with its Victorian coat rack and tall flight of narrow carpeted stairs, that she forgot all about Toff who was on the front doorstep outside waiting for her to open the door.

She took a deep breath to calm her nerves and moved on. She peered into one ground-floor room and then another, only briefly stopping to admire the old period furniture, delicate lace curtains, and fine colourful rugs. As she went she picked up small knick-knacks that took her fancy, old snuffboxes and china ornaments, and quickly stuffed them into her coat pockets. To live in such a beautiful place with so many fine and wonderful things would be like a dream come true. And it was all so cosy and warm, with the dying embers of a fire still glowing in the grate. Who were these lucky old ladies who lived here? she wondered. What had they ever done to deserve such luck?

Out in the hallway again, Nellie suddenly heard Toff rattling the front door letterbox. 'Nell!' he called in as loud a whisper as he dared. 'Nell, are you in there? Open up!'

Nellie made for the door. Then she changed her mind and stopped. She knew it was irrational but quite suddenly she wanted to do something on her own, and for herself. Impetuously she turned and went off to look for the kitchen.

She eventually found it at the end of a small passage, at the back of the house. Even before she reached the door, she knew it had to be

49

the kitchen, for the smell of cooking earlier in the day still drifted out into the passage, making her stomach yearn for whatever it was. As she reached for the doorknob, she desperately hoped that she was about to find some succulent leftovers of fried sausages or spam fritters or perhaps even a meat stew. Slowly, she turned the doorknob and went in. What greeted her was a shock that turned her blood to ice.

Glaring at her in the beam of her torchlight was the huge face of a large, savage-looking dog, eyes red, teeth bared, growling menacingly. Nellie's first instinct was to turn and run. But she knew that if she made even the slightest move, the beast would leap straight at her. So she remained as still as her paralysed body would allow, her back pinned against the open door. For a moment, she and the dog were quite motionless, just poised there sizing each other up. Desperately, Nellie tried to think of a way of getting out into the hall to call to Toff. But then a change seemed to come over her. She had already taken her decision and settled for doing this job without Toff's help. Fear was gradually replaced by a need for power, and without moving a muscle, she found herself talking to the dog.

'Sit!' she said, quite calmly.

The dog refused her order. His lips continued to quiver angrily.

Nellie took a deep breath. 'Sit!' This time her voice was stronger, more decisive.

Again, the dog refused her order.

Regardless of the risk, Nellie shouted at him.

'I said *sit*, you ugly great monster! *Sit*, or I'll knock yer bleedin' 'ead orf!'

To her utter amazement, the dog stopped growling, and after a moment of indecision he sat down with a thud.

Nellie summoned up enough courage to draw closer to him. Without faltering, she put out her hand and stroked his head. 'That's better, mate,' she said, somewhat breathlessly. 'Now s'pose yer tell me where I can find the grub.'

Toff was still outside on the front doorstep anxiously rattling the letterbox. His concern increased when he heard the drone of approaching aircraft, quickly followed by the first ack-ack fire of the night. 'Nell!' he yelled through the letterbox. 'What the hell are you up to?'

The street door promptly opened and Nellie appeared. 'Two pork trotters, two sausage rolls, some cheese, and a bottle of pickled onions,' she said triumphantly, holding up a bulging paper bag. ''Ow's that for a beginner?'

As the first wave of enemy aircraft thundered across the sky above and bombs whistled down in the distance, Nellie and Toff ran down the front steps of the house and were immediately joined by Nuts. All three made a wild dash for the main road in Highbury Grove, which was lit up by searchlights criss-crossing the sky and the flash of ack-ack shells as they exploded high above the protective net of barrage balloons. With debris now tinkling down on to the pavements around them, it was time to take cover.

'This way!' yelled Shortso, who was beckoning

to them from outside a pub in the Balls Pond Road. 'There's a place round the back!'

They hurried towards him, but before they had gone more than a few steps, there was a gigantic white flash that produced a myriad of sparks that set fire to a nearby tree. The three teenagers immediately threw themselves to the ground. When they eventually looked up they were horrified to see Shortso rolling himself over and over on the wet pavement, trying desperately to put out the flames which had engulfed his clothes.

Chapter 4

Christmas 1940 was a miserable time for the people of London. The festive spirit which had always existed at this time of year was completely absent, for during the last two months the Blitz had taken its toll, and in December alone thousands had been killed. On top of that, food rationing was biting hard, and the little luxuries that people had come to expect just weren't there any more. In some of the poorer parts of North London and the East End, a Christmas meal consisted of nothing more than the usual bowl of soup and some vegetables, and even in the more fortunate working-class areas it was almost impossible to get all the ingredients for a Christmas pudding. The air raids were relentless and people spent most of their time either in an underground shelter or risking their lives in their blacked-out homes. The only consolation was that Christmas Day itself was free of air raids.

Nellie spent much of the day following up a clue to her real identity. She had had a dream a couple of nights before, in which she saw herself with a whole lot of children and young people, running down some steps inside an old large building. When she woke up she remembered the dream but she didn't understand it. She wondered whether it was about when she was at school, and she tried very hard to make sense of where it might have been. But it was a casual remark from Toff that gave her a clue. He mentioned an orphanage in New North Road that had been bombed just a few weeks before. So on Christmas morning, Nellie left the gang's latest hideout in a bombed-out furniture store just behind Essex Road and made her way to the site of the old orphanage. When she got there, all she saw was yet another pile of rubble, which for the first few moments meant absolutely nothing to her. As she started to clamber over some charred timbers, which were now covered with a thin layer of cold white frost, she came across what looked like a notice board which was partly concealed beneath a frozen puddle of mud. She stooped down, and with some difficulty managed to pull the board free. It had one word printed on it: BARRATTS'.

'Does it mean anything to you?'

Nellie turned with a start, to find Toff perched on some bricks just behind her. 'What you doin' 'ere?' she asked irritably. 'Did you foller me?'

'As a matter of fact, I did,' Toff replied cheekily. 'D'you mind?'

Nellie felt self-conscious. He was smiling that smile at her again, and she didn't really want to respond. 'What d'yer want?' she asked.

'To see if you've found yourself,' Toff replied, hands dug deep into his overcoat pocket, looking at the noticeboard Nellie had just retrieved. 'Barratts',' he read. 'Does it ring any bells?'

Nellie's puzzled eyes searched the bleak scene around her. 'I *feel* somefin',' she replied, obliquely. 'Somefin' inside.' It was true. The sight of that noticeboard had triggered something; she could hear laughter, shouting, just like in her dream.

Toff kicked a piece of broken brick which went tumbling down the debris he was standing on to join another pile of rubble below. 'An orphanage is a place where kids come because they have no parents.' He paused, then turned to look at her. 'D'you reckon this is where you came from, Nell?' he asked gently.

Nellie suddenly felt quite numb. She was trying so hard to remember something, anything, that she wondered if she was just imagining the sound of children's voices, of being part of such a place. She stared hard at the broken bricks and mortar, the charred timbers, the arched windows in isolated walls that still stood. Then her gaze moved to the stone steps that had clearly once led up to the front door of the building. She jumped across to them, and stood there, trying to remember, trying to bring her life into focus and to know if she had ever been part of this strange, tragic place. Then, without turning to look at Toff, she said, 'If I did come from 'ere, then I don't want ter know. I want ter belong ter someone. I want ter be part of someone's family.'

Toff picked his way carefully across the rubble and joined her on top of the steps. 'You do belong to someone, Nell,' he said, staring into her eyes and putting both his hands on her shoulders. 'You're part of *our* family now. Me and the gang.'

Nellie lowered her head, but Toff's hand reached down and gently raised her chin. When he looked into her eyes this time, he saw that they were filling with tears. 'Merry Christmas, Nell,' he said with a smile.

'Merry Christmas, Toff,' Nellie replied.

'Martin,' Toff said firmly. He wanted her to call him by his real name.

'Martin,' replied Nellie, at last managing a smile.

Ethel Ackroyd was beginning to regret that she had never married. It was something she had thought about lots of times, especially since the start of the war, but not when she was of the right marrying age back home in the Yorkshire Dales. In those days she had known a lot of boys and could have had her pick of them in the village where she was brought up. She had had many a fling, but never with the right person, never with a boy she felt she could spend the rest of her life with. Now, unfortunately, it was too late. She was in her late forties, time had passed her by—or at least that was how she felt. Her work at Barratts' Orphanage was a kind of compensation. As far as she was concerned, all the unwanted children there were her own children, and she was able to share their problems and help them to sort out their lives. But there were one or two of them who refused to share their problems. Like Vicky Hobson. She was such a rebel, such a misfit, so like Ethel herself when she was the same age, which was perhaps why the girl had fascinated her so much.

'Penny for your thoughts,' said Mrs Hare. She and Ethel were watching the children playing musical chairs in the assembly hall of the school in which they had been given temporary accommodation. 'Bet you it's that young Vicky.'

Ethel looked at her and smiled. The old lady was a good soul, and a shrewd observer. 'She's out there somewhere, Mrs Hare,' she said. 'I won't rest 'til I find her.'

Mrs Hare sighed, and shook her head despondently. Since the bombing of the orphanage, she knew only too well how obsessed Ethel had become about losing Vicky Hobson. She also knew that Ethel was the only person who was convinced that the girl was still alive. 'I wouldn't hold out your hopes, dearie,' she said. 'Even if she did survive that bomb, why wouldn't she just've found her way back to us?'

Ethel turned to look at her with a pained

expression. 'Because she didn't want to, Mrs Hare,' she replied despairingly.

At that moment there was an almighty cheer, followed by shrieks of laughter, as the piano playing stopped and two children fought for the last musical chair. This provoked shouts and jeers, and some of the younger children called out excitedly, 'Cheat! Cheat!' Finally, Arthur Driscoll, who had been playing the piano, came down from the platform and, to prolonged cheers, triumphantly declared one of the children the winner. After that, the forty or so orphans filed into the dining hall for their Christmas afternoon tea party, most of which had been provided by contributions from various charitable organisations, and local people.

It was not until the early evening when the children were playing party games that Mrs Hare was able to continue her chat with Ethel. The two women were taking a breather from the festivities with a stroll around the school playground.

'What did you mean?' asked Mrs Hare, her puffy cheeks red from the cold. 'About young Vicky not wanting to come back to us.'

Ethel was reluctant to answer. She had her reasons for not wanting to talk about that afternoon, the afternoon before the air raid. But if she didn't talk about it to someone, she would go out of her mind. The guilt was just too much to bear. 'We had—a quarrel,' she said, with difficulty. 'Just a few hours before the bomb. I hit her, Mrs Hare. I slapped her face. She said she'd run away. She said she hoped I'd die.'

'What?' gasped Mrs Hare, clasping her hand over her mouth in shock.

'It happened when I started talking to her about the future. About what she wanted to do when she was old enough to leave Barratts', when she found herself a husband to settle down with and start a family. For some reason she flew into a rage and accused me of poking my nose into her private business. I told her that as I'd known her since she was a baby, I had every right to talk to her as her own mother might have done. But she wouldn't listen to me. She said I just wanted to know if she had any boyfriends, and what she got up to when she was out of sight. She called me an interfering old hag, an old maid.'

'The little vixen!' Mrs Hare said angrily. 'Didn't I always tell you what a packet of trouble she was? We all knew it.'

'You don't understand, Mrs Hare,' Ethel said, in anguish. 'Vicky was only telling me what I've been thinking about myself all these years. I know nothing about life outside the walls of the orphanage.'

Mrs Hare was fuming. 'You're a good woman, Ethel, and don't you ever think otherwise. What you've done for these children is nothing short of a miracle. There's not a person who knows you that doesn't love you.'

'Except a man,' replied Ethel.

Mrs Hare ignored this. 'Vicky was a wicked girl, my dear. Mark my words.'

Ethel laid her hand on the old lady's arm. 'No, Mrs Hare. What Vicky told me is the truth.

I was trying to live out my own life through her. And she knew it. That's why she wanted to get away from Barratts', away from me.'

The old lady's knuckles were white with tension. 'May God forgive me, but I say it's a good thing He took her.'

'Don't ever say such a thing, Mrs Hare!' Ethel cried, almost in panic. 'They never found Vicky, so as far as I'm concerned she's still alive. There are children running wild all over this city, children who've run away from home, children who ran away from evacuation. She could be out there with them—anywhere. If she is, I'm going to find her.'

From inside the school hall, the two women could hear the children singing 'Away In a Manger'. They stood there in the cold, frosty, evening air, their faces turned towards the blacked-out windows, listening.

The best part of Christmas for Nellie was to see Shortso sitting with her and the other boys eating Christmas dinner. She had been horrified to see him rolling about on the pavement trying to put out his burning clothes. He had been lucky to escape with only minor burns on his neck, hands, and legs. Anything more serious and they would have had no alternative but to get him straight to the hospital. And that could have meant all sorts of questions being asked. It brought home to Nellie more forcefully than anything how tenuous her life on the streets with these boys was.

Their Christmas meal consisted of a piece

of roast leg of chicken, some carrots, boiled onions, and a slice of fried bread. It wasn't the most traditional of Christmas meals, but beggars—and thieves—could not be choosers. At least it was all hot food. They had built a fire right in the middle of the gutted furniture store and cooked the food in an assortment of pots and pans that they had acquired since living out on the streets. There was no Christmas pudding but Rats and Bonkers had delighted everyone by producing two dozen mince pies which they had found in cardboard boxes in the storage room of a baker's shop. All in all, the meal was an unqualified success and much more fun than Nellie had ever imagined it would be. Nuts set the mood by appearing at the meal as a waiter, his hair greased down with lard and parted in the middle, a thin moustache created with soot, and a white towel draped professionally over one arm.

After the meal, everyone sat around squat-legged on the floor and told stories about Christmas from the time when they lived at home. Some of it Nellie found a bit childish, but she had to laugh when Nuts told of the Christmas when his dad dressed up as Santa Claus, crept into Nuts' bedroom late at night, and then tripped over the cat. It was all a welcome relief from the usual nightly routine of life on the streets, sneaking in and out of people's homes during the air raids and making off with their measly food rations. Nellie had come to accept that if they were to survive, there was no other way. But she didn't enjoy this false way of life. What she wanted, what she craved was a family of her own, a real family, whom she could be proud of and tell funny stories about too. And yet she couldn't shake that dragging sense that perhaps she had never had a family at all, and that if ever she did remember who she was and where she came from, the truth would hurt.

The last part of Christmas evening did, however, cheer Nellie up no end. Shortso, the back of his hands and face discoloured by dark red blotches from his burns, revealed a hidden talent. For the best part of an hour and a half, he played a mouth organ while Nellie and the gang joined in with some of the popular songs of the war, such as 'Run, Rabbit, Run', 'You Are My Sunshine', and 'She'll Be Coming Round the Mountain'. To Nellie's surprise and delight, everyone got up to dance, and the boys acted the fool by bowing and then dancing with each other. Their antics made Nellie roar with laughter, and for a precious hour or so she and the others simply enjoyed themselves and forgot all about the tensions they had to live with each day. The most touching moment came when Toff stood up and gallantly offered his hand to Nellie to dance. At first she refused, but after a great deal of cajoling and calls of, 'Come on, Nell!' she took hold of Toff's hand and allowed him to help her up. Shortso played a tune that was regularly bashed out on pub pianos. It was called 'Always', and it was perfect for a nice, smoochy dance. Nellie couldn't remember ever having danced before but she followed Toff's steps as best she could. After a moment or so, the space between them grew less, and it was not very long before their bodies were pressed very firmly against each other. The only light came from the old paraffin lamp, but somehow this only added to the atmosphere, so much so that some of the boys, either jealous of Toff's growing fondness for Nellie or grieved that a girl was intruding too much on their close bond of friendship, decided to call it a day, and one by one they left. Nellie and Toff seemed oblivious of this and continued to move to the poignant wail of the mouth organ. Finally, Shortso came to the end of the song, but Nellie and Toff kept on with their dance, locked in an intimate embrace. Shortso and the few boys still there decided it was time they left too, and they quietly retreated to the coal bunkers where they slept.

Nellie and Toff continued to sway to and fro to the evocative song that was now only a memory.

No matter how hard she tried, Ethel Ackroyd had never liked Lizzie Morris. The fact was that the child was sly, and whenever she was able to tell tales about any of the other orphans at Barratts', she would do so. It was a pity, because Lizzie was a pretty child, with a round, almost doll-like complexion, and long auburn hair that draped beautifully over her shoulders. She was a little on the plump side, which was unusual considering the wartime rations, but as she was only fifteen years old, most people put this down to puppy fat. Ethel tried to make allowances for the fact that she was the victim of a broken marriage—her parents had separated when she was at the vulnerable age of eleven. Unfortunately the child had used her situation to cause trouble for just about everyone. And that included her worst enemy, Vicky Hobson.

'I bet I know where she's gone,' Lizzie cooed mischievously, her large blue eyes slyly watching for Ethel's reaction. She and some of the orphans and staff were taking a Boxing Day afternoon stroll across Highbury Fields, and Lizzie had deliberately attached herself to Ethel. 'She's wiv one of those gangs who've run away from being evacuated. Vicky always liked bein' wiv boys.'

'How would you know such a thing, Lizzie?' asked Ethel, trying to sound as nonchalant as possible.

'Because Vicky told me she was going,' answered Lizzie.

Ethel stopped abruptly. 'She *told* you she was going to join the evacuees?'

Lizzie, delighted that her remark had had the desired effect, came to a halt too. 'Why yes, Miss Ackroyd,' she said demurely. 'I thought everyone knew how much Vicky liked being in boys' company.'

Ethel was irritated. 'She told you she was going to run away?'

'Yes, Miss Ackroyd.'

'When was this?'

'Just a few days before the bomb dropped.'

Despite Lizzie's reputation as an inveterate

liar, Ethel was alarmed enough to question her further. She took hold of Lizzie's hand and led her to the nearest park bench. 'Now I want the truth, Lizzie,' Ethel said, pulling the girl down beside her on the damp bench 'None of your usual made-up stories, just the truth.' Grimly she looked the child straight in the eye and asked, 'Are you telling me that Vicky had been planning to run away from Barratts?'

Lizzie shrugged her shoulders. 'I suppose so.' Her attention was drawn to a grey squirrel which was sitting up on its hind legs just in front of them. 'Oh look!' she squealed excitedly.

Ethel refused to be diverted. She took hold of Lizzie's arm and asked sternly, 'Did Vicky Hobson talk about being—unhappy at Barratts'?'

Lizzie squirmed. 'You're hurting my arm!'

Ethel persisted. 'Did she?'

'Yes!' howled the child. 'She never liked Barratts'. She said so over and over again. You can ask the others. They'll tell you. They'll tell you that as soon as Vicky got the chance, she was going to get as far away from you as she could!'

Ethel gasped, and released the girl's arm.

The rest of the party had gone on ahead but Martha Driscoll spotted Ethel and Lizzie on the bench. Suspecting that something was wrong, she left the others and began to make her way back.

Ethel tried to compose herself, and after a long, deep breath, asked calmly, 'Are you telling me the truth, Lizzie?'

By this time, Lizzie was giving the impression that she was terrified of Ethel questioning her. 'Yes, miss! Honest, miss!'

The squirrel quickly sensed the atmosphere and made a hasty retreat up into the huge chestnut tree from where he had come. An elderly couple walking their Scots terrier dog had to restrain the creature when, barking furiously, he slipped his leash and tried to make after the squirrel.

Ethel, undeterred by the commotion, continued to cross-examine Lizzie. 'What makes you so sure that Vicky is still alive?' she asked as calmly as she could.

Lizzie thought carefully before answering. 'Because that's the reason she never came down the shelter that night,' she said, flicking her long hair away from her face. 'I could tell that was the night she was goin' ter do it. I could tell that was the time she was goin' ter make a run fer it.'

Ethel stared at her.

'By the time the bomb come down,' Lizzie went on with an unpleasant smirk, 'she was more than likely already on 'er way.'

Ethel felt nothing but contempt for her. 'And yet,' she said icily, 'you didn't tell me or any other member of staff. Why, Lizzie? Why?'

The girl fixed her with a hollow smile. 'I'd never do that, miss,' she replied. 'You might've changed your mind.'

Without a moment's thought, Ethel allowed all her feelings of loathing for the girl to surface. Rising quickly from the bench, she slapped Lizzie across the face.

Lizzie screamed and tried to run away, but Ethel grabbed both her arms and started to shake her.

The elderly couple with the dog stared in horror.

'Ethel!' Martha Driscoll rushed forward and managed to prevent Ethel from slapping the girl again. 'No, Ethel! No!'

Lizzie quickly became hysterical, more for effect than actual pain. Sobbing out loud, she yelled, 'I hate you! I hate you!'

Ethel, her face blood-red with uncontrolled anger, suddenly found her arms pinned behind her back by Martha's husband, Arthur, who had rushed to his wife's help.

'Get back to the others,' said Martha to the girl.

Lizzie, her eyes glistening with tears, hurried off, sobbing loudly.

But when she had gone some distance along the path, she looked back briefly over her shoulder to see Ethel, Martha, and Arthur Driscoll in tense conversation.

And the tears very quickly gave way to a satisfied smile.

The night after Boxing Day, it was business as usual for the Luftwaffe. Once again the skies echoed to the wail of the air-raid siren, the drone of enemy aircraft, ack-ack fire, fire and ambulance bells, and once again everyone rushed off to keep their nightly rendezvous in the air-raid shelters. This also meant business as usual for the evacuee gangs.

Toff had decided to concentrate their efforts on the back streets around the Nag's Head in Holloway, where the terraces of three-storey Victorian houses provided rich pickings for the intruder. From earlier recces, Toff had discovered that during an air raid most of the working-class people who lived there retreated to the corrugated-iron Anderson shelters in their small back gardens, leaving the house unprotected. Unfortunately, break-ins were not without risk, for the area contained at least one air-raid precaution post to co-ordinate fire-fighting operations, with plenty of wardens and Special Constables patrolling the streets.

After her near disastrous encounter with the guard dog, Nellie had decided that she was no longer interested in taking part in any more jobs. It didn't matter to her that she had given in to jibes from the boys that breaking into people's homes was not for girls; as far as she was concerned, her own safety was far more important than personal pride. So on the evening of the gang's first post-Christmas job, she decided to take herself off to the pictures at the Rink Cinema in Finsbury Park.

Nellie chose the Rink because its rear exit door was easy to open, mainly because people leaving from earlier performances never bothered to close the door properly behind them. Toff had shown her the knack of getting into the place without paying and, more importantly, how not to be caught once inside. This involved finding her way to a row of empty seats in the upper circle and lying flat on the floor until the lights went down and the programme started. Everything went according to plan, except that when she lay face downwards on the cold lino floor between the seats, something wet and sticky attached itself to her nose. It was a piece of used chewing gum and it positively refused to detach itself completely from the end of her nose. When the lights went down, she was at last able to sit up in a seat, although she kept a constant lookout for the beam of light from the usherette's torch when she approached.

Nellie couldn't remember ever having been inside a cinema before, and she was overawed by the vastness of the long, narrow auditorium, visible in the flickering projected light from the screen. The cinema had once been an old tramway with a roller-skating rink at the rear. And the smell! It was so strange, a mixture of damp rot, sweet perfume, and cigarette smoke. But it was when the film itself came on that she discovered how entrancing it was to come to such a place. The names of the stars—Katharine Hepburn, Joan Bennett, Frances Dee—that came up on the screen at the beginning meant nothing to her, but the tale of four young girls growing up in America before the Civil War captivated her.

The film, which was called *Little Women*, had quite an impact on Nellie, for it was about a family, and it prompted all sorts of questions within her, such as why couldn't she have a mum and dad of her own, and brothers and sisters, like those lucky girls down there on the screen? Why did she have to live a rough life out on the streets with a bunch of misfits? And then she got to wondering why she just didn't go to the nearest police station and tell them her story, how she had lost her memory, and ask who she was and where she had come from. But what if she *did* find out who she was? What if she discovered that she came from that bombed-out orphanage and that she'd never had a mother and father or brothers and sisters? What would be worse, to know that she really did have a family of her own and didn't remember them, or that her whole life had been spent inside a dingy old institution?

At that moment a message appeared along the bottom of the screen, telling the audience that the air-raid siren had sounded but that the film would continue. Nellie was too engrossed in the film, in the story of that family, to let any more bombs ruin her life.

On the way back to the burned-out furniture store, the air raid was in full swing and the whole sky was bright red with the glow of burning fires. No buses were running so Nellie made her way on foot along Blackstock Road to Highbury and then to Essex Road. It was quite a long walk, but in the middle of an air raid it was definitely the safest way to get around, for whenever the fall of shrapnel was too great she was always able to take cover in a shop doorway. There was one scary moment, however, when she had to throw herself flat on her stomach after a bomb whistled down in the distance on to one of the streets near the

Arsenal football stadium. The sound of glass shattering all around unnerved Nellie, and it was several minutes before she recovered enough to continue her journey.

When she eventually turned into Essex Road and reached the furniture store, there had apparently been a direct hit on a pet shop on the main road, which caused chaos and pandemonium as distressed local people tried to rescue the puppies, kittens, birds, and other helpless creatures who were trapped, screeching in panic.

'We're in trouble!' called Nuts, out of breath as he ran to catch up with Nellie who was just about to take cover in the gang's own makeshift shelter. 'When I left Toff about 'alf an 'our ago, the rozzers were on to 'im. Fer all I know, 'e's already locked up in the clink.'

At that moment, there was another explosion just a couple of streets away, so both of them practically threw themselves into the bowels of the dark shelter.

Nellie's heart had missed a beat when she heard about Toff. Not that she was surprised that the law had caught up with him; it was inevitable that it would happen sooner or later. But she hated the stupidity of it all, the mad way in which this bunch of outcasts put their lives at risk every night. 'Well, wot're yer goin' 'ter do about it?' she snapped. 'There must be somefin' yer can do!'

'We can't do nuffin', Nell,' squealed Nuts in the dark. 'Just leave it ter Toff, that's all. 'E can talk 'is way out of a cast-iron box, that one!'

Both of them ducked as the place vibrated from a volley of ack-ack fire in the sky above them. This was followed within seconds by a hail of shrapnel raining down.

When the explosions were replaced by the incessant clanging of fire and ambulance bells, Nell could hear Nuts breathing hard. 'Nuts?' she called in the dark. 'Nuts? Are you all right?'

Nuts hesitated before replying. 'I d—dunno 'ow m-much longer I can g—go on like this,' he stuttered in a barely audible voice. 'One of these days, I'm goin' ter cop my lot.'

Nellie was taken aback. Until this moment, she had been under the impression that Nuts, like all the rest of the boys in the gang, was quite fearless of the air raids. It came as a shock to hear Nuts shivering as he talked. 'Then why d'you carry on livin' like this?' she asked, raising her voice over the chaotic sounds outside. 'Why don't yer all just give up and go back to yer own 'omes?'

Nuts thought for a moment before answering. ''Cos they don't really want us back. My lot don't, anyway.'

''Ow can yer say that?' replied Nellie, irritated. ''Ow can yer say that when yer don't even talk to them? Why don't yer just go back, sit down an' talk to them?'

'Yer don't know my mum, or me dad. *They* do the talkin'. *I* do the listenin'.'

There was another loud explosion. This time Nellie yelled out, for it was too close for comfort. As she did so, someone threw himself down into the shelter, almost flattening her.

71

'Anyone at home?' he called out.

'Toff!' Nellie felt a surge of excitement. 'Where've yer been?'

'I fawt they'd nabbed yer!' spluttered Nuts.

'They nearly did,' growled Toff, 'thanks to you and Shortso. If you'd done something to divert them, I'd have made a better break. Stupid nerds!'

'You're the stupid nerd!' barked Nellie, more out of relief than anger. 'Why d'yer 'ave ter take risks? Why d'yer 'ave ter go on wiv this stupid nickin' all the time?'

'Come off it, Nell,' replied Toff, trying to make light of it. 'We've got to eat, haven't we?' But when he tried to take hold of her hand, she pulled away.

'Why can't yer learn that this ain't worf it! None of this is worf it!' Nell was letting off the steam that had been building up within her ever since she was asked to do her first job. 'Yer livin' like animals! When yer goin' ter give up and be yer age?'

Nell would have been even more furious with Toff if she'd known he was grinning at her in the dark. 'Sorry you feel like that, Nell,' he said mischievously, 'because I've brought you a present.'

Nellie didn't reply. But she was curious.

'Well, don't you want to know what it is?'

Nellie remained silent.

'Hold out your hand, Nell. Come on now. I went to a lot of trouble to nick this for you.'

Nellie waited a second or so, then decided to do as he asked.

Toff felt around for her outstretched hand, then dropped a small metal object into her palm.

Nellie had no idea what it was.

Toff leaned forward and whispered into her ear, 'It's a lipstick. Just your colour. You're going to look sensational.'

Chapter 5

Despite the severity of the Blitz, that stalwart of British entertainment, the music hall, remained in business. At the start of the war, the government closed most of the theatres, cinemas, concert halls, and football stadiums, but as time went on, the civilian population was in dire need of having their spirits raised, and everything sprang back into life, albeit under strict wartime conditions. Among the greatest saviours of the day in London were places like the Shepherd's Bush Empire, the Wood Green Empire, the Chiswick Empire, and the Finsbury Park Empire. Here, fun-starved audiences were given the chance to forget the air raids for a couple of hours, and to be cheered by a performance of song, dance, laughter, mystery and illusion, and above all a wonderful line-up of character comedians. During the war, there was nothing quite like the music hall to get you into a party spirit and to help you forget the horror and reality of the bombed streets outside.

The Hackney Empire, in East London's Mare Street, was one such place, and even though it was late January, the Christmas pantomime season was still in full swing. Ever since Nellie had started to use the lipstick he had nicked for her, Toff had waited for an opportunity to show her off to people other than the gang, and a visit to the Hackney panto turned out to be just such an opportunity.

The panto this year was the good old favourite *Cinderella*. Owing to the blackout, most performances had to be in the afternoon. Nellie and Toff had no money to pay the admission charge, but needless to say Toff had a plan of campaign. This involved mingling with the audience filing up the stone steps to the gallery, and if the usherette asked them for their tickets, they would point to some unsuspecting man and woman ahead of them and reply indignantly that their mum and dad had the tickets, and had already shown them. Then all they had to do was either find two spare seats that weren't booked, or wedge themselves among the overflow audience standing at the back. The plan worked perfectly, and they even found two seats in the front row at the side. They watched anxiously when anybody came near them, just in case they were there to claim their booked seats, but when the house lights finally went down, they knew they were safe.

Nellie was as excited as the rest of the audience, which included quite a lot of children. The theatre, with its crimson stage curtains and gold tassels, seemed to her to be like a kind of fairy wonderland, albeit one that stank of Zubes cough drops, which were the only real substitute for rationed sweets. When the orchestra started to play a rousing popular tune and the curtains swung back to reveal a whole lot of people in brightly coloured costumes and make-up, singing and dancing, she felt her stomach turn over with excitement and exhilaration.

Toff was more excited to see Nellie so happy, and throughout the first half of the show he couldn't take his eyes off her. He thought she looked so sexy. The lipstick really suited her, and she had combed her usually straggly hair and pinned it back over her ears, which gave her a much more grown-up look. He was determined that at the right moment he would tell her he thought she looked sensational, that what she lacked in height she made up a hundredfold in personality and sex appeal.

While Cinderella was sitting alone in her kitchen, singing of her despair at being left to do the chores while her ugly sisters went to the Prince's ball, Nellie and Toff took a peek between the brass protective rails, down into the circle and stalls below. There was a party of excited children there, most of them with adults. After the interval, when they all filed back into their seats, Nellie noticed one young teenage girl gazing up towards the gods, apparently at her and Toff. Just before the lights went down again, the girl seemed to be jumping up and down in her seat, pointing up towards where Nellie and Toff were sitting, trying hard to get some of the adults with her to look. This worried Nellie, and she quickly slumped down into her seat. To her relief, the performance began again, and the girl in the circle just beneath them was forced to sit down and keep quiet.

Nellie soon forgot about her as she became caught up in the colour, costumes, and glittering set of the Prince's ball. But despite the spectacle and romance of the story and the popular songs, Nellie was impressed most of all with what was called in the programme, *A Speciality Act*. This turned out to be a tall, skinny middle-aged man with a funny foreign accent, who used different coloured lights and handkerchiefs to create all sorts of strange illusions. He even had a cupboard on the stage in which he made his young lady assistant disappear, and then made her reappear in one of the stage boxes. He was a wonderful character, with his pencil-thin black moustache, and constant exclamations of *''Ere iz my miracle!'*, and Nellie thought him an absolute revelation. Toff enjoyed it all too, but as he puffed on his fag and blew circles of smoke up into the hot, sticky atmosphere, he was far more amused by the youngsters along the front row of the gods who were mischievously pelting people in the circle below with dried peas.

At the climax of the show, when the Prince named Cinderella as the girl he would marry, the whole theatre burst into cheers and tumultuous applause. And when the show was finally over, the performers took a bow on stage and invited the audience to sing one last popular song with them, followed by 'God Save the King'. This brought the curtain down, and the lights up. As the audience rose from their seats to leave the theatre, Nellie turned to look down at the circle below, and once again she saw the young teenage girl calling out and pointing up at her. She nervously ducked out of sight, unaware who Lizzie Morris was, or why she was desperately trying to point her out to the principal of Barratts' Orphanage, Ethel Ackroyd.

It was only a matter of minutes after the audience had streamed out of the Hackney Empire that the wail of the air-raid siren echoed along the length of Mare Street. Everyone raced to get home to the safety of their shelters; queues of theatre-goers quickly formed at bus stops on either side of the busy main street, while others chose to make their way as fast as they could on foot.

One of the last people to leave the theatre was Ethel Ackroyd. She struggled to push her way through the crowds to get to the exit used by the gallery audience. It was a futile effort, for by the time she got there a male attendant was already bolting up for the night.

'Excuse me,' she said breathlessly to the man, 'did you notice a young girl coming out just a moment or so ago. She was about this high, with mousey-coloured hair, and—'

''Ang on, missus,' he said, looking at Ethel as though she was mad. ''Ow many people d'yer fink we 'ave up there?'

'But you'd know this one,' she said, holding on to the door he was trying to bolt. 'She's really quite small—and pretty.'

'Is she now?' replied the attendant tetchily. 'Well, believe it or not, I 'ain't got eyes in the back of me blinkin' 'ead, yer know!' Then he pulled the door from her grip. 'You better get down the shelters. Don't yer know there's an air raid on!' With that, he slammed the door with a loud thud and locked and bolted it from inside.

For several moments, Ethel stood there in a state of anguish and confusion, her eyes anxiously searching the last remaining members of the audience as they hurried out of the front entrance of the theatre. She didn't really know whether to believe what Lizzie Morris had said about catching sight of Vicky Hobson up in the front row of the Hackney Empire gallery. But it was just possible that Vicky had been there, and if she was, Ethel felt devastated that she could have missed her after being so close. On the other side of the road she could see the charabanc waiting for her to join the party of children she and the Mitchells had brought to the pantomime. Once she was quite sure that there were no more stragglers left inside the theatre, she reluctantly moved off, trying hard not to be angry with the hordes of careless young couples who bumped into her as she went.

She was much too fraught and preoccupied to notice that one of those couples was Nellie and Toff.

It was about half an hour before the first wave of enemy aircraft was heard, droning in from an easterly direction along the River Thames. In the distance, Nell and Toff could hear the first bombs whistling down, and the angry barrage of ack-ack fire that was doing its best to bring down as many of the raiders as possible before they reached central London.

'Looks like it's Stratford way,' called Toff, arm round Nellie's waist as they hurried along Balls Pond Road. He had to shout to be heard. 'We'd better make a dash for it!'

Nellie broke into a run, not only because it was dangerous to be on the streets in the middle of an air raid, but also to put some distance between herself and Toff. She wished he would stop treating her like a precious flower. In fact, she was becoming more and more anxious with the attention he was always showing her; it was almost a fixation. Not that she didn't appreciate Toffs concern for her. In many ways, she felt flattered. But she wanted to be her own person, to think things out for herself, and make her own decisions. She was also concerned that Toff was becoming too moony about her, and although she did feel something inside for him, it was all too complicated for her to understand, and the only solution she had was not to respond.

By the time they got back to the old furniture store in Essex Road, the bombardment was in full swing. Most of the gang were out on jobs, with the exception of Rats and Bonkers who were waiting in the underground shelter, still wearing the tin helmets they'd nicked from a local ARP post. Nellie was at least grateful that there was a candle burning in the shelter; there was nothing worse than sitting in the dark listening to all hell breaking loose in the skies above. But the place still smelt heavily of cat's piddle, and there was at least an inch of rainwater seeping up through the muddy floor from last night's downpour.

'We got two buckets of shrapnel terday.' Bonkers announced proudly.

'We took it up the post,' added Rats. 'This ARP geezer give us a tanner fer the lot.'

'We din't ask fer nuffin',' Bonkers continued, his outsize tin helmet wobbling on his head as he talked. 'We told 'em it was fer the war effort.'

''E told us our mums and dads oughta be proud of us,' said Rats. 'Much better than the tykes who nicked 'is 'elmets!'

Both of them burst into laughter.

'What was that?' Nellie's voice cut through the sound of the ack-ack gunfire outside.

'Nothing to worry about. Nell,' said Toff reassuringly. 'It's pretty busy up there tonight.'

'No, not that,' replied Nellie. 'Something else.' The sound of a kitten mewing was just audible. 'There!' she said.

Rats and Bonkers exchanged a guilty look.

'It's nuffin',' said Rats, shrugging his shoulders dismissively. 'Yer get a lot of mogs down 'ere.'

'Where is it?' Toff demanded firmly.

'It's nuffin', Toff, 'onest,' Bonkers said quickly.

'I've told you two, no cats, dogs, or any other pets! We don't have enough to feed ourselves, let alone strays.'

'But this one's different,' pleaded Rats. 'We found 'im on a site down Dalston. 'Is mum was dead.'

Bonkers added his own plea. ''E was buried under all this debris. 'Is bruvvers an' sisters too.'

'Where is it?' demanded Toff. 'Come on. Get it out of here!'

Rats and Bonkers exchanged another guilty glance, then Bonkers shrugged his shoulders and dug deep into his pocket. He pulled out a tiny ginger kitten which immediately let out a wail.

Nellie's face lit up immediately. She reached across and gently took hold of the small creature. It had so little fur on it, it could not have been born more than a week before. 'It's beautiful!' she gasped.

'Maybe,' growled Toff, 'but it still has to go.'

Nellie swung an angry look at him. 'Why?' she asked. 'It's only a kitten.'

'Please, Nell,' Toff said. 'They know the rules. We have to have some rules. No pets.' He turned to Bonkers and said firmly, 'Get it out of here, now!'

Bonkers knew from experience that it was no use arguing with Toff, so he quickly snatched the kitten from Nellie and made for the curtain covering the open entrance.

'Wait!' Nellie stood up quickly. 'Can't we at least wait till morning? It's cruel to put it out there on a night like this.'

Toff suddenly became angry. 'Give me that

thing!' he raged, grabbing the small creature from Bonkers' hand. The kitten started to screech.

This show of temper from Toff took Nellie by surprise. It was the first time she had seen him in a mood like this, and it was a side to his character that she did not like. 'No!' she yelled, suddenly barring Toff's way. 'Why der *you* always 'ave ter 'ave the last say about *everyfin'*?'

'Because I'm in charge, Nell!' Toff roared back. 'Someone has to take some responsibility around here.'

'That doesn't mean yer 'ave ter yell at people and be cruel ter dumb animals.'

'Don't be so stupid, Nell!' snapped Toff, trying to push his way past her.

Nellie refused to budge. 'It strikes me, you're the stupid one 'round 'ere, mate!' she said angrily, staring straight at him in the dim candlelight. 'If you're in charge, then yer shouldn't allow this lot to carry on livin' like this. Yer shouldn't allow them to sleep rough in smell-'oles like this, livin' on uvver people's rations and hard-earned pickin's!'

Toff wasn't prepared to take this kind of talk, not even from Nellie. 'I seem to remember that *you* didn't object too much when we took you in and looked after you!'

This remark infuriated Nellie even more, and her eyes were now sharp with rage. 'Look 'ere, mate,' she spluttered. 'I din't ask no one ter look after me. I'm capable of takin' care of meself, see! If you're so 'igh an' mighty, why can't yer go back ter yer own 'ome and try bossin' yer own folks around?'

Rats and Bonkers stood back in the shadows, dumbfounded by this angry exchange between Nellie and Toff.

Toff was clearly stung by what he considered to be Nellie's ingratitude. In a slightly cooler voice, he replied, 'You're not a prisoner here, Nell. No one's forcing you to stay. If you don't like the way we do things around here, you're at liberty to go.'

'That suits me fine, mate,' she replied haughtily. ''Cos that's wot I've bin wantin' ter do ever since I got 'ere!' She turned and made a move to leave. But as she did so, there was a powerful explosion just a few streets away. The force of the bomb knocked her off her feet, and as she and the others fell to the muddy floor, dust came tumbling down on to them from the makeshift ceiling. At the same time, the kitten Toff was holding tore into his hand with its tiny claws and bolted.

'Bloody thing!' Toff yelled, his hand bleeding. 'Come back!'

'Don't let 'im go!'

Rats and Bonkers were immediately up on their feet and making a dash for the door.

'You stupid idiots!' yelled Toff as the two boys rushed out after the kitten. 'You'll get yourselves killed! Get back here!' Then he turned and quickly pulled Nellie to her feet. 'Look what you've done!' he growled.

Outside the shelter, the whole world looked as though it was on fire. As far as the eye could see, sheets of flame crackled up into the dark night clouds, and every so often small puffs of menacing black smoke were punched into the sky by exploding ack-ack shells. In all directions, from Victoria Park in Hackney, Clissold Park in Stoke Newington, and Finsbury Park in Islington, magnificent great silver barrage balloons were bursting into flame, ignited by machine-gun fire from enemy aircraft. Rats and Bonkers went sprinting across this desolate landscape, their movements illuminated by the flames and the white light from a winter's moon as it dodged in and out of the clouds.

'Over here!' yelled Rats, as he caught sight of the elusive kitten who was scampering off towards the shell of an old furniture warehouse.

Bonkers was right behind him, and between them they tried to head off the small creature.

'Get back here, you idiots!' Toff yelled, trying to make himself heard above the sound of clanging fire and ambulance bells and distant bomb explosions. 'Leave the bloody cat!' he roared, now having to compete with someone else's voice booming out through a loud-hailer across the street, where a terrace of single-storey houses had just received a direct hit. 'You're mad! Let the thing go!'

Nellie watched in alarm as the two young boys clambered over the debris, calling out to the small kitten, stretching out their hands to try to retrieve it from a pile of fallen masonry. As she watched, she became aware of a new sound, a strange rat-a-tat-tat, like someone tapping their fingers on a drum, fast and furiously.

Her blood froze. Toff stared up into the sky behind him, where a sinister dark shape was descending at speed from the sky, swooping low over the burnt-out shells of the furniture store and warehouse.

'Rats! Bonkers!' Toff's voice was now close to hysteria. 'Get down! Get—'

His voice was drowned by the deadly sound of machine-gun fire which cut into the debris in two advancing columns directly towards Rats and Bonkers.

'Rats! Bonkers!'

It was too late. The young German pilot of the enemy Messerschmitt fighter plane had found his targets and very quickly brought the two boys down in a hail of machine-gun bullets.

'No ...!' Toff's anguish was immense.

Nellie was horrified by what she had seen. She was too scared to scream, and could only turn away and press her body against the outer wall of the burnt-out furniture store. She was shaking from head to foot, and was so cold she felt numb. When she was finally able to turn and look, she saw Toff crouched over the slumped, blood-stained figures of Rats and Bonkers.

He raised his head and saw Nellie watching him. The tears running down his cheeks glistened in the moonlight. 'I hope you're satisfied?' he called, his voice cracking with emotion.

Nellie clamped her hand across her mouth. She was too shocked and distressed to answer. In one swift movement, she disappeared into the

85

furniture store, made straight for her sleeping quarters, and collected the large shopping bag containing the few belongings she had acquired since joining the gang.

A few minutes later, shopping bag strapped across her shoulder, she made a discreet exit through the back of the old store and headed off on her own along Essex Road, which was rumbling to the sounds of yet another aerial onslaught.

The boiler and storage rooms in the bowels of Melbourne Road School were not the perfect places for forty or so orphans and staff to shelter in during an air raid, but as all the school's regular pupils had been evacuated at the start of the war, no proper shelter had been prepared. The basement rooms had been made as comfortable as possible, with mattresses and bedding taken from beds in the upstairs classrooms/dormitories. There were no separate rooms for the staff, and this had meant a great deal of organisation to ensure privacy for the male and female staff. Under normal circumstances, the children would have found it a great adventure to sleep in such unusual surroundings, but after their traumatic experience in the bombed orphanage, the sound of the nightly air raids was an unsettling experience for them all.

Tonight, however, the children had come back from the Hackney Empire in a happy mood, their spirits raised by the sight of the grotesque, ugly sisters being chased by Connie the Cow the sing-song with the principal boy, Buttons and the spectacle of the Prince's wedding to Cinderella. But as Ethel watched them all chatting excitedly and laughing about their treat, her mind was obsessed with the thought that Vicky Hobson had been in that theatre at the same time as all the other Barratts' orphans.

It wasn't until lights out that Ethel had the chance to relax and turn things over in her mind. Although the air raid was still rumbling on in the streets above, most of the children and staff were now asleep, and in the far corner of the main room, Ethel could hear the loudest snores of all coming from Mrs Hare. It was dark in the basement except for two paraffin lamps turned down very low. Ethel sat in a chair beside her bed, finishing a lukewarm cup of cocoa which Mrs Hare had made for her at least twenty minutes before. Then she leaned her head back against the chair, and closed her eyes. Her mind was racing. Could she believe that wretched child, Lizzie Morris? Had Vicky really been in that panto audience, and if so. why did no one else see her? Oh, why was Vicky doing this to her? What had she, Ethel, done to provoke such hate? Guilt. Guilt. Guilt.

''Scuse me, miss.'

Ethel's eyes sprang open. In the half-light, she could just make out a child's figure standing in front of her. 'Who is it?' she asked.

'It's me, miss.' The girl's squeaky voice was unmistakable.

'What do you want, Lizzie? Why aren't you asleep?'

Lizzie paused before answering. 'I couldn't sleep, miss. Not until I'd said sorry—for what 'appened this afternoon.'

Ethel stiffened, and her stomach went quite tense. 'What are you talking about?' she asked.

'About seein' Vicky, miss.'

Ethel felt the anger rising in her. Ever since she had come back from the theatre she had been tormented by the thought that Vicky had been there too. It would be absolutely contemptible if this child had been lying. 'Are you telling me that you *didn't* see her?'

'I'm not sure, miss,' replied Lizzie.

'Not sure?'

'Well, it looked like 'er, it really did. But there were lights shinin' in me eyes from the balcony upstairs and, well, I might 'ave been mistaken. It looked like Vicky, but then again, p'raps it wasn't.'

Ethel hated the way she felt about Lizzie. Every time she heard her weak, simpering voice, she felt like taking her by the shoulders and giving her a good shake. And as the child stood there in the dark, Ethel could imagine what she looked like, her tiny sharp eyes darting all over the place, her feigned look of innocence. It took all Ethel's strength to control her feelings of distaste, to keep herself cool and calm, and to remember that whatever she thought about her, Lizzie, like all the other children, depended on the orphanage for love and care. 'At the time you seemed quite sure,' she said. 'What changed your mind, Lizzie?'

Ethel could almost hear the mechanism in the child's brain working to think of an answer. ''Cos I knew 'ow upset you were, miss,' she replied. 'I'm not sayin' Vicky wasn't there, just that I'm not an 'undred per cent sure that she was.'

This time Ethel paused before answering. 'Thank you, Lizzie. I appreciate what you've said. Now go to bed, please.'

'Yes, miss.' Lizzie turned to go, then stopped. 'Miss,' she said, competing with Mrs Hare's snores.

'Yes?'

'I love yer, miss,' said the child, in her most unctuous voice. 'We all do. 'Onest we do.' Then lowering her voice to what was almost a sinister whisper, she added, 'If anyfin' ever 'appened to you, I'd be ever so upset.' Lizzie didn't wait for a reply. She scuttled off as silently as she had come. A few moments later, Ethel heard the rustle of bedclothes as the child tucked herself up in her eiderdown on the floor.

Ethel decided to go to bed too, but after that sickening declaration of love, she didn't think she would get much sleep.

Nellie had no idea where she was, or how far she had come. All she knew was that she had finally broken away from her extraordinary life with the vacs gang, and never wanted to know anything about them ever again. But the sight of Rats and Bonkers being mown down by machine-gun fire would haunt her for the rest of her life. And Toff was right, in a way she was responsible for what had happened to them. If only she hadn't argued with him about the kitten, if only she had accepted that what he had said about not keeping pets was common sense, perhaps those two boys would still be alive. Every time she thought about it, the skin all over her body went taut. She was consumed with guilt, and she had no idea how she was going to live with it. The large shopping bag containing her belongings seemed very heavy now, and as she struggled on her way, she was practically dragging it along the pavement.

Although the air raid was still in progress, during the past half-hour or so the intensity had subsided, and by the time she had made her way along Canonbury Road and reached Highbury Corner, the rumble of gunfire seemed to be confined to the far distance, probably somewhere over the London docks. Her only moment of panic came when she was approached by a Special Constable who asked why she was out all alone in the middle of an air raid. But after she had explained that she was on her way to join her mum and the rest of the family down the Tube, she was allowed to proceed unhindered.

Nellie didn't know why she had chosen to go down the main Holloway Road, for she could have gone in a southerly direction along Upper Street towards the Angel, Islington. But the road seemed to be very wide, and it gave her the chance to meander rather than to walk in a straight line.

Once she had got past the Highbury Picture Theatre, she found herself passing the Salvation Army Hall, the Central Library, and then a whole cluster of small shops that seemed to go on for ever. But the cold realisation dawned on her that she really had no idea where she was going, or how she was going to survive without food or somewhere to sleep. She might not have liked living rough with the boys up at Essex Road, but at least they had looked after her, at least she had felt safe in their company. And she could trust them, trust them all. Especially Toff.

She passed another cinema, the Regent, then made her way beneath the railway arch opposite Holloway Road Tube Station. As she passed yet another cinema, the Savoy, she could hear the rumble of gunfire getting closer again. Despite the weight of her cumbersome carrier bag, she began to trot, and when the sky was once again lit up by searchlights, she knew it would be only a matter of minutes before the first enemy raider was caught in the middle of them, like a fly caught in a spider's web.

She soon found herself running past a department store called Jones Brothers. There were no lights in the windows, and the large glass panes were patterned with sticky protective tape. Without warning, there was an angry barrage of ack-ack fire which was immediately followed by an open truck racing past her. It carried a multi-barrelled anti-aircraft gun on the back and a man was firing a rapid succession of small shells up into the sky. Now she was frightened, really frightened, and her first thoughts were of Toff. She found it hard to believe that at a moment like this he was the one person that she actually missed.

She ran across the road and took shelter in the doorway of what seemed to be a large restaurant right on the corner of Holloway and Tollington Roads. By now she was so exhausted, all she could do was to flop down on to the cold tiles and wait for the air raid to pass.

As she lay there, propped up against the glass door criss-crossed with protective tape, her mind was dominated by thoughts of Toff and the gang, and the night's events which had so shattered her life. And then, for one fleeting moment, she thought about herself, about who and where she was, and what she was going to do with herself now that she was out here on her own—truly on her own. How would she live? How would she survive?

Dazed with tiredness, eyes closed, her head slowly drooped and came to rest on her right shoulder. When she opened her eyes again, she saw a small hand-scrawled notice stuck to the restaurant window. It read:

'WANTED: Waitress. Must be prepared to work long hours. Good wages, food, and (if required) accommodation. Apply within.'

Chapter 6

Monsieur Pierre came out of his front door in Tufnell Park Road and took a deep breath of warm summer air. It was such a glorious June day that for the first time this year he was wearing his lightweight fawn summer suit, which perfectly matched his cream-coloured shirt and light-brown patterned Tootal tie. His shoes, which he had miraculously preserved since before the war, were dark brown and set off his brown trilby hat, which he always wore at a rakish angle. His sartorial elegance marked him out as a gentleman—of the theatre. Wherever he went he was noticed, for at six feet two inches tall, he towered over most people, but he was so painfully thin that anyone who met him for the first time felt like offering him some of their ration coupons to get himself a good meal.

His wife, referred to by Monsieur's legion of admirers as simply 'Madame', was quite different. Small and dumpy, she wore the same clothes day in and day out. They usually comprised a Woolworth's cotton dress, a long-sleeved black velvet jacket (a gift from her ancient mother), and a moth-eaten cotton hat with a green cockatoo feather stuck in the side. But now that it was early summer, she too had opted for a cooler, more seasonal look. She had discarded the velvet jacket. Although completely different in shape and size, this stylish pair were the perfect foreign couple—except that their real names were Albert and Doris Beckwith, and they came from Stepney in East London.

For the past three months or so there had been a lull in the air raids, and with the start of summer, there was cautious optimism everywhere. Not that anyone was complacent, for only the previous month there had been a terrifying all-night air raid with a heavy death toll, and only a few days before, the Prime Minister Mr Churchill had warned the British nation to be vigilant. However, the sun knew how to bring out the best in people and the streets were bustling with activity, with all the shop windows doing their best not to look too austere. It was a perfect day for 'Monsieur and Madame Pierre' to take their regular morning walk to their favourite Holloway restaurant, Beales.

In the winter the journey from Tufnell Park Road to the corner of Holloway and Tollington Roads took a laborious eight minutes, but in the summer, with the aid of his black ebony cane (a personal gift from the Maharaja of Jaipur), Monsieur set a brisk pace, and they always arrived in six and a half minutes precisely.

For a midweek morning, Beales was quite full today. Most of the people there were shoppers, for Jones Brothers department store was just across the road, and Holloway Road contained Woolworth's, Marks and Spencer, Selby's, and a veritable treasure chest of small shops such as Liptons, Sainsbury's, Lavells the sweet shop, Hicks the greengrocers, and the North London Drapery Stores around the corner in Seven Sisters Road. As it was only ten thirty in the morning, lunch was still an hour or so away, so Monsieur and Madame Pierre had plenty of time to have their usual cups of Lipton's tea, and whatever biscuits were available.

'Mornin', Pierre, Mrs Pierre,' said Nellie, looking as pretty as a picture in a waitress's cap stuck on top of her neatly permed head of tight brown curls, a black dress, and white apron. 'The usual?' she asked, waiting to memorise the order as she was still unable to read or write.

'But of course, ducks,' replied Monsieur in a broad Cockney accent that hardly matched his classy foreign appearance. 'Got any new bickies terday?'

''Fraid not,' she replied, shaking her head sadly. 'Lincolns or crackers.'

Monsieur sighed. He hated Lincolns and crackers. So dry, so bland, and not sweet. Oh, how he longed for the good old days before the war, the time of digestives, petit beurres and chocolate fingers.

'Never mind, Nellie dear,' said Madame, who had a lovely smile and an attractive mole on her right cheek with two dark hairs growing out of it. 'We're lucky ter 'ave anyfin' in these 'ard times.'

Nellie smiled, did a brief curtsy, then scuttled off to the kitchen.

'She's such a luvely gel,' said Madame, watching Nellie disappear. 'She shouldn't be

95

workin' in a place like this. She should be 'ome wiv 'er mum an' dad, bein' looked after.'

'You 'eard wot she told us,' replied Monsieur, resting both his hands on top of his cane as he took in the other customers, in the hope that at least one of them would recognise him as the great music hall illusionist. 'She's got no family. That's why she 'as ter live in accommodation next door.'

Although Monsieur and Madame had been regular customers at Beales since they got back from their provincial tour up north, they had only actually been waited on by Nellie three or four times. But the moment they saw her, they were impressed by her good manners and the way she kept her back straight and erect as she went in and out of the kitchen balancing trays of tea on the fingers of one hand. When they did eventually get talking to her, they liked her so much that they had asked the restaurant supervisor, Mrs Wiggins, to make Nellie their 'regular'. And today they had quite a treat for her.

When Nellie went into the kitchen, Mrs Wiggins was helping the chef peel potatoes for lunch. She was a kindly woman. When Nellie had first approached her for the job back in January, she had overlooked the fact that the girl had neither an identity card nor a National Security number, and taken her on without hesitation, saying that a girl of sixteen was hardly likely to be a Nazi spy! Nellie was the youngest person on the staff, for the three other waitresses were all middle-aged. They all got on well together, and once or twice Nellie had been invited back to the women's homes to meet the rest of their families. Nonetheless, Nellie was finding it a hard life, on her feet from eight in the morning until closing time at five thirty in the evening. But at least her room in the hostel next door to the restaurant was comfortable, and as the job included two good meals a day, she had no complaints.

'I want you to be extra nice to the gentleman and his wife today, Nellie,' said Mrs Wiggins, who had a rather elegant face which gave the impression that she should be above peeling potatoes. 'Mr Beckwith is going to allow us to put his photograph up on the wall,' she whispered, even though Hubert the chef had already heard the news. 'And he's also agreed to sign it. Don't you think that's wonderful, Nellie? It'll be so good for business to have a music hall star's photograph on our wall.'

'Won'erful,' replied Nellie, who was just as excited as Mrs Wiggins.

'We need some more spuds!' yelled Hubert.

'Coming up!' returned another male voice in the scullery adjoining the kitchen.

Nellie quickly prepared a tray of tea and biscuits for Monsieur and Madame. She poured boiling water from a kettle into the white teapot and collected two white cups and saucers and a small jug of powdered milk.

Behind her, Mrs Wiggins produced two Chelsea buns from a cardboard box that was tucked underneath the work counter. 'I want you to give these to the gentleman and lady.

Tell them they're with the compliments of the management.'

Nellie took the buns and put them on to two small tea plates. Then she picked up the tray, balanced it on one hand as she had been trained by Mrs Wiggins, and wound her way back through the kitchen mayhem to the swing doors.

'Oh, and Nellie!'

Nellie stopped and turned.

'Tell them we've got no marg,' said Mrs Wiggins. 'Apologise.'

Nellie nodded, and went into the restaurant.

When she reached their table, she found Monsieur smoking an Abdullah cigarette through a long cigarette holder and Madame reading an article in the *News Chronicle* about how the Germans had invaded the Greek island of Crete, and how many good British soldiers had died trying to protect their mates during the subsequent evacuation.

'I 'ate the war,' sighed Madame, putting her newspaper down to make room for the tea tray. 'I 'ate the Germans. All they can fink about is killin' and more killin'.' She looked up at Nellie. There was despair in the poor woman's eyes. 'Sometimes I fear fer the future. Not fer me, but fer the likes of young fings like you, and me own two kids.'

'Stop bein' so gloomy, Doris,' said Monsieur. 'The war won't last for ever. And anyway, we have some exciting times to look forward to.'

Madame smiled affectionately at her husband. He was such an escapist, but she loved him dearly.

'The supervisor told me to give you these buns,' said Nellie. 'Compliments of the management.' She put them on the table in front of Madame.

''Ow smashin'!' she said.

'Marvellous!' he said.

'Sorry there's no marg, though,' added Nellie. 'Nor any sugar.'

Madame shook her head. 'Don't worry about that, dear.' She bent her head forward to savour the smell of her bun. 'We're very lucky people, aren't we, Albert?'

Monsieur drew on his cigarette holder and exhaled a long thin trail of blue-grey smoke. 'That we are,' he agreed.

Nellie bowed briefly and turned to leave.

''Ang on a moment, love,' Monsieur said quickly. 'Got somefin' ter give yer before yer go.'

Nellie watched Monsieur hold the cigarette holder between his teeth, dig into his inside jacket pocket, and produce what looked like a small piece of paper.

'A little present from us ter you,' he announced with a flourish.

Nellie looked at the piece of paper in his hand as though it was something dangerous. 'What is it?'

'Take it, dear,' said Madame with a broad, friendly grin. 'It'll bring yer luck.'

Nellie took the piece of paper, looked at

it, but was none the wiser. She asked again, 'What is it?'

Monsieur pulled himself up in his chair to his full height. 'That, me dear,' he said, taking the cigarette holder out of his mouth, 'is a ticket to a star performance.'

Nellie's eyes widened.

Madame leaned forward and rested her hand on Nellie's arm. 'It's a ticket fer our next bookin', dear,' she said, voice low. 'Finsbury Park Empire. First 'ouse, Monday. Max Miller's top of the bill, but Albert's closin' the first 'alf.'

Nellie looked back at the piece of paper she was holding between her thumb and first finger. Suddenly it seemed like magic. 'Fer me? A ticket—fer the feater? *Free?*'

'As free as air, darlin',' exclaimed Monsieur loudly.

'It's our way of sayin' fank yer fer the nice way yer treat us when we come 'ere,' said Madame. 'It's a nice, comfy seat in the stalls, third row from the front, right in the middle.' She leaned closer again. 'You'll be sittin' wiv our two boys,' she whispered. 'You'll get on like an 'ouse on fire.'

Nellie was overwhelmed and didn't know what to say. 'F—fank yer,' she spluttered. 'Fank yer very much.'

Madame was delighted to see such a smile come to Nellie's face, and she squeezed her arm affectionately. 'Somefin' ter look forward to, dear,' she said.

Monsieur looked pleased with himself. No,

more than that. He was over the moon. This was mainly because a young couple at the corner table had recognised him and sent their small son across to ask him to sign the back of an empty cigarette packet.

When Nellie got back to the staff hostel each evening, she was usually dead on her feet. The hours were indeed long, and for the best part of the day she spent her time going backwards and forwards between the restaurant and kitchen balancing a whole weight of dishes on a large metal tray. Not that her height or slight build in any way restricted her from doing what the rest of the staff did—in fact Mrs Wiggins had often remarked how sturdy Nellie was—but it was a soulless job that never seemed to get anywhere. It did have its compensations, however, like meeting different people such as Monsieur and Madame, and having a little money in her pocket to go to the pictures or take a bus up to Finsbury Park. And one of her great joys was that her room had a wind-up gramophone on which she could hear all the latest records by such popular performers as Bing Crosby, the Andrews Sisters, Anne Shelton, Donald Peers, and Harry Roy and his Band. In the staff sitting room there was also a wireless set, but it was always tuned to the news. Nellie absolutely hated the news because it was all about the war, and war to her brought back so many horrific memories.

Because most of the staff were middle-aged, in the five months or so since she had been at Beales, Nellie had made very few friends of her own age. She had met no one like Toff, and whenever she was at her lowest, she always thought of him. She was still tormented by the feeling that she was responsible for what had happened to Rats and Bonkers. The painful memory was worst at night as she lay in bed before going to sleep. But Toff's face was always there before her, with those gleaming dark eyes, jet-black hair greased back over his slightly protruding ears, and a swarthy complexion that gave Nellie a tingling sensation every time she thought about him. But Toff was in the past, and nothing in this world was going to persuade her to look for him.

Nellie's best friend at the restaurant was Hubert the chef. He was a funny little bloke, not much taller than Nellie herself, and his constant grumbling about the customers made Nellie laugh, mainly because she agreed with practically everything he said. Even his face made her laugh. It was small and round and Nellie often told him that he looked like a rabbit because even when his mouth was closed she could see the tips of his teeth. Hubert was in fact quite a sad character. Ever since he left school it had been his ambition to become a policeman, but his height and the fact that he wore spectacles put paid to that. It was also the reason why he had been turned down for conscription. But whenever Nellie was feeling fed up, it was usually Hubert she turned to. He was a real stay-at-home; he spent most evenings alone in his room, endlessly reading the sports pages of the *Daily Sketch* and smoking himself to death with foul Woodbine cigarettes. Tonight, however, Nellie was determined to get him out of his room.

'Come on, Hube!' She called, thumping on his bedroom door soon after she'd had her supper in the staff dining room. 'Don't be such a lazy ole git! It's a luvely evenin'. Put yer shoes on an' let's go out an' 'ave a walk.'

Hubert's door suddenly opened and a pall of choking cigarette smoke wafted out. 'Walk?' he bellowed, fag in mouth, and began to cough. 'Wot do we wanna walk for? I've bin on me plates of meat all day!'

Nellie laughed and fanned away the smoke with her hand. 'There's somefin' outside called fresh air,' she jeered. 'Why don't you an' me sample it?'

Despite Hubert's objections, a few minutes later they were strolling idly along Tollington Road. After a long hard winter stuck down the air raid shelters, many people were taking advantage of the warm weather to sit on chairs in their small front yards or chat amiably with their neighbours at the gate. The war seemed a long way away this evening. Not that anyone was under the illusion that it was all over; this was only a temporary lull and everyone knew it. But it was good to feel the evening sun on their faces and watch the sparrows and pigeons preening themselves on the leafy branches of elm and poplar trees.

Nellie enjoyed living in this part of Islington. It wasn't nearly as snooty as some of the boys in the gang used to tell her; she put down their resentment to the divide between North Londoners and those living in the East End, who considered themselves, quite rightly, to be the real London Cockneys. She admired the tall Edwardian houses on either side of the busy Tollington Road. Small back streets led to Seven Sisters Road on her left and the red-brick Shelburne Road School on her right, which was now being used by the Auxiliary Fire Service.

'Tell me about yerself, Hube,' Nellie said brightly as they crossed Hornsey Road.

'Wot yer talkin' about?'

'Tell me about yerself,' Nellie said again. 'You know, about where yer come from, yer mum an' dad an' all that.'

Hubert scratched his head. His stroll was more of a shuffle, and he never once took the fag from his lips. 'I 'ad a mum an' dad once. That I do know.'

'Of course yer 'ave a mum an' dad, yer twerp!' said Nellie. 'Everyone does. Wot I mean is, where are they now?'

''Ow should I know?' replied Hubert, whose fag was now almost burning his lips. 'Down Romford, I reckon. That's where they live.'

'Don't yer ever see them?'

Hubert turned with a start to look at her. 'Wot do I wanna do that for? I don't like 'em. They don't like me.'

Nellie stopped, shook her head, and sighed. 'Yer know, I don't understand boys,' she said. 'None of 'em seem ter get on wiv their folks at 'ome.'

104

Hubert shrugged his shoulders, pulled the fag butt from his lips and threw it to the pavement. 'Wot's so special about 'ome?' he asked.

Hubert's response bewildered Nellie, and then she asked herself, what *is* so special about home? Well, for one thing it meant being part of a family, your own family, with a mum and dad who cared for you, who took the trouble to talk to you when you were in trouble, who allowed you to be yourself and didn't keep questioning you about where you went and what you did. Home was about love, and being loyal and faithful, and thinking about other people and not just yourself. 'I wouldn't mind one of me own,' she said with a glance at Hubert. 'They say what yer've never 'ad, yer never miss,' she added wistfully. 'Not in my case, it 'ain't.'

They moved on past the Globe pub where Bessie, the regular tinkler, was already bashing out a favourite song on the old joanna. Although it was only eight o'clock in the evening, the customers were in boisterous mood, belting out a spirited rendering of 'Boiled Beef and Carrots'. Further along the road, Nellie and Hubert stopped for a few moments to watch a team of workmen, stripped to the waist, pulling down the remains of some houses that had recently been devastated by a high-explosive bomb.

'The fing is,' said Hubert, who was lighting up another Woodbine, 'we all 'ave ter make our own way in this life. Take me, fer instance. I'm a square peg in a round 'ole, that's me.

I coulda bin workin' down the Ritz if it weren't fer me old man. When I told 'im I couldn't get in the police force 'cos I wasn't tall enough, 'e practically told me I was a liar. An' yer should've 'eard 'im when I said I was goin' ter work as a cook. Called me all the bloody pansies under the sun.' He took a deep drag of his Woodbine and nearly choked. 'So don't talk ter me about 'ome. Ter me, it's all overrated.'

Nellie only half heard what Hubert said, her attention was focused on the workmen. 'Yer know, it's a funny feelin' not knowin' who yer mum an' dad was,' she said, 'or if yer 'ad any bruvvers or sisters or aunts an' uncles. There are times when I feel—empty, as though I've got no stomach. Take the people who lived in those 'ouses over there,' she said, indicating the bomb site. 'I wonder 'ow many of them were families.'

Hubert was concerned that she was getting maudlin about her lack of identity. He moved round to stand in front of her. 'It's not important, Nell, believe me. It's not who yer are that matters, but what yer are.'

Nellie, eyes glazed, appeared to be looking straight through him. 'That's not what Miss Ackroyd says,' she answered.

Hubert scratched his head again. 'Who's Miss Ackroyd?'

Nellie blinked. 'Wot d'yer say, Hube?'

'I said, who's Miss Ackroyd?'

Nellie looked totally nonplussed. 'Who? I don't know wot you're talkin' about.'

Chapter 7

A few days later, Hitler committed what Winston Churchill later described as one of the greatest blunders in history: the Nazi leader invaded Soviet Russia. For the people of London, this meant a continuation of the lull in air raids, as it was obvious that from now on, the Luftwaffe would need to deploy much of their aggressive air power to a second front. And so the pubs were packed again, parks were crowded with people enjoying the hot summer sunshine, and places of entertainment such as cinemas were gradually reverting to their normal opening hours.

The Monday first house performance at the Finsbury Park Empire was full to capacity, not a seat was empty. This was unusual for a first house, for most people didn't get home from work until six o'clock or so, which made getting to a six fifteen first house show almost impossible. But this particular week there was a good reason for the great demand for tickets, for top of the bill was one of the great stand-up comedians of the music hall, the 'Cheeky Chappie' himself, the one and only Max Miller. This ribald entertainer was a star wherever he went, despite the fact that on occasions he had been in trouble with the authorities for his blue jokes and outrageous humour. Nonetheless he was an idol for countless millions of music hall and wireless fans, and an appearance on the Moss Empires circuit meant the clicking of cash tills all over the country. And if a performance by this famous London comedian wasn't enough, the lead supporting act of Monsieur Pierre, 'Illusionist Extraordinaire', made the whole evening irresistible.

Nellie arrived at the theatre before the doors had even opened. The fact that she was able to get there so early was due to Mrs Wiggins who, thrilled to know that Nellie was to be Monsieur's guest at the show, let her off work the moment she had done the three o'clock afternoon tea shift. When she got there, there was an aura of excitement in the foyer, a real buzz that this was not only the start of a new week's shows but the first night of a 'special'.

The moment she got inside, she was thrilled to be given a programme of her own, which had been thoughtfully organised by Monsieur and Madame. Her very own programme! And when the usherette showed her personally to her seat, she felt as though she was Lady Muck herself! Waiting for her in row C, third row centre stalls, were Monsieur and Madame's two sons, Sid and Lenny. Sid, at thirteen, was the older of the two brothers and looked like a carbon copy of his dad, except that he had a mole on his right cheek, just like his mum. Young Lenny was two years younger than his brother, and looked nothing like either his mum or dad. In fact he was quite plain, with a perpetually sulky expression, tight blond curls, small metal-rimmed spectacles, and two large upper front teeth which, according to his brother, made him look like Count Dracula. 'Bet you're lucky to have a famous star for a dad, ain't yer?' was one of the first questions Nellie asked her companions. But as the only response she got was a bored shrug, she decided to look around the theatre and look at her programme until curtain up.

To Nellie, the auditorium of this lovely music hall was truly beautiful to look at. Like the Hackney Empire, where she had seen *Cinderella,* the curtains were scarlet plush and gold, and looked dazzling in the glare of the spotlights. She swivelled round in her seat to look at the upper circle and the gods, where she would have been sitting if she hadn't been given a free ticket. The atmosphere was quite unlike anything she had ever experienced. It was a hot night, and everywhere she looked she could see a mass of faces gazing down towards the stage, all fanning themselves with their programmes, and even in the posh seats in the four boxes bordering each side of the stage, men had removed their jackets and ladies were in short-sleeved summer frocks, wiping their foreheads with their handkerchiefs. Nellie herself, however, was as cool as a cucumber. She was wearing a second-hand cotton summer dress she had bought from a market stall in the Caledonian Road the previous Saturday afternoon. In fact, although the two sons of Monsieur and Madame made it only too obvious that they couldn't care less what their companion for the evening was wearing, Nellie looked radiant with her hair tied behind her head with a piece of blue ribbon, and a thin layer of dark red lipstick which she had picked up from a jumble stall in the same market.

When the lights finally went down, Nellie was in such a high state of excited anticipation, she thought she would never last until the interval before having to go out to the Ladies. But as soon as a bright white spotlight picked out the arrival of the orchestra conductor in his long black tails, bow tie, and white carnation, her worry vanished. Suddenly, the orchestra was playing a riotous overture of 'Here We Are, Here We Are, Here We Are Again!' and as one the whole audience joined in the chorus.

The first half of the show consisted of five acts. Nellie couldn't read, so her programme was only good as a souvenir to cherish, and every time the secondary stage curtains parted, each new act was, for her, a delightful surprise. First came some chorus girls dancing in a line. This made Nellie snigger, for the girls' costumes were very scant and provoked quite a few wolf whistles from some servicemen in the audience, and also Nellie's two young companions. This was followed by a strong lady who tore up telephone directories, a wonderful ventriloquist named Albert Saveen with a saucy but lovable dummy called Daisy, and a crooner who also did impersonations of Arthur Askey, Sir Harry Lauder, and Winston Churchill. But the moment Nellie, and presumably her two companions, had been waiting for finally arrived as a booming voice announced over the theatre's tannoy

110

system, 'And now, ladies and gentlemen, the Finsbury Park Empire is proud to present, straight from his success at the Grand Theatre, Leeds, the irrepressible, the incorrigible, the master of mystery and imagination, the man who can work miracles, the Illusionist Extraordinaire, Monsieur Pierre!'

The theatre erupted in applause and cheers, with Nellie clapping her hands so hard they began to sting. The house lights went out, and as the curtains slowly began to part, a small spotlight picked out what looked like a toy snake which gradually began to rise and waver to and fro towards the audience. It was such a creepy image that Nellie began to sink down into her seat, but she sat bolt upright when, with a clash of cymbals, the snake suddenly vanished and in its place appeared a skeleton! Some of the female members of the audience screamed, including Nellie, but when the lights were suddenly turned up again, the skeleton disappeared, to be replaced by the extraordinary figure of Monsieur Pierre himself. When Nellie had recovered from her shock, she was thrilled to see her friend Monsieur bowing to the audience, who were giving him a rapturous reception. She stared goggle-eyed at the stage setting. Question-mark motifs hung all over the drapes, and different coloured lights flashed on and off, eerily illuminating the upright coffin-like cabinet centre stage. The biggest surprise for Nellie was to see Madame sitting at a grand piano to the side of the stage. She looked so different in her black evening dress, trimmed with black fur round the neck, and her hair neatly permed into tight black curls. When Monsieur started his act, she played music which perfectly matched the mood of the mysterious illusions created by the star.

The act itself lasted almost twenty minutes, and consisted of Monsieur Pierre, with the help of a young female assistant, performing a series of tricks which gave the audience the impression that they were watching something that was not really there at all. Nellie was fascinated by it all, but when she turned to comment on the act to her two companions, both of them were leaning back in their seats, eyes closed, obviously bored, chewing toffees that their dad had managed to get them on the black market.

Monsieur Pierre, immaculate in a one-piece suit of black satin, a green sash draped across his chest, an ultra tall top hat perched on his head, and with his eyes made up with thick pencil lines and mascara to match his black moustache, performed his illusions with flair, panache, and extraordinarily agile movements. He appeared as light and nimble on his feet as a ballet dancer, and his frequent heavily-accented calls of 'See me! I am invincible!' and ''Ere is my miracle!' were made with a theatrical flourish that would have impressed even the most sceptical of onlookers. Once or twice Madame glanced briefly at Nellie in the stalls, which brought a blush to her cheeks because she had the feeling that the whole audience was looking to see who and where she was—which of course they weren't.

Monsieur's *pièce de résistance* was accomplished with the aid of his female assistant, who had spent most of the time with a fixed grin on her face, gesticulating towards the 'Master' as though she herself had performed all the tricks. The final illusion consisted of putting the female assistant inside the upright wooden coffin and making her disappear, to reappear instantly from the wings of the stage. 'Now you zee 'er—now you don't!' proclaimed Monsieur, triumphantly, and with great humour. The audience burst into thunderous applause, which went on for several minutes, before the red plush curtains came down, then opened just wide enough for Monsieur to take a bow. After calling on Madame and the young assistant, all three joined hands, took a bow together, then disappeared into the wings.

During the interval, whilst the Safety Curtain came down to allow projected advertisements for local shops and services, Nellie did her best to make conversation with her two companions. 'Wasn't yer dad marvellous!' she enthused as the lights went up.

Sid sat up in his seat and shrugged his shoulders. 'He was OK,' he replied non-committally. 'I've seen him before.'

'Lots of times,' chimed in Lenny. It was more or less the first time the two of them had opened their mouths all evening.

'If *I* 'ad a dad like that,' said Nellie, a touch irritated with them, 'I'd be really proud.'

'Yeah, I bet,' sneered Lenny with a smirk. 'Just fink wot 'e could do ter you if 'e put *you* inside that coffin.' He and his brother sniggered.

'Just fink wot *I* could do ter you two if I put *you* in there!' Nellie retaliated.

The two boys stopped sniggering.

'Don't worry,' she added mischievously. 'I'd make sure yer was dead first!'

When the show was over, Nellie, the two boys, and the rest of the audience filed out through the main foyer where the second house crowds were lined up waiting for admittance. For Nellie, the evening had been wonderful, what with seeing Monsieur perform his own act on the stage and then rolling with laughter at Max Miller's dirty jokes at the end of the second half. In fact just being inside the theatre had somehow inspired her; it had such an aura, an atmosphere that was so different from anywhere else. And that persistent pungent smell of sweet perfume and cigarette smoke. It was intoxicating!

Nellie had promised to go backstage to visit Monsieur and Madame after the show. As she accompanied the boys to the stage door, they passed the entrance to the gods where a long queue had formed waiting for entrance and any return tickets.

'Straight in, miss!' called the stage door keeper without even inquiring who she was. It was obvious that he had seen Monsieur and Madame's boys many times, and as she was with them, he had no need to waste time asking questions. 'Dressin' room number two.'

114

Nellie followed the two boys through the stage door and found herself in a narrow corridor with plain green plaster walls. After going down some stone steps, they turned into another narrow corridor. As they did so, a door opened suddenly, and a man's head peered out.

''Arry!' he yelled. 'Get us a bottle of Guinness, will yer?'

Nellie stopped dead. It was the great man himself, Max Miller.

''Allo, 'allo, 'allo then,' he said, still removing his make-up with a piece of cotton wool smothered in cold cream. 'Back fer some more punishment, eh, lads?'

''Allo, Mr Miller,' the two boys said in unison.

'This gel's wiv us,' groaned Lenny. ''Er name's Nellie.'

'Is it now?' replied Miller. 'Please ter meet you, young lady,' he said to Nellie with a nod of the head.

Nellie's mouth dried up, and when she replied it was more of a croak. 'Fank yer, sir,' she said. 'I fawt you was marvellous ternight, sir. I larffed ever so much.'

Max Miller's face lit up. 'Hey!' he said brightly. 'That's really nice of yer ter say so, duckie. Yer must come again—soon.' With that, he returned to his dressing room, where voices inside indicated that he had visitors waiting for him.

Nellie watched him close the door before following the two boys, who had already

115

disappeared into their parents' dressing room further down the corridor.

'Come on in, darlin'!' Monsieur's voice boomed out from inside the dressing room. The door was wide open.

Nellie peered in and saw Monsieur at his dressing table, also removing make-up with cold cream. But when she saw his reflection in the dressing-table mirror, it took her some time to bring the Monsieur she was used to into focus, for his head was bald, with just a fringe of greying hair over his ears and around the lower part of his head. Not that she thought his lack of hair made him any less striking, but his appearance was so different from the well-coiffeured look she was used to.

'Come in, Nellie dear! We're just goin' ter 'ave a nice cup of tea.'

Nellie turned her attention to Madame, who had just finished boiling up a kettle of water on a small gas ring in the corner of the room.

'We always 'ave our tea in between first an' second 'ouse,' Madame said with her usual comfortable smile. 'Gives us a chance ter rest an' unwind.'

Nellie smiled back. Sid and Lenny, she noticed, were occupying the only armchair in the room, and were tucking into a plate of cheese and pickle and spam sandwiches.

'So wot d'yer fink, Nellie?' asked Monsieur, talking to her reflection in the mirror while he continued to remove his make-up. ''Ow'd d'yer like the act?'

116

'I fawt yer was t'rrific, sir,' she answered timidly, quite overcome by the strange room she was in, with the blinding lightbulbs round the dressing-table mirror dazzling her eyes. 'Fanks ever so much fer givin' me the ticket.'

'Pleasure, darlin'!' he said, taking a deep drag on an Abdullah fag through his cigarette holder. 'Now yer know 'ow we feater folk really live.'

Yer can say that again! Nellie thought to herself, her eyes watering in the smoke-filled room. She was fascinated by the weird paraphernalia stacked around the place. The room itself was quite small and bare, with plain green distempered walls, but Monsieur and Madame's different costumes draped on hangers on various hooks and the props from the act made everything seem exotic and glamorous. Even the coloured handkerchiefs and the magic lantern Monsieur had used looked as though they were alive, and Madame's black velvet costume and fur collar made her look not only slimmer but also quite mysterious.

'I must say, you were a lovely audience, dear,' Madame said from the washbasin where she was adding water to some powdered milk. 'Very appreciative.'

'You was too slow on the lantern trick,' sniffed Lenny, his mouth stuffed full of spam sandwich.

'Bull!' snapped Monsieur. He was combing his jet-black wig which was mounted on a stand. 'It was dead on!'

'Lenny's right, Dad,' said Sid, less sourly than his brother. 'The kaleidoscope effect got held up 'cos you was a bit late.'

As usual when her sons criticised the act, Madame intervened. 'I must say,' she said sweetly, only too aware that as the two boys had seen the act so many times, they were picking holes in it, 'I didn't notice it, dear. From where I was sitting, it looked wonderful.'

Such a perfect wife, thought Nellie.

''Ow would *you* know?' snapped Lenny. 'You can't see nuffin' from where *you* sit.'

Nellie felt as though she could have strangled the boy. Both children were clearly spoilt brats although Sid, the older one, was slightly less objectionable than his brother.

Just then, there was a knock on the door and without being asked to come in, Monsieur's young girl assistant poked her head in. 'Mind if I go an' 'ave a breaver, Albert?' she rasped. She was a brassy looking girl, with long blonde hair piled on top of her head, held down with a gawdy rhinestone coronet. 'Eddie Sparks 'as asked me ter go 'an 'ave a cuppa wiv 'im at the tea stall outside the park gates.'

'Off yer go,' replied Monsieur, who was already applying fresh make-up ready for the second house show. 'Make sure you're back by the 'alf.'

'Righto.'

The girl was about to close the door and go, when Madame called to her. 'Ange, dear before you go, come an' say 'ello to a friend of ours. Nellie, this is our Ange. She's a foreigner,' she said jokingly. 'From down Streatham way. Ange, this is Nellie.'

Ange, who was still wearing her rather skimpy stage costume, came into the room and offered her hand. 'Pleased ter meet yer.' Her voice was more like a squeak.

'Me too.' Nellie took her hand, which was limp and sweaty, a bit like a wet kipper, she thought. As Ange turned to go, Nellie noticed that her costume was too tight for her; her rather large bum looked, to say the least, somewhat constricted.

'An' put some clothes on,' said Monsieur, watching his assistant's reflection in the mirror. 'You go out like that an' you'll 'ave 'alf the British Army after yer!'

The girl slammed the door behind her as she left.

'I know wot she's after,' growled Lenny, downing a glass of Tizer.

'Don't be rude, Lenny,' said his mum handing Nellie a cup of tea. 'It's none of your business, son.'

'Who cares?' remarked Monsieur. 'As long as she don't get boozed before the 'alf. I don't want 'er fallin' about all over the place.'

'Before the 'alf?' said Nellie, looking puzzled.

''Alf an 'our before the act goes on,' explained Madame. 'We 'ave a lotta funny slang in the feater.'

For the next half hour, Nellie had tea and some sandwiches with Madame while Monsieur drank brown ale, poured from a quart bottle which he kept on one side of his dressing table. For Nellie it was not only a fascinating experience to be in the dressing room of a famous music hall performer, but a comforting feeling to know that she was in the presence of a family, a *real* family. Monsieur and Madame obviously cared for each other and, lousy brats though they were, they cared for their kids too. It sent pangs of longing through Nellie's veins, and maybe because of this, it gave her the feeling that somewhere in her former life she too had been part of a family. For call them what you will—Monsieur Pierre and Madame, or just plain Albert and Doris Beckwith—to Nellie they were a true inspiration.

'Oh, by the way, Doris, me darlin',' said Monsieur from the ensuite toilet where he was washing his hands in the chipped enamel sink, 'after the show ternight, yer'd better go on 'ome wiv the boys. I've got a meetin' wiv Charlie 'Orton.'

Madame turned with a start. 'Oh Albert,' she said, clearly taken by surprise. 'Not ternight. Not the first night.'

Monsieur was now wiping his hands on the towel in the toilet. 'Can't be 'elped, darlin',' he said, sounding apologetic. 'Business is business. Eddie reckons there's a chance of gettin' a spot in the new show at the Palladium. Can't miss out on that.'

Madame looked thoroughly downcast. But she quickly composed herself and smiled bravely. 'It's all right, dear. I quite understand.'

Even though Madame had clearly had to cope with this kind of disappointment before, after such an unblemished happy evening, for Nellie it was a strangely disturbing moment.

By the time Nellie left the Finsbury Park Empire, the second house had already begun. As she passed the gods entrance, she could hear the happy chorus of 'Here we are, here we are, here we are again!' bursting forth from the orchestra pit and auditorium, and even as she made her way beneath the railway arch in Seven Sisters Road, in her mind's eye she could still see the stage and everything that had taken place on it.

As she passed the vast white tiled frontage of the magnificent Astoria Cinema and started to make her way back along Isledon Road towards the hostel, her mind was dominated not by Monsieur Pierre's performance but by Albert and Doris Beckwith and their two young sons. For some inexplicable reason they had focused her attention on something that had been on her mind since she and Hubert had gone for their evening stroll just a few days before. Who *was* Miss Ackroyd? Where did the name come from when she had no recollection of any such person in her life? She wondered if Miss Ackroyd might perhaps be her *own* name. Maybe the memory of her former life was at last beginning to filter back. Perhaps, after all, she hadn't come from that orphanage. Perhaps she did have a family of her own, and the bombing of Barratts' Orphanage that same night was pure coincidence. Suddenly her spirits were raised, and she started to imagine a whole new scenario, a mum and dad of her own, maybe brothers and sisters. From there, she imagined all sorts of things, that the Ackroyd family were probably at that very moment trying to find her, that she was on a missing persons list at the local police station. Or did they believe that she had been blown to pieces by a bomb somewhere? Would they have simply accepted her death as inevitable, in view of her disappearance? Whoever the Ackroyd family were, wherever they were, they must be heartbroken. What should she do? What *could* she do? And once again the answer came to her. Nothing. She would do nothing because the truth scared her. If what she had imagined was not true, how would she ever be able to face up to the future?

As she climbed the stone steps leading to the hostel, one of two terraced houses next door to Beales Restaurant, a light summer drizzle began. She found her keys, opened the front door, and hurried in.

Inside her room, she opened the blackout curtains which she had drawn before she went to the theatre. It was still light outside, but dull and grey, so she decided to go to the sitting room. As she expected, no one was there, which gave her the chance to turn on the wireless in the hope that there was something more than the boring old news bulletin. Unfortunately she had missed *Monday Night at Eight* on the Home Service, and the nine o'clock news had indeed already started. She quickly re-tuned to the forces station and immediately recognised one of her favourite singers, Anne Shelton, who was the main guest on a variety programme called *Northern Music Hall.*

Settling back in a rather austere armchair, she was soon carried away by the sweet sounds of 'You'll Never Know', sung in those characteristic velvet tones that had made Anne Shelton such a popular wartime singer. After a few moments, the door opened and in walked Hubert.

'Wotcha!' he called. 'So 'ow'd it go?'

Nellie turned to look at him. ''Ow'd *what* go?' she asked.

'The Empire, yer nut! Finsbury Park. 'Ow was the show?'

Nellie knew she was no longer going to be able to listen to Anne Shelton, so she got up and switched off the wireless. 'It was smashin'. Specially Monsewer Pierre.'

Although there was no fire in the grate, Hubert went and stood with his back to it, took out one of his dreaded Woodbines, lit up, and started coughing, as usual. 'Wot about old Maxie Miller?' he asked. 'Plenty of dirty jokes, I bet.'

Nellie grinned. 'Oh yes,' she replied.

Hubert waited a moment. 'Well, come on then. Let's 'ear some.'

'Don't be daft,' said Nellie, curling up side-legged on the sofa. 'I can't remember jokes. They all sound the same ter me.'

'Gels!' Hubert spluttered, disappointed. 'Yer miss all the best parts.'

''Ad a good time wiv Mr Beckwiff, an'

123

'is missus. I really like 'em.' Even as she spoke, Nellie felt a nagging feeling inside. She couldn't exactly understand why, only that she had been concerned by Madame's expression when her husband told her he had to go out on business after the show that night. 'As a matter of fact, they've asked me over ter 'ave tea wiv 'em on Sunday afternoon. They're playin' at Chiswick Empire all next week.'

Hubert flopped down into the armchair that Nellie had just vacated, put his feet up unceremoniously on to a small highly polished coffee table in front of him, leaned his head back, and smoked his cigarette. 'Looks like you're well in there,' he said, again coughing and spluttering. 'Unless they 'ave ter close down the 'alls and picture 'ouses again.'

Nellie turned with a start. 'Close them down again? Why should they?'

'Churchill's warned we might get some more air raids. It was on the six o'clock news. Could be worse than ever.'

'Oh no,' groaned Nellie. 'Not again. I fawt it was all over.'

After a moment's pause, Hubert looked across at her. 'Ever fawt about gettin' out of this place, Nell?' he asked gingerly.

'Wot d'yer mean? Leave Beales?'

'I mean leave London. Go somewhere safe. Out in the country. We could go down Guildford way. That's in Surrey. I 'eard they're lookin' fer staff at this 'otel down there. I could cook, you

124

could do wot you're doin' now.'

Nellie looked puzzled. She wasn't sure she'd heard right. 'Yer mean leave 'ere an' get a job in the country? You an' me, tergevver?'

Hubert looked quite hurt. 'Well, don't make it sound like I'm tryin' ter kidnap yer!' He sat up in the armchair. His feet only barely touched the floor. 'I just fawt yer wouldn't wanna stay 'round 'ere no more if fings start 'ottin' up again.'

Nellie suddenly felt guilty. She had never suspected that Hubert had felt anything for her before, and his consideration for her welfare touched her. 'You're smashin', Hube,' she said, smiling affectionately at him. 'You're probably right. I'd 'ate it if fings did get—well, bad.' Then added, 'I've 'ad enough of this war.'

'Then wot's stoppin' yer?'

Nellie lowered her eyes. 'Instinct,' she said.

Hubert looked slightly embarrassed. He got up and stubbed out his cigarette in the nearest ashtray. 'Just an idea, that's all,' he said, shrugging his shoulders. He made for the door. 'If yer change yer mind ...' he said brightly as he went.

'Fanks, Hube,' Nellie replied. 'You're the tops.'

'It's nuffin',' said Hubert, opening the door. 'Oh, by the way. Your pal turned up terday. The famous Miss Ackroyd.'

Nellie's eyes widened; she felt a tingling sensation up and down her spine.

'Seems she ain't a ghost after all,' Hubert said with a grin.

Chapter 8

Nellie had never been into Finsbury Park before. Under normal circumstances she would have felt happy at the prospect of a stroll beside the few remaining flower beds and those that had been turned into vegetable allotments to help the war effort. But her reason for being there on such a sunny and warm Tuesday evening filled her with deep apprehension. Who was this Miss Ackroyd who, until the night before, had only been a name which had suddenly sprung to life from out of her subconscious. And why had she agreed to meet her, a woman about whom she knew nothing whatsoever? As she made her way through the main park gates and headed off in the direction of the old boating lake, she knew that her past, which she had so far carefully avoided, was about to catch up with her.

It was now almost six o'clock in the evening, and most of the people there were families enjoying the last few hours of a perfect summer's evening. Nellie's legs felt quite shaky, for they were trying to move faster than she really wanted them to, and when the boating lake finally came into sight, she thought they would collapse beneath her.

There was only another hour or so left before the last of the rowing boats had to be called in, but with the absence of air raids there was a relaxed atmosphere everywhere. People were strolling on the path round the lake or having sparse picnics on the grass verges. Children ran up and down playing tag while their mothers watched and dreamed of the day when their servicemen husbands would be back from the war and able to see their own children growing up.

Which one of all those faces out there was Miss Ackroyd's? Nellie's legs, which now felt like lead, came to a halt, and she slowly looked around, waiting for one of those people to come up to her.

'Hello, Vicky.'

The voice came from behind, but as the name meant nothing to her, Nellie did not turn immediately. When she did, she saw a tall, thin but sturdy woman, and for a split second, no more, she thought she recognised her short auburn hair, large soulful eyes, and gaunt face. But the recognition disappeared as quickly as it came. 'Miss Ackroyd?' she asked timidly.

The woman stretched out her hands. Her face crumpled up, and there were tears in her eyes. 'Oh, Vicky. I knew I'd find you one day. I always knew.' But when she moved forwards to embrace her, Nellie stepped back.

'I don't know who yer are,' she protested. 'Me name's not Vicky.'

Briefly, Ethel Ackroyd looked hurt. But realising that she had moved too quickly, she composed herself, lowered her arms, and remained still. 'Don't you remember me, Vicky?

I'm Miss Ackroyd. From Barratts'. From the orphanage.'

Nellie's expression turned to stone.

Ethel waited a moment before continuing. 'I've been searching for you, ever since it happened. That night. That terrible night.' There was pleading in her eyes. 'I never gave up. I never would give up.'

If the truth of her past was gradually unfolding before her, Nellie was still unwilling to acknowledge it. 'I—I don't know wot yer talkin' about,' she said, staring up into Ethel's eyes.

Ethel paused again before answering. 'Will you come and sit with me for a few minutes, and let me tell you?'

They made an odd pair, one tall, the other pint-sized, Ethel in a clean white blouse and dark brown skirt, and Nellie in her Sunday best cotton dress. But when they sat on a bench seat beneath a huge chestnut tree overlooking the lake, they became more equal, both in size and character.

'On the night the orphanage was bombed,' Ethel began, in her soft Yorkshire voice, 'everyone told me you were dead. But I refused to believe them.' She turned to look at Nellie with a warm smile, her eyes still moist. 'I didn't know why. I still don't. It's just something I felt—here.' She placed her hand against her heart. 'You've always been very special to me, Vicky.'

Nellie was puzzled and uneasy.

Ethel smiled reassuringly at her. 'Oh, I know how difficult all this must be for you to take in.

But from that first day you were brought to the orphanage, I knew that you were different from the other children.'

Nellie continued to look blank.

'You don't know what I'm talking about, do you?'

Nellie shook her head.

'Don't you remember anything? Anything at all about your time with us at Barratts'?'

Nellie shrugged her shoulders. 'I'm not sure,' she said.

'You were quite a handful. No worse than many of the others really, but you certainly had a mind of your own. A sharp tongue, too. Mrs Hare, our cook, got very cross with you at times. Do you remember Mrs Hare, Vicky?'

'I'm not sure,' she said again.

'I had to take your part against her quite a few times, I can tell you. But I didn't mind. I admired your spirit.'

'Who am I, Miss Ackroyd? I want ter know about me mum an' dad. Where are they? *Who* are they? Why did they put me in an orphanage?'

The sudden intensity of Nellie's questions took Ethel aback. Gently taking hold of her hand, she started to tell her all she wanted to know. For the next hour or so, the two of them sat there as the evening sun became more crimson and began to caress the ripple of waves drifting lazily across the lake.

Ethel told Nellie everything about the tragic circumstances of her parents' death, how, soon after she was born, her dad had died in an accident working on a building site, and how her mum had been so distraught that she had thrown herself into the path of an oncoming Tube train.

As she listened, Nellie stared forlornly out at the lake. For a few brief moments, she felt as though she could see two faces reflected in the water out there, the faces of those two tragic people who had brought her into the world. For Nellie, it was a moment of deep despair. It was as though she had entered a long dark tunnel with two other people and emerged alone.

Ethel watched her carefully. She wanted to tell the child that everything was all right, that once she had accepted what had happened to her parents, she would forget all about them. But Ethel knew only too well that it wasn't like that. She had had to tell so many children the awful truth about why they had been put away in an orphanage. It was never easy. It was painful, and always would be. 'I can tell you this much though,' she said softly. 'Your parents would have been very proud of you.'

Nellie's eyes flickered, as though she had just woken up. Then she slowly turned to look at Ethel. 'Proud?'

'You have some remarkable qualities, Vicky. I recognised that even when you were a small child.'

Nellie stared at her in disbelief. 'A few minutes ago yer was tellin' me I was quite a 'andful.'

Ethel smiled at her. 'That's right. But for those who took the trouble to understand you,

you had quite a lot to offer.'

Nellie was puzzled.

'Listen to me, Nellie. There's a lot more to a person than what she knows. It's what she *is* that counts. Yes, it's true, you were a handful. In fact you were a troublemaker. At times I was very angry with you. But for all your worst qualities, there was always something to compensate.' She relaxed her body and leaned back on the bench. 'You know, Vicky, when I was your age, I was a bit like you, a mind of my own, full of myself. I really thought I was the cat's whiskers and that everyone admired whatever I said.' She paused a moment. 'I only learnt the truth about myself as I got older. I discovered that being the centre of attention only turned people away from me. I lost friends, and made enemies.'

Nellie was embarrassed. 'I'm sorry, Miss Ackroyd,' she said. 'I don't know wot this's got ter do wiv me.'

Ethel hesitated before replying. 'You were my friend, Vicky.'

Nellie was lost. 'Me?'

'Whenever I was at my lowest, the one person I could talk to was you. Not the staff, nor the other children, but *you*. Oh, you were pretty hopeless with your school studies, that's why you could hardly read or write. But you had other qualities. You had an instinctive knowledge about people, about their weaknesses, and how they think. You were the only person I knew who could see right through me. Even when you were a child, when you were behaving like a monster, you knew what I was thinking, how

131

I was feeling. You had a way of talking to me, of listening to me. Whenever I was down in the dumps, whether it was about lack of money for the orphanage or something personal, like the way I looked, you were the one who always knew, who always understood. You were also the only one who knew how to hurt me.'

Nellie stared hard at her. 'Hurt you?'

Ethel turned and smiled. 'You once called me an old hag, a spinster who wouldn't know how to find a man if she tried.'

Nellie's face crumpled up and she turned away.

'Oh, you mustn't be upset, Vicky,' said Ethel. 'What you said was true. You were always perceptive enough to know more about me than I ever knew myself. That's why I admired you. That's why I was distraught when I thought I'd lost you.'

For a brief moment, there was silence between them.

Nellie was first to speak. ''Ow did yer manage ter find me?' she asked.

Ethel straightened up and stretched her neck. 'I searched everywhere for you, all over Islington, Hackney, Stoke Newington—everywhere. I finally followed a lead to a pub in Essex Road. They told me there about a gang of evacuees who were living rough out on the streets. I managed to track down one of them.'

Nellie's look was an inquiring one.

'A boy called Martin. Martin Hecht.'

Nellie's eyes widened. 'Toff! You talked ter Toff?'

'It took quite a time to find him. He'd gone back home to his parents in Highgate.' Ethel lowered her eyes as she continued. 'He told me quite a lot about you, and where I could find you.' When she looked up, Nellie was staring hard at her.

'Toff knew I was workin' at Beales?'

'Yes. Apparently his father is a doctor at the Royal Northern Hospital just down the road from the restaurant. You may not have realised it, but you often waited on his table.'

It took Nellie a moment to take this in. Then she looked up suddenly. 'If Toff knew where I was, why didn't 'e come ter see me?' she asked, indignantly.

Ethel briefly lowered her eyes. When she looked up again, she found Nellie glaring straight at her. 'I gather he felt guilty about some of the things he said when he last saw you. But he seemed very concerned about you, Vicky. That much I do know.'

'Toff concerned about *me?*' Nellie said acidly. 'That's a larff, that is!' Even as she spoke, she thought how false her words sounded. The very mention of Toff's name had sent a longing through her veins. So many nights she had lain awake thinking about him. So many times in her dreams her mind had recalled that special Christmas night when Shortso played 'Always' on his mouth organ while she and Toff smooched around the muddy floor of the old gutted furniture store. Why did the very mention of his name fill her with such longing?

'Martin is a very sensible young man, Vicky,' Ethel said, breaking Nellie's line of thought. 'He said you'd been through a terrible ordeal, and that you needed love and attention.'

Nellie sprang to her feet, crossed her arms, and glared angrily into the water. 'Yeah, well, I don't need 'is advice, fanks all the same!' Now quite agitated without really knowing why, she turned to Ethel and said, almost apologetically, 'Look, Miss Ackroyd, if it's all the same ter you, me name's not—well, wotever it was I used ter be called. I don't want a name that reminds me of the past, especially *my* past. I want ter be the person I am now, the person I'm goin' ter be in the future.'

Ethel waited a moment, then got up and joined Nellie at the water's edge. 'Nellie's a good name. I like it,' she said calmly, and with complete understanding. Still looking into the water, she added, 'I'd like you to come home, Nellie.'

Nellie swung a look at her. ''Ome?' she asked. 'Yer mean go back ter the orphanage?'

'You wouldn't have to stay there for ever. I'm sure we could soon find foster parents for you. A nice family who'd take care of you.'

'I can take care of myself,' Nellie said firmly, avoiding eye contact with Ethel.

'You're only sixteen years old, Vicky.'

'Stop calling me that name!' she snapped. 'Once an' fer all me name's Nellie!'

Ethel tried to calm her down. 'I'm sorry, Nellie. I'm just worried about you, that's all.

You shouldn't have to be fending for yourself at your age.'

'If I'm old enough to work fer me livin', I'm old enough ter fend fer meself.' She stooped down to pick up a chestnut leaf that had fallen from the branch of the tree above them. Without realising what she was doing, she started to pick the leaf to pieces. 'I'm sorry, Miss Ackroyd,' she said guiltily. 'I don't want yer ter think I'm ungrateful, but I've got the right to a life of me own. I don't want ter go back ter the orphanage. I want a 'ome of me own, a mum an' dad, an' a family I can call me own.'

Ethel was becoming desperate. 'But we can help you to do that, Vick—we can help you to do that, Nellie.'

Nellie turned and stared at her. 'I don't want yer ter do that, Miss Ackroyd. I want ter do it meself.' She opened her hand and released the remains of the chestnut leaf.

Ethel realised that she could go no further. After a brief moment of hesitation, she returned to the bench and collected her handbag. 'I'll send along your identity card and ration cards,' she said, trying hard not to sound anxious. 'Now I know where you are, I won't worry so much.' Despite a sinking feeling in her stomach, she tried a weak smile. 'In the next few weeks, the orphanage is moving out into the country. As soon as we get settled, I'll send you the address.' She paused. 'If you ever need help—anything, no matter how big or small—I want you to promise that you'll get in touch with me. Will you do that for me, please, Vicky?'

135

Nellie resisted the urge to be annoyed at being called by her real name again, and merely nodded her head.

Ethel took just one step towards her and offered her hand. 'Then I won't trouble you any more. From now on, you're on your own, Vicky. Just you and the wide, wide world. As far as everyone else in my world is concerned, you no longer exist.'

Nellie took Ethel's hand and shook it. For a brief moment, she felt a sense of guilt.

Ethel smiled affectionately. She wanted to cry but was determined not to. Then she turned, and started to go. But after a few steps, she stopped and looked back.

'You're a remarkable girl—Nellie,' she said. 'I'll never forget you.' And then she was gone.

Sunday was Monsieur Pierre's favourite day of the week. This was so for many reasons, but most of all because after the end of the second house Saturday show, for at least twenty-four hours he could discard the mystery and panache of his stage persona and revert to his everyday plain and simple Mr Albert Beckwith. Therefore, to Albert, Sunday morning was always known as his 'bliss morning', which meant that he could lie in bed, have tea and two pieces of toast brought up to him by his ever loving wife Doris, and scour the pages of the *Sunday Pictorial* from start to finish. Doris herself had her own way of relaxing. For her, just being at home with her family was bliss enough, and there was nothing she adored more than preparing Sunday lunch which, despite the rationing, always consisted of a roast, followed by baked rice pudding or apple pie (sweetened with saccharin tablets) or just occasionally a nice jam roly-poly. Sid and Lenny also enjoyed Sundays, for by then they had usually finished their homework, which left them free either to go out with their mates around Tufnell Park Road where they lived, or to have them all in to play table tennis in the conservatory at the back of the house.

It had been a triumphant week for Monsieur Pierre at the Finsbury Park Empire. The show had been a complete sell-out and more bookings were coming in for not only the Moss Empires circuit but also other provincial theatres and several one-night stands. After a depressing and unproductive time during the height of the Blitz, things were certainly looking up. But although Sunday in the Beckwith household was always a day of rest, it was also a time to prepare for the next date, which in this case was a week's engagement at the Chiswick Empire in West London, starting the following day.

'Got ter do somefin' about that gel, yer know,' yawned Albert, who had just got up and was still in his patched silk dressing gown, his bald head not yet covered with his toupee, which his two boys invariably referred to as their dad's 'rug'.

'Which gel's that, dear?' asked Doris, who was at the kitchen table, scraping potatoes.

'That little tart, Ange. D'yer know she 'ad the cheek ter ask me fer a raise last night? Bloody nerve.'

As she scraped the new potatoes, Doris's glasses were splashed with water from the saucepan in front of her. 'Well, she's probably right, dear,' she said, peering at Albert over the top of her specs. 'She's been in the act for the best part of a year now. P'raps we ought ter up 'er anuvver 'alf-crown or so.'

Albert nearly had palpitations. ''Alf a crown! Yer expect me ter give that—that little—you expect me ter give 'er anuvver 'alf a crown? She's already on a quid a week! An' fer wot? Fer tartin' round the stage in the altergevver, doin' absolutely bugger all!'

'Watch yer language, Albert!' whispered Doris, turning to look over her shoulder into the conservatory to make sure the two boys hadn't heard. 'Ange only does wot yer ask her. After all, she's only s'posed ter be there ter assist you.'

'Oh yes,' growled Albert as he searched for his packet of Abdullahs in the kitchen dresser drawer. 'Then why does she carry on as though she's the star of the bleedin' act?'

Once again Doris took a sly look over her shoulder into the conservatory. 'You mustn't keep goin' on like that about Ange, dear. She's only young. She means well.'

Albert found his Abdullahs, took one out, and lit it. In the seclusion of his own home, he never used a cigarette holder.

'Is that why you was late last night, dear?' Doris asked suddenly, but casually.

Albert stopped what he was doing but did not turn to look at her. 'Wot d'yer mean?'

'Yer didn't get in till well after one o'clock,'

said Doris, still concentrating on the spuds. 'Was it Ange who kept you back? Or Eddie?'

Albert was taken slightly offguard but he managed to keep his composure. 'Actually,' he replied, 'I went fer a drink wiv Max. If yer remember, I told yer I might do. It *was* the end of the run, yer know.'

Even though Albert had his back towards her, Doris looked across at him with an affectionate smile. 'Of course it was, dear,' she said benevolently. 'But I'm surprised you went drinkin' with Max. Let's face it, good ol' Max Miller ain't known fer dippin' inter 'is own pocket, now is 'e?'

Doris chuckled to herself. But Albert was not amused. Well, not entirely.

Nellie had not enjoyed her week. It had started well enough, with her free visit to the Finsbury Park Empire and tea with the famous Monsieur and Madame in their dressing room after the show. But from Tuesday onwards, after her traumatic meeting with Miss Ackroyd in the park, it was downhill all the way. Hubert was the first to notice it. He always knew when Nellie was down in the dumps because she virtually dried up and didn't talk to him more than she had to. And since Tuesday, she had gone off to her room after work each afternoon and hardly emerged until breakfast the following morning.

Nellie had indeed spent a great deal of time in her own room. She had a lot on her mind, so much to think about and churn over. An orphan, no mum or dad, no family, no one she could call her own ... She kept telling herself that she wished she'd never been told about her former life. Why couldn't she go on living a lie? Why couldn't she just go on being Nellie and never know one lousy thing about a person called Vicky. Each night, as she lay in bed in the dark, staring up into a void, she tried desperately hard to cry but somehow the tears just wouldn't come despite the fact that she couldn't stop feeling sorry for herself. The crunch came on Saturday evening. It happened quite suddenly when, after hours of lying around doing nothing all day, she felt a strong urge to visit a certain place that she had not been to for some time.

The interior of St Mary Magdalene's Church in Bedale Street looked much the same as the last time Nellie had been there, shortly after the bombing of the orphanage. The only difference now was that it was not biting cold, for it was a summer's evening, and there were several people there, some of them kneeling in prayer in the pews, one or two waiting outside the confessional box in the side aisle.

Nellie entered quietly through the main entrance which was wide open. But before she could get inside, she had to pull back a large curtain which was hanging in front of the doors, screening off the interior of the church from the street outside.

The first thing she noticed was the intense feeling of peace, for although there was a hum of

140

worshippers quietly saying the rosary or offering up prayers to the statue of Mother Mary just in front of the first row of pews, the air seemed so pure and untarnished. For a moment Nellie felt as though she was intruding, especially when an elderly woman, accompanied by what looked like her young grandson, turned round to glance at her. But when the woman gave her a warm smile, she felt reassured.

She made her way silently to a pew near the back of the church. It was the same pew where she had sought refuge the night she had strayed into the building more dead than alive. She had no intention of doing what everyone else was doing, for she had never prayed before, and even the idea embarrassed her. So she just sat there, hardly moving, staring straight ahead at the altar, which seemed miles away. Then she closed her eyes. Alone now with her thoughts, she began to see herself, on that night, that horrifying night, her face and arms bruised, feet lacerated, blood seeping out of the deep cut in her leg. She could see herself stretched out on the same bench she was sitting on now. But what she saw more clearly than anything was that she was alive—bruised, cut, dazed, but alive. And then she could see Rats and Bonkers—and Toff. There they were, standing over her, whispering, peering down at her anxiously. She could almost hear Rats' voice: 'She's a gel. We don't 'ave no gels wiv us!' The image brought a smile to Nellie's face. She was alive! Nothing in the whole wide world could change that. She was alive! And her whole life was ahead of her.

Her eyes were still closed as tears gradually began to trickle down her cheeks.

Tufnell Park Road was quite an affluent part of Holloway. It was a fairly wide, long side road leading off the main Holloway Road, and the terraced Edwardian houses in it were three or four storeys high. Even though some people in the adjoining streets thought there was a certain air of 'kippers and curtains' about the place, there was no doubt that quite a few of the residents there were not short of a bob or two.

It took Nellie only a few minutes to reach number 147A, for Tufnell Park Road was a short walk from Beales Restaurant and her hostel. It was a good walk, because that's how Nellie felt. The traumas of the past few days had given way to a new determination to get on with her life, and see what she could make of it. That's why she was really looking forward to having tea at the home of Monsieur and Madame.

'Oh, we're just a couple of silly ol' Cockneys who've struck lucky in the world,' said Madame, soon after she had shown Nellie into the front room.

'Not so lucky!' protested Monsieur as he joined them. 'We've 'ad ter work dam 'ard fer our livin'.'

The moment Monsieur entered the room, Nellie was immediately in awe of him. He was wearing his toupee and after a hearty Sunday roast followed by an hour's nap, he was as bright as ever, looking very dapper in his casual cream-coloured trousers, striped short-sleeved summer shirt, and a green polka-dot cravat. As ever, Madame had not tried to compete, but she did look rather pretty in a simple pale blue cotton dress cut just below the knees.

Nellie adored the front room, for it was so unusual. A huge aspidistra plant was climbing up as far as it could in front of the lace window curtains, and there seemed to be mass of ornaments scattered all over the room—snuff boxes, a little Dutch china boy and girl in traditional clothes, and lots of novel items such as a miniature brass theatre programme cover, inscribed 'Theatre Royal, Drury Lane'. The furniture was very ornate, and it seemed to Nellie to be more for show than for practical use. The floor of the room was covered with a multi-coloured Persian carpet which was just beginning to show its age. Nellie was particularly fascinated by the array of framed photographs adorning the walls. It seemed that every space had been taken up with portraits of famous music hall entertainers, some of them signed. It was a wonderful gallery of Monsieur and Madame's fellow artistes and friends, and to Nellie at least a sign that this house was quite unlike any other in Tufnell Park Road.

Monsieur and Madame told Nellie stories about their travels around the country and their performances in places like Huddersfield, Bristol, Birmingham, Manchester, Liverpool,

Leeds, Sunderland, and even as far away as Glasgow and Aberdeen in Scotland. They brought out some scrapbooks of the different shows they had been in, leaving Nellie quite overwhelmed with the sheer magic of it all.

It was not until they sat down to tea that Nellie was persuaded by her hosts to talk a bit about herself. 'Nuffin' much ter tell really,' she said lightly. She was far more interested in the kitchen where they were having tea, for it was so well equipped, with a beautiful gas cooker, a large oak dresser, and a round table which had been set with a lovely blue lace tablecloth and a china tea set that Nellie thought must have cost a bomb.

'Come on now, Nellie dear,' insisted Madame. 'Tell us about yer mum and dad. 'Ow many bruvvers an' sisters 'ave yer got?'

''Ope ter Gawd they ain't as bad as our pair!' growled Monsieur, glaring at Sid and Lenny who were sitting opposite Nellie at the table and who hadn't waited to be asked before pouncing on the fish paste sandwiches.

'Ain't got no mum, nor dad,' Nellie finally admitted. Somehow she felt less self-conscious about saying it than she had expected.

Monsieur and Madame exchanged looks.

'No mum or dad?' said Madame.

'Nor bruvvers or sisters.' added Nellie. 'I was the only one. Me mum and dad died soon after I was born. I lived in an orphanage up New Norf Road.'

For a moment there was a shocked silence

144

apart from the sound of munching coming from the two boys.

It was eventually Madame who spoke. 'I'm so sorry, dear,' she said with the utmost sincerity. 'Wot a terrible fing, not 'avin' people of yer own ter care for yer.'

Nellie shrugged her shoulders. 'Just one of those fings.'

'Are yer sure they din't kick yer out or nuffin'?' quipped Lenny.

'Lenny!' snapped his mum. 'Don't say fings like that!'

Nellie took no notice of the boy, merely pulled a face at him and replied, 'No. They din't kick me out. The only person who could do that was 'Itler.'

Again, Madame and Monsieur exchanged a glance.

Nellie realised that it was better for her to tell the whole story, and so during much of teatime that is what she did.

Monsieur and Madame listened with rapt attention, interrupting every so often to ask questions about how she had managed to survive on the bombed streets, and with such a bunch of juvenile delinquents. Nellie found herself constantly defending her old mates, despite the fact that they had never really accepted her as one of their own. Even Sid and Lenny were quiet throughout; at times they seemed almost inspired by the sheer adventure of it all.

When Nellie had finished telling all she could tell, Madame asked her about the future. 'Surely

145

yer can't go on living in one room in an 'ostel for the rest of your life,' she said. 'It ain't natural.'

Nellie shrugged. 'I'll stay there till the war's over. Then I'll look around for somefin' more permanent.'

When tea was over, Nellie and the family sat out in the garden. It wasn't a very big garden, for the Anderson shelter took up quite a bit of it, but it was more than Nellie had ever experienced and she felt very grand lounging back in a striped canvas deck chair, staring up into the evening sky as the light gradually faded. For a time, she and Monsieur played darts with the two boys, who cheated like mad and created a fuss every time their dart missed its target. When both of them had gone to bed, the three adults stayed outside, watching day turn to night, and the sky gradually filling with a galaxy of bright, shining stars. It wasn't long before Nellie could smell the pungent aroma of Monsieur's Abdullah cigarette. Because of the blackout, she couldn't see either him or his wife, but she could feel their presence so much.

'Yer know,' came Madame's voice in the dark, close by, 'I don't know 'ow I could 'ave coped if I'd bin in your position. Sometimes I don't fink we realise 'ow lucky we are. Wot say you, Albert?'

Monsieur didn't answer immediately. But Nellie heard him inhale, then blow out a lungful of smoke. 'Everybody should 'ave someone in this world,' he said in a solemn voice, which

was rare for him. 'Sometimes life can be bleedin'
unfair.'

On the garden wall, two moggies were locked
in mortal combat, growling and hissing and
claiming every inch of territory for themselves.

'D'yer ever get lonely, Nellie?' Madame asked,
quite out of the blue.

Nellie thought about it for a moment.
Strangely enough, the worst pangs of loneliness
she had had for a long time had been during
tea at the kitchen table. Watching the family
together had only made her realise how much
she had missed out on. 'Sometimes,' she replied.
'But then I reckon most people do from time ter
time.'

There was a long pause. The two moggies
finally gave up the struggle and went their
separate ways.

'Yer know, Nellie,' Madame said, 'I know
I ain't yer mum, and never could be, but
if—just *if* yer ever need someone, well, someone
ter talk to, I'm never really far away, yer
know.'

In the dark, Nellie felt Madame's hand take
hers and squeeze it.

'Wot I mean is,' Madame continued, 'I've
always wanted a daughter of me own. Someone
ter talk to, ter listen to. That's somefin' I've
never 'ad. D'yer know wot I mean, Nellie?'

'Let's not beat about the bush,' came
Monsieur's crisp East End voice. 'Wot she
means, wot we boaf mean is, when yer want
a 'ome ter come to, yer've got one—right
'ere.'

Chapter 9

The summer of 1941 was a glorious time for Nellie. The evenings were long and hot, and apart from an occasional Luftwaffe intruder, the lull in the air raids continued.

Nellie had come to enjoy living in the Holloway part of Islington. Although it was quite a busy area, sometimes it seemed like a village. As well as her regulars in the restaurant, she got to know all sorts of people in the shops, they were so friendly and full of good humour. Sometimes she and Hubert would go to the pictures, for there were at least five cinemas within walking distance, and other times they would just stroll for miles, exploring the maze of little back streets behind Holloway Road all the way up to Archway in one direction, or to Camden Town in another, or up to Highbury Corner and the Angel. And when they went on bus rides, there was always something new to discover. On August Bank Holiday Monday, they even went on a number 14 bus to Piccadilly Circus and strolled around the West End. For Nellie it was a wonderful experience, for although she was disappointed to find that the statue of Eros had been removed to a safe place for the duration of the war, she had the chance to see Nelson's Column in Trafalgar Square for the first time in her life, and feed the flocks of pigeons there. When she and Hubert passed the National Gallery on the north side of the square, Nellie was amazed to see so many people queuing up to get inside for a lunchtime piano recital given by someone called Myra Hess. Despite the war, everyone was doing their best to go about their lives in as normal a way as they could.

On 14 September, Nellie was surprised to receive a birthday card from Miss Ackroyd, which told her she was seventeen years old that day. So, for a special treat, Hubert took her 'up West' to see a musical revue at the London Palladium. The star was a comedian called Tommy Trinder who brought the house down with his hilarious routines, and the show itself was a dazzling spectacle. The Palladium was a much bigger place than the Finsbury Park Empire, but being inside a theatre once again made Nellie think of Monsieur and Madame, whom she had not seen since they went off to fulfil a series of engagements in the provinces.

Over the previous few weeks, Hubert had become a really close friend of Nellie's. She found him good company, for they spoke the same language and both loved a good gossip about people. They spent most of their spare time together. It helped that Hubert was physically the same height as Nellie; she frequently had to use her finger to lift stray strands of his straight brown hair out of his eyes. Of course he smoked too much, chain-smoked in fact, and it worried her that he often burst into uncontrollable fits of coughing. Hubert was becoming an important part of her life, so much so that she began to rely on him. And it was not long before that, too, started to worry her. It was her fault, not his, for Hubert was just as independent as she was and never showed that he was in the least romantically inclined towards her. Nonetheless, she felt the time had come to start looking for other friends.

The opportunity came one Saturday afternoon when she was in Saville's Record Shop in Holloway Road, sorting through some of the latest gramophone records. As usual there were plenty of teenagers in the booths, listening to a variety of songs such as Bing Crosby and the Andrews Sisters singing 'Don't Fence Me In', and Glenn Miller and his Band playing 'Little Brown Jug'. In the next booth to where Nellie was trying to listen to the latest hit record of Spike Jones and his City Slickers, there was a boy listening to an orchestra playing some noisy classical music which he was pretending to conduct. This really irritated Nellie, so she banged on the window and mimed to him to turn the sound down. The boy shrugged his shoulders and ignored her. Furious, she took off her own record, marched straight into his booth, and turned off the gramophone he was using.

'Wot's up wiv you, mate?' Nellie snarled. 'You deaf or somefink?'

The boy, who looked about a year older than Nellie, looked astounded. 'Here!' he gasped, in a faintly Irish accent. 'What the hell d'yer think you're doin'!'

'I can't 'ear myself breave in there!' snapped Nellie. 'There's me tryin' ter listen ter Spike Jones, an' all I can 'ear is that muck!'

The boy crossed his arms angrily and glared at her. 'That is not muck! It happens ter be Rachmaninoff!'

'Well, 'e's too loud, whoever 'e is. So just turn 'im down, or else!'

'Or else?' The boy put his hands on his hips defiantly. 'Or else *what,* may I ask?'

'Or else I'll break the bleedin' record over yer bleedin' 'ead!' Nellie shouted.

The angry exchange was causing the other customers in the shop to stare at them. Nellie was aware of this, so she quickly strode back to her own booth and put on her Spike Jones record again, this time turning it up full blast.

In the next booth, the boy glared at her, put on his record, and also turned up the volume.

The combination of Spike Jones and Rachmaninoff's second piano concerto was formidable, and half the customers in the shop left.

Eventually, the challenge was too much for Nellie, so once again she flung open the door of her booth and went next door, where the boy was waiting for her.

''Scuse me!' called a voice from behind.

Nellie turned, to find the harassed middle-aged shopkeeper glaring at her. 'In't it about time you two lovebirds kissed an' made up?' he asked.

The wail of the air-raid siren was totally unexpected. It had only been heard a few times since the disastrous raid on London on the night of 10 May, and nobody seemed to be prepared.

Nellie was fast asleep in bed. At first she thought she was dreaming the sound, but when her eyes sprang open in the dark and the siren's wail continued, she leapt out of bed and rushed to the window. She pulled back the blackout curtain and looked out.

In Tollington Road below, she could see people rushing to and fro all over the place. ARP wardens were hurrying to their post in nearby Shelburne Road School, and several families were emerging from Hertslet Road just round the corner, some of them still wearing their night clothes under their coats, making for the nearest air-raid shelter alongside the Savoy Cinema in Loraine Road.

Nellie was still at the window when the siren stopped wailing. She quickly got dressed and rushed along the passage to knock up Hubert. She thumped on the door and called out, 'Hube! Are yer in there, Hube? We've got ter get ter the shelter!' There was no response. In desperation, she tried the door handle. To her surprise, the door opened.

'Hube?' she called again. 'Are yer in 'ere, Hube?'

As she peered inside, the first thing she heard was someone groaning. The blackout curtains had not been drawn, and by the light of the full moon she saw Hubert stretched out face down on the floor.

'Hube!' she cried in alarm. Quickly crouching

down beside him, she tried to turn him over. But he was a dead weight, and almost impossible to move. He also stank of booze. 'Hube!' she cried again. 'Wot's 'appened to yer? Wot 'ave yer bin up ter, yer stupid twerp!'

Hubert's only response was to groan again.

At that moment came the first salvo of anti-aircraft gunfire. The whole house shook.

'Hube!' Nellie tried to shake some life into him, but it was no good. Desperate, she looked around the room for something she could use to sober him up. She spotted a jug of water on the washstand. She rushed across, lifted it out of the china basin and struggled back to Hubert with it. Without another thought, she poured the water over his head.

There was an almighty explosion somewhere outside, which shook the very foundations of the place. Nellie leapt up with a loud yell and dropped the water jug.

'Hube!' she yelled, again crouching down and trying to help him up. 'We've got ter get out of 'ere! There's an air raid. We've got ter get ter the shelter.'

To her relief, Hubert stirred, and turned over. 'W—wot's goin' on?' he groaned, slurring his words. 'Wot's g—goin' on?'

'Give me yer arm,' yelled Nellie over the sound of ack-ack fire and emergency service bells clanging out along Holloway Road outside. ''Ang on ter me!'

Hubert put his arm round Nellie's neck and with her help managed to get to his feet. But he was very wobbly, and he had to grab on to her to keep his balance.

''Old on!' she said. But even as she spoke, he collapsed on to the floor again.

Nellie knew there was no way she could get him to the shelter. The next best thing was to try and get him and herself under the bed. She grabbed hold of his arm and using all her strength started pulling. 'Come on now, Hube!' she yelled. 'Give us a bit of 'elp, fer Gawd's sake!'

Hubert groaned again and tried to lever himself out of the pool of water he was lying in and along the floor. It was a slow, laborious process.

With the sound of enemy aircraft droning overhead, ack-ack gunfire intensifying outside, and the emergency services racing along both Holloway and Tollington Roads outside, Nellie finally succeeded in getting Hubert under his own bed. There was barely enough room for them under there, but Nellie was convinced that this was their best chance of shelter.

It was almost daybreak when the siren sounded the all clear. By that time, both Hubert and Nellie, still wedged hard under the bed, were fast asleep.

Luckily, the Saturday night air raid was not as serious as it had seemed while it was taking place. The explosion that had shaken the entire area turned out to be a magnesium bomb which had come down somewhere around Manor House, more than a mile away, and the majority of damage elsewhere was superficial, mainly caused by jagged fragments of anti-aircraft shells. But there was no denying that the sudden attack had caused great alarm around Holloway and beyond, and many people feared that this might be the start of a new Blitz.

When Nellie opened her eyes on Sunday morning, the room was flooded with bright sunlight. Her entire body ached, for she was still wedged under Hubert's bed, and her feet were prickling with pins and needles. 'Fanks fer nuffin', Hube!' she groaned, turning over and trying to pull herself out from under the bed. But when she looked, Hubert had already gone.

By the time she had managed to stand up, the door opened and in walked Hubert, carrying two cups of tea.

''Ere yer go then, Nell,' he said rather sheepishly. 'Somefin' ter wet yer whistle wiv. Sorry fer last night. Must've mixed me drinks or somefin'. Reckon I owe yer one, eh?'

Nellie rubbed her eyes, then glared at him. ''Onestly, Hube,' she croaked hoarsely, 'wot d'yer fink yer was up ter? Yer was boozed out of yer mind!'

Hubert went to his bed, sat on the edge of it, and put his cup and saucer down on the small bedside cabinet. 'I went round the corner, ter the Eaglet,' he said, taking out a fag. 'There was this darts match. Din't know no one, but I got dragged in.'

'Sounds like it,' said Nellie, propping herself on the windowsill, sipping her tea. 'When did you start boozin' then? I've never seen yer sloshed before.'

Hubert lit up his Woodbine and spoke through the smoke. 'Just one of those fings,' he replied.

Nellie shook her head disapprovingly. 'Yeah, well, you're lucky we din't get our 'eads blown off. Did yer 'ear that racket goin' on last night?'

'Din't 'ear nuffink,' Hubert replied, adding, 'You was a brick, Nell. I don't know wot I'd 'ave done wivout yer.'

Nellie shrugged her shoulders. She didn't mind Hubert having a drink if he wanted one. After all, he worked damned hard in that kitchen from Monday to Saturday. But she was curious about his odd behaviour over the last week or so. She had always accepted that Hubert was a very self-contained individual who seemed to have no hobbies except smoking Woodbines and reading kids' comics and the sports pages of the newspapers. But just lately he had been more withdrawn than ever, keeping himself to himself, and going out on his own in the evening.

'By the way,' Hubert said, after taking a mouthful of tea without exhaling the smoke he had just inhaled, 'did I tell yer I've given in me notice?'

'Wot!' gasped Nellie.

'Remember the job down at that 'otel I told yer about? The one near Guildford. I've decided ter take it.'

Nellie took a moment before answering. 'Hube,' she said, suddenly feeling all let down inside, 'why din't yer tell me?'

'I did ask you ter come wiv me. Remember?'

'Yeah, I know, but,' she took a quick gulp of tea to steady her nerves, 'why all the rush? Yer din't mention anyfin' about it durin' the week.'

Hubert drew hard on his fag. 'Once yer've made up yer mind ter do somefin', I say yer should get on wiv it.'

Nellie noticed that he seemed to be addressing the floor rather than her. She went across to him. 'Hube, I don't understand. I fawt yer liked it 'ere. A room of yer own, free grub ...'

'Well, I don't!' he snapped, suddenly springing up from the bed and moving away from her. 'Anyway, why d'yer 'ave ter keep askin' me questions? If you like it 'ere, that's OK by me, but just stop askin' me questions all the time. Right?'

Nellie was taken aback. 'Right.' Her reply was more startled than angry. She put down her cup and went to the door. 'Fanks fer the tea,' she said and quietly left the room.

Later on in the morning Nellie heard a rumpus. She was spread out on a tiny patch of grass in the hostel's small back yard, alone, but only too aware that every so often Hubert was taking crafty looks at her from his bedroom window on the first floor. After the scene she had endured no more than an hour before with him, her mind was racing. Why had he spoken to her like that? What had she done to offend him? Did this mean that they were no longer friends? She was deeply depressed by it all. But most of all, she was bewildered by the fact that he was leaving his job at Beales at such short notice.

The rumpus in the next-door back yard of the restaurant suddenly snapped her out of her soul-searching. There were men's voices, voices she hadn't heard before, the sound of dustbins being moved around, then a door opening and closing. Since the restaurant wasn't open on a Sunday, Nellie was intrigued and worried, so she got up, went back into the house, and made her way quickly to the street outside.

She was shocked to see a police car parked in Tollington Road near the front entrance of the restaurant, and when she went to investigate, she found the front door wide open. She went inside to see what was going on.

'It's all right, dear,' a voice called the moment Nellie entered the dining room. It was Sarah Wiggins, the supervisor. With her was a uniformed policeman. 'There's been a little—problem,' she said rather cagily as she came across to Nellie. 'There's nothing for you to worry about.'

On the other side of the dining room, Nellie could see two of the kitchen girls talking to a second policeman. They were Molly Clarke and Brenda Kitson, both of whom lived in the hostel accommodation next door, but whom Nellie rarely saw. They looked fraught and anxious. 'Wot's 'appened?' Nellie asked. 'Wot're the rozzers doin' 'ere?'

Mrs Wiggins sighed deeply. 'Somebody got into my office last night, Nellie,' she replied, voice low. 'They broke into the safe and took last week's takings.' She shook her head

158

despairingly. 'I blame myself,' she said. 'I should have banked it all on Friday. It was so careless of me.'

Nellie looked around. 'But 'ow did they get in? They must've done it durin' the air raid last night.'

'No, Nellie,' Mrs Wiggins said, slowly shaking her head. 'Nobody broke in.'

Nellie was puzzled.

Mrs Wiggins sighed. 'The police think it's an inside job.'

The Savoy Cinema in Holloway Road was not the most attractive cinema, but at least it was brand new. It had opened only the year before, in February 1940, at the height of the 'phoney war', that strange period when the idea of air raids seemed nothing more than bluff. However, it did not arrive without controversy, for to accommodate it, part of Jones Brothers department store had had to be demolished. Nellie quite liked the place because it was just a few minutes' walk from the hostel, and the pastel colour of the interior made her feel that she was in very contemporary surroundings. This being Sunday, there were just two separate performances, afternoon and evening. After the drama of the day's events, it had come as a bit of a godsend for Nellie when Brenda and Molly, the two kitchen girls from the restaurant, asked her to accompany them to the afternoon show.

Today's film was showing Peter Lorre as the notorious Japanese detective Mr Moto, but as

Brenda and Molly chatted incessantly, Nellie feared she would not be hearing very much of Peter Lorre's performance.

'So what did they ask you, Nell?' Brenda was quite a pretty girl, with lovely blue eyes and light blonde hair that was permed into tight curls. But her voice was so high-pitched, Nellie felt the whole audience could hear her. 'The two flatfoots. Did they ask yer where you were last night an' all that?'

Nellie had to lean forward to reply, because Brenda was sitting on the other side of Molly, to her right. 'I just told 'em I was back at the 'ostel, listenin' ter the wireless.'

'Bet they asked yer wot the programmes were,' said Molly.

'I remembered most of them,' replied Nellie, her voice much lower than her two companions'. *In Town Ternight, Music 'All,* then *Saturday Night Feater.* Wot about you two?'

'We was at the dance down the Irish Club,' said Brenda.

'Din't get back 'till after midnight,' sniggered Molly, which sent both her and Molly into hoots of laughter.

Nellie was glad she wasn't sitting between them. ''Ow much did they take from the safe then?' she asked. 'Anyone know?'

'That younger flattie told me it was over forty quid,' squeaked Brenda, leaning forward to answer Nellie.

'That ought ter buy someone a few bottles of gin on the black market!' sniggered Molly.

Once again both girls burst into laughter.

Nellie was relieved when the house lights began to dim and the beautiful new cream-coloured stage curtains curled up to give way to Pathé News.

The news was all about the meeting at sea between Winston Churchill and President Roosevelt the previous month, and then lots of awful newsreel film of the war between Russia and Finland. Nellie couldn't bear to watch the screen; news about the war was something she never wanted to hear or see. In any case, her mind was still on the break-in. What did Mrs Wiggins mean about it being an 'inside job'? Did she mean a member of the staff? And if so, who did they suspect? If the burglary took place during the evening, as the flatties said it did, then she knew for a fact that, apart from herself, all the staff staying in the hostel had gone out for the night. If it was a member of the staff who'd nicked the forty quid, they must've been either pretty desperate or boozed half out of their mind. Then she remembered Hubert, stretched out blind drunk on the floor of his bedroom.

The crowing cockerel brought Pathé News to an end. When the house lights went up again, Brenda and Molly were surprised to see Nellie sitting bolt upright in her seat, her face ashen, eyes staring in a cold fix.

'Nell!' said Molly anxiously. 'Is anyfin' wrong?'

Nellie turned quickly to look at both her companions. 'Did they mention anybody?' she asked breathlessly. 'Did they mention a name?'

161

Molly and Brenda exchanged a puzzled look. 'Did *who* mention a name?' asked Brenda.

'Wot yer talkin' about, Nell?' asked Molly.

Without saying another word, Nellie sprang up from her seat and started to leave.

'Nell!' called Brenda.

'Wot's wrong, Nell?' called Molly. 'Come back!'

As the house lights started to dim again, Nellie had already pushed her way past the irritated people sitting in the same row and was heading for the exit.

Although she had only been inside the picture house for less than an hour, Nellie had to adjust to the bright sunlight as she came out. As the feature film hadn't yet started, there were still a few people filing in, and when she pushed her way through them, there were some angry calls of, 'Wot's yer 'urry, mate!'

Nellie's feet couldn't carry her fast enough. She ran all the way along the Holloway Road, straight past Jones Brothers, and in a few minutes she was within sight of Beales. At once, her worst fears were realised.

The police car that she had seen earlier in the day was now parked directly outside the front door of the staff hostel, and before she reached it she caught a glimpse of someone being led down the outside steps of the hostel, accompanied by two grim-faced policemen. 'Hube!' she yelled from the other side of Tollington Road.

Hubert, arms held firmly by the two officers, paused briefly and looked across the road towards Nellie. But before Nellie could reach him, he was quickly hustled into the car.

'Hube!' she yelled again, almost walking straight under a motorbike as it rushed past to beat the traffic lights.

But the police car was already on its way along Tollington Road, making for Hornsey Road Police Station. As it went Hubert, wedged in the back seat between the two policemen, turned half-heartedly and Nellie caught a glimpse of his face before the vehicle disappeared round the corner of Herstlet Road.

Nellie, distraught, stood helplessly on the pavement. She couldn't believe it. She couldn't believe that Hubert, ordinary, harmless Hubert, was a thief.

'There's nothing we can do now, my dear.'

Nellie turned, to see Mrs Wiggins standing just behind her. She looked crushed and miserable.

'Wot're they doin'?' Nellie croaked, her voice breaking. 'They can't take Hube! They can't!'

'There's nothing we can do for Hubert now, Nellie,' replied Mrs Wiggins. 'He's been a foolish young man.'

'But 'e din't do nuffin'!' she insisted. ''E couldn't've done. Hube's a good, kind, 'onest person. 'E wouldn't nick nuffin' from nobody! It's a lie! I tell yer, it's a lie.' She went right up to Mrs Wiggins and said defiantly, 'If they try ter pin it on Hube, I'll tell 'em 'e was wiv me all night. I will! I swear ter God I will!'

Mrs Wiggins shook her head slowly, then took hold of both Nellie's hands. 'You can't do that, Nellie. It would be wrong. You see, this is not the first time. Hubert's been in trouble before.'

Chapter 10

November was Monsieur Pierre's least favourite month of the year. The early winter mists played havoc with his bronchitis and it was also generally a rest month in the music hall before the onslaught of the Christmas panto season. Madame, however, rather enjoyed the respite, for it gave her the chance to catch up with all the household jobs she was unable to do while they were on tour, and also to be with Sid and Lenny who had to spend most of their schooldays staying with their grandparents in Hilldrop Crescent. But during this period, at least one of their regular treats remained untarnished: the daily morning trip to Beales Restaurant.

The place was quite full when they got there, which was just the way Monsieur liked it because there was always the chance that someone would recognise him and ask him for his autograph. For Madame, it was the smell of bread baking in the kitchen ovens and the heady aroma of Camp coffee that immediately made her feel at home.

'Mornin', sir! Mornin', madam! Can I take yer order, please?'

Monsieur and Madame turned with a start. The voice was unfamiliar. So was the face.

'Mornin', me dear,' replied Monsieur, both

hands balanced on the top of his cane. 'An' where's Nellie terday?'

'Who, sir?' asked the girl, who was so young, she seemed hardly out of school. 'Oh, Nell. Nell's gone, sir.'

'Gone?' asked a surprised Madame.

'Yes, madam. She left a few weeks ago.'

Monsieur and Madame swung a startled look at each other.

After a moment's pause, Monsieur spoke. 'Young lady, be so good as ter ask your supervisor if she can spare me a moment of 'er time.'

The girl looked puzzled, and wondered if she'd done anything wrong. 'Very good, sir,' she said, and scuttled back to the kitchen.

Mrs Wiggins was already coming out of the kitchen, and making her way straight to Monsieur and Madame's table. 'Mr Beckwith. Mrs Beckwith.' She had a broad. welcoming smile on her face. 'How good to see you again. I do hope you had a successful tour.'

'Extremely so, fank yer, Mrs Wiggins,' replied Monsieur, nodding his head graciously.

Madame leaned forward, and with lowered voice asked, 'Wot's 'appened to our young Nellie?'

Mrs Wiggins' expression changed and she sighed before she answered. 'Yes, it's very sad, isn't it? She left us, I'm afraid. A few weeks back. We had—some problems here, and she decided, well, she didn't want to stay on.'

'Problems?' asked Monsieur suspiciously. 'What sorta problems?'

Madame lowered her voice even more. 'You didn't—I mean, she wasn't—'

'Oh no,' replied Mrs Wiggins immediately. 'Nellie was a lovely girl, very hard-working and conscientious.' Aware that some of the other customers were looking at her, she leaned closer to Madame. 'It was her own decision. I'm sure you'll understand that I can't really say any more than that. Staff matters are always confidential.'

Once again, Monsieur and Madame exchanged a glance. Beales' homely atmosphere suddenly seemed less homely.

''Ave yer any idea where Nellie's gone?' asked Madame anxiously.

'I did hear that she's taken a cleaning job. A dentist's surgery up by Archway, I believe. It seems such a waste. Nellie's far too intelligent to be doing that kind of work.'

Soon after eight o'clock in the morning, Nellie drew back the blackout curtains. The nights were getting longer now and, like everyone else in war-weary London, she found it depressing to have to observe the strict blackout restrictions from five thirty in the evening to eight in the morning. She had already been at work for over an hour, cleaning by electric light, and in the confined space of the dental surgery, it wasn't so easy to see into the dark corners. However, by eight o'clock she had swept the faded carpet in the waiting room with a hard brush, dusted the receptionist's desk, and generally tidied the place. Now she had to start on the surgery itself.

Mr Horrocks, the dentist, didn't arrive until just before nine, and by then the lino floor had to be swept, scrubbed spotless with carbolic soap, and then wiped clean and dry with a floor flannel. This part of the job she hated most, for it played havoc with her knees and always left them bruised and sore. It was not her job to touch any of the surgical instruments but she made sure that the leather dental chair was wiped clean, and never finished off her two hours' work without leaving the place absolutely spick-and-span.

The cleaning job was a poor substitute for Beales Restaurant. But once it was proved that Hubert had been responsible for breaking into Mrs Wiggins' office and stealing the money from her safe, and the management decided to press charges against him, Nellie decided that life there without the only true friend she had known was untenable. This was Hubert's third conviction for burglary, and as he had now turned twenty-one years of age, he was serving a six-month sentence in the horribly grim Pentonville Prison in Caledonian Road. Ever since it had happened, Nellie had lain awake at night thinking about him, wondering whether his criminal activity was in some way a revenge for what he saw as his own inadequacies, such as failing to get into the police force. She thought he was a fool, that all boys and men were fools for having this tendency to nick things from other people. And she thought about Toff and the vacs gang, and how stupid they were too.

The dental surgery was situated above a

tobacconist's shop, and at about five minutes to nine, Nellie heard loud footsteps coming up the narrow stairs from the street door. She recognised them as Mr Horrocks'; he always made heavy weather of the morning ascent. She braced herself for his habitual effusive greeting.

'Hello there! And how's our little girl today?'

It never changed, every morning the same. There he was, a middle-aged man, dressed more like a City broker than a dentist, in his bowler hat, navy blue jacket and pinstriped trousers, a rolled umbrella over one arm, a copy of the *News Chronicle* under the other.

'Thought you'd be gone by now, young lady,' he said, taking off his bowler and hanging it on the waiting-room coat stand. He wasn't a bad looking man for his age, with dark bushy eyebrows and only a tinge of grey hair above the ears. But Nellie thought he had terrible teeth for a dentist. 'Mind you, I'm glad you're not,' he continued. 'Always glad to sit and have a little chat with our Nellie.'

Nellie had stacked away her cleaning utensils and was already putting on her hat and coat. ''Aven't got much time, sir,' she said quickly. 'Got ter get ter my uvver job by nine.'

'You're a good girl, Nellie.' Mr Horrocks took off his jacket, placed it on a coat hanger and hung it on the same coat stand. 'In my newspaper today they're talking about the number of girls around town who are not doing their bit to help the war effort. They can't say that about you. Three jobs in one day. You certainly do your bit for your country.'

'Fank yer, sir,' Nellie said, making for the door.

But Mr Horrocks was there before her, blocking her way. 'By the way, Nellie,' he said, a bright gleam in his eyes. 'I was wondering whether you'd like to come out to dinner with me one evening, up West.' He lowered his voice. 'I know a little place where they do meals on the black market. Get anything you want—roast beef, chicken stew, fresh eggs, pork and dumplings ...'

'Fanks all the same, sir,' Nellie replied, trying to open the door. 'I don't get much time ter meself.'

'Come now, Nellie,' said Mr Horrocks, voice low, holding his hand against the door. 'A young girl like you should *make* time.'

Nellie could hear the receptionist's footsteps coming up the stairs, so she felt brave enough to reply, 'But wot would yer wife say, sir?'

A few minutes later, Nellie was out on the street. It was pouring with rain and she hurried into the entrance of the Archway Underground Station, which was just a few yards from the dental surgery. There were plenty of people around, for it was still rush hour. with heavy traffic passing to and fro along Holloway Road to the south, Junction Road to the west, and Highgate Hill and the main arterial Archway Road to the north. Nellie watched the seething mass of humanity rushing here, there, and everywhere, puppets on a string dancing to a tune none of them could hear. She noticed how

169

many more women and girls there were among that throng; the call-up to active service had taken its toll of the male population. Her mind became numbed by the thought of the humdrum existence these people, including herself, were leading. How could they live like this, making the same journey day in and day out, travelling on crowded buses and Tubes in the morning, returning at the same time every evening? Then she caught sight of the scrawled headline on a newsvendor's placard: 'ARK ROYAL SUNK: A HUMAN TRAGEDY'.

There was nothing humdrum about death, about war. Every one of these people she was watching was, in one way or another, a part of the tragedy.

''Ello, Nellie.'

Nellie hadn't really taken in the faces of the small group of people who, like herself, were sheltering from the rain in the Underground entrance. But when her eyes focused properly, she immediately recognised the woman who had spoken to her. It was Doris Beckwith—Madame. 'Mrs Pierre!' She could hardly believe her eyes.

Madame's face was partly hidden by the rainhood she was wearing. 'I saw yer come out of the dentist's,' she said, raindrops dripping from the end of her nose.

'I don't know wot ter say,' Nellie said, suddenly feeling self-conscious in her dowdy winter coat. But she was genuinely pleased to see Madame. 'Wot're yer doin' up 'ere?' she asked.

Madame smiled, and put her arm round

Nellie's shoulder. 'S'pose we go an' 'ave a cuppa tea, an' I'll tell yer.'

A few minutes later they were in a dingy workmen's cafe in Junction Road. There was no waitress service, so Madame collected a tray and they both queued up for two chipped mugs of tea. They found seats at a table right in the middle of the cafe, which they had to share with two grubby looking elderly plasterers who were tucking in to plates of dried scrambled eggs and toast with a scrape of margarine.

'We was very upset ter 'ear yer'd left Beales,' said Madame, taking off her rainhood and putting it on her lap. 'It was Mrs Wiggins who put me on ter comin' up 'ere. She told me about you workin' at the dentist's.'

Nellie lowered her eyes guiltily.

Madame leaned across and covered Nellie's hand with her own. 'She din't tell me *why* yer left,' she added.

For the next half an hour, Nellie tried her best to tell how she had felt after Hubert had been charged with the break-in at Mrs Wiggins' office. Madame listened sympathetically. After the two men had left the table, she got up and moved to the seat alongside Nellie. Just by them was a wood-burning stove which struggled to heat the place.

'You once told me an' Albert that yer never wanted ter leave Beales,' said Madame. ''Ow are yer managin'?'

Nellie shrugged her shoulders. 'Monday ter Friday I do three part-time jobs a day,' she said. 'Apart from the dentist's, I do cleanin' up the

171

Mayfair picture 'ouse in Caledonian Road, and I scrub out a school 'all, up 'Ornsey Road.'

'An' yer make a livin' out of that?'

Nellie again shrugged her shoulders. 'I manage,' she replied, leaning across to the stove to warm her hands.

'But where're yer staying, Nellie?' asked Madame, taking a sip of her rapidly cooling tea.

'I found a room. It's not much, but it's all I need. It's over a pub, down 'Olloway Road.'

Madame shook her head despairingly. Around them, the cafe was gradually losing its breakfast customers and one of the assistants was clearing the tables and wiping them with a damp cloth.

'Look, Nellie,' Madame said, 'I've bin talkin' it over with Albert. We 'ave a suggestion ter make. Remember the last time we saw yer, back at the 'ouse in Tufnell Park? Remember wot Albert said about there always bein' a 'ome for yer there wiv us?'

Nellie quickly turned away, embarrassed. 'No, fanks all the same, Mrs Beckwiff,' she said.

'Why not? There's a room there. It's only goin' ter waste.'

Nellie shook her head. 'I couldn't do that, Mrs Beckwiff. You've bin marvellous ter me already. I'm not goin' ter be a stone round yer neck.'

Madame smiled. 'Don't be so silly, child,' she said. 'You'd never be a stone round my neck—nor anyone else's. Now look.' She stretched her hand forward and turned Nellie's face towards her. 'I'm sure yer must know by

172

now that from the first time we saw yer, Albert an' me took a shine ter you. You're like the daughter I always wished I'd 'ad.' She took her hand away from Nellie's face, and the two of them were now staring straight into each other's eyes. 'We'd like ter do somefin' for yer—for you, an' fer us.'

'Wot d'yer mean?'

'I'm sayin' that I don't fink a girl of your age should be gettin' down on 'er 'ands an' knees scrubbin' floors. That's a job fer older people. Yer've got a good mind on yer, Nellie. Yer should be puttin' it ter better fings.'

'I 'ave ter earn me livin'.'

'There are better ways.'

Nellie suddenly felt uneasy. 'Dunno wot yer mean.'

The cafe assistant came up to their table and glanced down into their mugs. 'Finished?' she asked.

'Yes, fanks,' replied Madame, placing the two mugs on the assistant's tray.

'I want ter ask yer somefin', Nellie,' said Madame when the assistant had gone. 'That night you come up ter see Albert's act, at the Finsbury Park Empire. Did yer enjoy yerself?'

'Yer *know* I did!'

'Then 'ere's an idea for yer,' Madame continued quickly. 'Wot d'yer say to a job in the music 'all?'

Nellie stared at Madame in disbelief. 'The music 'all? *Me?*'

'Why not?' said Madame eagerly. 'It's a tough life, but a good'un, full of surprises and interestin' times. An' yer get ter meet lots of nice, warm-'earted people. Yer could come an' work wiv Albert and me. We'd look after yer, show yer the ropes.'

Nellie was dumbfounded. 'But I don't know nuffin' about the music 'all,' was all she could say.

Madame took hold of Nellie's cold hands and squeezed them. 'Yer don't 'ave ter know nuffin', Nellie,' she said reassuringly. 'There are plenty of jobs yer can do, far better than the rubbish you're doin' now. In fact, I know somefin' yer could do that yer'd really like, somefin' that's really werfwhile.'

Nellie, taken aback and nervous, shook her head.

Madame squeezed her hands tighter. 'Listen ter me, Nellie,' she pleaded. 'Yer deserve a chance in life. After all yer've gone through, yer deserve a chance ter get on an' 'ave a family who care for yer.' She leaned closer. 'Come an' live wiv us, Nellie. Come an' let us be yer family. I promise yer, yer can trust us. We'll take care of yer. Yer won't regret it, 'onest yer won't.'

Chapter 11

'Roses is red, violets is blue.'

''Ow'd d'yer know they're blue?'

''Cos I saw 'em 'angin' out on the washin' line this mornin'!'

The only person who ever laughed at Ruby Catmonk's jokes was Ruby herself. And when she laughed, the whole wardrobe room knew it, for it was such a chesty laugh, so hoarse, so coarse, it could deafen anyone at ten paces. But she was a good soul, remarkably well preserved for her seventy-odd years, with dyed bright ginger curls which were really an obstinate silver-grey straining to get out. She made no concessions to her weight, despite the fact that countless doctors had warned her that if she didn't knock something off her fourteen stone, she'd one day tumble over and fall right through the stage floor. Her great joys in life were fags and black market gin, and she was the best seamstress on the British music hall circuit.

Nellie and Ruby got on like a house on fire from the moment they met. Monsieur and Madame had introduced them in the tiny backstage room that was used for costume repairs at the Finsbury Park Empire, and in no time at all Nellie was learning the art of needlework. She even had some lessons on Ruby's ancient Singer sewing machine, and by the time she'd finished the week, she knew practically everything there was to know about running repairs to both male and female theatrical costumes. Madame was right. This certainly was a job that was worthwhile.

Since her meeting with Madame just two weeks before in the workmen's cafe up at Junction Road, Nellie's life had been transformed. Everything had happened so fast. That same day she gave in her notice at all three part-time jobs and left her digs over the pub in Holloway Road to move in with the Beckwith family at number 147A Tufnell Park Road. For Nellie, it was like a dream come true, for she had her own room with a window overlooking the back garden, pretty green floral curtains and wallpaper to match, a single bed and brass bedstead, covered with a huge beige eiderdown and two soft flock pillows. The moment she got there, she just had to throw herself on the bed and bounce up and down on it. She had her own dressing table, chest of drawers and a spacious built-in wardrobe that took up almost one whole wall of the room, although she had hardly any clothes to put in it. The other walls, like the rooms downstairs, were covered with framed photographs of music hall artistes. She hadn't the faintest idea who they were because she couldn't read their names.

Nellie's most exciting time had been the first day at her new job. When Madame suggested that she should become the personal dresser to Monsieur and herself, she was certain that she would never be able to cope with such a job. She didn't even know how to use a needle and cotton, so how could she be expected to keep them in good repair? But once she met up with Ruby Catmonk, all her doubts were dispelled.

It was now just three weeks before Christmas, and rehearsals for the annual panto were in full swing. This year it was to be *Babes In the Wood*, and the cast was headed by the favourite music hall and radio duo, 'Wee' Georgie Wood, who was playing Simple Simon, and his partner,

Dolly Harmer, as his mother. Apart from his usual 'Illusionist Extraordinaire' act, Monsieur Pierre was cast as a foreign-sounding Baron Hardup. He had to wear a variety of colourful costumes which included silk robes, a turban, and a selection of exotic outsize hats.

Watching rehearsals from the empty stalls was a fascinating but in some ways unnerving experience for Nellie. There seemed to be so much frenzied activity everywhere, with performers walking around the stalls trying to memorise their lines, chorus girls and boys practising their musical scales, featured artistes singing snatches of songs, members of the orchestra tuning their musical instruments, dancers limbering up and stretching their bodies with alarming flexibility, 'speciality' acts such as Monsieur Pierre with Ange his assistant and Madame going through some of their new material, and the panto director constantly on the move as he shouted instructions to everyone, from lighting people to sound engineers. The atmosphere was often charged with tension, but the more the show took shape, the more excited Nellie became.

A couple of days before opening night, she was in the costume room ironing one of Monsieur's fancy shirts when the door was flung open by a highly irate Ange.

'Nell!' she growled indignantly. 'I fawt I told yer I wanted these two top buttons taken off the uniform. If you're goin' ter do this job, then fer Gord's sake do it properly.'

Nellie put down the hot flat iron and looked

at the red military-style uniform jacket Ange was dangling before her. 'Sorry,' she answered, a bit taken aback. 'I was goin' ter take them off but Madame told me not to. She said she didn't want yer ter show too much cleavage.'

Ange was outraged. 'Bleedin' cheek!' she yapped. 'I'm the one that's wearin' it, not 'er!'

'Well, yer'd better get yerself some tits first, gel,' sniffed Ruby as she bent to pick up her fag end from the floor where Ange's sudden entrance had sent it flying from the edge of the table she was working at. 'It's no use tryin' to show somefin' that's not there!'

Ruby's acid remark infuriated Ange. 'And we can do wivout your clever comments too, fank yer very much, Ruby Catmonk! Just remember somefin'. Albert Beckwiff's act ain't nuffin' wivout me.'

'Goes wivout sayin',' replied Ruby sarcastically, with only a passing glance at the girl over the top of her tortoiseshell specs as she tried to puff some life back into her battered fag end.

Ange glared at her, then threw the tunic on to Nellie's ironing board. 'Just do it!' she snapped, and stormed out of the room, slamming the door behind her.

'Pardon me fer breavin'!' snorted Nellie. 'Is she always like that?'

Ruby's only response was to laugh. 'Don't take no notice of our Ange,' she chortled. 'Nobody else do.' She took one last puff of her fag end before stubbing it out in the lid of an old Zube tin on her work table. 'Got ideas above 'er station, that one. Dunno wot ol' Albert sees in 'er—'cept the obvious.'

Nellie took Ange's tunic and put it on a hanger alongside others that were marked 'The Great Pierre'. She felt like throwing it on the floor and trampling on it.

Ruby watched her over the top of her specs and grinned. 'I know 'ow yer feel, Nell,' she said sympathetically. 'But yer'll get used to it. There's plenty more of 'er kind around treadin' the boards.'

'I fawt they said people in showbusiness 'ad 'earts of gold,' Nellie said.

Ruby looked up from her sewing. 'Yeah,' she replied. 'Only sometimes the gold's really only brass.'

Ruby's comment brought a smile to Nellie's face, but it also made her think. Although the music hall was glamorous and exciting, it had an ugly side, just like anything else in life—except maybe Ruby. She was of the old school, a former chorus girl who had had to give up the bright lights after a dancing accident on stage when she was only nineteen years old. Every time Nellie looked at the tatty old posters of past shows peeling from the walls of Ruby's tiny domain, she knew where the old lady's true affections lay. 'So wot d'yer fink I should do, Rube?' she asked. 'Shall I take off 'er lousy buttons or shall I go an' ask Mrs Beckwiff?'

Ruby shot her a cautionary look. 'Take the bleedin' fings off,' she said firmly. 'Never play one against the uvver. She's a mischief-maker, that one. If she can put the knife in yer back, she'll do it.'

179

Nellie was puzzled. 'But why? Wot 'ave I done ter hurt 'er?'

'Yer ain't done nuffin', gel,' replied Ruby. 'She's jealous, that's all. To 'er, you're a threat. That one can't cope wiv competition.'

'Competition?'

Ruby took off her specs, rubbed her eyes, and looked at her. 'Albert an' Doris 'ave taken to yer, Nell. They're good people. If I know them, they'll take care of yer as if yer was one of their own.' She pointed her specs at Nellie to emphasise her words. 'But wotever yer do, keep out of that gel's way. She's a dose of poison, Nell, a real madam. If she takes agin yer, Gawd 'elp yer!'

Babes In the Wood opened just two nights before Christmas and was a huge success. The theatre was packed to capacity at every performance. Despite the depressing fact that, after the Japanese attack on Pearl Harbor just two weeks before, Britain and America had joined forces to declare war on Japan, the raucous atmosphere of the Finsbury Park panto raised everyone's spirits.

Living with the Beckwith family made Nellie realise how much joy and happiness life could bring. Her only problem was the two Beckwith boys, Sid and Lenny. From the moment she had moved in, they had made it clear that they resented her. They were full of sarcastic remarks about her height, and made her feel as though she had been dumped in an orphanage by a mum and dad who never really wanted her. Nellie tried to ignore their jibes, putting it down to jealousy because they were no longer the centre of their parents' attention. Their spite usually only surfaced when Monsieur and Madame were not present, and it was a matter of some concern to Nellie. She did her best to befriend the brothers, and make them take to her, but this proved difficult, and even harrowing, as she discovered during the Christmas festivities.

For Nellie, spending Christmas with her adopted family fulfilled all her dreams. Monsieur and Madame were both determined to make her a part of it all and she was swept along by the excitement of helping Madame do the shopping and wrap up presents for everyone. Then, on Christmas Eve, Madame asked Nellie to take the boys out to do their own personal shopping. Their first destination was the North London Drapery Stores in Seven Sisters Road.

'OK then,' Nellie said as Sid and Lenny dutifully followed her up the main staircase to the ladies' clothes department on the first floor. 'Who's got all the lolly?'

'Yer don't fink we're goin' ter tell you, do yer?' sneered Lenny, overtaking Nellie as he raced his brother up the stairs. 'It's our pocket money. We can do wot we want wiv it.'

'Course yer can do wot yer want wiv it,' Nellie said as she reached the top of the stairs. 'As long as yer know 'ow much yer've got ter spend on presents.'

'Wot yer talkin' about?' asked Sid. 'Who said anyfin' about buyin' any presents?'

Nellie did a double take. 'Well, wot we doin'
'ere then? I fawt I was s'posed ter be 'elpin'
yer to buy yer mum and dad's Christmas
presents.'

'Give over!' squawked Lenny. 'Who d'yer fink
we are?'

'We don't buy presents fer mum an' dad,'
explained Sid.

'We don't buy presents fer no one,' added
Lenny. 'Don't yer know it's Christmas? It's a
time fer kids, remember, not grown-ups.'

Nellie was taken aback by their comments.
As she watched them hurrying off towards the
children's department, she could hardly believe
how little they cared for their parents.

There were plenty of shoppers milling around
the rails of ladies' clothes. It was surprising
really, for the garments seemed drab and
unimaginative, dreary grey two-piece suits and
pill-box hats, plain blouses and narrow, straight
skirts, for to save labour and material, no
pleating was allowed. Nellie wasn't impressed
with anything she saw, and thought to herself
that even if she had the money and ration
coupons to spend, she certainly wouldn't use
them here. But she had managed to save a little
of her earnings and was determined to find a
small present for Monsieur and Madame, and
something for the two boys.

'Come an' see wot we've found, Nell.' Sid
was tugging her arm and she allowed him to
lead her into the children's department where
Lenny was standing among a group of other
boys watching an electric train race round a

vast track. Pleased that she had been asked to join them, Nellie stood there watching with everyone else, happy to know that Sid at least was showing some sign of accepting her.

''Ow long you goin' ter stay wiv us, Nell?' Sid asked, quite suddenly.

Nellie was surprised by the question. 'Wot d'yer mean?' she asked.

Sid repeated the question. ''Ow long yer goin' ter stay? At our 'ouse, workin' wiv Mum an' Dad?'

'I dunno, Sid,' she said. 'I reckon it's up ter them.'

Sid kept his eyes on the model train. 'It's not the sorta place fer someone like you,' he said, his voice flat.

Before Nellie had a chance to respond, the air was pierced by the wail of an air-raid siren, which was soon joined by the deafening sound of the fire alarm inside the store itself.

Within moments, shoppers were streaming down the stairs. Some hurried out into the street, while others, including Nellie, Sid, and Lenny, made for the shelter in the store basement. It was the first air-raid alert for some weeks and no one was taking any chances.

After a quarter of an hour or so, the siren wailed again, this time for the all clear. During that time there had been no sound of ack-ack gunfire, bombs, or panic. Nobody in the shelter knew quite what had caused the alert, only that this was a sinister reminder that the war was still on.

A few minutes later, Nellie left the store with

Sid and Lenny, and all three made their way home along Seven Sisters Road. Sid didn't refer again to his conversation with Nellie in the store. And neither did Nellie.

On Christmas morning, Nellie woke up to the smell of a fifteen-pound turkey cooking in the kitchen oven downstairs. It was a wonderful smell, and a rare one, for in this time of acute meat rationing, finding any size turkey was an achievement. But Monsieur had his connections, and despite his patriotic fervour, he was quite prepared to use the black market for personal luxuries.

When Nellie looked at the small alarm clock on her bedside cabinet, she was surprised to see that it was still only eight o'clock in the morning. She and the family had not got to bed until two in the morning after a Christmas Eve party at the theatre.

In the kitchen downstairs, Madame was already hard at work preparing the potatoes, Brussels sprouts, parsnips, carrots, and cauliflower, and her homemade Christmas pud was bubbling away on the gas hob. Nellie adored watching Madame in the kitchen, for she was a wonderful cook, nothing fancy, but good, wholesome English food which her own mother had brought her up on in Stepney.

Monsieur was, as expected, the last to appear, and he didn't really come alive until after he'd coughed on his first Abdullah of the day. Sid and Lenny had been up for hours, pestering their mum to hurry up with the chores so that they could get down to what they considered the only important business of the day, namely, opening their Christmas presents.

After a sparse breakfast of tea and toast, Nellie helped to clear up, and at eleven o'clock on the dot, Monsieur's ancient parents arrived, together with his younger brother Louis, and Louis' wife Merle. Nellie liked them all, especially Monsieur's mum, Lillian, who was fat and cuddly and never stopped putting her two sons in their place. Her husband, Maurice, was a dear old thing; although he was bent over with back problems, he never stopped beaming at everything and everybody. Louis was quite unlike Monsieur—portly, with a bushy moustache which he constantly twitched and a full flock of light brown hair, and he stood a good six inches shorter than his elder brother. His work was very different too; he was a fitter for the Gas, Light, and Coke Company, and wouldn't say boo to a goose. Louis' wife Merle was a pretty little thing who only spoke when she was spoken to. She seemed a bit self-conscious of the fact that her accent betrayed that she came from a 'better class' of family up in Palmers Green.

While the women had a cup of tea, the men opened a quart bottle of brown ale, despite the fact that it was still only mid-morning. A few minutes later, Madame's mother, a widow, arrived. Edna had a barbed tongue and treated everyone, including her son-in-law's family, with suspicion and resentment. Madame actually preferred her mum-in-law, and never felt at ease when the two families were together.

Just before midday, Sid and Lenny's great moment finally arrived. Everyone gathered round the six-foot Christmas tree in the living room where the presents, wrapped in brightly coloured paper, were piled high. Nellie loved the way everyone treated her as a member of the family, for they had all bought her something.

'It ain't much, dear,' said old Lillian as she watched Nellie open her gift, a small bottle of eau de cologne. 'But you're a pretty little fing, an' at least it'll make yer pong nice!'

Nellie joined in with the old lady's laughter. She was thrilled. To her, eau de cologne was the equivalent of getting the most expensive perfume in the world. Nellie was overwhelmed by the trouble everyone had gone to. She received real silk stockings from Monsieur and Madame, and a woollen scarf from Louis and Merle. Monsieur and Madame gave Louis and Merle two new cushions, and they had bought cigarettes for Monsieur and some new popular sheet music for Madame. Apart from practical presents to wear, Sid had additional carriages for his model train set, a game of Lotto, and a new cricket set. Lenny was swamped with comic annuals, a Meccano set, a chemistry set, and numerous puzzle games. Monsieur gave his wife some money to buy a new dress, and Madame gave her husband a pullover she had knitted herself, together with a bottle of whisky she had bought on the black market from a stagehand working at the Chiswick Empire. The only one who didn't fare too well was Edna, who seemed to receive much the same present from everyone: three pairs of gloves, two packets of hair curlers, and three potted chrysanthemum plants. But she accepted all her gifts graciously, particularly the two bars of Lifebuoy soap, for all soap was rationed and in very short supply. The most telling moment for Nellie came when Monsieur and Madame opened the presents that she had bought for them. Sid and Lenny had already opened theirs and dismissed them without so much as a thank you—a pack of playing cards for Sid, and a model of a Spitfire fighter plane for Lenny. Nellie had never had anyone to buy presents for until now and she was quite nervous.

'I know wot she got fer you, Dad!' Lenny proclaimed smugly.

'Ssh!' Madame scolded him. 'It's s'posed ter be a surprise.'

Lenny ignored his mum and continued, 'I was wiv 'er when she got it in the Drapery Stores. She paid three bob fer it. It's a fag case.'

There was an intake of breath from everyone present.

'Lenny!' Madame was furious.

'That weren't very nice, dear,' said Lillian, shaking her head.

'Wot difference does it make?' Lenny sniffed dismissively. 'It's only a present.' Then, to everyone's horror, he turned to his mum. 'She got *you* a new hand mirror.'

'No, Lenny!'

There were cries of protest from everyone.

Monsieur refused to take any notice of his

son and carried on opening his small, carefully wrapped parcel. When he took out the modest tin cigarette case he found there, he let out a gasp of delight that made everyone feel as though it was made of pure gold. 'Nellie!' he said, looking up at her with a start. ''Ow did yer know? This is just wot I needed!' He went up to her and gave her a big kiss right in the middle of her forehead. 'Fank yer, gel!' he said with a stony glance towards Lenny. 'This is the best present I've 'ad fer years.'

Nellie's distress turned to real delight.

Madame's reaction was much the same. 'Oh, Nell!' she exclaimed. 'Wot a beautiful mirror!' Then, after throwing her arms around Nellie and hugging her, she asked. ''Ow did yer know pink was my favourite colour?'

Nellie felt embarrassed. 'I knew yer wanted a new one. I 'eard yer say so, in the dressin' room at the Empire.'

Madame hugged her again. But, over Nellie's shoulder, she directed an icy look at Lenny.

Nellie thoroughly enjoyed the Christmas lunch. She had never seen so many people crowded round one table before. There were no formalities; once Monsieur had sliced the turkey, everyone tucked in and helped themselves to the vegetables, homemade blackcurrant jelly, and gravy, and while it was all going on, Monsieur, Louis and Maurice sank the best part of two bottles of brown ale, leaving the solitary bottle of red wine, left over from before the war, to the ladies. When it was time for the Christmas pudding, needless to say it was Lenny

188

who discovered the traditional threepenny piece in the middle of his portion; everyone knew Madame had sneaked it in while she was serving it. Everyone pulled Christmas crackers and donned paper hats, and then collapsed back into their chairs, their stomachs full. Old Lillian was the only one who seemed to have any energy to make conversation.

'So, Nellie, dear,' she said, using a paper napkin to wipe the remains of Christmas pud from her lips. ''Ow'd d'yer like livin' wiv the Beckwiff family?'

A broad smile spread across Nellie's face. 'I fink they're the most won'erful people in the world,' she said, turning to look at Monsieur and Madame.

Everyone, except Sid and Lenny, used either their fingers or a piece of cutlery to tap on the table in agreement.

'I hear yer've now got your papers fru from that children's 'ome,' said Louis, always the practical one. 'Be able ter get yer identity card, I reckon.'

'And her ration card,' added Merle, who, on hearing the sound of her own voice, quickly shrivelled up again.

'It was no problem really,' explained Nellie. 'Miss Ackroyd, the woman in charge, she sent everyfin' fru. She said I was very lucky ter live wiv such a nice family.'

'We're the lucky ones,' said Madame, squeezing Nellie's hand.

Nellie smiled back at her.

'This is no ordinary family, yer know, Nell,'

Louis snorted, after gulping down half a glass of beer. 'They're all exhibitionists. Even Mum an' Dad 'ere. Did yer know they used ter be a double act—"The Flying Equilibrists".'

'An' a great act we were too,' boasted Lillian. 'Weren't we, Dad?' she added, turning to her husband who was sitting at her side.

'The best!' he said modestly.

'So tell me, Lou,' said Monsieur, 'wot's so ordinary about you an' Merle?'

'We don't 'ave ter work evenin's,' Louis joked.

Everyone laughed, and there was a chorus of ''Ear! 'Ear! Yer can say that again!'

During the meal, Madame's mum, Edna, had said very little, preferring to eat her food and make the most of any alcohol that was going. Unlike her opposite number, Lillian Beckwith, she had never had anything to do with the music hall; she came from a family of bricklayers. But she loved singing popular songs, and when Doris was young, Edna had encouraged her to take up piano lessons. 'Nuffin' wrong wiv the music 'all,' she said now, on the verge of being a little tipsy. 'At least it 'elps yer ferget this bleedin' war.'

For a brief moment, her comment brought a hush to the after-lunch chat. Until now, all talk of the horrors of the past two years had been carefully avoided.

'I'm not sure you're right, Edna,' said Lillian soberly. 'A lot 'as 'appened in these two years that some of us'll never ferget.'

Several pairs of eyes turned to look at Nellie.

Nellie tried hard not to react. The devastating

190

experience of surviving the bomb explosion at Barratts' Orphanage was now behind her, and she had no wish to try to remember anything about it. But she did remember the Christmas she had spent with Toff and the vacs gang back in the gutted-out furniture store. In that split second, she could see Toff's flashing good looks smiling at her, wanting her. And she wanted him. She wanted him more than she had ever thought possible. But where was he now? Would she ever see him again?

'Best not ter look back, eh, Nell?' said Monsieur sympathetically. 'You're our little gel now.'

Sid and Lenny exchanged a strained look, then without saying a word they got up from the table and left the room.

On Christmas evening, several music hall friends of Monsieur and Madame turned up, and in no time at all there was a party. Practically every one of the friends did a turn, either a song or an impersonation of people like comics George Robey and Harry Bennett or popular music hall favourites such as Marie Lloyd, Randolph Sutton, Ella Shields. It was a very theatrical occasion, with everyone talking shop, and Nellie could understand what Louis had meant when he said this was no ordinary family. After a while the party turned into a knees-up, with Madame bashing out song after song on the piano, and the guests doing everything from the hokey-cokey to a spoof ensemble tango. Nellie loved it all, and joined in the laughter along with the rest of them. She was amazed by Madame's resilience and abounding energy she was the only one who had had nothing alcoholic to drink. 'I've got nuffin' against it, dear,' she said. 'I just don't like it, that's all.'

During the course of the evening, Nellie and Merle went off to the kitchen to make some sandwiches from the leftovers of the midday meal. Nellie got on well with Merle, despite the fact that the two of them hardly spoke the same language. But once they were alone together, Merle was far more outgoing, and Nellie was able to talk to her more freely about the family.

'Hearts of gold?' said Merle, in response to a comment from Nellie. 'Oh yes, Doris and Albert've got that all right. In fact I can't imagine more generous people. They'd do anything for anyone. Except themselves, of course.'

'Wot d'yer mean?'

Merle shrugged her shoulders. 'Oh, I don't know. Sometimes I get the feeling that they're always on stage, always acting. I'm a good bit younger than Lou, and I notice these things.'

Nellie, cutting bread while Merle sliced the remains of the turkey, stopped briefly to look at her. 'Wot d'yer notice, Merle?' she asked.

Merle looked up. She was indeed younger than her husband; she had a lovely complexion and large brown eyes, with hair swept back behind her head. 'They don't know how to be themselves,' she replied.

Nellie thought hard about this for a moment,

192

but she still didn't quite understand.

'Don't get me wrong,' continued Merle. 'I adore Albert and Doris. They're the best brother-in-law and sister-in-law you could ever have. But sometimes they exhaust me. Especially Albert. Always on the move, always playing to the gallery. I just wish sometimes they could be more of a husband and wife than an *act.*'

The sound of Madame playing the piano filtered through the open serving hatch. It was a lovely, poignant love song, 'Let the Rest of the World Go By', and when Nellie turned to look out through the hatch, she was enchanted to see Monsieur singing the words of the song, his arms lovingly folded round her neck and breasts. It was a wonderful picture, and in complete contrast to what Merle had just said. If this wasn't being a husband and wife, she thought to herself, what was?

Most of Monsieur and Madame's friends, didn't leave until well after midnight. But as most of them lived within walking distance, there was no real problem about getting home. By the time the family finally said goodnight and went to bed, Nellie felt exhausted and exhilarated. Her mind was so full of all that had gone on during the day that she found it almost impossible to sleep, and for nearly an hour she lay awake reviewing all the images before her and asking herself over and over again what she had done to deserve the kindness of her new mum and dad.

Eventually she dropped off to sleep, but about

three o'clock in the morning, her eyes flicked open. She had heard something, something downstairs, a movement.

Getting out of bed, Nellie put on the pale blue carpet slippers Madame had given her on the day she had arrived, then quietly left her room.

It was dark on the landing, but she could see a small chink of light coming from the kitchen downstairs. Carefully holding up her nightie, which was a little too long for her, she began to creep down the stairs. As she went, she could smell the remains of the cigars that Monsieur, Louis, and Maurice had been smoking in the living room earlier in the evening. The cigars had been given to Monsieur by a director of the Moss Empire circuit after the first night of the panto, and they had clearly been of a good quality, but the sweet-smelling tobacco smoke they produced was overpowering.

By the time she reached the bottom stair, she began to wonder if someone had merely left the light on in the kitchen, for there was no sound coming from there, and there was certainly no sign of life from the upstairs rooms.

She paused a moment, and listened. At first, no sound. But then she heard someone sniffing, as though they had a bad cold. As quiet as a mouse, she tiptoed slowly towards the kitchen door which was very slightly open. She put her head round the door, and the first thing she noticed was a strong smell of spirits.

Madame was sitting at the kitchen table, her back towards the door. The sniffing sound

Nellie had heard turned into a sob. And on the table beside Madame was a bottle of gin, from which she poured what appeared to be a rather large measure.

Chapter 12

The grey stone walls of Pentonville Prison looked grim enough at the best of times, but against the dim winter light of a January afternoon, they looked positively soul-destroying. Most local residents hated the place, for it was a huge eyesore spread out along a great stretch of the Caledonian Road between Holloway and King's Cross, and there had often been complaints that it was neither ethical nor fair to have two prisons within the boundaries of the London Borough of Islington, Pentonville for men and, less than a mile away, Holloway for women. But there it stood, a monument to the horrors of modern-day life, housing both petty criminals and convicted murderers, a joyless place, particularly at the time of an execution when the black flag of death was raised and the gruesome chapel bell pealed its toll of doom.

This was the first time Nellie had come to visit Hubert in gaol. She had wanted to come soon after he had been put in there, but he had sent a message to say that he was too depressed to see anybody, even her. However, using Ruby Catmonk to write a letter for her, Nellie had managed to make contact with Hubert, and he had at last agreed to see her.

Nellie walked the mile or so to the prison. It was quite an easy journey from Tufnell Park Road, for she was able to take short cuts through Dalmeny Road, Camden Road, and Hillmarton Road, which eventually brought her out into Caledonian Road just a few hundred yards from the prison itself. She had deep forebodings about visiting such a place. And when she got there, her fears were justified.

Outside the main gates, a small group of visitors had already gathered, some of them quite rough-looking but most of them very ordinary people, their faces showing anguish more than anything. Once inside and signed in at the reception area, Nellie and the others were shown into the waiting room where they were allocated individual chairs positioned in front of a long counter which had a barrier of wire mesh down its length. Despite being just one of many visitors waiting to see a prisoner, Nellie felt very self-conscious, almost as though she was a criminal herself. No matter how she felt, however, nothing could have prepared her for her first glimpse of Hubert.

''Ello, Nell,' he said, as he sat down on a stool on the other side of the wire mesh. 'Fanks fer comin'.'

Nellie took a moment to focus on him. In just a few months, he had changed beyond recognition. 'Hube!' She had to lean close to the barrier for him to hear her clearly. 'I've missed yer so much.'

'Missed yer too, Nell.'

For a brief second, they just stared at one another.

Nellie tried hard to smile, but she was so distressed to see her old mate looking so emaciated. He had always been as skinny as a drumstick, but now he looked so ill, so pale and drawn. ''Ow they bin treatin' yer then?' was all she could ask.

Hubert's parched skin practically cracked with his wry smile. 'They keep me on me toes, Nell, that's fer sure.'

Nell's stomach churned over inside. She felt into her small shoulder bag and brought out two packets of his favourite Woodbines. 'Got these for yer,' she said. 'Lucky ter get them fru though. They searched me at reception.'

Hubert pulled the packets underneath the barrier. 'Yer shouldn't 'ave, Nell,' he said. 'I got no right ter expect anyfin' from yer.'

There was an uneasy silence between them. There were so many questions Nell wanted to ask him, so many things she wanted to say that might help. Finally, Hubert broke the silence.

''Ow've yer bin, Nell?' he asked. 'Are yer 'appy wiv this family?'

Nell's faint smile broke the gloom. 'Oh Hube, I can't tell yer 'ow won'erful they are ter me. They couldn't treat me better if I was their own daughter.'

'Yer deserve it, Nell,' he said earnestly. 'If anyone deserves a bit of luck, it's you.'

Nell lowered her eyes awkwardly, then raised

them again. 'Did yer know I'm learnin' ter read an' write?'

Hubert grinned. 'You?'

'It's this woman up the Empire,' replied Nellie with sudden enthusiasm. ''Er name's Ruby. Ruby Catmonk. Wot a name, eh! Anyway, I work wiv 'er, sewin' an' fings. An' she's givin' me lessons. Not official like, but a few words 'ere an' there. A'tually, I'm gettin' on really well. I could read the noticeboard outside. "H.M. Prison, Pentonville." Wot does the H.M. stand for?'

Hubert's grin broadened. 'His Majesty's.'

Nellie looked puzzled. ''Is Majesty's? Wot's this place got ter do wiv the King?'

'Good point, Nell,' Hubert replied. 'Good point.'

After her sudden burst of talking, Nellie sat back in her chair and there was another awkward pause. Then she again leaned forward. 'Why did yer do it, Hube? Why did yer 'ave ter get inter this mess?'

Hubert lowered his eyes in anguish.

The room was filled with the buzz of prisoners talking to their visitors. It was a strange sound, for their voices echoed round the green varnished walls. The smell of carbolic used to scrub the lino floors pervaded the place.

Hubert's eyes flicked up again and he stared at Nellie's face behind the wire mesh. 'It's a part of me, Nell,' he said candidly. 'I just can't 'elp meself.'

'But free times, Hube!' Nellie said, pressing forward so that her lips were almost touching the wire mesh. 'I can understand it 'appening on the spur of the moment, but free times. Why?'

Hubert thought for a moment before answering. ''Cos it's the only way ter get anyone ter take notice of me.' he replied. 'I'm fed up wiv bein' stopped from doin' all the fings in life I want ter do. When I left school, I 'ad plans, all kinds of plans. I wanted ter go in the army, then the police force. I wanted to find the right gel, save up, get married, 'ave me own family an' settle down. But every way I turned, it never 'appened. There was always somefink, someone ter stop me, someone ter tell me I was just a toerag who 'ad no right ter nuffink at all.' He paused only long enough to take a deep sigh. 'Well, maybe they was right—no, they *was* right. I *don't* 'ave the right to expect anyfin'.'

'You're right, Hube, yer don't.' Nellie's lips were now pressed right up against the wire mesh. 'But it doesn't mean yer 'ave ter stop tryin'.'

Shaking his head, Hubert leaned back in his chair.

'Listen ter me, Hube!' Nellie said fiercely. 'Just listen!'

A burly uniformed prison officer came forward and gently eased Nellie back from the mesh. 'Not so close. please, miss,' he said firmly but politely.

Nellie obeyed, waited for him to go, then resumed what she was saying. 'Look, Hube, just 'cos we find it 'ard tryin' ter get the fings we need most, doesn't mean that we 'ave ter go around breakin' inter uvver people's 'omes and offices. *I've* 'ad ter struggle too, Hube. I've never 'ad anyone ter stand up fer me an' fight my battles. But I'm not goin' ter give up tryin'. I'm not goin' ter keep takin' it out on uvver people. An' I'll tell yer this,' she leaned towards the wire mesh again, then remembered the prison officer watching her and sat back. 'I'll tell yer this,' she continued, her voice low, 'I won't give up tryin'. I won't give up tryin' ter get on wiv my life, in me own way, wivout 'urtin' everyone round me.'

As he listened to her, Hubert kept his head lowered. When she had finished, he looked up with a strained expression on his face. 'I asked yer ter come 'ere, Nell,' he said, with obvious anguish, ''cos I wanted ter say g'bye.'

Nellie immediately felt a sense of panic. 'Goodbye? Wot yer talkin' about?'

Hubert leaned forward as far as he dared, and looked along the line of other prisoners to make sure no one was listening. 'When I get out of 'ere, I'm goin' away, Nell.'

'Where?'

'It doesn't matter where. I'm just going, that's all.'

Nellie felt as though all the blood was draining from her body. 'But yer can't go anywhere, yer can't survive wivout a job. 'Ow yer goin' ter get a job after yer've bin in this place?'

Hubert sighed again. 'Let me worry about that, Nell.'

'Let me 'elp yer, Hube. I'll talk ter Mister

Beckwiff. I'm sure if I talked ter 'im 'e'd 'elp find yer a job.'

Hubert was suddenly very firm with her. 'No, Nell! I said, let me worry about it.' Abruptly, he got up from his stool.

'Hube! Why are yer doin' this? Don't yer like me any more?'

Hubert felt his whole body tense. This was his supreme test. This was the moment he had been preparing for during the past few days while he had been rehearsing this meeting with Nellie. For a moment, he just stared at her. Then slowly he raised his hands and pressed the palms against the wire mesh. 'I like yer all right, Nell,' he said, his voice a croak. 'I could never stop likin' *you*.'

Nellie got up from her seat. She, too, raised her hands and placed her palms against his through the mesh.

After a brief moment, and without speaking another word, Hubert turned and quickly strode back to the door leading to the cells, where a prison officer let him through.

Nellie watched him go, cold and numb, and as the door slammed behind him, she shivered.

Nellie felt total despair. Making her way down the ramp from the main entrance of the prison, she hardly realised that she was back in Caledonian Road again. Her legs told her that it was too much to expect them to take her all the way back to Tufnell Park Road without help, so she crossed to the bus stop on the opposite side of the road. Within moments of her leaving the prison, huge hailstones began pelting down on to the pavement. There was no place to shelter at the bus stop, so she took cover beneath the railway bridge which spanned Caledonian Road. As far as the eye could see along the main road, hailstones thumped down, reducing visibility practically to nil. Nellie felt as though she was on an alien planet. After a moment, several other people ran to join her, but she paid no attention to them. All she could think about was Hubert, the torment he was enduring, and the cold hard fact that she might never see him again.

'Well, hello.'

Nellie barely heard the voice addressing her from behind, so she ignored it.

The gentle Irish-sounding voice was not deterred. 'I hope your taste in music's improved since we last met.'

Nellie turned with a start. Standing just behind her was the young bloke she had almost come to blows with in Saville's Record Shop in Holloway Road a few months before. Her lips pursed. 'Wot *you* doin' 'ere?' she asked sniffily.

'Much the same as you, I reckon,' the boy replied. 'I don't usually enjoy walkin' in a hailstorm.'

Nellie shrugged dismissively and diverted her gaze.

Looking at the back of Nellie's head, the boy smiled. He knew he was irritating her. 'It's still Spike Jones, is it?' he asked.

Nellie swung back to him. 'Wot d'yer say?' she asked tetchily.

'Spike Jones and his City Slickers. You know, your favourite type of music.'

Nellie knew he was getting at her, so she turned away again.

'Actually, I quite like them meself,' the boy said, his Irish accent now more pronounced. 'Not quite in the same class as Rachmaninoff, but pretty close.'

This caused Nellie to smile. After all, even she had to admit that the cacophonous sound of Spike Jones and his City Slickers was about as similar to classical music as Hitler was to Yorkshire pudding. 'Well, yer don't get many laughs from Rick Mani whatever 'is name is!' she quipped.

This broke the ice, and both of them chuckled together.

'Patrick,' the boy said, offering his hand.

Nellie hesitated briefly, then shook it.

'Are you goin' to tell me yours? You do have one, I suppose.'

'Nellie.'

Patrick grinned. 'Pleased to know you, Nellie.'

The hail finally eased off, and the small group that had been sheltering beneath the railway bridge dispersed. The storm had left the air bitingly cold, and the hailstones covered the pavements, making them treacherous, but as Nellie and Patrick moved out into the street, the sun broke through and lit up the whole of Caledonian Road, transforming it into a much more attractive place than it had been ten minutes ago. By the time the two of them had reached the bus stop, a rainbow arched across the sky, forming a multi-coloured backcloth to the silver barrage balloons that were bouncing up and down at the ends of their umbilical cables, their bulbous silver shapes glistening in the sunlight.

A long queue had formed at the bus stop, and it was obvious that they were in for quite a wait.

'So how far d'yer live?' Patrick asked, pulling the hood of his fawn-coloured duffel coat as tight as he could over his head.

'Not far from the Nag's Head,' she replied vaguely. She thought he had a bit of a nerve asking such a question on so short an acquaintance. Still, she had to admit he was really good-looking and he had a devastating smile. But it wasn't his looks or smile that fascinated her now, it was his gentle manner and soft-spoken accent, so different from the boys she had known so far. Different from Toff, with his direct no-nonsense, plum-in-the-mouth delivery, and the boys in the vacs gang who, like herself, fractured the English language with their rough Cockney slang. Different also from Hubert, sitting back there in his prison cell, lighting up his beloved Woodbines.

'Looks like you've got company on the number fourteen then,' said Patrick, who kept on looking at Nellie's lips as he talked.

'Huh?' Nellie was miles away. 'I'm sorry, wot did yer say?'

'I said, d'yer mind if I join you on the bus?

I live up Hornsey Rise way.'

Nellie shrugged her shoulders. 'It's a free country,' she said, briefly aware that she had made eye contact with him. Embarrassed, she quickly looked away to see if there was any sign of a bus approaching.

'My pals tell me I'm the shy sort,' said Patrick. 'What do you think, Nellie?'

Nellie turned back to him. 'I dunno,' she replied. 'D'you fink yer are?'

Now it was Patrick's turn to shrug his shoulders. 'Well, I suppose I've got a bit of a cheek to be chattin' you up. Especially after our last meeting.'

'Chattin' me up? *Are* yer chattin' me up?'

Patrick was still looking at her lips. 'Yes, I am. D'you mind?'

Nellie didn't know how to respond. She found it disconcerting the way he kept staring at her lips. 'Like I told yer,' she said, 'it's a free country.'

Patrick smiled and leaned towards her ear, whispering, 'Tell me something, Nellie. What d'you think of Paddys?'

'Paddys? Irish people, yer mean? Dunno. You're the first one I've met.'

'A lot of people think we're dubious.'

'Wot's that?'

'They don't trust us.'

This remark was a little louder than Patrick had intended, and it prompted an elderly woman standing just in front of them to turn round and glare at him.

'Every person's a diff'rent person,' Nellie said

205

after a long moment's thought. 'What part of Ireland was yer born in then?' she asked, trying to sound as though she was only making casual conversation.

'Actually I was born in London, where I live now in Hornsey Rise. But me mam comes from County Donegal, and me dad's from Muswell Hill. He's in the Army. And by the way, would you care to have a drink with me some time?'

Nellie thought she hadn't heard right. One minute he was talking about his mum and dad, the next he was trying to date her. 'Wot d'yer mean?' she asked.

'I'm inviting you to have a drink with me. You know, in a pub. Any time you like. Tonight if you want.'

Nellie looked at him in disbelief. If this bloke was shy, then she was a Chinaman. 'I'm not allowed ter drink in pubs,' she replied. 'I'm under age.'

'You can drink a lemonade, can't you? Or even a shandy.'

'Are all Paddys like you?'

'Some of them,' Patrick answered, quick as a flash. Then with a broad grin and a mischievous twinkle in his eye he added, 'But none of them are as charming and tactful as me.'

For a brief moment, Nellie looked him over. Then she laughed.

The Theatre Royal in Drury Lane was one of London's oldest playhouses. Its origins went back as far as the year 1616, and during its long and distinguished history, its most celebrated patron had been Charles II. Some of the most famous actors in the land had appeared at the theatre, and although the building itself had had several incarnations, its colourful past had now become folklore.

Nellie had never been inside such a famous and beautiful theatre, and when she first entered the elegant cream and gold-leaf auditorium, with its red plush fauteuils, stalls, three circles and stage-side boxes, one of them with a royal crest proudly displayed above the canopy, she was overawed by the sheer grandeur of the place. One of the joys of working for Monsieur Pierre was experiencing moments like this, the chance to enter an empty auditorium with its rich galaxy of past artistes and audiences surrounding her. She could almost see the performers in their colourful costumes, and the audience in all their finery, laughing, applauding, gasping with horror or ecstasy.

But today Nellie's presence did not involve a live performance. Today Monsieur Pierre was giving the first audition he had given since he set out to become a music hall performer back in the early 1930s. He was prepared to do whatever was asked of him, for today he was auditioning for a place with the Entertainments National Service Association, or ENSA. There was no disgrace in auditioning for such an organisation, for what mattered was the chance to entertain the armed services.

The day had started early for Nellie. She had got up at six o'clock in the morning to make sure that Monsieur Pierre's stage costume was carefully ironed, his vast black cloak folded neatly and packed into his suitcase, his white gloves stretched, and his tall black top hat brushed, steamed, and free of every particle of dust. Madame's dress had also to be attended to. She would be wearing her long blue sequined gown which Ruby Catmonk had only recently restored to full glory after nearly nine years of continuous stage wear. The only panic was Madame's tall ostrich feather, which she always wore in the back of her hairpiece, and which overnight had become limp and obstinate. But with careful combing using a fine nailbrush, and some nail varnish to keep it in line, even the feather lived up to expectations. Needless to say, Monsieur's young assistant, Ange, left everything to Nellie, contributing nothing to the huge task of getting all the costumes and props on time to the theatre.

Nellie enjoyed the journey to Drury Lane, for it was the first time she had ever travelled in a taxi. On the way, Madame pointed out the sights, some of which Nellie had already seen when she and Hubert had strolled around Piccadilly Circus and Trafalgar Square together the previous August Bank Holiday Monday. Monsieur spent most of the time puffing on an Abdullah through his short, slender cigarette holder, silently miming the words of his act.

The dressing room allocated to Monsieur and Madame seemed to Nellie to be not much bigger than the one they occupied at the Finsbury Park Empire. But it was certainly better furnished, with an elegant chaise-longue

covered in fine yellow brocade and a wrought-
iron radiator that made the room warm and
cosy. Nellie laid out Monsieur and Madame's
costumes, then left the room while they got
changed. She made her way to the stage where
she helped a stagehand to identify the props
belonging to Monsieur's act.

When Monsieur and Madame were fully
costumed, Nellie checked to see that there
were no hairs, or dust, or creases lurking on
their garments.

'No sign of Ange, I s'pose,' said Madame,
sounding as though she was used to the late
appearance of Monsieur's stage assistant.

'I ain't seen 'er yet,' replied Nellie. 'If yer
like, I'll go up an' see if she's in the supports'
dressin' room.'

'I wouldn't bovver,' said Monsieur dismissively as he practised various dramatic poses in
front of the dressing-table mirror. 'If I know
'er, she'll turn up just as we're goin' on.'

Nellie made her way back into the auditorium,
and on the dot of eleven o'clock, the auditions
began with a wonderful act by Billy Reid and
his accordion band, who were already famous
in the music hall and on the wireless. Nellie sat
on her own at the back of the stalls and watched
with huge enjoyment, quietly joining in with the
songs. They were followed by a tap-dancer who
juggled clubs and rubber balls at the same time,
a comedian who told conversational jokes about
his 'affairs', a pair of male acrobats who were so
daring Nellie was convinced one of them was
about to be catapulted into the front row of the

fauteuils, and finally a female impersonating a singing soldier. Nellie had a wonderful time, and felt that the whole show was being put on just for her alone. But the proceedings were continually spoilt by the voice of a middle-aged man in Army uniform who was sitting in a seat three or four rows from the front, flanked by one male and one female assistant. Nellie was horrified by the way the man kept yelling at the artistes on the stage, 'Get on with it! How d'you think you're going to perform an act like that in the back of a lorry?' He sounded really nasty and Nellie only hoped that when it was time for Monsieur and Madame to come on stage, his manners would have improved.

'Wot d'yer fink of our Basil then?' It was Ange, speaking into Nellie's ear from the seat behind. ''Is name's Basil Dean. 'E's in charge of ENSA. A real charmer, that one. Most people'd like ter cut 'is bleedin' 'ead off!'

'I'm not surprised,' replied Nellie. 'I 'ope 'e's not like this durin' our act.'

'*Our* act?' Nellie could hear the indignation in Ange's voice. 'Since when 'as this act bin anyfin' ter do wiv you?'

Nellie could have bitten off her tongue. 'That's not wot I meant, Ange,' she said, almost apologetically. 'I just meant that I'd 'ate ter see that geezer down there talkin' ter Monsieur like that.'

'Don't you worry about that,' whispered Ange. 'Me an' the ol' man know 'ow ter take care of ourselves. Oh yes, an' 'ow!' Then she leaned closer, adding, 'As a matter of fact,

210

me an' Albert can give as good as we take, if yer get my meanin'.'

'What the hell's going on back there?'

Nellie froze as Basil Dean's voice boomed out from the fauteuils.

'If I hear one more person chatting during my auditions, they're out! Do I make myself clear?'

Nellie shrank down in her seat. She imagined Ange had done the same. Only when the next act was called did she have the courage to sit up again. When she turned to look round, Ange had gone.

Basil Dean had the good sense not to talk to Monsieur in the same way that he had addressed some of the other artistes. Monsieur was known for his sharp East End tongue, and one word out of place from Basil Dean would have unleashed a torrent of good old-fashioned costermonger fury. Nellie was amused when at the conclusion of Monsieur's act, the irascible producer even managed a compliment. 'Well done, Mr Beckwith,' he said. 'I'm sure you'll be a great asset to ENSA. The troops will love you.'

As Nellie set about packing up the props and costumes, Ange's lewd insinuations were far from her mind. But as she made her way back to the dressing room to collect the costume case and take it to the stage door, she came face to face with the reality behind Ange's words. There, partly concealed behind some scenery at the back of the now deserted stage, were Monsieur and Ange.

To her horror, Nellie realised that the Great Pierre and his young assistant were locked together in an intimate embrace.

Nellie told no one about what she had witnessed in the Theatre Royal, but during the following days it caused her a great deal of anxiety. Questions flooded her mind. Was this the reason why Madame had been so concerned about her husband going out so many times after the show, supposedly with either his agent or the theatre manager? Was this why Madame was a secret drinker? What was it about that little tramp, Ange, that attracted Monsieur to her? Was it really possible that he was having an affair with her, and that she was in a position to blackmail him? Nellie began to worry. She wanted to talk to Ruby about it, but the old lady was too close to everyone in the theatre, and she might dismiss her accusations as malice, motivated by her dislike of Ange. But she had to talk to someone. She just had to.

Nellie thought of Hubert. He understood her so well, probably better than anyone else she knew. So, one afternoon a few days after the Drury Lane auditions, she made her way along Caledonian Road to that grim, grey building. She checked in at reception and asked to see Hubert. To her surprise, she was told that prisoner Hubert Pickering had been released on parole just forty-eight hours earlier—and prison regulations did not allow a forwarding address to be given.

Chapter 13

The spring of 1942 was a particularly good time for daffodils. At least, that's how it appeared in the back garden of 147A Tufnell Park Road, for the fifteen inches or so of soil that covered the top and sides of the corrugated iron Anderson shelter were a riot of yellow which positively gleamed in the light of the early morning sun. A few weeks earlier, white snowdrops had been the dominating feature, but during February they had been engulfed by a heavy fall of snow, and by the time the thaw finally came, all that remained were soggy limp stalks with none of the beautiful white petals that provided so much hope in the depths of a hard winter. In the past year, there had been relatively few visits from Field-Marshal Goering's Luftwaffe bombers, which meant that the Anderson had seen very little use. Just occasionally, however, Monsieur did use it as a retreat from his two sons, who distracted him when he was trying to work out new ideas for his stage act. The only problem was that the shelter was also a haven for stray cats who left the place stinking of urine.

Early in March, Monsieur, Madame, and Ange left on a three week ENSA tour of army bases around the United Kingdom, and the boys went to stay with their grandparents. Nellie was left on her own in the house, for with strict security regulations and small budgets, ENSA could not make provisions for artistes' personal staff. She was very disappointed, for she had never travelled outside London, but at least she wouldn't be lonely because she was now seeing the Irish boy, Patrick, on a fairly regular basis.

Despite his gentle, smooth manner, Patrick Duvall was quite a brash character, who used his irresistible smile to conquer anyone he talked to. Not that Nellie ever felt conquered by him. In fact, he puzzled her. She found it curious that he spoke with such a marked Irish accent when he had been born in London. The fact that his English dad was away in the Army didn't entirely explain why he should have picked up his Irish mum's way of talking to such an extent. Just how Irish Patrick really was intrigued her, and it was with a certain amount of trepidation that she agreed to go with him to 'Mulligan's Friday Night Out', an Irish evening at the Arcade Dance Hall, just opposite the Nag's Head in Holloway Road.

'Funny night ter 'ave a dance,' Nellie said as they made their way into the Arcade next door to the Marlborough Cinema.

'Ha!' laughed Patrick. 'Shows how much you know about Paddys. Friday night's pay night. Straight in the Nag's Head across the road, then over here for the dance. Anyway,' he added, holding Nellie firmly round the waist and kissing her quickly on the tip of her nose, 'it was my namesake's day last Tuesday. You don't think we're going to forget blessed Saint Patrick, do yer?'

The dance hall was crammed, for this part of Islington had a large population of Irish people. As it was a celebratory night, there was a good mixture of young and old, and the music was traditional, including the best of Irish jigs and folk songs. And Patrick was right, quite a few of the men had obviously come straight from the Nag's Head. Spirits were high but Nellie was impressed by the cordial atmosphere and laughed openly every time a complete stranger came up to her spluttering things like, 'Darlin'! Where have yer been all my life?'

'D'yer know all these people?' Nellie yelled over the whoops of delight and clapping to the rhythmic Irish group dancing.

'You must be jokin'!' he replied. 'Looks as though half the Borough of Islington's in ternight!'

He grabbed Nellie round the waist and led her into the middle of the crowd who were doing what Nellie considered to be a mixture of 'Knees Up Mother Brown' and a Highland fling. About halfway through the dance, while she was in the middle of changing partners, Patrick signalled to her that he was going out for a couple of minutes. Nellie nodded back, and did her best to keep up with some rowdy young men who were now dragging her into what seemed to be an impromptu Irish tap dance. After the dance had finally come to an exhausting end, there was still no sign of Patrick.

As she edged her way slowly towards the

215

exit door, to search for him, her tiny figure was swamped by the crowd and all she could really see were the light fittings dangling down from the ceiling above her. It wasn't an easy task getting out of the hall, for every young man Nellie tried to pass did his best to waylay her. By the time she did finally manage to reach the main door, the accordion band on stage was launching into its next group of songs, and the great sway of dancers started to swarm back on to the floor.

A bouncer was standing by the door, his hand on the blackout curtain.

''Scuse me,' Nellie said, 'd'yer know a bloke about this 'igh, brown eyes, dark wavy 'air? 'Is name's Patrick.'

The burly man burst into laughter. 'Patrick?' he chortled, in a thick Irish brogue. 'Now there's a new one if ever I heard it! Sorry, me darlin'. I've never heard a name like that in me whole blessed life!'

Nellie thought he was bonkers, and left.

It was quite chilly in the arcade just outside the dance hall, and as she hadn't brought her coat with her, Nellie didn't want to hang around there for too long. There were a few people around, most of them young couples snogging in the dark corners of the various shop doorways, but when she moved out further towards the street, the place seemed deserted. She decided to have a quick look out into Holloway Road before she went back to the hall, just in case Patrick was chatting up some bit of skirt she didn't know about. The sky was full of dark night clouds, and it was difficult to see anything clearly, but the main road, too, seemed deserted. It was quite late and most of the last buses and trams of the day had gone.

She was about to turn back into the arcade when she heard men's voices coming from a brick public shelter close to the side exit of the Marlborough Cinema. Even though she was some distance away from it, she was positive that one of the voices she could hear was Patrick's. She decided to investigate.

As she approached the shelter, the voices became more distinct, and it sounded to her as though a quarrel was going on. All the voices had a strong Irish accent. She was standing outside, shivering in the cold and wondering what to do next, when the door of the shelter was suddenly flung open and two men appeared. Neither of them saw Nellie, for she immediately ducked into the shadows. One of them turned back and called out, 'It's up ter you, Pat! This is the last time, so I'm warnin' yer!'

A third man came out of the shelter, and paused. Although it was pitch dark, Nellie knew at once that it was Patrick, for she recognised that well-scrubbed odour she had come to know so well. 'Enjoyin' yerself?' she asked.

Her voice coming out of the darkness took Patrick completely by surprise. He whirled round, grabbed hold of her and raised his fist.

'You lay yer 'ands on me, mate, an' it'll be the last fing yer ever do!'

'Nellie!' Patrick immediately released his grip on her. 'What are you doing out here?'

'I might ask you the same question,' she replied angrily. 'Am I mistaken, or did yer ask me out wiv yer ternight?'

'I'm sorry, Nellie, truly sorry. I—I had ter see these two blokes. It was business. I—I just had ter—' He stopped suddenly, and his voice hardened. 'How long were you standing out here?'

Nellie shrugged. She was shivering with cold. 'Long enough,' she replied. 'But don't worry. I din't 'ear nuffin.'

'Not that it matters,' said Patrick dismissively. 'It was nothin' important.'

Nellie didn't believe a word of it, but she didn't say so.

Patrick suddenly noticed she was shivering. 'Yer poor thing,' he said, taking off his jacket. 'You're freezin'! Here.' He quickly placed the jacket round her shoulders. Then he leaned close to her. 'I'm sorry,' he said softly. 'Will yer forgive me?'

'Wot's there ter fergive?' There was more to Nellie's reply than her tone implied, but Patrick didn't realise it. He put his arms round her and hugged her tight. Then with one hand he raised her chin and kissed her full on the lips. Nellie didn't resist. They had kissed many times before, and she loved the feeling. As his lips pressed against her own, she let the tip of his tongue slide against her teeth.

'Let's go back to your place, Nellie,' he whispered. 'I want you so much.'

Nellie pulled away quickly. 'No, Patrick,' she said firmly. 'It wouldn't be right.'

'Don't you want me?'

'That's not what I meant.'

Gently he pulled her close again, his face against her cold cheek. 'I don't mind if it's your first time,' he whispered. 'I won't hurt you, Nellie. I'd never hurt you.'

'It wouldn't be right,' she insisted.

'But everyone's away,' he said, lovingly biting the lobe of her ear. 'Why wouldn't it be right?'

'Because ...' Nellie desperately searched for a reason. 'Because it's not my house. Because, Monsieur and Madame—they trust me.'

'Then trust me too, Nellie,' he replied softly. 'I know how fond you are of your family, I know what they've done for you. But you're entitled to a life of your own, Nellie. You're not a kid any more. You're a woman.'

Nellie wanted to tell him that in the eyes of the world she was still a kid, for she was not yet eighteen. But the words wouldn't come. She just couldn't say what she knew she had to say. She was too aroused, too infatuated by this smooth-talking boy, too overwhelmed by the attention he was giving her. And he was right. She *was* a woman; at least, she felt like one, and she wanted to know what it was like to *be* a woman, to experience all the emotional and physical feelings of *being* a woman.

That night, Nellie slept with Patrick, in her own bed, in her own room at 147A Tufnell Park Road. It was her first time, and she was nervous, consumed with guilt. But Patrick kept his word. He was gentle—and kind—to her,

219

and never once made her feel that what she was doing was wrong. But no matter what he said, in the aftermath of a night of love-making, she felt a sinking feeling of shame and despair, and that she had betrayed the trust Monsieur and Madame had placed in her.

Patrick left before daybreak. While they were together, she never once mentioned the two men she had heard him arguing with in the air-raid shelter. If he was in some kind of trouble, she didn't want to know. Not just yet anyway.

It was well after ten o'clock in the morning before Nellie got out of bed and raised the blackout curtains. As her room was on the second floor at the back of the house, she could look down on the row of small back gardens along the terrace. For as far as the eye could see, a profusion of stately daffodils swayed to and fro in the slight morning breeze, like groups of happy faces turning up towards the sun. Nellie felt a bit like them, for she, too, was in the springtime of her life, exploring, reaching out for all the things that until now had seemed so beyond her.

As the day wore on, however, her feelings of guilt and shame began to dominate. The more she thought about the night she had spent with Patrick, the more she felt she had betrayed the family who had embraced her. What could she do to put things right? For most of the morning, she just wandered aimlessly around the house, unable to concentrate on anything, not even the children's book Ruby Catmonk had given her to help her reading. What could she do? Oh God, what *should* she do? Should she own up and tell the truth, or should she just keep quiet about her one night of love with Patrick? For that's what it was, just one night, nothing more. She would never do such a thing again, never! In any case, as physically exciting as she had found the whole experience, Patrick lying in bed with her was just a body, a boy's body. It wasn't what she had really wanted. It wasn't Toff. Oh God, should she tell Madame? Surely she of all people wouldn't turn her back on her. After all, she had often told her to think of her as her own mum, so wasn't she the one person she could turn to for help and advice?

It was the middle of the day before Nellie made up her mind what to do. She didn't want to eat anything, but she was determined to be practical. She would do something positive for Madame and Monsieur. She would clean the house from top to bottom, so when the family came back in a couple of days' time, they would find everything spick-and-span and smelling of carbolic and furniture polish. This was the way to deal with things; she should stop fussing about what was right and wrong and show Monsieur and Madame how much she loved them by letting them see how beautifully she had looked after the house while they were away.

She made herself a cup of tea, then set about cleaning the house. She started on the top floor with the two boys' room. Needless to say, it was in a disgusting state, for it never occurred to them to put anything away once they'd used it. But Nellie was determined to sort it out, for once Sid and Lenny got back from staying with their grandparents, the room would once again revert to looking like a rubbish dump. On the second floor, she swept the carpet in Monsieur and Madame's bedroom, and also the runner which ran along the landing. By the time she had scrubbed the bathroom floor and used Vim to clean out the washbasins, toilet pan, and bath, the place smelt like new. Downstairs, she swept out the conservatory, cleaned the inside of the windows, and watered all Madame's potted plants. The kitchen was the most difficult and obstinate of all; the gas stove in particular needed a great deal of elbow grease to get it clean. By four o'clock in the afternoon, she had achieved everything she had set out to do. But she was absolutely exhausted. She had made herself another cup of tea and a spam sandwich, but as soon as she settled down on the settee in the freshly dusted sitting room, she just closed her eyes and went right off to sleep.

About half an hour later she was awoken by the slamming of the front door and the sound of someone rushing up the stairs. It took her a moment to focus, but when she did, she realised it must have been one of the boys, for no one else apart from her had door keys. She hurried out into the hall and shouted up the stairs, 'Sid? Lenny? Is that you?'

The only reply was the slamming of the boys' bedroom door on the top floor.

'Sid! Lenny!'

Nellie started to worry. The boys were not

due back from their gran and grandad's until their parents returned in a couple of days' time. She hurried up the stairs to the top floor, and called again.

'Sid! Lenny!'

'Get out of it!' came a shrill, hysterical yell from Sid. 'It's nuffin' ter do wiv you!'

'Wot's up, Sid? Wot's wrong?'

'Go away!'

Nellie crossed the landing and went into Sid's room. 'Sid! Wot's up?'

Sid was lying face down on his bed. He was sobbing his heart out. 'Leave me alone, will yer!' His voice was barely audible for his mouth was pressed hard into the pillow. As Nellie drew closer, he turned round and growled at her, 'This is *my* room! Leave me alone!'

'Sid!' Nellie was shocked, for the boy's right eye was closed and swollen, and his nose and lower lip were bleeding. 'Wot's 'appened?' she asked anxiously, sitting on the edge of his bed. 'Who did this to yer?'

Sid recoiled from her like a scared animal, grabbing the blood-stained pillow and hugging it to his body as though trying to protect himself. 'Keep away from me!' he blurted. 'I don't like yer! I don't like yer!'

This irritated Nellie. 'No, mate! An' I don't like you neivver. But the least yer can do is tell me wot 'appened!'

Sid cowered away from her, which made her feel guilty, and sorry for him. She tried a more gentle approach. 'Tell me wot 'appened, mate,' she pleaded softly.

The boy sensed Nellie's concern, and after a moment's silence he responded to her. 'I 'ad a fight at school.'

'Who wiv?' Nellie asked, watching him carefully.

'This boy. 'E's always pokin' fun at me, always pickin' on me.'

'Why?'

''Cos 'e don't like me! 'E calls me a lump of East End shit.'

Nellie's eyes widened in anger. ''E wot?'

''E usually 'as a go at me in the playground durin' break. Pushes me around all over the place, showin' off ter the uvvers. After school terday 'e waited fer me outside the gates. Then 'e started again.'

'Wot 'appened?'

'I took a swipe at 'im.'

'Why?'

For a moment, the boy looked embarrassed, and diverted his gaze. ''E called Dad a music 'all pansy.'

Nellie was outraged. 'A *wot*?'

''E's always sayin' fings like that. 'E reckons all people who work in the music 'all are eivver pansies or layabouts. 'E tells everyone Dad's a cheat and don't know the first fing about doin' magic tricks.'

'Oh, 'e does, does 'e?' Nellie replied. 'So yer took a swipe at 'im, did yer?'

Again, Sid looked embarrassed. 'Well, it wasn't exactly a swipe. I just, well, pushed 'im away, that's all.'

Nellie was simmering, but she tried to contain

224

her anger. She got up from the bed and went to look out of the window. She thought how stupid boys were, how all they ever wanted to do was to prove how tough they were, and to fight, and to cause as much upset to people as they possibly could. It made her think of Toff and the vacs gang, and how full of bravado they all were, living like street urchins instead of going back to their own homes and making peace with their mums and dads. It was all so pointless, such a waste of time and energy. Life should be about getting on with people, not about making enemies all the time. And this poor young quivering creature who had always treated her with such disdain was no different; he was like all the rest of them, all show, not a brain between his ears to work things out properly. But something had to be done about this pile of rubbish at the school, there was no doubt about that. Anyone who said the kind of things about Monsieur that that snipe-nosed little bag of wind had said needed to be taught a lesson.

'Tell me somefin', Sid,' she said, turning from the window. 'Wot would yer say ter givin' this pal of yours a bit of 'is own med'cine?'

Sid looked up with a start. 'Don't be a nark,' he replied. ''E's older than me. An' much taller.'

Nellie crossed her arms. 'So wot?' she replied defiantly.

''E towers above me!'

'The taller they are, the 'arder they fall.'

The boy punched the pillow he was still

holding against his stomach. 'You don't know nuffin'. You're only a gel.'

Nellie gritted her teeth. This was not the first time this sort of thing had been said to her, and it got up her snout. 'Try me,' she said, with a fixed smile.

The boy looked at her warily. 'Wot d'yer mean?'

Nellie, arms still crossed, walked slowly back to him. 'I mean, why not see 'ow much a gel *really* knows?'

''Ow?'

She uncrossed her arms, moved closer to the bed, and sat on the edge of it. 'D'yer want ter get yer own back on this pal of yours?'

''E ain't my *pal!*' the boy snapped. 'An' anyway, I've told yer. Everyone's scared of 'im. ''E'd make mincemeat out of me.'

Nellie smiled wryly. 'Not after *I've* worked on yer,' she said with a gleam in her eye.

'Wot d'yer mean?' Sid asked suspiciously.

Nellie stood up. 'S'pose we get yer cleaned up first. Then I'll show yer.'

Chapter 14

Monsieur and Madame were absolutely exhausted. Although they had been told that touring army bases around the country with ENSA would be a tough assignment, nothing had prepared them for the long hours, late nights, and very basic working conditions. They were, in effect, on duty twenty-four hours a day. To the troops, the touring artistes were a link with their homes, and understandably they were very demanding.

'The best place though,' said Madame, removing a long hatpin, 'was the show we did in an aircraft 'angar, up near Newcastle. Must've been more than two thousand boys crammed in there—Army, marines, Air Force. They went wild. It was just like a football match.'

'Better crowd than the Sunderland Empire,' said Monsieur, who had flopped on to the settee, his feet resting on a footstool. 'An' that's on a good night.'

Nellie was thrilled to see them again. To her, the house had seemed so empty during the long three weeks they had been away, and now, suddenly, with their return, it had come to life. It was also good to see them getting on so well together. From the moment they first stepped into the house, Nellie had noticed how Monsieur had referred to his wife as 'me dear ol' dutch', and how Madame had responded with loving looks. The concerns Nellie had felt since she had unwittingly glimpsed Monsieur embracing Ange were thankfully dispelled. Whatever had been going on before, there was no doubt in her mind now that Albert Beckwith was devoted to his beloved wife Doris.

'I 'ope yer didn't get too lonely when we was away,' said Madame, placing her arm round Nellie's shoulder affectionately. 'It's a big 'ouse

227

ter sleep in all on yer own.'

'Oh no, Mum,' Nellie replied, heart in mouth.

'Weren't yer scared of sleepin' on yer own, wiv nobody 'ere?'

Nellie felt her heart racing. 'No, Mum,' she said, trying to sound convincing. 'I just pretended you an' Dad were in the next room.'

'I wish we 'ad been, Nellie dear,' Madame said wistfully. 'I do wish we 'ad been. You're so precious to us, yer know. We 'ated goin' off an' leavin' you like that. But it was worf doin' the tour. Yer should've seen the look on those boys' faces. Gawd bless 'em.'

Nellie wanted to tell her. She wanted to tell her so badly about her night with Patrick here in Monsieur and Madame's own house. But she couldn't do it; the words just wouldn't come. Not yet. Not now. Not until the right moment.

She took a quick look at Monsieur to see if he had noticed anything strange in her behaviour. Clearly he hadn't; he was nodding off on the settee, his new day-wear black toupee slowly shifting down towards his left ear.

The following day, Sid and Lenny didn't get home from school until almost four thirty. Nellie was waiting for Sid in his room. Lenny knew what had been going on for the past couple of days, so he came too. Luckily, Monsieur and Madame had gone up to Bond Street to look for some new sheet music for the act, and they were not expected back until after six. This left

228

Nellie clear to carry on with the lessons she had been giving Sid.

'Now don't ferget wot I told yer,' she said, her two fists positioned up in front of her in a classical prize-fighter's pose. 'Keep yer mitts up in front of yer, and never leave yer face unprotected fer one single minute. Got it?'

'Got it.' Sid, one foot in front of the other, both fists raised and clenched, was copying Nellie's pose as closely as he could.

Nellie waited for the right moment, then moved in a flash. 'Right! Let's go!'

She and Sid launched into a sparring match, darting back and forth, moving from one foot to the other with the grace of ballet dancers. Every so often Nellie would strike out towards Sid's face, and Sid would duck.

'Keep yer mitts up, Sid!' she commanded. 'Don't look at the floor! Keep yer eyes on me!'

Sid did as he was told, and took a crafty right-hander at Nellie.

Nellie ducked. 'That's it! That's it! Keep it light on yer 'eels, Sid. Light as a fevver, mate. Not so 'eavy.'

Sid did as he was told, and used his feet as though he was learning how to dance instead of learning how to box.

Lenny sat cross-legged on Sid's bed, watching in awed fascination. When his elder brother had told him that Nellie had been taught how to box by one of the vacs street kids, whose old man was once a pro, he quite literally fell about laughing. A pro was one thing, but a girl teaching a boy how to box was just plain stupid! If Sid was going to defend himself against Alfie Clipper, then in Lenny's opinion his brother was about to be annihilated. But as he watched Nellie dancing about barefoot, he couldn't believe his eyes. Time and again his big brother had nearly been laid out by this half-pint-sized girl who moved with the speed of a bullet and whose punch looked as deadly as the world heavyweight boxing champion's himself, Joe Louis. If either Sid or Lenny had ever doubted Nellie's claims that she had been taught how to box by some snotty-nosed runaway kid out on the streets, then those doubts were rapidly dispelled.

Nellie was teaching Sid how to box in as professional a way as she knew how. As far as she was concerned, the Alfie Clippers of this world were the amateurs, and they would always lose out to an opponent who used their brains rather than just their fists.

'Wake up, Sid!' Nellie yelled as strands of her hair swished across her face and eyes. 'If yer wanna teach that great big pile of 'orse manure a lesson, then yer'd better move yer arse!'

Listening to that kind of language, Lenny was absolutely convinced that Nellie was definitely not like any girl *he'd* ever known!

Nellie and Sid continued to spar, unaware that in Monsieur and Madame's bedroom directly beneath them, tiny particles of flaking paint were falling from the vibrating ceiling.

''Ang on a minute, Nell!' Sid shouted, panting heavily. ''Ang on!'

Nellie immediately came to a halt and lowered her fists. 'Wot's up now?' she asked, completely composed.

'I wanna ask a question,' said Sid, swallowing hard, sweat pouring down his forehead. All of a sudden he seemed to be all legs, thin and gangling. 'You said if I cover me face wiv me left fist, I should use me right ter do the strike.'

'Right,' replied Nellie. 'So why aren't yer doin' it?'

''Cos I'm so busy concentratin' on me left fist, I keep fergettin' about the uvver one.'

'Then don't!' growled Nellie. 'Yer 'ave ter co-ordinate.'

'Do wot?'

'Concentrate!' yelled Lenny.

Sid swung round to glare at his younger brother. 'Mind yer own business, Len!' he snapped.

'Watch me, Sid,' Nellie said, raising her fists again. 'Just watch me, then do exactly as I show yer. OK?'

'OK,' sighed Sid. 'But I don't fink I'm gettin' the 'ang of all this.'

'Up wiv yer mitts!' commanded Nellie.

Sid raised his rather pathetic little fists.

'Now, like this.' Nellie proceeded in slow motion, first covering her face with her left fist.

Sid copied her every move.

'An' like this.' Nellie slowly moved her right fist towards Sid's jaw. 'Cover yerself!' she yelled. 'Don't let me reach yer chin, yer berk!'

Sid immediately covered his chin and deflected Nellie's slow-motion blow.

'That's it! That's it!' Nellie was delighted as Sid pushed her blow away. 'Now fer Gawd's sake, do it like that *all* the time.' She raised her fists again. 'Right. So I'm Alfie Clipper, an' I'm coming after yer,' she said aggressively. 'So wot yer going ter do about it?'

Sid's face turned to stone and he immediately went on the attack with a left, then a right, then a left, and finally with a right upper cut which caught Nellie completely off guard, walloped her hard on the chin, and sent her flying to the floor.

This was greeted with wild applause from Lenny.

Sid was horrified. 'Nell!' he shrieked. He dropped to his knees and crouched beside her. She was lying flat on her back, eyes closed.

'Nell!' he shouted again, trying to shake some life back into her.

'Is she dead?' asked the ever cheerful Lenny.

'Nell!' spluttered Sid, pushing, shoving, digging Nellie, and fearing the worst. 'Say somefin' ter me, Nell! *Please* say somefin'!'

After a moment, Nellie's eyes opened. She felt quite dazed, and didn't even attempt to raise her head. 'Wot d'yer mean, say somefin', Nell! Yer bleedin' near killed me.'

Sid was distraught. 'I'm sorry, Nell! I'm really sorry.'

Nellie turned to look at him, and tried to focus. 'Wot d'yer mean, you're sorry, yer stupid berk! You just laid me out fer the count.

232

Now yer can do the same ter Alfie bleedin'
Clipper!'

'Jack and Jill ... went up ... the hill ter ... ter
fe—tch a pail of ... water ...'

It wasn't easy for Nellie to read. No matter
that it was a children's book of nursery rhymes,
it took a long time to understand letters and
words, and how they were put together, and
what they meant when they were put side by
side. Being unable to read at the age of nearly
eighteen was a major disadvantage for Nellie.
The fact that she was now able to make at least
some sense of written words was due entirely
to Ruby's tireless patience. The old lady was a
tower of strength to Nellie, and in just a few
short months she had become more than just a
friend; she was also her mentor.

Once or twice a week, Nellie went for her
lessons to Ruby's tiny flat in Blackstock Road,
which was just a few minutes' walk from the
Finsbury Park Empire. The flat was situated
above a funeral parlour which Nellie found
disconcerting. It was a peculiar feeling to know
that she was learning to read children's books
and newspapers while a whole lot of dead
people were being washed and laid out in
the room directly beneath her. But Ruby was
a good teacher in every way; she gave Nellie
the confidence to read, and also the chance to
confide in her.

'Fank Gawd I'm not Jack an' Jill!' Ruby
sniffed as she peered over her specs at the
nursery rhyme. 'The way you're readin' it, no

wonder it took the poor buggers so long ter get up that bleedin' 'ill!'

Nellie laughed. She didn't take offence at anything Ruby said, for she knew it was only meant to help her. 'I'm sorry, Rube,' she replied above the loud purring coming from a large ginger tom cat on Ruby's lap. 'Accordin' ter Miss Ackroyd from the orphanage, I never was no good at readin' an' writin'. Why can't I remember anyfin' about those days, Rube?'

'Maybe it's 'cos yer don't want to,' said Ruby, gently lifting Caesar the cat on to the floor to join his four pals who were all strays collected by Ruby. 'Sometimes the mind plays funny tricks wiv yer. It tries ter tell yer somefin', especially if it's got somefin' troublin' it.' She rested her arms on the table in front of her. ''Ave yer got somefin' troublin' yer, Nell?'

Nellie shrugged her shoulders and shook her head.

Ruby smiled. 'Sure?'

Nellie hesitated, and leaned back in her chair. It was difficult to keep anything from the old lady. Ruby was so shrewd, she was practically a witch. Nellie needed advice, she needed it badly, and who better to give it to her than Ruby? 'I'm worried about ... Mum an' Dad,' she said eventually.

Ruby sat bolt upright in her chair. The movement dislodged a bright ginger curl of hair which flopped untidily over her forehead. 'Albert and Doris?' she said anxiously. 'Yer ain't fallen out wiv 'em, 'ave yer?'

Nellie quickly shook her head. 'No, Rube,

nuffin' like that. Well, not yet, any rate.' She leaned across to Ruby, and looked directly into the old lady's face. And what a face it was. It was so heavily lined that Ruby herself had often remarked that a tram would have no trouble finding its way about. 'The fing is,' this was difficult, and Nellie hesitated again. 'The fing is, there's somefin' I 'aven't told 'em, somefin' I should've told 'em but I'm too worried that if I do, they'll want ter kick me out.'

'Who is 'e?' Ruby asked without a moment's hesitation.

Nellie gaped at her. 'Er, wot d'yer mean?'

'So yer've got boyfriend trouble,' Ruby said, stretching for her packet of Capstans.

''Ow'd yer know?' Nellie asked, eyes wide with amazement.

Ruby extracted a fag and laughed. 'I weren't born yesterday, yer know!' she roared. 'If a gel your age didn't 'ave some kind of boy trouble, I'd fink there was somefin' wrong wiv yer.' She stuck her fag between her lips and gave Nellie a measured look over the top of her specs. ''Asn't put one in the oven for yer, 'as 'e?'

'No, course not!' replied Nellie, embarrassed. Then she added, 'Well, I 'ope 'e 'asn't.'

Ruby lit her fag, then got up and went to the sideboard, where she picked up a bottle of gin. 'So who is 'e? Wot's it all about?'

Nellie took a deep breath before replying. ''Is name's Patrick. 'E's an Irish boy. I—slept wiv 'im one night last week.'

235

Ruby came back with the bottle of gin, unscrewed the top, and poured some into the cup of tea she had made a few minutes before. 'Where?' she asked uncompromisingly.

Nellie bit her lip anxiously. 'Back 'ome,' she replied. 'In my bedroom.'

Ruby raised her eyebrows, said nothing, then moved to pour some gin into Nellie's cup.

'No, Rube,' she said, covering the cup with her hand. 'I'm under age.'

'Yeah,' replied Ruby. 'So am I.' She pulled Nellie's hand away from the cup and poured a dash of gin into it. 'Go on,' she said.

'Nuffin' more ter say. The fing is, I shouldn't've done it, Rube. It wasn't right. I shouldn't've taken 'im back. Not to Mum an' Dad's 'ouse.'

Ruby took a gulp of her gin tea. 'Where else would yer take 'im? To a bleedin' graveyard?'

'Yer don't understand, Rube. Mum an' Dad trust me. They left me alone in the 'ouse—their 'ouse. I was supposed ter be lookin' after fings.' She sighed, and put her hands round her cup. 'I feel as though I've let them down.'

Ruby sat back in her chair and rocked with loud laughter. There was a flurry of different coloured moggies as they fled for cover under the table, the sideboard, and out into the kitchen.

Nellie looked hurt, and not a little surprised. 'Wot yer laughin' at?' she asked.

'People wiv guilt complexes always make me laugh,' the old lady replied. ''Onest, Nell, I don't know wot you're gettin' yerself all worked up about.' She leaned forward in her chair, cup of tea in one hand, and her fag in the other. 'Let's face it, gel, wot difference does it make *where* yer do it? The important fing is, did yer *want* ter do it?'

Nellie lowered her head.

'Well, did yer?'

Nellie nodded.

'So good luck to yer!'

'But wot about Mum an' Dad?'

'Wot about 'em?' Ruby asked. 'Albert an' Doris are broadminded people. They come from the music 'all, from the feater. Yer can't survive long in this business, gel, unless you're broad-minded.'

Nellie wasn't convinced. 'But that doesn't mean wot I've done is right, does it?'

Ruby considered that for a moment, then thought that if she was honest, she would have to agree with the girl. She picked up her cup of gin tea, got up from her seat, and went to the window. 'I want ter tell yer somefin', Nell,' she said, finally emerging from her few moments of silence. 'I knew this feller once—oh, it was long before you was born, when I was still only a kid your age. I was in this variety show at the old Met, down Edgware Road, in the chorus.' She turned briefly to look at Nellie. 'I'm tellin' yer, I 'ad damned good legs.' She faced the window again. 'Anyway, he was a fiddler, played violin, in the pit. 'E was a year or so older than me, real knockout looks, the sort yer lie in bed only dreamin' about. I'd seen 'im lots of times durin' the run, but I only met 'im properly at the party

237

on the last night of the show. But we sort of got tergevver, and I fell for 'im, 'ook, line an' sinker.

'One night,' Ruby continued, 'we met up an' went fer a drink at a pub up near the Angel, 'an after chuckin' out time, 'e asked me ter go back wiv 'im to 'is digs up Liverpool Road way. I said I couldn't 'cos my mum was waitin' back 'ome an' she'd know wot I was up to.' She paused, waiting for a noisy lorry to pass in the busy Blackstock Road below. 'It wasn't the last time 'e asked me. Oh no. 'Alf a dozen times, I reckon. But every time I said no. The fact is, I knew it was wrong. Even though I wanted 'im more than anyfin' else in the 'ole wide world, I knew I 'ad no right ter ...' She stopped to take a quick gulp of her gin tea and a puff of her fag. 'Ter cut a long story short, one night I said yes. 'E took me back, an', well, it was just wonderful. All I ever dreamed about, an' better. The only trouble was, me mum found out. Don't ask me 'ow—it must've been one of the gels in the chorus or somefin'—but she found out, an' she never talked ter me again. It was a cruel fing ter do. But yer see, I'd hurt 'er.' There was pain in her voice now. 'I always regret that I never told 'er. If I 'ad, I think she'd've respected me for it. The trouble was, I never told her nuffin'. I never asked 'er for advice, I never took 'er inter me confidence, I never once told 'er that she was any use ter me at all. But she was. No matter 'ow narrow-minded she was, she was still my mum. All I 'ad ter do was talk to 'er.'

Nellie got up from her seat at the table, went across to the old lady, and put both her arms round her waist.

'It's silly 'ow we let fings prey on our mind, ain't it, Nell?' said Ruby. 'But one mistake—'cos that's wot it was—practically destroyed my life. When my mum died, we 'adn't so much as passed one single word ter each uvver fer over forty years.'

Nellie hugged her tightly.

'And the stupid fing is, I never saw me feller again after that one night of passionate love. Oh yes, 'e was off, mate, like a flash of lightnin'. I did 'ear that 'e copped 'is lot in the last war, in the navy, went down in a sub or somefin'. I din't shed no tears, though. Wot's the point? Anyway, there were plenty more where 'e come from, most of 'em from music 'alls up an' down the country.' She grinned briefly. 'All us ol' pros stick tergevver, yer know.'

For a few moments, Nellie stood there, her arms round the old lady's waist, her chin on her shoulder.

'Tell me somefin', Nell,' asked Ruby, softly. 'D'yer want ter go steady wiv this boyfriend of yours?'

Nellie shrugged her shoulders and sighed. 'I'm not sure, Rube.'

'Well, just remember, Nell,' Ruby said. 'Yer've got a mum an' dad of yer own now. Don't 'ide fings from them. It ain't worf it. They'll fink much better of yer if yer talk to 'em.'

As she spoke, there was a chorus of miaows from the moggies in the kitchen.

'All right! All right! Muvver's comin'!' Ruby called as she hurriedly made for the kitchen. 'I know it's yer bleedin' dinner time.' She paused briefly to say to Nellie, 'I tell yer, by the time I finish wiv this lot, I ain't got much ration left fer meself. They couldn't care less there's a war on!'

Nellie couldn't help laughing as she watched the old lady disappear into the kitchen. Then she looked around at the shabby surroundings where Ruby had spent so much of her life. She couldn't help wondering how someone so special had managed to survive in a place that was hardly big enough to swing a cat in, let alone five cats.

It was exactly four o'clock in the afternoon when young Sid Beckwith left Tollington Road Boys' School at the end of the day's lessons. A few minutes later, his brother Lenny came out of the building and they made their way across the playground towards the school gates. They had got halfway across when, as anticipated, they were confronted by a tall, well-built boy who looked about fourteen.

'So wot's all this then, Becky?'

Alfie Clipper had his own pet name for most of the boys in the school, including Sid Beckwith. He was a lumbering sort of boy, whose legs and arms seemed out of proportion to the rest of his thick-set build. If it hadn't been for his perpetual snide grin, he could have been quite a reasonable-looking boy.

'I was told yer wanted ter see me. Right?'

Sid pushed his younger brother to one side. 'Right,' he replied.

Alfie took one step towards him, and stared him out. 'If people *wish* ter see me, they *ask*,' he said. 'I take it you're *asking*.'

'No, Clipper,' Sid replied. 'I'm telling yer. I 'ave somefin' ter say to yer.'

Alfie was becoming irritated. He took a step closer. 'Then say it!'

Although a good proportion of the pupils had been evacuated, there was still a sizeable number of boys at the secondary school, and a small crowd of them started to gather, but not too close; they knew all about Alfie's ferocious temper.

'I want an apology, Clipper,' said Sid, with no apparent trace of fear.

'You wot?'

'You called my dad a pansy. I want you to apologise.'

Alfie could hardly believe his ears. For a moment he just stared at Sid in disbelief. He was already working out how he was going to knock the living daylights out of this gangling son of a music hall poof. 'An' wot d'yer intend ter do about it if I don't?' he asked in the silliest namby-pamby voice which was meant to amuse his spectators.

Sid beckoned to Lenny, and passed him his school satchel. Then he took off his black school cap with the white badge, and handed that to him as well. Last of all, he took off his black school uniform blazer. Then he turned back to Alfie and fixed him with an icy stare. 'Say you're sorry, Clipper,' he said firmly, 'or I'll knock yer head off.'

Alfie threw down his satchel and lunged at Sid.

Sid was ready for him. Up went his two clenched fists in the pose that Nellie had shown him, and as Alfie came at him, he covered his face with his left hand and with his right hand struck Alfie with a sharp upper cut to the jaw.

There was a great roar from Lenny and the other boys watching as Alfie staggered under the unexpected blow. But Alfie was quite a lump, and he quickly regained his balance, straightened up, and with a ferocious look on his face launched himself at Sid again.

But Sid was prancing around as light as a daisy, ducking and weaving, while Alfie lumbered after him like a bull in a china shop. When this got him nowhere, he tried to grab Sid round the neck and land a series of heavy blows on his face and stomach. Once again, Sid was ready for him. He ducked out of the way before Alfie could get anywhere near him. Then he swung round behind Alfie, tapped him on the shoulder, waited for him to turn, then punched him, once, twice, three times in quick succession, just as he had practised with Nellie.

Alfie started to reel, and a trickle of blood appeared on his lip.

'Say sorry, Clipper!' called Sid, twirling and curling round Alfie.

Alfie suddenly let out a huge roar, swung

round, and aimed a heavy thump at Sid.

Sid ducked down, then immediately leapt up again and landed a really hard upper cut on Alfie's jaw, and then another blow to his left eye.

Heavy and cumbersome as he was, Alfie was knocked off balance and sat down hard on his rump.

The crowd, now swollen by many more boys from the school, went wild.

Dazed, Alfie shook his head and tried to focus.

'Say sorry, Clipper!' demanded Sid.

Alfie glared at him. 'Piss off!' He struggled to his feet. But the moment he managed to stand up, Sid thumped him one straight on the jaw again. Alfie went down on his knees then slumped to the ground.

Sid moved in for the kill. Placing his foot on Alfie's chest, he stooped down, his fist clenched menacingly a few inches away from Alfie's face. 'Say sorry, Clipper, or else!'

'Get off!' yelled Alfie in panic. 'All right, I'm sorry! Leave me alone, will yer! Leave me alone!'

Sid hesitated a moment, then withdrew his fist and his foot. 'I'm warnin' yer, Clipper,' he growled, pointing his finger menacingly at Alfie. 'You ever say fings like that about my dad again, an' I won't let yer off so lightly!' He swung to the crowd of boys who were watching in awed admiration. 'Somebody get this cry-baby out of 'ere!'

Sid coolly took his blazer and cap from his

brother, and put them back on. Then he slung his school satchel over his shoulder and with Lenny at his side made his way to the school gates—where Nellie was waiting for him.

Chapter 15

Easter 1942 was a special time for the Beckwith family. It was the twentieth anniversary of Monsieur and Madame's wedding, and the first public holiday the whole family were able to spend together since the war had started. And to Nellie's delight, that included her.

Soon after eight o'clock on Good Friday morning, Sid and Lenny were bundled off to the baker's shop at the end of Tufnell Park Road to buy two bobs' worth of hot cross buns. And they were hot, steaming hot, straight out of the oven, smelling of delicious mixed spice and topped with the traditional marzipan Christian cross. It was a miracle that twenty-four of those buns ever managed to arrive home intact, but it helped that Nellie went with the boys.

The fact that Sid and Lenny had actually asked Nellie to go with them was in itself quite an achievement. Since Sid's crushing defeat of Alfie Clipper, in both brothers' eyes Nellie could do no wrong, and from that moment on she was the one they turned to for advice, sympathy and, more significantly, companionship. To them, Nellie was now truly one of the family, and they rarely went anywhere or did anything without consulting her first. They trusted her, not as a sister but as an elder brother. Nellie made it clear that just because she had taught them how to defend themselves, scrapping with people was not something they should do unless there was a real reason for it.

Nellie's only real worry now was her guilt about the night she had spent with Patrick while Monsieur and Madame were away. Ruby was right. Until she had talked it over with her adopted mum and dad, her mind would remain in torment. The only trouble was how and when to do it.

The opportunity came on Easter Monday, when Monsieur announced that he had managed to acquire enough petrol to take the family on a day's outing to the seaside. The chosen resort had to be reasonably close to London, for petrol was difficult to come by and if Monsieur's ancient Morris ran out of petrol en route, the chances of getting a fill-up would be remote. Clacton was top of the list, mainly because Monsieur and Madame had played there at the Hippodrome several times, and also because Clacton and Southend were the only two seaside resorts where Sid and Lenny could get their favourite Rossi's ice-cream cornets.

Mercifully, it was a bright and sunny Easter Monday morning. There was still quite a chill in the air, but not a cloud marred the azure blue sky. To ensure that the family could get away early, everyone was assigned a job. Madame and Nellie made the sardine and fish paste sandwiches, then packed them into a picnic basket together with some apples and pears, two flasks of tea, a bottle of brown ale for Monsieur, and a bottle of ginger beer for the two boys. In the street outside, Monsieur gave a last-minute polish to 'the old gel', his beloved Morris motor car. By the time he'd finished, he reckoned it could compete with Max Miller's prize Rolls-Royce. Luckily, he didn't notice the burn mark on the faded blue paintwork, which had been caused by hot cigarette ash dropping from the Abdullah wedged between his lips.

Action stations came at eight-thirty on the dot. With Monsieur driving, Madame at his side, and Nellie squeezed between the two boys on the narrow back seat, the great trek east began. The illuminated indicator arm shot out to the right, and Daisy, as the Beckwith family car was known, moved proudly out into Tuffnell Park Road.

By the time they reached the outskirts of London, Nellie felt as though she was encased in a block of ice. There was no heater in the car, and during the winter months passengers were obliged to keep warm by huddling beneath a blanket. Nellie also had a hot water bottle on her lap, but despite this her legs felt numb with cold and she seriously doubted she would ever be able to stand on her own two feet again.

Things got better once they reached the fringe of Epping Forest and the sun grew stronger, which also helped to clear the condensation from the inside of the car windows. Nellie could now concentrate on the scenery, and she craned her neck to look out of the window past Lenny's big head. She had never seen a large forest before, and she loved the way the sun kept popping up and down behind the leafless branches of the trees as the car hurried past. The fine Bank Holiday had brought out people from all parts of North and East London, and despite the mud after a few harsh weeks of spring rain, the damp forest picnic areas were already thronged with day-trippers.

'Yer know somefin'? Essex in't nearly as flat as I fawt.' Whenever he wanted to say anything, Monsieur had the disturbing habit of taking his eyes off the road and turning to look at Madame at his side. From the back seat it wasn't easy to hear what he was saying, for his teeth were firmly clamped on his cigarette holder, with the strong Abdullah smoke filling the car. He certainly looked the part; his brown and white checked jacket, plus-fours, flat cap, and white driving gloves were clearly the envy of every other motorist.

'Oh, I know, dear,' replied Madame, who had a happy smile on her face as she took in the rural scenery. 'Didn't you see that hill when we passed the uvver side of Braintree?'

'I saw two 'ills,' chimed in Lenny.

'I only saw one,' said Sid.

'That's 'cos yer was 'avin' a kip,' quipped Lenny.

'I must say, I'd love ter live out in the country,' sighed Madame wistfully. 'So much fresh air, and space. Wot d'yer reckon, Nellie?'

Nellie leaned forward to answer her. 'I love

the country,' she replied. 'But I still love London. 'Specially Tuffnell Park Road.'

Nellie's reply brought a warm smile to Madame's face, and she reached back to rest her hand on her shoulder. Nellie immediately responded by covering Madame's hand affectionately with her own.

'Well, I tell yer one fing,' Monsieur said. 'There's bin a good dozen cars or so on this road in the last ten minutes. Where do they all get their petrol coupons from? I'd like ter ask. Why don't people just stay at 'ome where they belong? Don't they know there's a war on?'

The authorities had relaxed regulations forbidding unnecessary travel to any of the south and east coast seaside resorts, and Clacton-on-Sea was pulsating with life. Not since before the war had so many day-trippers crammed into the town, despite the fact that most of the beach areas were sealed off with barbed wire. By midday, queues had formed outside every fish and chip shop along the promenade, and even the ever popular funfair, which had been closed since before the war, was partly operational again to cater for the surge of weekend visitors. Clacton bristled with pride and new-found confidence; its Edwardian and Victorian terraced shops and houses basked in the Easter sunshine, and even the landladies of the bed and breakfast mock-Tudor bungalows were able to display 'NO VACANCIES' notices at their lace-curtained windows. The warm spring sunshine had induced some men to wear grey flannels and summer jackets, while a lot of young girls wore their brightest cotton dresses with a turban, and one or two had even opted for the only real fashion of the war, the one-piece siren suit. However, no one took the lull in aerial bombardment for granted, and many a day-tripper was vividly reminded of what had happened during the Blitz as they strolled past buildings that had been gutted by incendiary bombs or reduced to rubble by high-explosive bombs. Most people made a mental note of the exact location of the nearest air-raid shelter, but the hope was that for one Bank Holiday at least, the shelters would not be required.

Nellie was overcome with excitement. This was the first time she had seen the sea, and she couldn't believe how different its colour was to the sky. This was the east coast, where the water seemed grey and muddy but calm and inviting, although Monsieur had told her about the landmines that had been buried on the beach to deter enemy invasion. Yes, she said to herself as she stood alone for a few minutes on some stone steps overlooking the stretch of seafront, they *are* out there, those people who had brought so much death and destruction to her home city. Just on the other side of that water, they were waiting for the day when they could march into the streets of this lovely old seaside resort, just as they had done in all the cities and towns of Europe.

''An 'ere, my gel,' said Monsieur grandly after helping himself to a chip from his wife's three penn'orth which were smothered in salt and vinegar and wrapped up in a page of the *Daily Herald*, 'yer 'ave one of the great wonders of the world!' He raised his cane and flourished it towards the majestic if somewhat jaded edifice that was Clacton Pier.

'If God gave everyone birds and bees and grass and trees,' Madame said to Nellie in a low voice, 'He also gave Albert this place!'

Nellie gazed at the fine old Victorian pier reaching far out over the water on its iron struts. Much of it was boarded up but the remains of an old billboard above the entrance, announced a past summer season of variety shows starring a host of talented music hall performers. 'I fink I'd be scared sittin' in a feater watchin' a show wiv the sea rushing underneaf me,' Nellie said.

'Never!' objected Monsieur, with a grand gesture of his left hand which was still holding the now cold chip. 'Once that orchestra started ter play, the curtain rose, an' the dazzling bright lights tore into yer soul, the sea beneath yer din't exist. I tell yer, Nellie, there's nuffin' like a show by the seaside ter send people 'ome in the best of moods. As a matter of fact, I gave one of me best performances 'ere. Same bill as the great Randolph Sutton.'

Nellie turned to Madame for enlightenment.

'Wonderful singer, dear,' she explained, then launched into a few bars of his popular song, 'On Mother Kelly's Doorstep'.

'It didn't matter that we were paid peanuts fer a summer season,' continued Monsieur. 'It was the atmosphere. Just us on stage, an' the

250

payin' customers. It was magic. Pure magic.' He looked at Nellie. 'It'll come back,' he said confidently. 'Get this ruddy war over, an' it'll come back.'

Madame wrapped her scarf round her head to keep her ears warm in the cool sea breeze. 'Let's 'ope so, dear,' she said. 'Let's 'ope so.'

Sid and Lenny managed to find a space on one of the promenade lawns overlooking the sea, and among the formal gardens of late daffodils and early tulips the family laid out their picnic. When they had eaten, Sid and Lenny became restless for both Rossi's ice cream and a trip to one of the two amusement arcades which had opened up for the Bank Holiday weekend, so Monsieur took the boys off, leaving Madame and Nellie to finish their cups of tea in peace.

Elated as she was at the prospect of her first day ever by the seaside, Nellie knew that this was her chance to talk to Madame in confidence. It was now or never. 'Yer've been so good ter me, Mum,' she began. 'I don't know what I'd've done wivout you an' Dad.'

Madame was sitting on a low canvas chair which she always took with her on outings. 'We're the one that should be fankin' you, Nellie dear,' she said, warming her hands round the cup of tea from her vacuum flask. 'Yer've given this family a new lease of life. Albert was only sayin' so the uvver day. An' as fer Sid and Lenny, well, it's a miracle.' She leaned across and smiled at Nellie. 'We know wot yer did fer young Sid. 'E told us everythin'.'

'Oh Mum,' Nellie sighed. ''E shouldn't've. I told 'im it was somefin' fer 'im an' me, an' not ter go worryin' you about it.'

'Yer taught 'im 'ow ter fight.'

'I showed 'im 'ow ter defend 'imself. There's a big diff'rence, Mum. That's why I wanted 'im to know 'ow ter fight in the proper way, not ter go in there like any uvver scrapper down the street.'

'Yer taught 'im more than that, Nell. Yer taught 'im all sorts of fings, about gettin' back 'is confidence and self-respect. You're a wonderful gel, Nell. We're all proud ter 'ave yer in the family.'

Nellie felt her insides churning over. 'Mum,' she said quickly, lowering her eyes and biting her lip, 'there's somefin' I've got ter tell yer ...'

'An' there's somefin' I want ter tell you too, Nell.' Madame eased herself off her chair and squatted alongside Nellie on the picnic blanket. 'Albert an' I, we've been talkin' it over. We want ter adopt you—I mean official like.'

Nellie's eyes widened. 'Mum!'

Madame smiled, and took Nellie's hand. 'Yes, Nell. That's wot I want ter be, yer mum. Not yer real one, of course. There's no way we can put that right. But someone yer can talk ter, someone yer can feel belongs to yer. That goes fer Albert too. We want yer ter be our daughter. An' Sid an' Lenny want it too. They want yer ter be their sister.'

Nellie felt as though she was going to cry. But all this wonderful show of love and affection from Madame was only making it more difficult

252

for her to say what she had to say.

Madame was watching Nellie carefully. She was worried by her silence and lack of response. 'Is there anyfin' wrong, Nell? D'yer not want us to adopt yer?'

Nellie looked up quickly. 'Oh, I do, Mum,' she said eagerly. 'I can't fink of anyfin' in the 'ole wide world I'd like more. You an' Dad are wot I've dreamt about, me own family, people I can care about and call me own.' She stopped abruptly and felt anguish rising up through her body. 'But I can't do it, I can't let you an' Dad do it until—until ...'

'Wot is it, Nell?' asked Madame gently. 'I'm yer mum. Yer can tell me.'

Nellie waited a moment, then told Madame everything about her relationship with Patrick, and the night they had spent together in her bedroom. By the time she finished, she couldn't look Madame in the face. To make matters worse, Madame had listened to everything she had said in total silence, staring out to sea as though trying to pretend that what she was hearing was nothing more than a dream. Or at least, that's what Nellie thought. But when she ended with the words, 'I'm sorry, Mum. I'm truly sorry fer lettin' you down,' she was astonished to hear Madame roar with laughter.

'Oh, Nellie!' she said, throwing her arms round her. 'Why do yer even fink yer 'ave ter apologise ter me? It's all right, Nellie. It's perfectly all right.'

Nellie was bewildered. 'Yer mean—wot I did, it's all right?'

Madame looked her straight in the eye. 'No, Nell,' she said. 'It'd be wrong of me ter say it's all right ter do—wot yer did. All I'm sayin' is, it's somefin' that 'appens. As a matter of fact, the same fing 'appened ter me when I was your age.'

Nellie stared at her in disbelief.

Madame smiled, her voice becoming a touch more serious. 'Yes. It's a situation we all 'ave ter face up to at some time in our lives. When you're young, it's a big adventure, like knowin' you're doin' somefin' yer shouldn't do. But when it's all over, that's the time yer 'ave ter start askin' yerself questions.' She leaned closer again. 'Tell me, Nell. This boy, Patrick. D'yer love 'im? Is 'e the one yer want ter spend the rest of yer life wiv?'

Nellie paused a moment, then shook her head. 'I like 'im,' she said. 'I like 'im a lot. But I don't love 'im. I don't fink I ever could. I just don't know enough about 'im. 'E's just a mate—nuffin' more.'

'That's all right then. No 'arm in that.' Then she added tentatively, 'As long as there're no—complications?'

Nellie, embarrassed, shook her head and lowered her eyes.

With a reassuring smile, Madame put her hand under Nellie's chin and gently raised her head. 'Fanks fer tellin' me, Nell. After all, that's wot mums are for.'

Nellie and Madame sat on the seafront lawn and talked for over an hour. Nellie felt as though she had known this wonderful woman all her life, and thought to herself that she would rather have her for a mum than anyone else. And Doris Beckwith felt the same way about Nellie. She was truly someone she could talk to, share a laugh with, and get on with. Above all, Madame felt she had gained a daughter to whom she would one day be able to tell the truth about the heartache and suffering she was being subjected to.

It was mid-afternoon when Monsieur returned with the two boys, both of whom looked the worse for wear after consuming four Rossi's ice-cream cornets each, and two more bags of chips.

'My legs're gettin' cold!' griped Sid to his mum. 'Why can't I wear long trousers now? Most of the uvvers at school wear 'em. I'm too old fer shorts.'

'I've told yer, Sid, yer've got ter 'ang on fer anuvver year or so. The Government says there ain't enough material around ter put all boys your age in long'uns.'

Sid groaned. Lenny sniggered.

''E's bin moanin' on like this all afternoon,' complained a weary Monsieur. 'As if they boaf 'aven't cost me enough on those ruddy pin machines!'

'Somefin' tells me we'd better be on our way, dear,' replied Madame, helping Nellie to fold up the picnic blanket. 'By the time we get back 'ome, it'll be—'

A loud explosion drowned the rest of Madame's sentence. There were yells and screams from people everywhere, followed by

255

a wild dash to the nearest air-raid shelters.

'Wot is it?' gasped Madame. 'Is there an air raid?'

Simultaneously, the air-raid alert sounded from the top of the police station a couple of streets away.

'Let's get out of 'ere!' shouted Monsieur.

'No, Dad!' yelled Sid. 'Look out there! Look!'

The family turned to where Sid was pointing. Far out to sea they could see a vessel under attack from a dive bomber. Above it, the sky was criss-crossed with vapour trails; a fierce dogfight was taking place between at least a dozen aircraft.

'My God!' gasped Monsieur, quickly focusing his binoculars. 'It's a warship! Jerry's tryin' ter bomb it! Oh my God!'

'Over 'ere, Nell!' yelled young Lenny who, with his brother, had climbed up on to a wooden bench overlooking the beach. 'Yer can get a smashin' view up 'ere!'

Both boys gave Nellie a bunk up, then huddled together to watch the action.

'No, please, let's get to the shelter,' begged Madame anxiously. 'They've sounded the alert. Jerry could start bombing over 'ere any minute ...'

'Bravo!' cheered Monsieur, closely echoed by the crowd now watching along the promenade. 'They've got one of 'em! Our boy's 'ave got one of 'em! Look at 'im! 'E's on fire!'

'It's a Messerschmitt!' yelled Lenny, his knowledge based on his model aircraft kits.

'Down, yer bugger, down!' yelled Monsieur.

Nellie stared out at the incredible battle being fought out before their eyes. The cloudless, crisp blue sky was now streaked with dozens of thin white vapour trails, and as the blazing German fighter twisted and turned down into the sea, it left a trail of oily black smoke. Its pilot was clearly visible, holding on for grim death to the cords of his flickering white parachute which fluttered down helplessly, only opening just before it hit the water. One fighter plane chased another, and Nellie was sure they would collide as they twisted and turned, chasing, circling, diving, skimming the waves. She could see and hear the tracer guns as two enemy bombers dived towards their naval target. And the sound of fury, determination, and annihilation. No wonder it was called a dog-fight. There were no rules, just a free-for-all.

'Stuka!' yelled Lenny, pointing out to sea and jumping up and down excitedly on the bench.

'It's a Heinkel!' came a yell from another youngster nearby, hanging precariously from a promenade lamppost.

'Don't be daft!' Sid growled back. 'Anyone can see that's a Stuka dive bomber!'

''E's right!' Monsieur pronounced, his binoculars glued to his eyes. ''E's got a couple of sniffers on 'is tail!'

'Spitfires!' yelled the know-all.

''Urricanes!' replied Monsieur. 'They're 'eadin' this way!'

'Oh please, Albert!' pleaded Madame, starting to panic. 'Do let's get ter the shelter!'

Nellie could see the three fighters roaring in from the sea. 'Come on, you two,' she said urgently. 'Mum's right.'

She had hardly spoken when the German fighter bomber came twisting and turning in from the battle, hotly pursued by two RAF Hurricanes. And as the enemy plane approached, it made straight for the shoreline, its machine guns blazing, strafing the beach, the bullets sending up small funnels of sand on the way.

'Everyone down!' yelled Monsieur. He threw himself on to his wife, bringing her and himself to the ground, shielding her with his body. 'Down!'

Nellie grabbed both Sid and Lenny by their necks and shoved them to the ground beneath the bench they had been standing on.

Within seconds, one of the two Hurricanes had caught up with the intruder and filled his tailplane with machine-gun bullets. The enemy bomber banked straight out to sea, but before it had reached more than half a mile or so, there was a loud explosion and the entire aircraft disintegrated.

Some of the more daring onlookers on the promenade stood up and started cheering.

'He's down!' yelled an elderly woman whose basket-weave hat had been crushed in the excitement.

Then someone else, a teenage boy, yelled out. 'Look at that! There's nuffin' left of 'im!'

There was a huge cheer from everyone, and as Nellie turned to look, the promenade crowd threw caution to the wind and lined the seafront, waving and shouting, cheering and applauding. Monsieur helped Madame to her feet and as they both turned to look out to sea, he put his arm round her waist and hugged her.

Then an extraordinary thing happened. As the exultant cheers faded away, there followed a strange, unnatural silence. Nellie looked along the promenade at the quiet faces of all the people, now tinged with the red glow of the sun which had begun its downward journey towards that mystical line between sea and sky. No one spoke. No one even cleared their throat. It was as if every person there had been joined together by some unseen force. There was now no sound of battle either; the ferocious dogfight had come to an end, leaving the warship free to continue its journey and the remaining enemy bombers to retreat. Silence, but for a hungry seagull squawking for scraps as it swooped low over the heads of the crowd. Until finally one solitary voice began to sing, 'Oh, I do like to be beside the seaside ...' Slowly, barely audible at first, it grew stronger and was joined by another voice, then another, and another. It built to a crescendo until the air along the Clacton-on-Sea promenade was filled with one of the most beautiful and stirring sounds Nellie had ever heard.

This was a Bank Holiday Monday that she, and everyone else, would remember for a very long time.

Chapter 16

Nellie hated Monsieur Pierre's latest addition to his act, which he called 'Biting the Bullet'. It involved a volunteer from the audience being asked to fire a handgun directly at Monsieur, who had first been blindfolded and had his hands tied behind his back. The intention was to shock, startle, and trick the audience into believing that Monsieur had caught the bullet between his teeth. The bullet in the gun was, in fact, a blank, and Monsieur would put a real cartridge in his mouth while the trick was being set up. But Nellie was intensely nervous of the idea, for two reasons. First was that the last person who had tried the stunt had been killed when a real bullet was accidentally inserted into the gun instead of a blank. Secondly, she thought Monsieur was tempting fate by trying out the idea at the Wood Green Empire where the earlier accident had taken place on the same stage in 1912. The artiste who was killed was called Chung Ling Soo, although he was no more Chinese than Monsieur was French.

For three weeks before the new illusion was to be shown for the first time, Monsieur spent a great deal of time with his old mate, Gus Maynard, who was a member of the local Home Guard unit and knew about handling guns. The rehearsals were carried out, like all Monsieur's 'illusions', under great secrecy, although Madame told Nellie that permission had been given to use a target range at an ammunitions factory somewhere in the East End. Both Madame and Nellie were relieved every time Monsieur arrived back home in one piece after a rehearsal; they dreaded the moment when the new act would be tried out on the first day of the Great Pierre's week's booking at the Wood Green Empire.

Top of the bill that week were Elsie and Doris Waters, better known by their stage names Gert and Daisy, two of the most loved Cockney performers of their time. Nellie got to meet them during music rehearsals, and they were so friendly and jolly she felt as though she had known them all her life. They had worked on the same bill as Monsieur many times before but they, too, were nervous about his new 'illusion'.

'You tell Bert Beckwiff from me, Nell,' said Elsie, the plump one of the two, 'e should keep away from guns and bullets an' things. Far safer wiv his Indian rope trick. Wot say you, Gert?'

'Yer can say that again, Daisy!' answered Doris, following her sister's lead and using the style of their stage act to convey her concern.

Elsie Waters could see the anxiety in Nellie's eyes. She dropped the Cockney persona and reverted to her everyday gentle suburban voice. 'Don't worry, dear,' she said reassuringly, 'old Bert's a survivor. He's always dreaming up one mad lark after another.'

'Tell him from us,' added Doris, 'he'd better

get through the week if he wants to get paid on Saturday!'

Nellie felt cheered as she watched the two great artistes disappear down the corridor to their dressing room.

Before first house that evening, Nellie had to get in early to make sure that Monsieur's new jet-black wig was combed properly. It was one of the jobs that she didn't particularly relish, for she was sure the hair had been taken from a dead horse. For the act that week Madame had decided to wear a long burgundy chiffon dress, with a large vermilion sash over her left shoulder and an artificial rose pinned to the right side of her waist. Unfortunately, during a Sunday night performance at the Wigan Hippodrome the week before, the hemline of the dress had got caught under Madame's piano stool.

The torn material had been stitched up by the local theatre seamstress, but when Nellie checked over the dress before the morning rehearsal, she was none too pleased with the hasty repair. So one hour before the show began, she sat in Monsieur and Madame's dressing room and used the expertise she had learnt from Ruby to sew up the tear.

Monsieur and Madame arrived just a few minutes later, and Nellie immediately noticed the strained atmosphere between them. They said no more than was absolutely essential to each other, and Nellie's fears about tonight's act increased.

On the half, the time when all artistes were expected to be in the theatre, Nellie went upstairs to make sure that Ange had arrived. Monsieur's assistant was having to share a dressing room with two other girls who were not leading artistes, much to Ange's disdain. They were a tap-dancing duo called the Sisters Tapp who had been around the halls for quite some time and knew the ropes, and Ange soon found out that when it came to bitchy repartee she had met her match.

Nellie knocked on the dressing-room door only once before opening it and peering in. 'Monsieur says you're to watch yer timin' on the Magic Box bit ternight,' she called. ''E says 'e don't want yer smilin' too much till 'e brings out the glass of beer at the end.'

'Tell 'im ter get stuffed!' came Ange's reply.

Nellie took a step into the room. 'Wot did yer say?' she asked. She couldn't see where Ange was.

'I said, tell 'im ter get stuffed!'

One of the Sisters Tapp leaned back in her chair at the dressing table and nodded to the right of the door.

Nellie looked behind the door. Ange was stripped down to her knickers and bra, standing in the small washbasin, sponging down her legs with Lifebuoy soap and cold water. 'Ange!' she gasped, horrified. 'Wot yer doin'?'

Ange paused only long enough to swing her an icy glare. 'Wot d'yer fink I'm doin'? Catchin' up on me beauty sleep?'

'You'd 'ave a job!' quipped one of the Sisters Tapp in a broad Geordie accent. She and her sister sniggered.

'Yer shouldn't be doin' that, Ange,' Nellie scolded. She pointed to a notice pinned to the wall above the washbasin. 'Yer can see wot it says on this notice: "Standing in washbasins is strictly forbidden".'

'Oh, well done, yer clever gel!' sneered Ange. 'Didn't know yer could read anyfin' but kids' books.'

'Meee-oww!' squealed both Sisters Tapp.

'It's dangerous,' insisted Nellie. 'There've bin a lot of accidents. If that basin collapses, yer could hurt yerself bad.'

'Wishful finkin', Nell?' Ange turned off the water tap and climbed out of the sink. 'If it's *my* job you're after, ferget it. I'm a pro, mate.'

All this was too much for the Sisters Tapp, who exchanged a bored and impatient look and got up from the dressing table simultaneously.

'If you'll excuse us,' said the older of the two acidly, '*we* 'ave a show ter do.'

They checked their sailors' mini uniforms and fishnet stockings in the long mirror, then turned off the electric lights framing their dressing-table mirror and left the room, the steel taps of their dancing shoes clip-clopping down the corridor.

Nellie closed the door behind them and turned angrily to Ange. 'Just exactly wot d'yer mean about me bein' after your job?'

Ange sat down at her dressing table to dry her feet and legs on a towel. 'You know wot I mean, lil' ol' Orphan Annie!' she said nastily. 'Can't wait ter step inter my shoes, can yer? Bright lights an' sweet music, an' yer fink you're a star. Well, yer got anuvver fink comin', Miss

Blue-Eyed an' Innocent.' She was glaring at Nellie. 'I'm 'ere ter stay.'

'I don't want your job, Ange,' snapped Nellie. 'I like wot I'm doin', an' I'm grateful ter Monsieur an' Madame fer givin' it ter me.'

'Fer Chrissake cut out all that crap about Monsieur an' Madame. They're nuffin' more than Bert an' Doris Beckwiff from Stepney. Common as muck!'

'Ter me they're Mum an' Dad!' Nellie's voice was raised. 'They're the salt of the earth!'

'Ha!'

Ange's dismissive grunt infuriated Nellie. 'I love them fer wot they are, not *who* they are!'

'Oh, so do I,' replied Ange silkily. 'I love 'em boaf, specially Bert—oh, sorry, *Monsieur.*'

'An' wot's that s'pposed ter mean?'

'You know very well,' replied Ange with a smirk on her face. She went back to the washbasin, wiped it round with her towel, then returned to her seat at the dressing table. 'I take good care of Monsieur, Nell, an' *'e* takes good care of *me.*'

Nellie watched the reflection of both herself and Ange in the brightly illuminated mirror as they sized each other up. Ange started applying her make-up, using first her basic Five and Nine greasepaint sticks. 'Yer've got a lot ter learn about the feater, mate,' she said, rubbing the foundation into her cheeks. 'Specially wot goes on *after* the show.'

Nellie turned away and made for the door. The combination of the smell from Ange's greasepaint and the heat generated by the dozen or so electric light bulbs round the dressing-table mirror was stifling her.

'Yer mustn't let it get yer down, Nell,' Ange called, using a deep red carmine stick on her lips and watching Nellie carefully in the mirror. 'We all 'ave ter get on in this world, don't we?'

Nellie paused at the door. 'You're right, Ange,' she said quietly. 'An' some of us like ter dream, don't we?'

They were interrupted by a banging on the door. 'Overture and beginners, please!' yelled the call boy's voice from the corridor outside.

The show—the real show—was about to begin.

First house Monday at Wood Green was full. The people of nearby Harringay, Turnpike Lane, Palmers Green and Stoke Newington knew what they liked, and with favourites like Gert and Daisy, the Great Pierre, the Flying Ellisons, and popular stand-up comedian Billy Bennett, on the bill, there wasn't a seat to be had. Most regulars had their own particular evening for visiting their local music hall, but tonight they swarmed into the traditional red plush and gold auditorium because the word had got around that the Great Pierre was going to attempt something really daring this evening.

At six fifteen, the house lights dimmed and the conductor took his place in the centre of the orchestra pit. Nellie was in her usual place, standing on her own at the back of the stalls. There were five acts to go before Monsieur took the stage but her stomach was already churning. She was also concerned that Patrick had not yet turned up, which irritated her after all the trouble she had gone to to get him a complimentary standing room only ticket. By the end of the overture, however, he crept in, and sneaked his arm round Nellie's waist.

'Where've yer bin?' Nellie whispered as the Sisters Tapp took the stage with a frenzied tap routine to the strains of 'I Got Rhythm'.

'Business,' replied Patrick, close to her ear.

'Wot kind of business?'

'I've just robbed a bank and nicked ten thousand pounds.'

Nellie chuckled at Patrick's flippant reply, but she was still curious to know what work he did. Although she had been seeing him for several weeks, she knew as little about him now as she did when they first met.

The Sisters Tapp left the stage to tumultuous applause, and everyone settled down to a thrilling high slack wire act, the Flying Ellisons, which was followed by what Nellie thought was one of the funniest stand-up comedians in the business. Billy Bennett, billed as, 'Always a Gentleman', was a portly little man with a boozer's flushed face, blood-red nose, and a bushy brown moustache. He came on stage looking like everyone's favourite uncle, wearing a bowler hat, three-piece brown serge suit, and highly polished brown leather shoes. 'I'm 'ere to talk on behalf of the workin' class,' he opened, and for the next fifteen minutes he sent wave after wave of laughter through the audience as he passed comment on the world as he saw it, and recited from his own repertoire of humorous wartime poems.

Nellie and Patrick both rocked with laughter, and for those few minutes Nellie forgot about the ache in her stomach that kept telling her that there was only one more act to go before the Great Pierre took the stage. That act was the 'Novelty Juggler' Frank Marks with his lovely young assistant, Iris. At first, Nellie found little to interest her in the act which consisted of juggling with up to eight clubs at a time. But then she remembered what Madame had once told her about supporting acts like this being the very life and heart of the music hall, where people worked long hours to make a name for themselves and were often only there to keep the audience warm until the appearance of the top of the bill.

There was a gasp from the audience as the house lights dimmed and the act culminated with a dazzling array of wildly flashing clubs whirling high into the air, each one lit up by a tiny coloured light, and all to the rousing orchestral accompaniment of Johann Strauss's 'Thunder and Lightning Polka'.

Once again thunderous applause rocked the theatre, and as the secondary stage curtains swished gracefully together, Nellie felt her stomach rise up into her mouth. Patrick could feel the tension in her body. He knew the reason for it and gave her waist a reassuring squeeze.

At last the moment arrived. The house lights dimmed from stalls to gods, and the entire theatre was plunged into almost total darkness.

Nellie could feel the current of excitement and anticipation running through the auditorium; there was dead silence, but for one young teenage girl who sniggered nervously. Then, from the orchestra pit, came the sound of a cymbal, quivering and hissing like a snake, and as it built in volume a bright white spotlight no larger than a tennis ball picked out the ghostly white face and thin black moustache of a figure dressed from head to foot in black, swirling round and round, arms out stretched, massive black cloak swirling through the air as if in slow motion. Gradually the spotlight expanded to reveal the whole face until, quite suddenly, the hissing cymbal came to a loud climax, whereupon the figure froze, statue-like, in the centre of the stage, dark, pencil-lined eyes fixing the audience with a menacing stare.

'Ladies and gentlemen!' The auditorium echoed to the sound of the stage manager's voice booming out over the theatre's loudspeaker system. 'The Wood Green Empire is proud to present THE GREAT PIERRE!'

The theatre erupted with applause as Monsieur took a very theatrical bow. Simultaneously, the curtains behind him opened to reveal a sinister black backcloth with, on one side of the stage, Madame at the grand piano, only just visible in a subdued blue spotlight, and on the other side of the stage Ange, poised like a figure of death in a black hood and long black cloak that reached to the floor. Monsieur turned with a dramatic flourish of his white-gloved hands and the stage became bathed in green light, Madame started to play, and Ange let her cloak drop to reveal her scanty stage costume of glittering green sequins.

Nellie's eyes travelled over Madame's burgundy dress, checking that the repair she had made just a short time earlier was no longer visible. Satisfied that it wasn't, she turned her attention to the act.

First came the juggling with swords, which at times gave the impression that they were sliding in and out of Monsieur's body. That was followed by the Magic Box trick, in which Ange, orchestrated by Monsieur, had to pull a variety of unlikely objects out of the box—a white mouse which ran up Monsieur's arm and disappeared into his white-gloved hands, an electric lightbulb which flashed on and off without any sign of a connection, several kitchen utensils, a large ginger tom cat, and finally dozens of Union Jack pennants which, together with Madame's rousing accompaniment of patriotic piano music, brought a round of applause from the audience.

Then came the old favourites, such as sawing the lady (Ange) in half, the Indian rope trick, in which a length of rope coiled uncannily on its own out of a woven basket like some dangerous reptile, and the most extraordinary sight of all, the levitation of a human form (Ange again) which rose up from the stage like a laid-out corpse, lit only by a chilling red spotlight. It was all heady, mesmerising stuff, and Nellie never ceased to be amazed by the tricks. No one was allowed to know how they were done; Monsieur always insisted that during his act, nobody was allowed to watch from either the wings or the flies above. Even at home he worked on his tricks behind the locked door of his workroom on the top floor of the house and not even Madame was privy to the innermost secrets of the Great Pierre.

Finally, it was time for the climax of the act, the moment that Nellie and the entire audience had been waiting for. It was heralded by a roll of drums in the orchestra pit, and the melodramatic voice of the stage manager.

'Ladies and gentlemen!'

Roll of drums, terminated by the clash of a cymbal.

'Tonight, Monsieur Pierre will embark on the most dangerous, the most death-defying illusion of his entire career. Before your very eyes, a volunteer from the audience will be asked to fire a bullet from a handgun directly at Monsieur Pierre ...'

Gasps from the audience.

'Monsieur will then attempt to *catch the bullet between his teeth ...*'

More gasps from the audience.

Monsieur stepped into the bright white spotlight, bared his teeth and with one gloved finger pointed to where he intended to 'Bite the Bullet'. Then he quickly stepped back out of the spotlight.

'Ladies and gentlemen,' continued the booming voice of the stage manager, 'this illusion requires the utmost concentration by Monsieur Pierre. He therefore asks each and every one of you to be absolutely silent throughout the remarkable event you are about to witness. If you wish to clear your throat or blow your nose, please do so now.'

It seemed that the entire audience wished to do so; the auditorium was suddenly filled with the nervous sounds of throats being cleared and noses being blown.

Nellie did neither. Her blood had turned to ice, and she was so tense she could hardly breathe.

'And so, ladies and gentlemen,' continued the dramatic voice, 'we come to the moment of truth. First of all, we ask if we have a volunteer in the audience tonight who would like to fire the fatal bullet at this great and fearless artiste?'

There was a deathly hush. Ange, who had spent much of the act adopting various absurd poses and who always acknowledged the applause at the end of each turn as though it was all meant for her, shielded her eyes from the stage footlights and peered out into the audience to see if anyone was offering their services.

'Come now,' called the stage manager. 'One person, just one courageous person who is willing to put Monsieur to the test.'

'Over 'ere!' came a man's voice from the back stalls. 'I'll 'ave a go!'

The audience craned their heads as one to see who was volunteering.

With a spotlight covering her, Ange moved to the steps on the left-hand side of the stage and went down to meet the man who, to Nellie's relief, turned out to be Monsieur's old Home Guard mate, Gus Maynard.

'A volunteer!' proclaimed the stage manager's voice triumphantly. 'Let's give him a big hand, ladies and gentlemen.'

The audience was too wound up to demonstrate very much enthusiasm, so while Ange led Gus up on to the stage, Madame played some mood-setting music.

Nellie's heart was thumping. But, scared as she was, Ange's squeaky little voice started to echo through her mind: *'I take good care of Monsieur, Nell. An'· 'e takes good care of me.'*

The audience watched with bated breath as Monsieur greeted his 'volunteer', gave him the handgun, and went through the motions of showing him how to use it, making quite sure while he did so that the barrel was kept pointed down towards the floor.

Once again, the house lights were turned off, leaving only two spotlights, one on Monsieur on one side of the stage, the other on the apparently courageous 'volunteer'.

A roll of the drums. A clash of the cymbal.

Monsieur raised his arms out from his sides and turned towards the 'volunteer', who raised the handgun and took aim.

'*Allez!*' called Monsieur, in very Cockney French. He rarely spoke during his act, but this was one of the few French words he had taken the trouble to learn. '*Un ... deux ... trois ... SHOOT!*'

Nellie turned her head away and crunched up in terror as the shot was fired.

The audience gasped, squealed, shouted, and one or two women even screamed.

Nellie looked up. Monsieur had fallen to his knees, seemingly in pain as he covered his face with his white gloved hands.

'Oh Gawd!' howled Nellie, causing several people in the back stalls to turn round and look at her. "E's bit' it! 'E's bit' it!'

The wave of horror that swept through the audience suggested that the tragedy of 1912 had just been repeated. But just when one or two people felt distressed enough to get up from their seats, Monsieur suddenly recovered himself, stood up, and with a flourish took his hands away from his face to reveal the bullet lodged firmly between his clenched teeth.

The conductor of the orchestra, who was just as relieved as the audience to know that Monsieur's illusion had worked, immediately prompted his musicians to give this dramatic climax to the act a triumphant orchestral flourish.

Nellie didn't know whether to laugh or cry; her relief and excitement were so great that she just threw her arms round Patrick and hugged him tight.

On stage, Monsieur took the bullet from between his teeth and held it up for all to see, while his adoring audience shouted, cheered, whistled, squealed, applauded, and stamped their feet in appreciation and admiration. As the main house curtain came down behind Monsieur, he took bow after bow on his own in the spotlight, until he was finally joined by

Madame on one side and Ange on the other, and hand in hand they bowed and curtsied together.

It was yet another triumph for the Great Pierre.

After the second house show, Monsieur and Madame's dressing room was crammed with wellwishers. Monsieur, a glass of brown ale in one hand and the smoke from his Abdullah fag wafting up from the holder in his other hand, lapped up all the attention he was getting. Madame was pleased that her husband's new illusion had been both safe and successful, but she was less happy about the way Ange was standing alongside Monsieur, attempting to hog as much of the limelight as she could. Nellie had brought Patrick to meet her mum and dad and he, too, was full of praise for the way the act had held the audience absolutely spellbound. Monsieur graciously acknowledged the compliment and opened up the conversation with Patrick. ''Aven't 'eard from any of your boys just lately,' he said expansively while admiring himself in his dressing-table mirror over Patrick's shoulder.

Patrick exchanged a puzzled look with Nellie. 'I don't foller you, sir.'

'The IRA,' Monsieur said lightly. 'They seem ter be keepin' themselves ter themselves these days, fank the Lord.'

Patrick stiffened visibly. 'I don't know nothin' about the IRA, sir,' he said.

'But you're Irish, ain't yer?'

275

Madame was embarrassed. 'Don't be silly, dear,' she cut in quickly. 'Not all Irish people belong to the IRA.'

'Well, let's face it,' responded Monsieur, determined to continue with what he considered to be a bit of harmless fun, 'most of 'em ain't on our side in this war, are they? I mean, look wot they done in nineteen forty just before the Blitz—that bomb down Whiteley's store in Bayswater, and the one outside that 'otel in Park Lane. Not exactly an act of friendship, would yer say?'

'Patrick don't 'ave nuffin' ter do wiv politics, Dad,' Nellie interceded; she could see the tension rising in Patrick. 'That's right, ain't it, Patrick?' She turned to look at him, even though she was unsure she believed what she had just said.

'I doubt anyone in their right mind believes in politics,' said Madame, trying to defuse the atmosphere. 'There's no time for it durin' a war. We all 'ave ter stick tergevver.'

Monsieur was at last beginning to realise that perhaps he had gone too far. 'You're absolutely right, me dear,' he said, giving Patrick a friendly smile. 'No offence meant, Pat lad. As a matter of fact, some of me best pals are Paddys.'

Patrick looked at Nellie. His expression was thunderous. 'I'd better be goin',' he mumbled. 'Got an early call termorrow.'

'I'll see yer out,' said Nellie and followed him anxiously to the door.

'No need,' replied Patrick. 'I can find me way. G'night, Mr Beckwith, Mrs Beckwith. It

276

was a grand act.' He quickly pecked Nellie on the cheek, then left.

Madame looked mortified. 'Go after 'im, Nell,' she said, very concerned. 'Tell 'im we didn't mean nuffin'.'

Nellie rushed out of the dressing room and caught up with Patrick just as he was leaving by the stage door. 'Patrick!' she called anxiously. 'Don't go. Yer mustn't take any notice of Dad. 'E's just excited, that's all. 'E din't mean wot 'e said.'

Patrick stopped and swung round. 'Oh, he didn't, didn't he?' he snapped angrily. 'Well, let me tell yer somethin'. That man is nothin' more than a pile of horseshit!'

Nellie immediately stiffened. 'Don't talk like that, please, Patrick. 'E's my farver!'

'Then go back ter 'im!'

'Fer Chrissake, wot's 'e said that's upset yer so much? Yer'd fink 'e'd stabbed yer in the back or somefin'!'

'As far as I'm concerned, he has!' Patrick turned and started to walk away from her.

'Wot's up wiv you?' Nellie barked. 'You got a guilt complex or somefin'?'

Patrick stopped and again swung round on her. 'And what's that supposed ter mean?'

'If yer've got nuffin' ter 'ide,' Nellie replied, 'I don't see wot you're gettin' so worked up about.'

'I have *nothing* ter hide!'

Although it was now late and dark, there were still a few people strolling home from the Silver Bullet pub just round the corner. Suspecting there was some kind of lovers' tiff going on, they gave Nellie and Patrick a wide berth.

'D'yer realise I know nuffin' about you, Patrick?' Nellie said, trying to lower her voice. 'Ever since I met yer, yer've never told me exactly where yer live, wot yer do, or anyfin' about yer folks. That's wot I call secretive.'

Patrick glared at her 'OK! OK! So tell me, wot d'yer want ter know?'

Nellie hesitated for a moment, then took the plunge. 'Who were those two blokes yer was wiv that night yer took me to the Irish dance at the arcade down the Nag's 'Ead? You was 'avin' a barney wiv two blokes in the air-raid shelter.'

Patrick froze. 'So that's it,' he said contemptuously. 'You *were* spying on me.'

'Don't be stupid!' Nellie shouted. 'Yer suddenly leave me all on me tod in the middle of a dance 'all, then 'cos I come lookin' fer yer, yer tell me I'm spyin' on yer!'

'Then how d'yer know we was arguing?'

''Cos I *heard* yer. I'm not deaf, dumb, an' blind, yer know!' She walked right up to him, kept her voice as low as possible, and challenged him. 'Who were they, Patrick? Are yer mixed up in somefin'—in the IRA?'

For a moment, there was no response from Patrick. He just stared at her in silence. Then he turned away and started to walk off.

Nellie wasn't having it and bellowed after him. 'Yer can't just keep fings from me, Patrick! Sooner or later, yer'll 'ave ter tell me!'

Patrick swung round angrily. 'They're my brothers! My own family! We were discussing something personal. Is that good enough for yer, Nellie? Are you happy now?'

Nellie was at a loss for words. With mixed feelings, she watched Patrick stride off in the dark. As he disappeared out of sight round the corner into Seven Sisters Road, she was convinced that this was the last she would see of him.

Chapter 17

The number 14 bus took for ever, at least that's what it seemed like to Nellie. She had already had to endure a journey of half an hour, for the bus was early, and the driver was taking his time, despite the fact that Hornsey Rise was no more than ten minutes or so away at the most. Even before she got to the bus stop in Caledonian Road, she knew she would have to wait. There seemed to be something about London buses; they never came on time. They blamed it all on the war.

Nellie had no idea where Patrick lived. He had never given her the address, only that he lived with his parents in a house somewhere near a small park just off Hornsey Rise. She had to find him. No matter how long it took her, she had to find him and apologise for what she had said to him outside the Wood Green Empire the night before. Every time she thought about it her stomach turned over. Why did she have to assume that he was mixed up with a bunch of Irish spies just because she had overhead him having a row with two men that she hadn't even heard properly. If he said the row was personal, about family matters, then who was she to disbelieve him? She cringed at the thought of her behaviour but was determined to put things right. The only trouble was how to find him.

The bus finally limped to a halt at the junction of the busy main Hornsey Road and the rather posh-looking Hazelville Road. Nellie decided to get off so that she could stroll around a bit and make a few inquiries. Luckily, she did not have to be at the theatre until first house that evening; it was only mid-morning now so she had plenty of time on her hands. But where to start?

First she searched for a park, but after looking around and asking several rather bemused passers-by, there didn't seem to be much on offer except a small area of grass close to where she had got off the bus. Like so many other parts of Islington, Hornsey Rise had its share of bomb damage. There were the inevitable empty sites piled high with rubble, and gaps in the neat rows of Edwardian and Victorian terraced houses. Even so, this part of the borough seemed to Nellie to be more affluent than those small back streets behind the Nag's Head. There were more trees, and more space, and people walked with their heads up and seemed to know where they were going, unlike some of those in Seven Sisters Road, who appeared to be mesmerised by either the pavement or the shop windows when they walked.

Nellie reached the highest point of the 'Rise' after walking around for nearly an hour and a half. The view from the top wasn't the most exciting in the world, but she could see Holloway stretched out in the distance below, and behind her the leafy outskirts of Crouch Hill with a distant view of the radio mast on top of Alexandra Palace towards Wood Green. By this time, her feet were killing her, and as soon as she found a bench which overlooked Hornsey Road, she stopped to rest for a few minutes.

It was a lovely summer's day, and the sun was picking out colours magically, when under normal circumstances the same objects looked grey and drab. Even the single-decker buses climbing up Crouch Hill glowed a spectacular red in the midday sun, and Nellie thought that if she had been an artist, she would have liked to capture a scene that was at first glance so ordinary but also so alive. Then she thought of why she was here, and how futile and pointless it all was. How could she possibly find Patrick among all these streets and houses? It was like trying to find a needle in a haystack. As her eyes scanned the patchwork of rooftops laid out in the valley beneath her, her attention focused on the steeples of three churches. Surely they were worth a try. At least one of those churches would be Roman Catholic, and surely someone there would know an Irish family in the neighbourhood by the name of Duvall.

The Reverend Archie Scott at St Luke's was certainly the most likeable of the vicars Nellie called on during her trek round the three churches in Hornsey Rise. In fact, he couldn't have been nicer. Unfortunately he was a bit on the vague side and seemed more interested in telling Nellie about the night an oil bomb fell just behind the church and blew in their only stained-glass window. The fact of the matter was that he hadn't a clue who the Duvall family were, or where they could be found. Nellie didn't have much luck at St Thomas's either, for the vicar there was a ferocious Church of England Bible-puncher, and the mere mention of the words Roman Catholic was enough to give him palpitations. Finally, Nellie found her way to the Church of Our Lady, which was situated in a quiet back street between, rather appropriately, a pub and an undertaker's parlour. The only problem was that when she got there, a funeral Mass was in progress, and when it was over, Father Michael O'Halloran had little time to spare for Nellie. However, an elderly Irish nun named Sister Marie Louise came to the rescue.

'Duvall?' she asked, peering over the top of tiny rimless spectacles. 'Yer don't mean our little Patrick, do yer?'

Nellie's eyes lit up. 'Yeah, that's 'im!' she said eagerly. 'Patrick. Patrick Duvall. D'yer know 'im?'

'Know him? Ha! Little scoundrel! I've known him since he was nothin' but a glint in his mother's eyes. And his brothers too. They're all young scoundrels, all of three of 'em!'

Nellie breathed a sigh of relief. She smiled at the old lady who was chuckling merrily to herself as though she was reliving her whole relationship with the Duvall boys. So it was true what Patrick had told her the previous night. He *did* have two brothers.

'Are you a friend of the family?' asked the old nun whose sunny smile was in complete contrast to her pallid complexion visible beneath her white coif.

'Sort of,' replied Nellie. 'Fing is, I've bin away a bit, an' I've lost their address.'

The old lady was still fondly thinking of the Duvall boys. 'They're good people, that's for sure,' she said, with a nod of the head. 'Those boys have stuck together through thick an' thin. I tell you, harm one an' yer harm the lot. Their mother an' father must be proud of them. An' so is our Lord God the Father.' She looked up towards the church ceiling, and with two fingers of her right hand, crossed herself. Nellie briefly lowered her eyes.

'Do all the bruvvers live tergevver then?' she asked.

'Mercy, no!' came the quick reply. 'Tom and Seamus are still at home with their parents. I'm afraid they'll both be called up in the next few months, God help us.'

Nellie was puzzled and wanted to ask more, but before she could do so the old lady was called silently away by one of the other sisters.

'Number Fourteen Winsford Place,' said the

old nun quietly before she scurried off. 'It's a tiny little mews just off Hornsey Lane. Yer can't miss it. Give that rascal Patrick my love!'

Nellie watched her go, relieved to know that at least Patrick was held in such high regard.

An hour and a half later, Nellie at last found the elusive Winsford Place. The elderly nun had said it was just off Hornsey Lane, but Hornsey Lane stretched for what seemed like a couple of miles from Crouch End Hill to Highgate High Street. Winsford Place turned out to be far scruffier than the name suggested. There were about two dozen small houses in all, facing each other on either side, and like most other properties in the borough they clearly needed a coat of paint and extensive renovation. Some of the windows were still boarded up from the Blitz two years before, and weeds were growing out of cracks in the stucco on the flat roofs. All the houses had just two floors, and it seemed to Nellie that it would be quite a crush for any fair-sized family to live in.

Number 14 was the last house on the right-hand side. It was joined to a large brick wall which seemed to form part of a junk yard full of old motorcar tyres. The small paved area in front of the house had three over-full dustbins, one of which was used for pig swill and was very smelly in the afternoon sun.

Nellie made her way to the front gate. The latch was broken and made a sharp grating sound when she opened it. The front door had both a doorbell and a rusty door knocker. Nellie chose the bell, but when she tried pushing it, it seemed to make no sound at all, so she banged on the door with the horseshoe-shaped door knocker. There was no response. When Nellie peered through one of the smoked glass door panels, she could see no sign of life at all. All the curtains at the ground-floor bay window were drawn, so she couldn't even get a glimpse of how the Duvall family kept their place. Eventually, she gave up, but as she turned away, she came face to face with a young woman not very much older than herself.

'Are yer lookin' fer someone?' she asked, with a slight Irish brogue.

'Oh, yes,' replied Nellie, a bit sheepish, and feeling as though she'd just been caught trying to break in. 'I was wonderin' whevver the Duvall family lived 'ere.'

The girl's face relaxed. It was actually quite a sweet face, although rather tired and drawn. 'Yes, we do,' she replied. 'Can I help?'

'I'm lookin' fer Patrick,' said Nellie awkwardly. 'Is 'e at 'ome?'

''Fraid not,' replied the girl. 'He doesn't get back from the pub till after three.'

Nellie was puzzled. 'Pub?'

'The Hornsey Arms, it's just up the lane. He works behind the bar there.'

Nellie didn't say anything for a moment. There was nothing wrong with Patrick working in a pub, but it just hadn't occurred to her that someone like him would be doing such a run-of-the-mill job. 'But this is the right 'ouse?' she asked. 'This is where 'e lives wiv 'is mum an' dad?'

'His mum an' dad!' The girl roared with laughter. 'Over my dead body!'

Nellie was beginning to feel decidedly ill at ease. 'Can I ask,' she said, 'who are yer?'

The smile disappeared from the girl's face. 'I was about ter ask you the same question.'

The two girls stared briefly at each other in silence.

'I'm a friend of Patrick's.'

'My name's Bridget,' replied the girl, stony-faced. 'I'm Patrick's wife.'

Nellie felt her stomach turn inside out. She wanted to say something, but she didn't know what. All she could do was grab hold of the broken front gate and open it. 'I'm sorry ter 'ave bovvered yer,' she said.

The girl stood aside to let Nellie pass. Behind her was a baby's pushchair containing a beautiful child, a little boy. It started to grizzle as Nellie rushed off.

'Can I tell Patrick who called?' called the girl.

Nellie stopped only long enough to turn and say, 'I wouldn't bovver. If yer ask me, I reckon 'e's got quite enough on 'is plate.'

Ange was in one of her spiky moods. Nellie knew it the moment she got back to the house from Hornsey Rise, for she could hear Ange outside in the conservatory, ranting to Monsieur about the way she was being treated by the Wood Green Empire management. Nellie couldn't bear the sound of Ange's voice at the best of times, but today it was more shrill and

286

ugly than ever. As she climbed the stairs to
her bedroom, she could hear her shout, 'Yer
couldn't do the act wivout me, an' yer know
it! You keep that bloody woman's nose out of
my business, or I'll tell 'er wot I *really* fink of
'er!' Even after she'd gone into her bedroom
and shut the door, Nellie could hear that
bossy, demanding little voice, and it nauseated
her. Why did Monsieur keep bowing to her
demands? What hold had that trumped-up,
brassy little cow got over him?

She threw herself down on the bed and stared
up at the ceiling. What a day it had been!
Why couldn't life just be simple? Why couldn't
people behave like civilised human beings and
be grateful for what they had. How she hated
Patrick for lying to her, for leading her on as
though she was some cheap little pick-up from
the street. And then she thought back to the
night when they had slept together in the very
same bed she was lying on now. Her flesh crept
at the thought of how stupid she'd been. Men!
They were nothing but liars and cheats. One of
these days she'd get her own back. One of these
days ...

A few minutes later, Nellie heard the front
door slam. She got up and made her way
downstairs.

Monsieur was still in the conservatory. Nellie
felt really sorry for him, for he was sitting bent
forward on a wickerwork chair, his elbows on his
knees and his head buried in his hands, looking
as though he had the worries of the world on
his shoulders. Which wasn't surprising after

listening to Ange ranting on, thought Nellie. 'Anything wrong, Dad?' she asked tentatively.

Monsieur looked up with a start, clearly surprised. 'Nell,' he said anxiously. 'Din't know yer was 'ome,'

Nellie smiled warmly. 'I was listenin' ter the wireless up in my room,' she said, trying to allay his fears. Then she sat on another wickerwork chair beside him. 'Is everyfin' all right, Dad? I mean wiv Ange, an' all that?'

'Ange?' he replied brightly. 'Course there's nuffin' wrong. Wot gave yer that idea?'

'I just wondered, that's all,' replied Nellie. 'I saw yer talkin' to 'er when I came in.'

Monsieur was getting a little agitated. 'Oh, it was nuffin', nuffin' at all. We was just talkin' over the new act. You know our Ange. She's a bit 'ighly strung. Always gets 'er knickers in a twist when I 'ave ter change anyfin'.'

Nellie leaned across and put her arm round his shoulders. 'Yer mustn't let 'er bully yer, Dad,' she said gently. He was obviously under some pressure. 'It's your act, not 'ers.'

'Bully?' said Monsieur, quickly reaching for his packet of Abdullahs. 'Oh no, Nell. Yer've got it all wrong, gel. Ange ain't tryin' ter bully me. Oh no. She's just—finkin' of the good of the act, that's all.'

Nellie watched him carefully as he got up, looked for his cigarette holder, and wedged an Abdullah into it. In the background, a small imitation antique clock chimed the hour. Nellie turned to look outside the conservatory window, where a blue-tit was tapping for scraps of bread.

Whilst she waited for Monsieur to light up his cigarette, only one thought dominated her mind after all she had been through that day. Why was it that men had to be so deceitful? Once they were married, they had the best of all worlds—a wife, kids, a good home, and yet it wasn't enough. They wanted adventure, to take risks with their marriage. Why did they do it? Was it because they wanted to stay young, or was it that they just had to prove something to themselves? Maybe it was the same thing. Deep down inside, she was in despair. After all she had learnt in so short a time, how could she ever love a man? But then she thought that maybe there was someone out there whom she could love.

Monsieur had lit his Abdullah and now started coughing. 'Why do I smoke these bloody fings!' he said angrily, pulling the cigarette holder out of his mouth and glaring at it. 'This is nuffin' ter do wiv me, Nell,' he spluttered in an outburst of pent-up frustration. 'This is part of my uvver self, somefin' that comes ter life just once a night up on some stage somewhere.' He found the nearest ashtray and firmly stubbed out the Abdullah. Then he opened a small drawer in the wickerwork table and took out a packet of Woodbines, a much cheaper brand. 'This is what I'm all about, Nell,' he said, lighting up again. 'Bert Beckwiff from Stepney, not Monsieur Pierre from bloody Frogland.' He inhaled a lungful of smoke, then took the fag out of his mouth and smiled at it. 'Yes, Nell. This is wot I'm all about. This is no music 'all illusion.' Nellie got up from her seat, went across to Monsieur, and lightly kissed him on the forehead. 'See yer later, Dad,' she said with a warm, affectionate smile. Then she turned to go.

'Nell?'

Nellie stopped and looked back.

'I'm sorry fer the way I talked ter yer bloke last night,' he said awkwardly. 'I 'ad no right. Will yer fergive me?'

Nellie smiled weakly at him. 'Don't be silly, Dad,' she replied. 'I don't 'ave nuffin' ter fergive yer for. Anyway, yer was probably right. Paddys are all the same.'

Monsieur was watching her carefully. 'No, Nell,' he said, showing uncharacteristic sensitivity. 'All *people* are the same. We all 'ave faults, we all make mistakes. I know I've made a good few of 'em in my time, an' don't worry, you'll make quite a few yerself as time goes by. But it don't mean we're all bad. It just means we're weak. An' that's somefin' we all 'ave ter pay fer, one way or anuvver.'

A sharp summer thunderstorm cracked loudly over the Wood Green Empire just as the first house audience was arriving. The approach roads to the theatre were carpeted with a swaying mass of dark umbrellas, and by the time they reached the theatre itself, they looked like a vast field of mushrooms. Those without umbrellas had to sit through the performance in wet clothes.

There was quite a thunderstorm brewing

inside dressing room number 5, too. Ange had accused Gladys, one of the Sisters Tapp, of nicking her bottle of wet white, a liquid powder used for covering blemishes. The row had become so fierce that Gladys, a tough Geordie who was known in the music hall business for her quick right hook, was very close to sending the 'little tart from Clapham junction' on stage with a black eye. Nellie saved the situation by finding the precious bottle of wet white on top of the toilet cistern in the ladies' room next door, where Ange had apparently forgotten it.

During the first house performance, Nellie stayed in Monsieur and Madame's dressing room. The agony of watching someone firing a revolver at Monsieur every night was too much for her and as she had quite a lot of sewing to do, she decided to keep away from it all. Before they went on, Monsieur and Madame discussed the act, what changes should be made and how best they could improve things. Nellie was proud of how professional they both were, and listened to everything they said with interest. She had heard the the act discussed so many times, she felt she knew it off by heart—apart from what Monsieur called 'the secrets of the trade'. Even Ange was only permitted to know what was absolutely essential to her part in the act.

There was always a long wait between their first and second house appearances. Usually, neither of them felt like eating until after the final curtain of the night, but tonight Monsieur's appetite was whetted by the smell of someone backstage eating chips; so Nellie volunteered to go out and get them all some fish and chips from the shop just round the corner in the High Road.

The thunderstorm had now given way to a less angry sky, and as Nellie left the stage door and made her way out on to the main road, the pavements were glistening in the short bursts of mid-evening sunshine. The storm had cleared the air, and Nellie felt relieved to get away for a few minutes from the clammy atmosphere of the backstage dressing room.

As usual, there was a long queue outside the fish and chip shop, and Nellie hoped that by the time she got to the counter, they would not have sold out. Fish and chips were, as Monsieur kept telling her, 'the poor person's slap-up meal', but as fish supplies were being hit hard by the war in both the North Sea and North Atlantic, fish was not as easy to come by as it used to be.

''Ow's me ol' mate doin' ternight then?' asked Gracie, the doyenne of Islington fish and chip shops. Gracie and her husband Mitch were great characters, the salt of the earth to their customers, Gracie always immaculate in clean apron and turban, and Mitch in his white jacket and straw boater hat. 'Tell 'im from me, 'e nearly give me a 'eart attack last night', Gracie said, piling a scoopful of chips into an old copy of the *Daily Herald*.

''Onest ter Gawd, I fawt 'e'd copped 'is lot when that stupid geezer fired a shot at 'im on that stage!' added Mitch.

A few minutes later, Nellie was on her way

back to the theatre, her string bag filled with generous pieces of cod and chips for Monsieur, Madame, and herself. As she turned into the small back alley where the stage door was located, she found her way barred.

'Hello, Nell.'

Nellie didn't even have to look up to know that it was Patrick. She didn't reply, merely tried to walk past him.

'Nell,' he said, placing himself right in front of her. 'Give me a chance to explain, please.'

Nellie couldn't bring herself to look at his face, so she kept her eyes lowered. 'There's nuffink to explain,' she replied coldly. Then she made another attempt to move round him.

Again, Patrick blocked her way.

'I should have told you, Nell,' he said, both hands clutching her shoulders. 'I had no right to—to ...'

'You 'ad every right ter do wot yer like, Patrick,' Nellie said impassively. 'It's a free country.'

'I didn't want to deceive you, Nell. You've got to believe that.'

Nellie finally looked up at him. 'I believe yer, Patrick,' she said, without any feeling at all.

'I fell in love with you, Nell,' he continued, his voice anguished. 'I'm still in love with you. I don't want us to lose what we have.'

'Lose wot we 'ave?' Nellie asked. 'Wot do we 'ave, Patrick? Din't your mum, or your dad, or your bruvvers, or that good priest up your local church ever tell yer, it ain't possible ter love two people at the same time?'

'Oh, but it is, Nell! I love you, I love my wife, and I love my baby.'

'So wot yer goin' ter do, Patrick? Share us around a bit, one night fer me, one night fer 'er?'

Two stagehands approached, and Patrick waited until they had disappeared through the door before answering. 'You don't understand, Nell. I love all three of you, but I love you most of all.'

Nellie looked straight through him. 'Then yer've got a problem, ain't yer, mate?'

'I've been trying to summon up enough courage to tell you for weeks. That night you saw me quarrelling with my brothers. It was nothing to do with the IRA. I'm not a traitor, Nell. I love this country, and I'd never do anything to harm it. It was *you* we were quarrelling about. They wanted me to get rid of you. They told me my place was at home, with my wife and my child. They told me I should go to see Father O'Halloran, to confess my sins. They told me I was a disgrace to myself and all our family.'

'Is that a fact?' replied Nellie. 'Good ter know some people know wot's right an' wrong.'

'D'you feel nothin' for me, Nell? Nothin'? After all we've had together?'

Nellie paused a moment before answering. 'Yes, Patrick. I do feel somefin' for yer. I feel you've destroyed my confidence in all the fings I believe in most. I trusted you, Patrick. I trusted yer so much that I slept wiv yer, the first an' only time I've ever slept wiv any feller. I did that knowin' that I was betrayin' my family, my own family, the only ones who've ever meant anyfin' ter me.' She pushed him to one side. 'Wot kind of a person d'yer fink I am, Patrick Duvall?'

'Someone special, very special. Someone I truly love, and can't do without.'

Nellie looked at him just one last time. 'Sorry, mate,' she said, unsmiling, and without emotion. 'That's your problem, not mine.' With that she disappeared through the stage door.

At the conclusion of the second house show, Monsieur informed his wife that he had an important meeting with his agent, which meant that he wouldn't be able to come straight home with her and Nellie. Madame took this news in her stride, or appeared to; she had become used to these sudden 'important' meetings after the show and had long ago decided that it would be useless to complain. So as soon as Nellie had finished helping both Monsieur and herself to hang up their stage costumes, Madame suggested that they leave their usual taxi for Monsieur and take the bus.

Although it was now quite dark outside, there was still a wonderful glow in the midsummer air, which hung over the rooftops as if to suggest that it would not be many hours before it was light again. Both Madame and Nellie thought that the air was now so light and fresh that they would walk to the bus stop at Turnpike Lane, which was about ten to fifteen minutes further down the road.

'Yer know, Nellie,' Madame said as they strolled quietly along the High Road, watching the last of the theatre crowds making their way to their buses. 'Before the war, from down 'ere yer could see the light on top of the mast at the dear old Ally Pally.'

Nellie turned to look up in the direction Madame was indicating. But she could see no sign of that great glass exhibition hall called Alexandra Palace. High on top of the hill at Alexandra Park, for, like all other buildings throughout the capital, the war had extinguished all its lights.

'When we was young, Albert and I used ter go roller-skating up there.' The nostalgic smile on Madame's face was tinged with sadness. 'That was before we 'ad the kids, of course. They was good days. Me and Albert used ter share so much tergevver.'

Nellie was careful in her reply. 'D'yer wish it was like that now, Mum?'

Madame shrugged her shoulders. 'Fings can never be the same as they were at the beginning. After all, times move on. We all 'ave ter change, don't we? At least, that's wot people keep tellin' us, so it 'as ter be true, don't it?'

'I don't fink change means better,' replied Nellie. 'We shouldn't ferget fings as though they never existed.'

'Wot about you, Nellie?' asked Madame. 'Would you like ter remember the past? Your time at the children's 'ome an' all that?'

Nellie was surprised by the question. But it made her think. 'I sometimes fink about Miss

Ackroyd,' she replied. 'She seemed a good woman. I'd like ter see 'er again one of these days.' She linked her arm through Madame's as they walked. 'But she couldn't mean as much ter me as you do. Nobody could.'

Madame smiled and gave her arm a squeeze.

'Mrs Beckwiff!'

Both women stopped and turned. Standing just behind them was Dandy, the younger of the two Sisters Tapp.

'Dandy!' Madame said. 'Wot's wrong, dear?'

Dandy was out of breath, having run the length of the road to catch up with them. 'You'd better come quick, Mrs Beckwiff,' she spluttered in her broad Geordie accent, clearly in some distress. 'Mr Beckwiff asked me to come after you. There's been an accident!'

Madame and Nellie hurried back to the theatre and made their way straight to dressing room number 5. A group of people were already there, gathered around a near hysterical Ange who was stretched out on the floor, screaming, her legs lacerated and bleeding.

'Dear God!' said Madame, immediately kneeling beside the girl. 'Wot's 'appened, Ange? Wot 'ave yer done to yerself?'

'We tried to tell her, Mrs Beckwiff,' said the distraught Dandy. 'We told her not to do it!'

'Told 'er not ter do wot?'

'What do yer think?' came the acerbic voice of Gladys, the other Sister Tapp. 'She was washin' 'erself, standin' in the washbasin.'

At this, Ange let out a piercing scream.

'Send for an ambulance!' called one of the

stagehands. 'For Gawd's sake, somebody send for an ambulance!'

Madame leant over Ange, tried to comfort her, and use her handkerchief to mop up the blood on her legs. 'It's all right, Ange,' she said repeatedly. 'Everyfing's goin' ter be all right, I promise yer.'

This only sent Ange into another fit of sobbing.

Nellie looked around the room. Her eyes came to rest on the ashen, stunned face of the only member of the group who was standing well back.

It was Monsieur.

Chapter 18

Nellie had never been so scared in all her life. Only twenty-four hours before, she had been quite content to do her job as personal dresser to Monsieur and Madame. Now here she was, less than an hour before curtain up on the first house show, waiting anxiously to make her debut as the so-called glamorous assistant to the famous Illusioniste Extraordinaire, the Great Pierre. Even to think about it made her feel faint.

Ange's accident in the washbasin had landed her in hospital. Both her legs and part of her back were so badly cut, she needed many stitches. No matter what Nellie felt about

Monsieur's assistant, she would never have wished such a thing on her. It was a tragedy for Ange, and for Monsieur's act. The week's engagement was not even halfway through, but everyone kept saying that the show must go on. Why did it have to go on? Nellie asked. Why couldn't an announcement be made that 'owing to unforeseen circumstances' the Great Pierre would be appearing for the rest of the week without his usual young female assistant? But in her heart of hearts, Nellie knew it was wrong to think like that. In many ways, Ange had been right. Monsieur's celebrated stage act could not work without help, without someone to be sawn in half, or to disappear from a wooden cabinet, or climb up a piece of rope suspended from nowhere, or levitate like a dead body. Someone also had to coax a member of the audience up on to the stage, or appear to do so, like Monsieur's regular 'plant', old Gus Maynard. If only Ange hadn't been so stubborn and stupid.

Both Monsieur and Madame had pleaded with Nellie to take Ange's place in the show. It was an impossible position to be in. She hated the idea of going on stage. She felt self-conscious about her height, her skinny legs, and everything else about herself. But Monsieur and Madame were not only her employers, they were now her own mum and dad. They had done so much for her, and come to her rescue when she was at her lowest ebb; now it was her turn to help them.

The whole day had been one mad rush.

It had started at six thirty in the morning, when Madame started fitting Nellie out in Ange's two costumes for the current act—the scarlet military-style uniform jacket with gold shoulder tassels, mini skirt, and silver boots, and the scanty green sequined dress with matching high-heeled shoes. The trouble was, Ange was three inches taller than Nellie, which meant that some pretty drastic alterations had to be made and rather fast. So, later in the morning, Ruby Catmonk was sent for, and she gladly got to work with her scissors, needle, and thread.

Most of the day, however, was taken up by a crash course in the basic art of assisting the Great Pierre. For the first hour or so, it was left to Madame to teach Nellie how to move on the stage, how to stand, how to pose, how to use all her feminine charms and how to react to the brilliant tricks as if she was seeing them for the first time. From late morning, the sitting room was cleared to make room to rehearse the act itself. From his private workroom at the top of the house, Monsieur produced various boxes, pieces of furniture, and other props that he used to practise on. For the levitation, Nellie merely had to learn how to lie like a corpse, covered from shoulders to feet with a large black sheet. Actual levitation could only take place on the stage. Nonetheless, lying absolutely still for several minutes at a time was not an easy task, despite Monsieur's somewhat sick suggestion that she should 'imagine yerself really dead, Nell'. The disappearing act was less arduous; the wooden cabinet in which the trick was performed was cunningly built to allow her to slip out of it at the rear without being noticed. 'Sawing the lady in half', however, was a nightmare. Crouching painfully inside the timber coffin, with only her head on show, she had to keep a fixed smile on her face while Monsieur began to saw and she could feel the sharp serrated blade brushing down past her knees inside. But how did he manage to show her feet, and then ask her to waggle her toes? 'Ah,' was all he would say. 'All in good time, gel, all in good time.'

When the time came for Nellie to leave for the theatre, she felt a nervous wreck. So much so that Ruby had to give her a good talking to.

'Take it in yer stride, Nell,' she said, peering over the top of her specs, her usual Capstan with all its ash intact dangling from her lips. 'But most of all, enjoy it! I mean, just look at yerself. Go on! Stop bein' so self-conscious!'

The old lady turned Nellie round so that they could both look at her in the full-length mirror.

'Don't, Rube,' Nellie protested, cringing with embarrassment at her reflection. 'I look awful!'

'Don't you believe it, gel!' scolded Ruby. 'Yer've got a neat little figure, slender 'ips, a bosom that makes Ange's look like table tennis balls, and as shapely a pair of legs as I've seen on any young gel since I was your age.'

'But I'm so small, Rube,' Nellie said with anguish. 'Just look at me, barely five feet two inches even in 'igh 'eels.'

Ruby quickly swivelled Nellie round towards

her. 'Listen ter me, young lady,' she said firmly. 'Small's beautiful! Don't yer ever ferget that. Wot you've got in these five feet two inches is worf six foot to anyone wiv a bit of know-'ow. You're a good-lookin' kid, Nell, believe me. When you walk out on that stage at first 'ouse, Bert Beckwiff's goin' ter 'ave a job stoppin' every red-blooded feller in that audience from gawpin' at yer.'

Nellie turned back to look at herself in the mirror again. 'But I'm not a performer, Rube,' she said, her face screwed up in anxiety. 'I've never wanted ter be in front of the bright lights.'

Ruby watched Nellie's reflection in the mirror again, and smiled. 'Whevver yer want ter or not, gel,' she said with more than a tinge of pride, 'ternight is *your* night!'

The first house audience was filing in. Some were still downing their drinks in the bars, while upstairs in the gods many had brought their own sandwiches. Eager faces were pressed against the brass safety rail, peering down with fascination at the rich people below. Wednesday mid-week evening shows were not traditionally the most sought-after tickets, but once again there was a capacity audience and the usual air of anticipation.

Backstage, Ange's accident in the washbasin had made it necessary for the Sisters Tapp to be moved into an alternative dressing room, which they only too willingly shared with Nellie. The atmosphere in the room was friendly and

302

cheerful as Gladys set about helping Nellie with her make-up, while Dandy worked on Nellie's hair.

'Take it from me, kiddo,' said Gladys, her Geordie accent at full throttle. 'Tonight you are going to be *the* number one sex bomb of Wood Green! Just wait till they get a whiff of you out there. There'll be a stampede to get at you!'

Both sisters laughed out loud, but not Nellie; she was too cold with terror even to smile. By the time the girls had finished with her, Nellie didn't recognise herself. Staring in the mirror, she reckoned she looked just like a tart. Thanks to the sticks of Five and Nine, she had a complexion that made her look more like Carmen Miranda in *Down Argentine Way*, and Gladys had used the deep red carmine so liberally that Nellie's lips looked as though they were bleeding. But the two sisters thought differently.

'You're a knockout!' exclaimed Dandy.

Gladys agreed. 'If I could look like that, I'd sell my body to the highest bidder!'

For a brief moment, Nellie felt just a grain of confidence. But the moment the sisters were called on stage to do their opening number, Nellie's stomach ached with panic. Now alone, she sat at the dressing table, staring in disbelief at herself in the mirror. Why had she ever allowed herself to get into this crazy nightmare? Everything inside her was telling her that the moment she set foot on that stage, she would just seize up and most probably die of fear. She tried to remember all the things Monsieur had told her—stand like this, don't react to that, never allow yourself to look as though you know what's going to happen next, always show your teeth to the audience, smile, smile, smile! She tried to focus on the rehearsal she had had on stage with both Monsieur and Madame, and she knew that climbing that suspended rope was not going to work. It was an impossible task even for someone more experienced than herself. What on earth had possessed Monsieur to ask her to do such a thing? But it was too late now. She had to go ahead with it all, regardless of how much of a fool she was going to make of herself, not to mention the celebrated name of the Great Pierre.

She focused on her reflection in the mirror again, and squirmed at the sight of herself togged up in a scarlet military tunic with gold tassels and make-up that made her look like a toy doll. And what about all those technical names that the stagehands kept throwing at her during that final rehearsal? How would she ever remember things like the gantry, the wings, spot one and mirror spot, floods, flaps, backcloth, stage left, stage right, and stage centre? It was like trying to learn Chinese. It was madness!

'Dear Nellie. Yer look t'rrific!'

Nellie looked up with a start. Madame was peering round the door at her.

'I'm so proud of you, my dear,' she said as she came across to Nellie. 'I can't tell you how grateful your dad and I are. If it wasn't for you, we'd 'ave 'ad ter withdraw from the show. It would 'ave done yer dad a great deal of 'arm, 'specially with Moss Empires and the Stoll people. Word gets around so fast.'

'Mum.' Nellie swung round on her stool to face Madame. 'I want ter ask yer just one last time,' she said, with pleading eyes. 'Are yer sure I can do this? If I let yer down, I'll never fergive meself fer the rest of me life.'

Madame gave Nellie a reassuring smile, crouched down, and taking hold of her hands said, 'Yer could never let us down, Nellie. You're one of us now. You're a Beckwiff. We're a team. All yer can do is yer best. Nobody can ask fer more.'

Nellie tried a weak smile. Then her mind started racing again. 'Wot 'appens when Ange gets well again?' she asked delicately. 'She ain't goin' ter take kindly ter me takin' on 'er job.'

Madame lowered her eyes. 'Ange won't be coming back, Nellie,' she said. 'The doctor at the hospital says her legs are going to be severely scarred for the rest of her life. There's no way she could ever appear on the stage again.' She took a deep breath, and looked up. 'She's bin a very foolish gel, Nellie. In every way.'

Nellie didn't need an explanation. She understood Madame's remark perfectly.

By seven o'clock in the evening, Nellie had begun to wonder whether the Novelty Juggler's act would ever come to an end. For twenty-five minutes or so, she had been waiting in the wings, watching the acts as they came on. Although she had seen all of them now several times, somehow they all looked so different from the side of the stage, unreal, and larger than life. She didn't dare to take a peek at the audience through the spyhole in the flaps, for if she did, she knew she would probably be sick. A few minutes before she was due to take her place on the stage, Monsieur and Madame joined her, and all three of them stood in silence waiting for the juggler's final bow.

When the moment finally came, Madame leaned across and hugged Nellie. 'Good luck, dear Nellie,' she whispered.

Monsieur squeezed her hands affectionately. 'Don't worry about a fing, gel,' he said with a wink. 'Just remember, smile, smile, smile!'

The closing music of the juggler's act played him and his assistant off stage. As they went, both of them gave Nellie a thumbs-up before disappearing to their dressing rooms.

The auditorium was in darkness. It was time for Monsieur, Madame and Nellie to take their places on stage. This was it. This was the moment of truth, the moment that Nellie had prayed would never come. Shaking from head to foot, she picked her way carefully in the dim light behind the front of house curtain, finally reaching her position at stage right. She immediately took up her pose, hands upstretched and hands dangling delicately high above her head, and her teeth bared. If anyone had approached her they would have thought she was a savage dog. To Nellie, the next few seconds were a living hell.

And then came the quivering, hissing sound of that terrible cymbal, which heralded the appearance centre stage of Monsieur, suave and sinister as ever.

'Ladies and gentlemen!'

The sound of the stage manager's voice booming out over the theatre's loudspeaker system sent a wave of panic through Nellie's body.

'The Wood Green Empire is proud to present THE GREAT PIERRE!'

As usual, the theatre erupted with applause and Monsieur bowed theatrically.

Gradually, the house curtains behind him opened to reveal Madame at her grand piano on one side of the stage, and Nellie on the other, both of them picked out in their own spotlights. Nellie was now ready to faint. The bright light was blinding her, and all she could think about was that beyond that light and all the other lights sat an audience of people who would now be watching every movement she made! Yes, she thought, the only solution was to faint. At least that was a legitimate way of getting out of this ordeal. But then she remembered what Monsieur had told her: 'Smile, Nellie! Smile, smile, smile!' Thankfully, Monsieur had changed the opening so that she did not have to appear as a figure of death, togged up in that ridiculous black hood and cloak, a device used by Ange to such effect.

Madame started to play, which was the signal for Nellie to drop her hands and arms—but not her fixed smile. The atmosphere on stage was stifling; the place was like a steam bath and it seemed as though the entire audience was smoking. But there were other smells too wafting in from the auditorium. Nellie couldn't identify them all, but she recognised cheap perfume, the familiar Zube cough sweets, cheese and pickled onions, and alcohol.

The first illusion involved the Magic Box, which Nellie had to collect, together with the small card table it was on, from the back of the stage. Although it was only a few steps from where she was standing, her legs felt like lumps of lead and she had no idea how she would get there. But somehow she managed to move and, with her fixed smile still beaming out brightly towards the audience, she placed the props over the chalk mark centre stage, where the spotlight picked it out. Then she moved to one side, followed by her own secondary spot.

As she did so, a chorus of wolf whistles and shouts of 'Cor!' echoed out from the auditorium. Nellie stopped dead and self-consciously looked down at herself, terrified that something was showing. Then she quickly glanced up at Monsieur, who had his back to the footlights, and she saw that he was grinning at her. The wolf whistles were clearly meant for her! Embarrassed, Nellie tried to slink back into the shadows, but the calls and wolf whistles from her male admirers in the audience continued, so she kept quite still and waited for the hubbub to subside. She was astonished. To think that, even for just a few seconds, she, Nellie, could be the centre of such attention! She couldn't believe that such a thing was happening to her. What was it Ruby had said to her? *'Listen ter me, young lady. Small's beautiful! Don't yer ever forget that!'*

From that moment on, Nellie found the confidence she was so desperately lacking and was gradually able to shrug off her self-consciousness. She was proud of what she'd got, and if they wanted to look at her, then good luck to 'em! In fact, she even began to enjoy herself, and as she collected the objects Monsieur pulled out of the Magic Box, she smiled and smiled and smiled out at her adoring audience for all she was worth. She was a star! Not in the same league as the Great Pierre, of course, but she had established her presence, without shame, even if it had been with a great deal of fear. At the end of the Magic Box sequence, Nellie waved her hand towards Monsieur, inviting the audience to applaud him to the rafters. She felt good, oh so good, and she resolved that never again would she let stage fright get the better of her. But even as she stood there, basking in her new-found confidence, fate decided that it still had one or two unexpected tricks up its sleeve. And the first appeared in the form of a howling wail which suddenly cut through the audience's cheers.

It was the sound of the air-raid siren.

The morning after the night before invariably brings the ring of truth, and more often shame. And so it was with Nellie. Lying in bed, exhausted by the ordeal of appearing on stage for the first time in her life, she felt nothing but shame, not only for those few exhilarating moments when she fantasised that she was a 'star', but also for the vanity of believing that she was more important during the act than the Great Pierre himself. How could she even think such a thing? she kept asking herself. She was no better than Ange. She cringed with embarrassment as she recalled herself during the first and second house performances. She hated the sight of herself, with that fixed, toothy smile, togged up in a scanty costume, with an artificial flower stuck behind her ear. It was shame-making, absolutely shame-making! She didn't want to be a 'star'. She never wanted to go on to a stage again as long as she lived, and she had every intention of begging Monsieur and Madame to find a replacement for Ange as soon as possible.

The air raid during the first house performance was the first such interruption the Wood Green Empire had had for some months, but the performance continued despite the threat of enemy action. The audience, given the choice of leaving the theatre or staying on to watch the show, decided to stay. In the event, two enemy raiders did manage to penetrate the defence system round the outskirts of London, but the only damage appeared to have been a stray bomb in Victoria Park, Hackney.

Nellie was never very good in the mornings, so she didn't get up until around eight thirty. She had a bath, got dressed, and went downstairs.

To her surprise, nobody was around. Sid

and Lenny would have already gone off to school, but there was no sign of Monsieur or Madame either, although they were usually up good and early every morning. 'Mum! Dad! Anyone at home?' she called. Still no response. Monsieur and Madame must have gone off early somewhere. She made her way to the kitchen. The moment she entered, there was a shout of 'Congratulations!' From a crowd of people gathered there: Monsieur and Madame, Sid and Lenny, Ruby Catmonk, and even Monsieur's old Home Guard mate Gus Maynard.

Madame embraced her in a tight, warm hug. 'Oh, fank yer, dear Nellie!' she said, her voice cracking with emotion. 'We were so proud of yer last night. Where would we 'ave bin if it 'adn't been fer you?'

Then old Ruby hugged her. 'What'd I tell yer?' she said with a mischievous twinkle in the eye.

Nellie was too taken aback to reply. She wanted to say that it was the most painful experience of her life, but old Gus was enthusiastically shaking her hand. 'You're a trouper, Nell, a real trouper,' he said, his eyes gleaming with admiration. 'I'm tellin' yer, that audience took to yer the moment yer set foot on that stage. Marvellous, Nell! Absolutely blinkin' marvellous!'

Sid and Lenny grabbed her round the waist and tried to make her dance with them. 'Nellie's on the music 'all! Nellie's on the music 'all!' they sang triumphantly.

'Stop it, boys!' protested Madame, trying to

restrain them. 'This poor girl's had a nerve-racking night. We've got ter give 'er a chance ter unwind.'

'Mum. Dad ...'

'Come 'ere, Nell,' said Monsieur, beaming. He took her in his arms and hugged her gently. It was not something he did very often, for he very rarely showed emotion. But this morning was different. 'Wot can I say to yer, gel?' He held her out in front of him and gazed at her admiringly. 'Last night yer showed yerself ter be a true pro—one of the best. An' Bert Beckwiff don't say that ter many people.'

'Dad,' Nellie said, 'I shouldn't've done that last night. When yer asked me ter do it, I should've said no. I had no right ter make such a fool out of yer.'

There was an immediate howl of disbelief from everyone.

'It's not true, dear!' protested Madame, and old Ruby shook her head.

'Yer saved the day, Nell!' added Gus. 'It's as plain as a pike!'

Nellie shook her head vigorously.

'Nell,' said Monsieur, 'don't yer understand? I'd never've asked yer ter do it if I thought yer couldn't. But yer did. In just one day, yer learnt enough ter go on that stage and give me the support I needed. 'Onest ter God, I'd've bin a dead duck wivout yer.'

'Gert an' Daisy said *you* was the real star of the show!' proclaimed Lenny.

'So did Billy Bennett!' added Sid.

Nellie covered her face in embarrassment.

Monsieur gently removed Nellie's hands. 'Don't be embarrassed, Nell. Every time yer do it from now on, it'll get easier. We'll 'ave lots of rehearsals. By the time we've finished, you'll be the best support on the 'alls.'

Nellie shook her head. 'No, Dad,' she replied firmly. 'I can't go on wiv it, not for ever. I'll do me best though, just till yer can find someone else.'

Monsieur exchanged an anxious look, first with his wife and then with Ruby.

'The bright lights are not fer me, Dad,' insisted Nellie. 'I don't like meself enough.'

'Plenty of uvver people do though, Nell,' chimed in old Gus. 'Take a butchers at this.' He picked up a copy of the *Daily Sketch* from the kitchen table. 'Just 'ere, down the bottom. See?'

Nellie took the newspaper.

Madame was uneasy. 'Nellie doesn't read proper yet, Gus,' she said. ''Ere, dear.' She stretched out to take the newspaper from her. 'Let me—'

'"Girl Saves Show."' Nellie was hanging on to the newspaper and reading out loud from it. '"Last night, a seventeen-year-old girl stepped in when the assistant to the Great Pierre stage act became involved in a backstage accident at the Wood Green Empire in Norf London."'

Monsieur and Madame exchanged a look of astonishment. Nellie was reading out loud, fluently, and without any help whatsoever.

'"Nellie Beckwiff,"' continued Nellie, '"who 'ad never before bin involved in featrical

313

work, took over at twenty-four 'ours' notice, ter rapturous applause from an appreciative audience. A spokesman at the featre last night was quoted as sayin' that in everyone's opinion, Nellie's cool an' professional nerve 'ad saved the Great Pierre's act from disaster. There was no doubt that she was headin' for a 'ighly colourful career in the music hall."'

Nellie lowered the newspaper and looked up at everyone. 'I've never 'eard such a lot of old cods in all me life!' she said.

'Nellie!' gasped Madame, hardly able to believe what she had just heard.

Nellie was bewildered to find everyone gawping at her. 'Wot's up?' she asked.

'Yer can read!' yelped Sid incredulously.

'All on yer own!' added young Lenny.

Nellie smiled. 'Ruby's bin teachin' me.'

'Try somefin' else, Nell,' said Monsieur, taking the newspaper from her and looking for another report for her to read. ''Ere! Try this.'

Nellie took the newspaper back from him, and after glancing at the report he was pointing to, slowly started to read out loud again: '"Berlin gets the jitters. Berliners are nightly awaitin' a raid by one thousand British bombers, as they believe their city ter be an inevitable target in the near future ..."'

Ruby listened with quiet satisfaction as Nellie continued, her pace quickening the more she read.

'I can't believe it!' cried Madame. She threw her arms round Nellie, and hugged

314

her. Everyone applauded, and patted Nellie on the back.

'It's not me that done it,' Nellie called to them all. 'There's the one that 'elped me,' she said, going across to Ruby, taking her hands and squeezing them. 'If it wasn't for Rube 'ere, I couldn't've done it. She's the best teacher anyone could ever 'ave.'

'Don't be silly, Nell,' said old Ruby, with a smile. 'I just gave yer a bit of a push, that's all. Yer've worked 'ard.'

'A few years ago, I couldn't do nuffink,' Nellie said, looking straight at her, 'I couldn't read or write, and accordin' to the Orphanage, I was 'opeless wiv all me school studies. I owe yer so much, Rube—so much.'

Madame was practically in tears. 'We all owe you, Rube,' she said, emotionally. 'Yer've given our Nellie a new lease of life. Now she can read, she can do anyfin' she wants.'

And from that time on, that is exactly what Nellie did. Between the first and second house shows at Wood Green, she read everything she could lay her hands on—newspapers, old magazines, the words on sheet music, even notices on the back of lavatory doors. Being able to read properly was like being born all over again, and once she was confident enough to read, with her mum's help, she even began to learn how to scrawl a few words. She was on her way. Thanks to Ruby Catmonk, there was no looking back.

Most rewarding of all, however, was the fact that Nellie was using her mind to the full. If learning to read and write had been one way to reach her lost memories, then losing her reluctance to talk to people about the war was another. Many a night she lay awake allowing memories of her past to come flooding back. Gradually, images appeared before her, and she could now visualise Barratts' Orphanage, and all the children and staff with whom she had shared her life.

But most of all, she remembered Miss Ackroyd. And she knew now that her life could never be fulfilled until she saw her again.

Chapter 19

Barratts' Orphanage had come up in the world. Its new premises, set in the middle of woodland just outside Harpenden in Hertfordshire, was an eighteenth-century manor house owned by an aristocratic local family. They had found the vast building too much to handle, let alone live in, so they had leased it to Hertfordshire County Council who in turn rented it to Barratts' for a minimum sum. After the stuffy, war-torn back streets of Islington, it was a veritable paradise for both children and staff. They relished the crisp, fresh air, the lush green fields and trees of every shape and size, with wonderful straggly branches that stretched up towards the sky.

Nellie reached the home after a journey from Holloway that took her the best part of three hours. She could have taken the train from Charing Cross, but as it was Sunday she decided to make a day of it and she took the Green Line bus from the Nag's Head to Barnet, a double-decker bus from there to St Albans, and a single-decker bus on to Harpenden town centre. From there, she still had a twenty-minute walk ahead of her, but it was such a glorious autumn day and she didn't mind a bit. The air was warm, and the trees and hedgerows were tinged with the most beautiful autumn hues.

As she made her way along an overgrown country lane and headed towards the big house on the other side of the fields, she was brimming with all kinds of emotions. It was well over two months now since her stage debut at the Wood Green Empire, and she had now accepted the fact that it was a way of life that she could embrace, as long as she kept her feet firmly on the ground and didn't make the same mistakes as Ange. There had only been four weekly bookings since then, which involved a tour on the Moss Empire's circuit in London and the provinces. In many ways it was quite fascinating, for she was seeing all sorts of new places and it was interesting how audiences reacted differently in different parts of the country. She was still getting wolf-whistles from the men, but in one of the older music halls in Leeds a woman in the audience had shouted out that it was a sin for a young girl like her to show her bare legs in public.

Learning how to read and write had somehow

triggered something in Nellie's memory. It had brought her past life into focus with uncanny detail. She remembered nearly every detail about the old Barratts' Orphanage in New North Road, about the staff, Mr and Mrs Mitchell, old Mrs Hare the cook, and Miss Ackroyd. Especially Miss Ackroyd. But she also remembered the children she had spent so much of her time with. Lucy, ten years old, with never a smile on her face; Jane, twelve years old, for ever drawing pictures of everything and everyone she saw; 'Big' Ben, fourteen years old, always being teased about his height, which was why he was Nellie's favourite. And then there was Lizzie, fifteen years old, the biggest troublemaker on God's earth, and Nellie's sworn enemy. But why? Try as she might, she couldn't remember any reason for the enmity between them, only that it had always been like that.

By the time she reached the huge iron gates of the big house, Nellie felt a sense of deep apprehension, and she was beginning to wonder whether it was a mistake to have written to Miss Ackroyd suggesting this visit.

The driveway was nearly half a mile long, covered in small shingle and overshadowed by tall elm trees which had already lost their fresh summer look and were now gradually beginning to shed their finely veined serrated leaves. But when the driveway finally opened out on to a wide paved courtyard, Nellie was less impressed than she had expected, for the big house was in need of urgent repairs. Some of its exterior walls were covered over with pebbledash, which robbed the vast building of its former elegance. Nonetheless, it was still a great improvement on New North Road; the grounds extended to four acres, with room for a football field for the boys, and a rounders pitch for the girls.

'Vicky!'

The sound of old Mrs Hare's voice sent a warm glow to Nellie's cheeks. There she was, running down a wide flight of steps from the house as though she was half her age. And she was exactly as Nellie remembered her, her white hair tied back in a bun behind her head, a coloured pinny tied round her vast tummy, and eyes that were as welcoming as a sun-drenched morning, despite the fact that the last time they were together, the old girl had ranted and raved at her and called her a mouthy little troublemaker!

'Oh, Vicky!' she cried, virtually sprinting towards Nellie and embracing her in a huge hug. 'I thought I'd never see you again!' Then she stood back to look at her. 'Oh, goodness, I almost forgot! It's not Vicky any more, is it? And just look at yer! You're so grown-up!'

'It's good ter see yer again, Mrs 'Are. Yer 'aven't changed a bit!'

'Vicky!'

This time it was Martha Driscoll, hurrying across the courtyard with her husband Arthur. 'Oh Vicky!' she called. 'This is wonderful, wonderful!'

'Look at her!' observed Arthur as he joined the rapidly expanding group of staff who were gathering. 'Too damned skinny! Don't they feed

319

you in the music hall?'

Laughter, tears, anxieties. Everyone wanted to see Nellie, and when some of the orphan children spotted her through the windows, she was soon in the centre of a jostling crowd. There they all were, a little older now but exactly as she remembered them—Lucy, now with a huge smile on her face, Jane, Big Ben, some of the younger kids from the upstairs dormitory, a bunch of boys she used to play football with. There were so many stories to exchange, and when Nellie first hugged Lucy, the poor girl burst into tears. It was all too much. But there was one face that Nellie was longing to see, and she didn't have to wait long. At the top of the long flight of stone steps stood Miss Ackroyd, tall and erect as ever, her short auburn hair shining in the midday autumn sun, her large soulful eyes brighter than Nellie remembered. And the moment their eyes met, they both broke out into a wide smile. Without another word, Nellie rushed through the crowd and quickly made her way up the stone steps to Miss Ackroyd.

'Hello, Nellie,' she said warmly. 'Welcome to Barratts'!'

It was a strange experience for Nellie, sitting down to Sunday lunch in Barratts' dining room with all the staff and orphans. It was as though time had stood still, as though everything was exactly the same as when she left. This time, however, she was sitting at the staff dining table, listening to that all too familiar sound of children eating their food and scraping their plates once they had finished. In some ways it was a rewarding sound, and it brought a smile to her face. As she looked up and down the trestle tables all around her, she could see herself sitting there, playing up with her mates Lucy and Jane while the staff were not looking. Subconsciously, she was also looking around to see if Lizzie Morris was amongst the faces along the trestle tables. But she wasn't there. And it made Nellie nervous. Luckily, the taste of Mrs Hare's Yorkshire pudding soon distracted her attention, as did the inevitable treacle tart and custard that followed as sure as night follows day. It was such a comforting feeling to be here, but also sad, for the children were still without a home—a real home—and none of them had the benefit of a loving family to support them. But Miss Ackroyd and the staff did all they could, and Nellie wondered what would have happened to the children if there hadn't been people like them to step in and take care of them.

After lunch, most of the children went off to play football or rounders, or take an afternoon stroll down to the beautiful lake in the grounds. This gave Ethel Ackroyd the chance to show Nellie around the place, and to speak to her alone.

'They often talk about you,' she said as they made their way towards the stream in the field behind the big house. 'Sometimes I hear the girls talk about that night, the night of the bomb, the night you made them all believe you were dead.'

'Is that what you believed?' Nellie asked.

'Not for one single moment. There was absolutely no doubt in my mind whatsoever. And when Lizzie told me that she'd seen you in the audience at the Hackney Empire, I knew that I'd find you alive somewhere.'

They reached a small and rather rickety timber bridge which stretched across the narrow stream. Pausing halfway across, they could hear the sound of some of the orphans shouting and laughing in the distance on the football field. Then both of them stopped to gaze at the water in the stream below, as it trickled over a large stone in strange kaleidoscopic patterns.

'The last time we met,' Nellie began, 'yer said fings about me that—disturbed me. Yer said I knew 'ow ter 'urt you.' She turned to look at the older woman. 'Wot did yer mean?'

Ethel hesitated before answering. 'I meant that you knew what I was going through. I've never had anyone to love me, Nellie,' she said, with difficulty. 'You knew that, but you wouldn't do anything to help.'

''Ow could I 'elp?' Nellie replied. 'I was only a kid. I din't know nuffin' about anyfin'.'

'Oh, but you did, Nellie,' insisted Ethel. 'You were always older than your years, more perceptive than anyone I've ever known. There were times when I felt I could talk to you as one woman to another, to tell you things about myself that I could never tell anyone else. But whenever I reached that point, you always shunned me and made me feel cheap.'

Nellie was consumed with guilt but she didn't

know why. 'I made yer feel cheap? Me? But 'ow? Wot did I do?'

'You ignored me, Nellie.'

Nellie was at a loss for words.

'You see, I once had a baby of my own—a little girl. It was born out of wedlock. I hardly knew the father.' Ethel was staring into the stream. 'It was a long time ago now, several years before the war, before I took over Barratts'. I didn't tell my parents. I couldn't! And so there was no one I could turn to.' The sun was glittering in the water and reflecting straight back into her eyes. 'The only solution I had was to dispose of the baby.'

Nellie was horrified. 'Yer mean yer got rid of it?'

'Yes,' replied Ethel, fighting back her emotion. 'I had an abortion. It nearly killed me.' She looked up from the stream and met Nellie's eyes. 'That's why I eventually came to Barratts'. I hoped it would be a kind of therapy, but it didn't work.' Her face was filled with anguish. 'You see, Nellie, I was always so desperate to have a husband and children, a family I could call my own. But I never knew how to do it the way other people did it. Instead I chose the first person who looked at me. It was a tragic mistake.' She took a moment to compose herself, and then continued. 'The problem was, it ruined my life. I could never have a relationship with anyone ever again. I was incapable of it. And *you* knew, Nellie. You could tell, just by looking at me. That's why you called me an old hag.'

'Oh Jesus!' Nellie said, covering her face with

her hands in horror. She remembered. Now she remembered *everything*.

'No, Nellie,' said Ethel, gently putting her hand on her arm. 'You were right. You have nothing to blame yourself for, absolutely nothing. I had no right to burden someone as young as you with my problems. It was just that you were always the only one I could trust, because you told me the truth.'

For a moment, Nellie was silent. 'I don't know what ter say,' she said, taking her hands away from her face.

'There's nothing *to* say,' said Ethel with a reassuring smile. 'But I had to tell you. You do understand that, don't you?'

Nellie paused a moment, then nodded.

Ethel smiled at Nellie again, put a comforting arm round her shoulders, and led her off the bridge. 'There is just one thing I want to ask you,' she said as they slowly moved on. 'Is it true that you wanted to run away from Barratts'?'

Nellie stopped with a start. 'Run away?' she gasped. 'Wotever d'yer mean?'

'That's what Lizzie Morris told me. She said that just a few days before the bomb explosion at Barratts', you told her that you were planning to get as far away from me as possible.'

Nellie suddenly became very angry. 'It's a lie!' she snapped. 'If she told yer that, it's a lousy, stinkin' lie!'

'But you did disappear.'

'That night,' replied Nellie, 'after the bomb

dropped, I din't know nuffin'. I didn't know who I was, where I come from or where I was goin' to. It all 'appened so quick, I din't know wot I was doin'. I never wanted ter run away from Barratts', Miss Ackroyd. I never wanted ter run away from you, nor anyone else. Yer've got ter believe me!'

They came to a halt. All around them was a vast landscape of rolling hills and green pastureland.

'I've always, believed you, Nellie,' said Ethel, the faint tones of her Yorkshire background audible. She looked at the diminutive figure at her side. 'I also love you, and admire you. Nothing will ever change that.'

Soon after tea with Miss Ackroyd, Mrs Hare, Martha and Arthur Driscoll and the rest of the staff, Nellie took her leave and made her way back to Holloway. But she left Barratts' with a heavy heart, and as she made her way along the shingled driveway towards the main gates, she turned to look back over her shoulder several times at the group of staff and orphans who had gathered to wave her off.

Nellie's day had turned out to be a mixture of elation and trauma. It was as though all those sixteen years of life had come into focus again, and as she now began the first part of her journey towards maturity, she could at least know that the shadows had been cleared, and she knew who and what she was. She found it a rewarding experience to see all those freshly scrubbed faces watching her as she ate lunch with the staff in the dining room. There was so much hope there, hope that their lives would tread the same lucky path as hers had. She did consider herself lucky, for she had found people who wanted her, and cared for her, people who were not prepared to see her spend the rest of her days in the care of an institution. And then she thought about Miss Ackroyd, and the candid way she had taken her into her confidence. As Nellie hurried along, all the old emotions of her childhood days came flooding back. How she loved all her mates back there in the dormitory, the late-night giggles, the fights and quarrels, the sharing of news and gossip about the staff, and, most of all, the feeling of just being together. But then she thought of Lizzie Morris, that sly creature who knew of her special bond of friendship with Miss Ackroyd, and who had done everything in her power to drive a wedge between them. It was Lizzie who had lied to Miss Ackroyd that she planned to run away, Lizzie who had made up stories to the other teachers about the awful things she was supposed to have said about them. Why, oh why did she do it? Nellie kept asking herself. Her instinct was to hate Lizzie, but at the same time she felt sorry for her. After all, like most of the children at the orphanage, Lizzie did not know what it was like to be loved and cared for by a family.

Ten minutes later, Nellie reached the main gates. As she opened and closed them behind her, she heard someone calling to her.

'Vicky!'

Running down the driveway towards her was the slight figure of a teenage girl wearing a dazzling white ankle-length dress with hemline frills. Nellie didn't have to look twice to know who it was, for she immediately recognised that round, insipid, doll-like complexion, and that long auburn hair that was now tied back with a white ribbon. It was Lizzie Morris.

'Vicky! Don't go!' As Lizzie reached the gate, she pressed her face up against it.

Nellie watched her in silence, a look of revulsion on her face. Then she slowly moved towards her.

For a moment the two girls stared at each other. Then Lizzie pushed her hand between the iron bars of the gate and stretched her arm out as far as it would reach.

Nellie watched her impassively. She hated that face more than any other she knew. But as she drew closer, her only action was to take hold of Lizzie's hand and shake it.

Then, without saying a word, she calmly turned and walked off.

During the next few weeks, Nellie continued to work on her role as assistant to the Great Pierre, and, as Monsieur had promised, the more she practised, the easier it became. She had now got used to the nightly ritual of climbing a rope, disappearing from a wooden cabinet, and being sawn in half, but she was never comfortable watching Gus Maynard fire that revolver at Monsieur. In fact, once or twice Monsieur had had to scold her for anticipating the shot by flinching before the wretched thing had even been fired.

During the second week of September, Nellie had her eighteenth birthday. The act had been booked in for a week at the Metropolitan Music Hall in Edgware Road, so the usual two evening shows had to be got through on the day she turned eighteen but this did not deter Madame from organising some lavish celebrations for her newly adopted daughter. In the morning, Nellie came downstairs to be given her first anklelength evening dress, made of navy blue velour and bought quite legitimately with Madame's own clothing coupons with the advice and connivance of Ruby Catmonk. Monsieur's gift was a row of imitation pearls to go with the dress, and Sid and Lenny contributed to a black evening bag, made by Ruby, and decorated with small white shirt buttons. Her special treat of the day was to be taken to her old workplace, Beales, for lunch. A delicious three-course meal, including boiled scrag end of beef, had been secretly organised by Madame with Nellie's former boss, Mrs Wiggins, who was genuinely thrilled to see how Nellie was blooming into such a lovely, well-composed young lady.

The biggest treat of the day was yet to come, for after the second house show in the evening an eighteenth birthday party had been arranged by Monsieur. Among the invited guests was the much-loved star of the show, the female impersonator from Lancashire, Norman Evans. Both he and all the show's supporting acts contributed a few bob towards a birthday present for Nellie, which turned out to be a framed poster of the week's theatre programme. She was thrilled, because her own name, Nellie Beckwith, had now been included in the billing beneath that of the Great Pierre and Madame. There was no cake, as the sugar ration did not stretch to such wartime luxuries, but once the front of house curtain had been raised, a table was set out on the stage containing sausage rolls, spam, cheese, and sardine sandwiches, a large fruit trifle made by Madame, and plenty of quart bottles of brown and light ale, stout, Guinness, and R. White's lemonade and Tizer. There were also one or two bottles of gin and whisky, which had been bought from the theatre bar before the first house show.

When it came to the birthday toast, Monsieur had an important announcement to make.

'Ladies and gents,' he bellowed. 'I'd like yer all ter raise yer glasses ter one of the sweetest little gels that ever walked the stage of the good old Met. Our Nellie has bin in our family now fer the best part of a year, and I tell yer, me, Doris an' the two boys don't know 'ow we've done wivout 'er yer all this time.'

There were cries of ''Ear 'ear!'

Monsieur turned to Nellie and addressed her directly. 'No, but seriously, Nell, bringin' you inter the family was the best fing we ever done. Yer mum an' I are proud ter 'ave yer as our daughter, and young Sid and Lenny 'ere don't know their luck gettin' a sister who can box the daylights out of any bloke twice 'er size!'

He waited for the laughter to die down, then continued.

'An' so, everyone, I'd like yer ter raise yer glass to our daughter, Nell, on 'er birfday. 'Ere's to yer, Nell. 'Appy birfday, and Gawd bless yer!'

Everyone raised their glasses and said, 'Appy birfday, Nell!' Then they all joined in a rousing chorus of 'Happy Birthday to you' which echoed out into the empty auditorium.

'Oh, yes, an' before I ferget,' said Monsieur over the hubbub, 'I've got some good news for yer, Nell. Me an' yer mum 'ave got an ENSA tour booking. We're goin' up norf—somewhere your way, Norman. Wot's more, they've agreed ter let us take you along too, Nell!'

This brought a burst of applause from the guests.

'Me?' Nell gasped. 'Are yer sure, Dad? I mean, I fawt they didn't want yer takin' a gel assistant wiv yer round the army camps.'

'Well, they do now,' replied Monsieur.

'If I was you, Bert,' called Norman Evans in the same disapproving female voice that he used in his 'Over the Garden Wall' act, 'I'd keep that girl handcuffed to yer, mornin', noon. an' night!'

This brought howls of laughter, and one or two wolf whistles from some of the stagehands.

'It'll be lovely 'avin' yer wiv us, Nellie,' said Madame. 'It's really thrillin' fer yer dad an' me.'

'Can't do wivout yer, Nell,' added Monsieur. 'Let's face it, you're part of the act now.'

He had hardly spoken when a voice called from the wings, 'Now ain't that nice. All comfy an' cosy.'

Everyone turned. It was Monsieur's former assistant, Ange.

There was an immediate hush as everyone watched Ange limp across the stage, her legs covered in thick surgical stockings. She came to a halt directly in front of Monsieur. 'Got it all nice an' sewn up now, eh, Albert?' she said acidly, a nasty grin on her face. 'Congratulations!'

Then she moved towards Nellie. As she did so, the other guests made way for her to pass.

'An' you, little Miss Wide-Eyes,' she said stingingly. 'Got it made, ain't yer, mate? Just wot you wanted.' And with a chuckle she added, 'Well, we'll soon see about that, won't we?'

Chapter 20

Nellie's first experience as an ENSA artiste came during November and the first two weeks in December, when she toured with Monsieur and Madame around some of the army bases in the North of England. It was hardly an easy assignment, for although the Navy, Army, and Air Force Institutes (NAAFI) provided the transport for artistes, the journeys were often undertaken in cold, unheated vans.

Most of the shows were played in quite small

venues such as NAAFI canteens, camp cinemas, or even the back of army lorries, so there was no room for the more elaborate stage props used in Monsieur's Great Pierre act. A far simpler routine and more moderate illusions had to be worked out, which included the disappearing white rabbit, strange electrical tricks, and even a 'second sight' item, which was a new and complicated routine. The ENSA revue they had joined for the tour was called 'Fickled Pink'. It was headed by a second-rate quick-fire comedian with the stage name 'Fickle Fred', whose act consisted mainly of an endless stream of jokes about his mother-in-law. Fred was always jealous of his supporting acts, and he was well-known for his wandering hands, so when Monsieur accepted his next six-week ENSA contract, he made quite sure it was not part of 'Fickle Fred's' company. As far as Monsieur was concerned, Nellie had quite enough lechers among the soldiers to cope with!

In March the following year, the Great Pierre road show was devised as a self-contained ENSA revue which used magic and mystery and song and dance in equal proportions. Monsieur was in charge of the show, and for support he took along the Sisters Tapp, a nimble-fingered accordion player called 'Maestro' Jack Pickle, and two rather po-faced balladeers named Ellington Manners and Millicent Withers. It turned out to be a winning combination; the armed services, which on this occasion included both RAF and army bases in southern England, lapped it up.

Having the Sisters Tapp in the company was a great comfort to Nellie. They had done much to help her overcome her stage fright before her terrifying debut at the Wood Green Empire only a few months before, and they had also shown her solid support when Ange had given her such a hard time while she was still Monsieur's assistant. Nellie had taken it for granted that after Ange's accident the Beckwith family would no longer be troubled by this vile-tempered troublemaker. But she was mistaken. Since the night Ange had appeared, uninvited, at her eighteenth birthday party, things had gone from bad to worse. Ange knew her stage career was over but she was determined that Monsieur was not going to get off so lightly. She wanted more from Monsieur than words of sympathy and a quick brush-off, and that meant just one thing—money. Nellie was not sure how much Madame knew about what was going on between Monsieur and Ange, but given the way in which Monsieur had been behaving since that ugly scene on stage at the old Met, Nellie feared the worst; she was convinced that her dad was being blackmailed by this troublemaking little bitch. However, until she found some way to help, all she could do was give as much love and support as she could to her newly adopted mum and dad.

During the last week of March, Nellie's life took an unexpected turn. The show was due to appear at a small RAF airfield in Kent, near the south coast. The airfield was called Hawkinge, and had been one of the foremost Battle of

Britain bases during the Blitz, but as visiting artistes were never allowed to reveal to anyone the location of camps where they performed, Nelly never asked where the show was taking place from one location to the next. What she did know was that on this occasion it would be performed in the NAAFI canteen before an audience of young airmen and women of all ranks.

As usual, they were a pretty rowdy lot, and the Sisters Tapp and Nellie both soon realised that the 'boys in blue' were no less licentious than members of the other armed services. But they were a courageous bunch of young people, many of them not much older than Nellie herself, who had been plunged into the thick of the fighting at a moment's notice, and been part of that immense effort to protect Britain's skies from the Luftwaffe. The show was a huge success including the accordion virtuoso 'Maestro' Jack Pickle, but also those endearing songsters, Ellington Manners and Millicent Withers, who, resplendent in full evening wear, launched into a fine rendition of 'songs old and new', which brought everyone joining in with them, despite the odd rowdy hoot, jeer, or whistle from one or two well-tanked-up young fighter pilots. However, as ever, the Great Pierre was the real hit of the show, involving the participation of some members of his blue tunic audience, whilst Madame clanged out background music on her well-battered upright piano. Needless to say, the most vocal reception was reserved for Nellie, who was wearing a brand new mini dress in pastel blue specially made for the road show by Ruby.

After the show, everyone who had taken part was invited to have drinks in the officers' mess, but at this stage of the tour Nellie was beginning to feel the strain of the daily routine of travelling from one base camp to another, doing a show, then being given hospitality by the same good-natured but repetitive kind of officers, so she declined.

Making her way back to her accommodation, which had been provided in the WAAF officers' quarters nearby, she paused for a moment on the parade ground between the NAAFI canteen and the building she was making for. It was a bitterly cold evening, and over her flimsy stage costume she wore a thick uniform topcoat, which she had been lent by a well-meaning squadron leader. The early spring moon was managing to show itself for only a few seconds at a time as it popped in and out of fast-moving clouds, The atmosphere inside the canteen had been unbearably stifling, for practically every serviceman and servicewoman seemed to be smoking. So, despite the cold, Nellie stood there briefly, taking in long, deep lungfuls of the crisp night air.

'Halt! Who goes there?'

Nellie nearly jumped out of her shoes with fright. Two dark silhouettes were standing right in front of her, shining a torch beam directly into her eyes.

'I say again' said the deep male voice, 'who goes there?

'It's me, Nellie,' she replied, teeth chattering with cold. 'Nellie Beckwiff.'

'ID card!' demanded a second male voice. 'On the double!'

Nellie's heart missed a beat. She had come out tonight without the green ENSA identification card that she had been instructed to carry on her at all times while on Government premises. 'I ain't got it wiv me,' she replied nervously. 'I left it back on me bed.'

'ID card number!' barked the second voice.

Nellie was now in a right two and eight. Surely these two idiots knew who she was. 'Don't be stupid! I can't remember me bleedin' number!' she protested. 'I've just come from the NAAFI. We've bin doin' the show—'

'You're under arrest!' growled the first voice.

'Wot?'

'At the double, intruder!' snarled the second voice.

'Intruder?' yelled Nellie. 'I'm not a bleedin' intruder. 'Ere, where yer takin' me?'

'To the guard room,' growled the first voice.

Before she had a chance to protest further, Nellie found her arms grabbed on either side by the two shadowy figures.

'Left, right, left, right, left!' bawled both men simultaneously as they frogmarched Nellie across the parade ground. 'Come on now! Get those feet up!'

'Lemme go! Lemme go!' spluttered Nellie, who had by now forgotten how cold she was. 'Wait till I tell your CO! 'Elp!'

A door was opened and Nellie found herself

being shoved inside some kind of building. The door slammed shut behind her. She began to panic, for she knew that the guard house at the main gates was in a completely different direction to where she had been taken. Now, left alone in total darkness, she feared the worst. Was this some prank by a bunch of randy young airmen who had got carried away by the sight of a few scantily clad girls in the show they had just seen? Yes, she tried to convince herself. That's what this was all about. She was sure she'd heard about this kind of thing happening to showgirls before. But why should they be frustrated when they had all those girls in Air Force blue around the place? It just didn't make sense. She could feel warmth coming from somewhere but she was still shivering with fear and apprehension. 'Is anyone there?' she yelled. 'Can anyone 'ear me?'

There was a movement behind her and a light was suddenly switched on. She turned with a start, to find a shadowy figure in uniform, arms crossed, sizing her up from the other side of the room. She was in some kind of an office, blackout curtains drawn at the windows.

''Ere, you!' she snapped, trying her best to sound tough. 'Who d'yer fink yer are bringin' me 'ere like this! I know your CO. Just wait till I see 'im!'

There was no response from the shadowy figure.

'Did yer 'ear wot I said?' Nellie shouted.

'Honestly, Nell,' came the shadowy figure's

337

voice, with a chuckle. 'You haven't changed a bit.'

Even before the figure stepped into the light, Nellie recognised that familiar, cultured voice. 'Toff!' she gasped. *'You!'* She lunged at him, spurting, 'Yer rotten sod! Yer set me up!' She didn't know whether to pummel him with her fists or to throw her arms round him. In the event, he solved the problem for her. He grabbed hold of her, pulled her to him, and hugged her tightly. In those few seconds, everything that had happened to her during those few eventful weeks with the vacs gang came flooding back—the dark, dingy nights down the air-raid shelter at the old furniture store, the endless jobs sniffing for food in people's homes, the constant danger of shrapnel, and above all the gang members themselves, living rough on the streets day after day, night after night, an utterly pointless existence. And then she thought of Rats and Bonkers, brought down in a hail of machine-gun bullets from an enemy aircraft as they tried to rescue a small kitten.

With her face pressed firmly against Toff's chest, she could smell the shaving cream he used and the Players No.1 tobacco smoke on the rough serge of his blue uniform jacket. After a moment, she looked up at him. He was smiling that smile again, the same one that had always made her feel so helpless every time their eyes met. At that moment, she would not have protested if he had wanted to kiss her. But they had never actually kissed before, and the last time they were together had been a deeply distressing experience. 'Wot're yer doin' 'ere then?' she asked. 'When d'yer get off the streets?'

'That was a long time ago, Nell,' he replied. 'A lifetime ago.' He was staring straight into her eyes. 'After what happened to Rats and Bonkers, none of us could face living out on the streets any more.'

'All of you?'

Toff nodded. 'There was no point. I went back home. It wasn't easy. My parents found it hard to forgive what I'd done. But we got over it. As soon I was eighteen I got my call-up papers. I joined the RAF.'

Nellie looked over his uniform to see if he had any flash tags. 'Are yer an officer?'

Toff laughed. 'No, Nell. Just one of the boys. I work here, in the Central Registry. We're not all flight crew. Some of us have to do the office work.'

Nellie was surprised. With his posh voice and cultured ways, she found it hard to believe that he was just a penpusher.

'I missed you, Nell,' Toff said quietly. 'I never forgave myself for the way I talked to you.'

He was stooping as he looked at her, and their lips were very close.

Nellie lowered her eyes. 'It wasn't just you,' she replied. 'It was everyfin'. Wot 'appened ter Rats an' Bonkers was more than I could take.'

Toff's mouth curved into an admiring smile. 'Well, you seem to have made the right decision,' he said, his eyes moving over her face and curled

339

hair. 'You look wonderful.'

Nellie suddenly remembered Patrick and felt uneasy. She gently pulled away. 'A lot of water's passed under the bridge since I last saw yer. The Great Pierre and his missus are my mum an' dad now. They adopted me.'

'Yes, I know,' replied Toff.

'Yer know? 'Ow?'

Toff fumbled around on a desk for his cigarettes. 'I know everything that's happened to you since you left,' he said. 'Right back to your job at Beales Restaurant.'

'Wot?'

'It wasn't easy to let go of you, Nell,' he said. 'A lot of friends helped me keep track of you.'

Nellie took a long, hard look at him. He was as tall and thin as she remembered him, with the same slight slant to his eyes, and rich black hair. In the stark light of the single electric light bulb, his skin looked almost olive coloured, and it was the first time she had noticed that his eyebrows were as dark as his hair. 'Yer knew where I was,' she said in a strained, incredulous voice, 'an' yet yer never come ter see me?'

'No, Nell,' replied Toff, lighting his cigarette. 'I felt I hadn't the right. I blamed you for what happened to Rats and Bonkers. I was wrong. I had no right to be part of your life.' He turned to look directly at her again. 'But I never stopped thinking about you, or wanting you.'

Nellie was embarrassed. 'It's bin good seein' yer again, Toff,' she said with an awkward smile. Then she turned to the door.

340

'No!' said Toff, hurrying to head her off. 'Don't go, please.'

'Look, Toff,' Nellie said, 'we ain't seen each uvver fer two years now. That's a long time. We ain't kids no more. Two years makes a big diff'rence. We begin ter see the future, ter know wot it's goin' ter mean one day, an' 'ow we'll cope wiv it. You say yer never stopped finkin' 'bout me.' She flicked her eyes down, then up again. 'Well, I fawt about you too, Toff. I used ter lie awake wonderin' where yer was each night, or whevver yer was even still alive. When I got me memory back, I was over the moon. I wanted ter tell yer 'bout it, but then I remembered 'ow yer looked at me that night when Rats an' Bonkers ... Yer looked at me wiv such 'ate. I know we only knew each uvver fer a few munffs, but the only fing I could remember was that look. Yer should 'ave come after me, Toff. If yer knew where I was, yer should've come after me.'

She turned and opened the door. But the moment she did so, Toff slammed it closed again. And in one swift movement he pinned her against the door and kissed her. It was a hard, passionate kiss, and as Nellie felt the moisture on his lips mingling with her own, a wave of excitement swept through her body.

When Toff finally pulled away, he rested his chin on her shoulder. 'Nell,' he whispered in her ear, 'I want to tell you something. Those few months, the months we spent together, it was like I'd known you all my life. What you and I endured together during those few months would have been like a lifetime to anyone else. We grew up before our time, Nell. War makes savages out of innocent people. But we survived. We've got to go on surviving.'

He leaned down, and kissed her again. When their lips parted, he whispered. 'This time, I won't let you go, Nell. Whatever happens from now on, I'll never let you go.'

At the end of the six-week ENSA contract, Monsieur, Madame, and Nellie arrived home to some unnerving rumours that Hitler was about to renew his aerial onslaught on London and the Home Counties. During the past month, there had already been a series of hit-and-run air raids on targets in the south-east, and some of the Nazi bombers had even penetrated the Greater London area, where single-engined fighters and fighter bombers had machine-gunned streets, a hospital, and a railway station. At least a dozen people had been killed, which prompted the authorities to issue warnings to everyone to be prepared for further attacks. All this came as quite a blow to the Beckwith family, for during the lull in air raids over the past months, Monsieur in particular had assumed that life was now back to normal and that the music hall was at the centre of that life. Nellie did not take such a view, and the moment she got back to Tufnell Park Road, she, Sid, and Lenny set about pumping rainwater out of the old Anderson shelter, which, due to lack of use, had filled up over the past few months.

A stack of mail was waiting for Monsieur.

Madame recognised Ange's handwriting on three of the envelopes, but didn't mention it when she handed them over to her husband. Nellie suspected what was going on, and she prayed that her mum knew nothing, for it would break the poor woman's heart. If it was true that Ange really was blackmailing Monsieur, Nellie was determined to do something about it. That little tart had to be put in her place once and for all.

Since her accident, Ange had been living in a basement flat in Harvest Road which was a quiet back street just off the main Hornsey Road. It was mid-afternoon when Nellie got there, and the first thing she noticed was that the blackout curtains at the front room windows were drawn, which was odd, since it was still a couple of hours before blackout time. After taking a deep breath, she opened the small iron gate, which squeaked mercilessly, and made her way down a few stone steps that were badly in need of repair. The small yard in front of the basement bow windows smelt of cat's pee, and there were tall weeds growing between the cracked paving stones which were littered with household rubbish. There was no bell or knocker, so she tapped on the door.

To her surprise, the door was opened immediately by Ange. She was wearing a long cotton dressing gown, a fag in her mouth. 'Well, if it ain't little Miss Wide-Eyes,' she snorted. 'Wot you doin' 'ere?'

'Come ter see yer, Ange,' replied Nellie, determined not to be provoked. ''Aven't seen yer since me birfday. I was wond'rin' 'ow you're gettin' on.'

''Ow very fawtful of yer,' Ange replied. 'Who sent yer? The boss, I 'ope.'

'No one sent me, Ange.'

Ange sized Nellie up for a moment. 'Yer'd better come in then.' She stood back to let her enter.

There were more smells in the small passage that led from the front door to the back yard. Nellie thought it smelt a bit like clothes that had just been ironed, and her guess was right, for when she followed Ange into the front room, an ironing board was set up there and a pile of clothes awaiting attention was heaped on a chair. It was quite dark with the blackout curtains drawn; the only light was provided by a battered looking standard lamp.

'Can't offer yer any tea, I'm afraid,' Ange said. 'Got no more ration coupons left till the weekend. But yer can sit down if yer like.'

'Fanks,' replied Nellie, trying to find somewhere that didn't have a pile of washing on it. She plumped for an armchair, after first allowing Ange to remove a soldier's army tunic that had been thrown there. 'So, 'ow's it goin', Ange?' she asked amicably. 'Legs 'ealed up OK?'

'You din't come 'ere ter talk about me legs,' said Ange abrasively. 'Wot d'yer want?'

Nellie paused a moment, then smiled. 'I fawt I'd ask you the same question, Ange. Wot's goin' on between you an' my dad?'

Ange roared with laughter. 'Yer *dad!* Ha!

That's a good one, that is. Wanna know somefin', Nell?' she said, hands on hips, fag in mouth, leaning down at Nellie. 'Yer should've stayed at that kids' 'ome. Yer wouldn't 'ave ter worry about randy ol' buggers there.'

Nellie's face hardened. 'Yer've bin writin' 'im letters,' she said calmly but firmly. 'Wot about?'

'None of yer business. Not yet anyway.'

'Is 'e givin' yer money?'

'Better ask *'im,* 'adn't yer?'

Nellie didn't like this conversation but she was determined to get the truth out of this little cow. 'I bet 'e gave yer money ter 'elp yer recuperate after yer accident!'

Again, Ange was amused. 'Is that what 'e told yer? Well 'e's a liar. That's wot your dad is. 'E's a piss-achin' liar!'

Nellie was getting angry. 'Don't talk about my dad like that, Ange!'

'OK, OK,' replied Ange, the picture of fair play. 'If that's wot 'e told yer, then you go right ahead an' believe 'im.'

At that moment, Nellie suddenly caught a glimpse of someone sneaking along the corridor outside. It was a well-built young man, bare-chested, with tattoos on his upper and lower arms, and wearing army trousers. Her eyes flicked back to Ange. 'Are yer tryin' ter blackmail my dad, Ange?'

For some reason, the word blackmail infuriated Ange. 'Look, mate,' she snapped, 'I don't *blackmail* anybody! But if they take advantage of me, they 'ave ter pay fer it!'

'In wot way did 'e take advantage of yer?' Nellie asked, her voice calm and controlled.

Ange tried to stare Nellie down, then she grinned. 'I'll tell yer somefin', after wot your lovin' dad 'as done, I reckon 'e must really 'ave the 'ots fer me.'

Nellie sat there staring at Ange, her face quite impassive. She had nothing but disdain and loathing for this dirty little go-getter. The very room she was sitting in smelt of Ange, her ironing, the ashtrays that were overflowing with cigarette butts, the half-empty beer glasses that hadn't been washed. The windows probably hadn't been opened in months. She decided to call Ange's bluff. 'You're a liar, Ange,' she said boldly. 'You're a liar, and yer know it!'

Ange's face went taut. Without looking at Nellie, she went to one of the overflowing ashtrays and stubbed out her fag. Then she went to a built-in cupboard at the side of the tiled fireplace. She found what she was looking for almost immediately. When she returned, she had a photo in her hand, which she held out to Nellie. 'Take a butchers at that,' she said triumphantly.

For a brief moment, Nellie kept her eyes on Ange's face. Then she took the photo and looked at it. It was of Monsieur, stretched out on some grass, lying in what appeared to be an uncompromising clinch with Ange.

'My friend yer just saw,' said Ange, ''e's a photographer in the army. Seein' 'ow the Great Pierre is so famous, seein' as 'ow 'e's always

346

bein' written up as such a lovin' family man, my friend reckons that picture could be worf quite a bit ter the papers. Specially the *News of the World* or the *People.*' She leaned down closer to relish Nellie's reaction. 'Wot der you fink, Nell?'

Nellie was in despair. Lying in bed in the early hours of the morning, she had to face the fact that Monsieur really had been involved with that cow of a girl. It was deeply depressing. As she lay, tossing and turning in the dark, the sight of that repulsive photo was like a recurring nightmare. Although Ange's flat was no more than fifteen minutes away from Tufnell Park Road, Nellie had taken the longest route back, wandering aimlessly around the little back streets behind the Nag's Head, fearful of how she would appear when she saw her dad again. Luckily, however, when she got home, she discovered that Monsieur and Madame had gone out for the evening. Madame had left her a piece of home-cooked dried egg and sausage tart to heat up in the oven, but she left it on the table and went to bed soon after nine o'clock.

It turned out to be a sleepless night. She kept asking herself how her dad had got himself involved with a bit of trash like Ange. Surely it must have been obvious to him, as it was to everyone else, that Ange was only interested in using him to further her own ambitions. Madness! Sheer madness! But Ange was clever, there was no doubt about that. She had exploited Monsieur's middle-aged vanity and would now use it to destroy both his marriage and his career in the music hall. Nellie's heart ached for Madame, for her mum. She now suspected that Madame knew everything that had been going on between her husband and that girl, she had probably known since it first started. It was heartbreaking.

Eventually, Nellie got out of bed. If sleep wouldn't come, there was no point in fighting it. She crossed to the window and pulled back one of the blackout curtains. It was a dark night; the sky had been invaded by thick black clouds and there was no sign of either the moon or stars. Her attention suddenly focused on the back garden below. To her astonishment, she could see a chink of light coming from the tiny entrance to the Anderson shelter, which was a wartime offence and also a dangerous invitation to any enemy aircraft. Quickly replacing the blackout curtain, she put on her dressing gown and slippers, and hurried downstairs.

When Nellie got to the conservatory, she found the back garden door wide open, which alarmed her. She collected the spare torch which was always kept on the ledge above the flower pots and made her way out into the garden.

It was a typical April night outside, with a stiff, ice-cold breeze battering the small back gardens along Tuffnell Park Road. Many of the early spring flowers were struggling to stay upright. Nellie pulled her dressing gown tightly round her.

As she approached the Anderson, she could see the protective blackout curtain which hung across the entrance flapping in the breeze, causing the light inside to be clearly visible. Obviously the Anderson door had been left open, which was odd. Peering in round the curtain, she was momentarily dazzled by the white glare of the paraffin lamp. There was an unpalatable smell of paraffin and gin. To her amazement, Madame was propped up in a canvas chair, her head lolling to one side. 'Mum!' she called, quickly climbing down the three steps into the stifling atmosphere of the shelter. 'Wot're yer doin' 'ere, Mum? Wotever are yer doin'?'

Madame's head suddenly straightened up, but she had difficulty focusing on Nellie.

'Mum, dear,' Nellie said gently, squatting beside her. She took the empty glass from Madame's hand. 'Wot're yer doin' down 'ere, all on yer own, in the cold? Come ter bed now, Mum. Come on ...'

Madame's eyes opened enough to be able to see who was talking to her. And then she smiled. 'No point, Nell,' she muttered, only just comprehensible. 'It's 'er 'e wants, not me,' and her head toppled over to one side again.

As Nellie tried to hold her in her arms, the same words came spluttering out over and over again.

'It's 'er 'e wants, not me ... not me ...'

Chapter 21

The crisis that was looming within the Beckwith family seemed inevitable. Fortunately, Monsieur had been fast asleep in bed during Madame's agonised outburst in the Anderson shelter, but in the cool light of day, Nellie realised that the time had come for her to have a heart to heart chat with her mum. The opportunity didn't come until the following afternoon, when they were able to slip away and have afternoon tea in the the cafe restaurant of the Gaumont Cinema on the corner of Tufnell Park Road. Decorated in Art Deco style, with potted palms and crystal chandeliers, the cafe was situated at the top of an ornate staircase which curved up to the mezzanine floor overlooking the spacious foyer below.

'I'm really sorry fer the way I be'aved last night, Nell,' said Madame with a pained expression. 'I've always tried ter keep this from the family, but just lately, well, it's all bin gettin' just too much fer me ter take.'

Nellie waited for the waitress to put down the tea tray, and then stretched across to hold Madame's hand. 'Yer shouldn't've kept it to yerself, Mum,' she said. 'Remember, I'm yer daughter. Yer can talk ter me about anyfin'.'

Madame tried hard to smile. But her eyes

were still red from a night of tears and heavy drinking. 'I know, dear,' she said. 'I know.'

Nellie poured her a cup of tea. 'Right. Now tell me,' she said, being very practical. 'When did yer first find out about all this?'

Madame sat back in her chair, and sighed. 'Oh, a long time ago, Nell. It seems ages now—before you come inter the family. The funny part is, when yer dad was lookin' round fer a gel ter 'elp 'im in the act, I was the one who chose Ange. She seemed such a pretty little fing, so sweet an' considerate.'

Nellie pulled a face. This was hardly the way she would have described Ange.

'But then,' continued Madame, 'after she'd bin wiv us just a few weeks, I noticed the way she kept lookin' at Albert. It was—too intimate. But the funny fing was, Ange always made more of it when I was around, as though she wanted me ter notice.'

While they talked, cinema-goers were leaving the afternoon film, and slowly making their way up the grand staircase to the mezzanine.

'Anyway, the first time I knew somefin' was goin' on was when we was doin' a week's contract up norf, at the Liverpool Empire. I caught a glimpse of 'er wiv 'er arms round his neck, just be'ind the flats on stage before the show.'

'Wos that the only time?' Nellie asked.

'Oh no,' replied Madame. 'I seen 'em doin' it lots of times since then—all over the place.'

'Wot about Dad?' Nellie asked. 'Does 'e know yer've seen all this goin' on?'

351

'I've no idea,' replied Madame, taking a sip of tea. 'But *she* does.'

Nellie's mind went back to that time at the Theatre Royal in Drury Lane when she had caught a glimpse of Monsieur and Ange together backstage. She remembered how Monsieur had had his back to her and might not have known that she was there. But Ange certainly did. 'Mum,' she asked, ''ave yer ever 'ad this out wiv Dad?'

Madame sighed again and shook her head.

'Why not? Wouldn't it've bin best to bring it all out in the open?'

'Yes,' replied Madame, rather primly, 'I've no doubt it would, Nell. But I 'ave the family ter consider. I don't want ter break up my family. They mean too much ter me.' She picked up her spoon and although there was no sugar in her tea, she began to stir it. 'Me only 'ope is that, in time, 'e'll feel the same way too.'

'I still think yer should talk ter 'im,' Nellie said, leaning across the table to her.

'You're very young, Nell,' she said with a faint smile. 'One day you'll know wot men feel when they're worried about gettin' older. They look fer change, fer somefin' new. When a younger woman comes along an' flatters 'em, they get restless, it reminds 'em of when they was young. I s'pose it's the same wiv some women too. When yer get ter a certain age, yer want love an' attention.' She stopped stirring her cup of tea and replaced the spoon in the saucer. 'It's easy ter fall in love, Nell, but it's much harder ter 'ang on ter it. As far as I'm concerned, if

352

Bert wants ter rock the boat, then 'e must do so. But as long as I still love 'im, *I* never will.'

Nellie was upset. 'Dad *does* love yer, Mum,' she said firmly. 'Wotever yer do, yer must never fink uvverwise. Fer some reason or anuvver, Dad's got 'imself in a mess. An' between us, we're goin' ter find a way ter get 'im out of it.'

On Sunday morning, Nellie played football in Finsbury Park with Sid and Lenny's team, the Tufnell Tigers. It wasn't her ideal way of spending a Sunday morning, but her two young brothers had conned her into it several weeks before when they had discovered, quite accidentally, that she had a pretty nifty right foot which could spin a ball into the net past even the best goalie. At first, the other members of the Tufnell Tigers were sceptical that a girl could have any talent on a football field, but the moment they saw her in action, she was in. Every team they had played since had complained that it was against the rules for a girl to play in a boys' game, but when they realised that she could dribble and foul with the best of them, they grudgingly accepted her.

This week they were playing a team called the Enkel Warriors which was made up of boys from some of the back streets behind the Nag's Head. During the match, Nellie caused the referee to give her a warning—she had punched one of the players on the head with her fist for stamping on her foot with his studded boots. There were always injuries at every Sunday morning match;

Sid invariably came home with either a gash on his leg or a black eye and, more recently, Lenny had lost a front tooth, which left a nasty gap. Lenny was a bit off colour during the match, and when he came off the field he had a hacking cough, so Nellie decided to get the two boys home as quickly as possible.

It was a twenty-minute walk from the park back to Tufnell Park Road, and on the journey along the busy Seven Sisters Road, Nellie thought she would sound out her two young brothers on what they knew, if anything, of the difficult situation that existed between their mum and dad. She felt that the two boys were old enough to talk sensibly about family matters, and if they were conscious of anything going on, she would do her best to reassure them. But when she carefully started to ask them oblique questions, the response was unexpected.

'Trouble wiv Mum is she boozes too much.' said Sid, bouncing the team's football as they strolled along.

Nellie was taken aback. 'Sid! That's not a nice fing ter say. Yer know Mum don't drink booze.'

Both boys laughed.

'Not much!' said Lenny, who was trying to control another fit of coughing.

'You should see 'er sometimes durin' the night,' added Sid. 'She can 'ardly stand up.'

Sid's comment sent a chill down Nellie's back. Even though she knew about Madame's drinking, she thought it best to sound surprised. 'Yer've seen Mum drinkin'?' she asked.

'Course,' said Sid. 'Lots of times. I was 'ungry once, an' I come downstairs fer somefin' ter eat. She was sittin' cross-legged on the floor in the kitchen wiv a bottle of gin.'

'Oh, well, I s'pose everyone 'as a nip of somefin' from time ter time,' she said dismissively. 'Specially people who work in the music 'all.'

'Dad don't like 'er bein' on the booze though,' Sid said. ''E told me so.'

''E told me too,' added Lenny, who had recovered from his coughing fit. ''E told me that if we saw Mum like that, we was ter leave 'er alone. 'E said she was only like that 'cos she was fed up.'

Nellie felt her heart racing. 'Did Dad tell yer *why* she was fed up?'

'Nope,' replied Lenny.

Lenny's blunt reply convinced Nellie that it would be unwise to pursue the topic. But for the rest of the walk along Seven Sisters Road, she felt uneasy about the effect this miserable business was having on the family. Sooner or later, something was going to give, and when it did, it would be nothing short of a tragedy. Deep down inside, she was beginning to feel a sense of disillusionment. All that time she had craved for a family of her own, and now she had one, there was a danger that it was disintegrating before her very eyes. The only comforting thoughts she had now were Toff's letters, which arrived regularly twice a week.

By the time they reached the Nag's Head and crossed Holloway Road, Nellie had decided that, even if it meant alienating herself from her own mum and dad, she just had to have it out with Monsieur.

When they got home, Lenny had another severe coughing fit, and Madame discovered that the boy had a high temperature. Concerned that he may be starting the flu, she made him some hot broth then duly packed him off to bed with a hot water bottle.

The following day, the Great Pierre was contracted to start a week's engagement at the Theatre Royal, Margate, in Kent. This meant that early on Monday morning, Monsieur, Madame, and Nellie had to travel down in a hired van which they needed to transport their rather cumbersome stage props. Madame was encouraged enough by young Lenny's condition to feel that she could undertake the engagement, so once she had ensured that Monsieur's parents, old Lillian and Maurice, were able to come and stay at the house to keep an eye on the boys, she left with the others.

Before the war, Margate had always been the ideal booking for any artiste appearing at the popular Theatre Royal. The white, sandy beaches were perfect for a day's picnic, and the seafront promenade was thronged with lovers and casual strollers who wandered from one fish and chip shop to another, queued up at the jellied eels van, or tried their luck in the dangerously addictive amusement arcades. Margate was, quite simply, a happy family resort, with an abundance of good bed and breakfast guesthouses, and countless select residential areas. Now it was wartime and the beaches were sealed off by barbed wire; it was also the end of April, which meant plenty of squalls and biting winds blowing in off the English Channel. But everyone found the tiny Theatre Royal a joy to play in despite the somewhat bleak conditions in the backstage dressing rooms, and Nellie soon made friends with some of the supporting cast, who included a trapeze act, an outsize xylophonist, a girl crooner, and a bird impersonator. Unfortunately, nobody got on too well with the rather tetchy orchestra conductor, called Reginald something or other, for he was a last-minute replacement for the regular conductor who was apparently down with laryngitis. The Great Pierre was top of the bill, and Nellie felt very grand when, for the first time ever, she was given her own dressing room, next door to Monsieur and Madame. And their digs, a lovely double-fronted Edwardian guesthouse overlooking the sea at Cliftonville, were a veritable palace compared to some of the places they had put up in.

The week's booking was an unqualified success, with the act being cheered to the rafters each evening, mainly by servicemen from the many surrounding army bases, who filled the small auditorium, often overflowing to the standing room only areas. For Nellie, it was a very happy experience. Lillian telephoned each day to report on Lenny, and the latest news was that he was now back at school. The thought of poor Grandma Beckwith using the ancient wall telephone at Tufnell Park Road tickled Nellie no end, for she knew the old lady was terrified of telephones and usually shouted into them as though the person she was talking to was at the other end of the garden.

As the week progressed, Nellie watched carefully for any signs of strain between Monsieur and Madame. If her dad knew about her mum's drinking, then surely he must also know that the poor woman suspected something? But they were professionals, both on and off the stage. They knew how to disguise anything that might disrupt their public or private lives. As Madame had confided to her, 'I don't want ter break up my family, Nell. They mean too much ter me.' So, for the time being, Nellie said nothing.

On Thursday, Nellie arrived at the stage door of the theatre to find a message waiting for her. It was from Toff. He had telephoned to say that he had managed to get a twenty-four-hour pass, that he would be coming to Margate for the day on Saturday, and would she please meet him off the train from Canterbury, which arrived at nine fifteen in the morning. Nellie was over the moon, and on Friday night she didn't get a wink of sleep. In fact, on Saturday morning, she got to the railway station fifty minutes before the train arrived, and by the time she saw Toff hurrying towards her along the platform, she was so excited she just threw herself into his arms as though she hadn't seen him for years.

A short walk from the station they stopped to have a cup of tea and a toasted bun at a market stall. It went down a treat, for neither of them had had time to have any real breakfast before they set out. The market was brimming with shoppers and fruit and veg stallholders soliciting business with shouts of, 'Come on now, gels an' boys. Let yer eyes be yer guide!' and, to gales of laughter, 'Don't give in ter Jerry, missus. 'E don't like sausage an' mash!' The war was still on, but it certainly hadn't dented anyone's sense of humour.

After a while, Nellie and Toff found their way to a covered seaview shelter. Above them were Nellie's digs high on top of the cliffs, and spread out before them was the untouchable stretch of beach which extended far beyond Margate towards the Thames estuary in the west and Ramsgate to the south. Although the sun was popping in and out of scattered white clouds, there was still a cold breeze which sent ripples across the incoming tide.

'D'yer fink it'll ever 'appen?' Nellie asked as she snuggled up to Toff to keep warm. 'I mean, Jerry's only just on the uvver side of that water. D'yer reckon 'e'll try an' get over 'ere?'

Toff's eyes scanned the cold, grey expanse of the English Channel. 'If you'd asked me that a year ago,' he replied, 'I'd have said yes. A lot has changed since then. A lot of good people have given their lives to make sure they can't get here.'

Nellie knew what he meant. If it hadn't been for the courage of a few young pilots during the Blitz, the German invasion would have taken place a long time ago.

'Most of the 'dromes around the coast took a real hammering,' Toff continued. 'There's a place called Sugar Loaf Hill, just between our place and the sea. It's a real landmark for our blokes trying to get back to base after an all-night raid. A sort of oasis in the middle of a desert, really,' he said. 'They say, when you get a view of Sugar Loaf, you're home and dry. Quite a few never make it.'

For a moment or so, they sat there, snuggled up together, just staring out to sea, listening to the breeze. Down on the beach below them, an armed soldier on patrol stopped briefly to adjust his tin helmet. He seemed such a slight figure against the full power of the incoming tide.

'Tell me about yer mum an' dad,' Nellie said out of the blue.

Toff, puzzled, turned to look at her. 'What on earth for?' he asked.

''Cos I'd like ter know,' she replied. 'After all, I've told yer all about *my* mum an' dad.'

'That's different,' replied Toff. 'Your parents are interesting. They do an interesting job.'

'They're just ordinary people, wiv ordinary problems—just like everyone else.'

Toff thought a moment, then reached into his overcoat pocket for his fags. He was in civvies, and to Nellie his clothes had style. He was wearing a chunky navy-blue overcoat, over grey flannels, a white shirt with blue cravat, and a white V-neck tennis pullover. 'They didn't take too kindly to my going into the RAF.'

'Well, yer can't do much about that, can yer?' said Nellie. 'There's a war on. You was bound ter get called up sooner or later.'

'That's not what I mean,' replied Toff, lighting up. 'What they didn't like was that I didn't take a commission.'

'Commission? Wot's that?'

Toff smiled at her. 'If they had to have a son conscripted, they'd prefer him to be an officer.'

Nellie pulled a face. 'Well, yer've got the brains fer it,' she said. 'Why din't yer?'

Toff took in a lungful of smoke and exhaled over her head. 'Because I don't want to do what's expected of me,' he replied drily. 'And anyway, I had enough of being in charge back on the streets. And look what happened there.'

They were silent again. Nellie put one of her hands in his overcoat pocket to keep warm.

'Are yer goin' ter let them meet me some time?' Nellie asked.

'No way!'

Toff's response was a bit brusque for Nellie, and she looked up at him sharply. 'Why not?' she asked.

'Because I say so. Because you'd have nothing in common with them, nor they with you.'

Nellie straightened up. 'Who are yer ashamed of? Me or them?'

'Oh, don't be so bloody silly, Nell!' he snapped. 'Why do we have to talk about my parents? You know how I feel about them.'

Nellie was taken aback. 'Yes, I do know,' she said indignantly. 'I just wonder why, that's all.'

Toff was getting irritated. He stood up. So did Nellie.

'It's funny, in't it?' she said, arms crossed, staring aimlessly out at the sea. 'There's me, always longed fer a family of me own. An' now I've got one, suddenly it don't seem real any more.' She hesitated, then linked her arm with his. 'An' then there's you. Good class family, well-ter-do, an' all yer want ter do is turn yer back on 'em.'

Toff threw his half-finished cigarette to the ground. 'Look, Nell,' he said intensely. 'My old man comes from good Jewish stock. He's a Jew, and wants to be nothing but a Jew. As far as he's concerned, his only son's a Jew too, and he expects me to behave like one. In his book, there's no room for compromise. D'you understand what I'm saying?'

Nellie's face was quite expressionless. 'Yes, Toff, I understand,' she said. 'So where does that leave me?'

Toff had no time to reply, for they were both distracted by the sound of someone calling to Nellie.

'Nell! Nell, up here!'

Nellie and Toff turned to look up towards the cliff path where Madame was shouting and waving frantically.

'Mum!' Nellie shouted back, at the same time rushing up to meet her. 'Wot's up? Wot's 'appened?'

They met halfway, with Toff following on behind.

Madame was fraught, she had not even had

time to put on a coat. 'It's Lenny!' she cried. 'Grandma's just telephoned. They've taken 'im ter 'ospital.' She was fighting for breath and had difficulty getting her words out. "E's ... collapsed ... they've ... taken 'im ... ter 'ospital. 'E's spittin' up blood, Nell. Spittin' up blood!'

Monsieur and Nellie took the last train of the day up to London from Margate. For both of them, it seemed an interminable journey, for it was a slow train which stopped at every station. And despite the fact that they were travelling first class, the compartment was unheated and filthy dirty with a layer of thick black soot from the steam engine all over the upholstered seats. Monsieur was also incensed that the strips of sticky protective paper on the windows were peeling off, and because there were no blackout blinds, the dim light available in the compartment had to be turned off. To make things worse, when they stopped at Maidstone, there was a routine security check. It seemed to take the two Special Constables forever to check one's identity cards. Monsieur said he would write a letter of complaint to the railway company about it all, but by the time the train finally pulled into Charing Cross, he had forgotten all about the journey and was only interested in finding a taxi to take them to the Royal Northern Hospital in Holloway Road.

After the traumatic telephone call from Grandma Beckwith, Madame had withdrawn from the last two shows of the week in Margate and gone straight back to London. As the Great

Pierre was top of the bill, it was decided that Monsieur and Nellie should finish off the last two shows of the week, with the help of the theatre orchestra's resident lady pianist.

If the news of Lenny's collapse distressed Monsieur, Nellie saw no sign of it. On the train he had said very little, preferring to sit in silence and stare out into the night, watching the distant dark shapes of the countryside fluttering in and out of the thick black engine smoke as the train sped by. It was the same in the taxi as it wound its way through the almost deserted streets of wartime London. No comment, nothing said. Only fear, hope, and prayers. Nellie had never known him to be so silent, and for so long. It told her quite a lot.

It was nearly half past one in the morning when they reached the ward where Lenny had been taken. Madame was waiting for them.

'It's pneumonia,' she whispered, her voice cracking and her eyes sore from crying. 'Apparently it was touch an' go. When they got 'im 'ere, 'e was coughin' 'is 'eart up. 'E looks terrible! I blame meself. I should never've left 'im. I should never've gone down ter Margate.'

'Calm yerself, gel.' This was the first time Monsieur had really said anything since he and Nellie had left Charing Cross Station. 'We 'ad no idea this was goin' ter 'appen. There's nuffin' we can do. Len's in good 'ands.'

Madame's face crumpled and she started to sob quietly to herself.

Nellie put her arm round her and hugged

364

her. 'It's all right, Mum,' she said comfortingly. 'Lenny's a tough little devil. 'E'll be OK, you'll see.' She wasn't sure she believed what she was saying. During the past month or so, she had noticed a subtle change in young Lenny's appearance. For a boy of thirteen, he was far too skinny. He had also lost his ruddy complexion and lacked bounce and energy when he was playing football with the Tuffiell Tigers.

'You can go in now,' said the night nurse softly. 'He's fast asleep, so just a few minutes, please.'

Due to the seriousness of Lenny's condition, he had been put in a small room by himself. When Monsieur, Madame, and Nellie filed in, they found him with an oxygen mask strapped to his face, a huge cylinder at the side of the bed.

Nellie flinched at the sight of Lenny. He looked so small, lying flat on his back in a bed that seemed to be far too big for him, with the oxygen mask strap caught up in the straggly curls of his mop of blond hair. She couldn't bear to see him like this. This was Lenny, this was her own brother. Inside she wanted to cry, to shout out loud. She wanted to bend down, to take him in her arms and say, 'Don't do this to us, Lenny! There's nuffin' wrong wiv yer. We love yer. Don't yer know that? We love yer!'

She, Monsieur, and Madame stood in silence beside the delicate, motionless frame of the boy. The only sound was that of Lenny breathing through the oxygen mask. It was an unnatural sound, a real struggle between life and death.

On one side of the bed, Madame gently covered Lenny's hand with her own. On the other side, Nellie did the same.

Monsieur remained silent, standing, watching. Then he put his arm on his wife's shoulder to comfort her. But she pulled away.

The house was empty when they arrived home, for with Lenny in hospital, Sid had gone to Grandma and Grandad Beckwith's for the night.

Nellie felt ill at ease. 'Why don't I make us all a cup of tea?' she suggested.

'Fanks, Nell,' said Monsieur, trying hard to put on a brave face. 'Good idea.'

'Mum?'

Madame said nothing. She just shook her head briskly, took off her coat and hat, and threw them carelessly on to a kitchen chair.

Nellie exchanged an anxious look with Monsieur as Madame went to a kitchen cabinet and took out a bottle of gin.

Monsieur quickly crossed to her and tried to take the bottle from her. 'No, Doris,' he said gently but firmly. 'It won't help.'

Madame wrenched the bottle back. 'Wot d'yer mean, it won't 'elp?' she growled angrily. 'Wot do *you* know about 'elp, *Monsieur?*' Her look cut straight through him, and her voice had a ferocity that Nellie had never heard before. 'If there's one fing I've learnt in life, Bert,' she continued, 'it's every woman fer 'erself!' She poured herself a half tumblerful of neat gin and took a gulp.

Monsieur and Nellie looked on helplessly.

'Please, Mum, don't,' Nellie pleaded, going to her.

Madame backed away from her, shaking her head vigorously. 'It's not your fault, Nell. This was bound to 'appen sooner or later. That's why our boy's in 'ospital. We should've seen this comin' but we didn't!'

'That's not true, Doris,' said Monsieur, making a move towards her. 'You're gettin' everyfin' mixed up.'

Madame held fast, holding up her hands in front of her face as though trying to shield herself. 'Mixed up?' she shouted. 'Mixed up? Is that wot it is, Bert? I'm mixed up because I failed to notice that my own son—*our* own son—was comin' down wiv pneumonia?'

'It's somefin' that could 'appen ter anyone,' Monsieur said defensively. ''Ow're we ter know these fings?'

'By noticin' our kids, Bert!' blasted Madame. 'By bein' wiv 'em when they need us.' She took another gulp from her glass. 'That's the trouble wiv us, Bert. Our 'ole lives live an' breave the Great Pierre. They live an' breave 'ow the act goes, 'ow people are goin' ter like it, an' 'ow they're goin' ter like you!'

'That's not true, Doris,' he snapped. 'That's an unfair, untrue fing ter say.'

'Is it? Then why aren't yer there when your family need yer? Why do they always come last when yer 'ave one of your so-called important *appointments* to go to?'

Nellie was appalled by her mum's ferocious

367

outburst. She had never seen her like this before. But as she stood there between them, deep in despair and disillusionment, a cold, hard fact was beginning to emerge. Even in the best of families, things were never exactly as they appeared. There would always be suspicion; mutual trust would always have to be worked for. Hard as it was to accept, nobody, not even her own mum and dad, was perfect.

Monsieur, clearly devastated, stood helplessly as Madame went out into the garden to her usual haunt, the Anderson shelter.

He turned to look at Nellie. ''Ow can she say those fings, Nell?' he said, totally crushed. 'I love 'er. I love all me family—an' that includes you.'

Nellie, who was herself reeling from Madame's words, looked at her dad. His face was racked with anguish, and he seemed as vulnerable as poor Lenny lying in his hospital bed. This was the moment, she decided. This was the moment when she had to tell him the truth. It was now or never. He pulled back a kitchen chair and sat down, and she joined him at the table. With calm dignity she said the words she knew she had to say. 'She knows, Dad. She knows about you—and Ange.'

Monsieur slowly looked up. Despite his height, sitting at the kitchen table he looked small and bent. 'I don't know wot you're talkin' about, Nell,' he replied, a look of genuine bewilderment on his face.

'Mum knows you've been 'avin' an affair wiv Ange.'

Monsieur was thunderstruck. He quickly shook his head. 'No, Nell! It's not true. It wasn't like that. I swear ter God, it wasn't like that at all.'

Nellie's face crumpled up. 'Dad. Everyone knows. They've seen yer.'

'Everyone don't know nuffin'! OK, so I 'ad a kiss an' a cuddle wiv 'er a coupla times a while back. It was stupid but it ain't ever gone any furver than that. I swear ter God it ain't!'

Nellie lowered her head briefly, then quickly raised it again and stared him straight in the eyes. 'Dad,' she asked with pain and embarrassment, 'wot about that snapshot? You an' 'er bunked down tergevver on the grass?'

Monsieur's eyes widened with shock. 'Yer've seen that? 'Ow d'yer see it?'

'It don't matter 'ow or where I've seen it, Dad. The fact is, I've seen it.'

Monsieur quickly searched for his packet of Players, took one out and lit it. 'I was set up, Nell,' he said, inhaling deeply and trying to speak with a throat full of smoke. 'One day, before you ever come, she asked me ter meet 'er in Finsbury Park. She said she wanted ter talk over one or two fings she found difficult ter do in the act. It was all rubbish, of course. Anyway, we sat down on the grass, just up near the lake—there were plenty of people around. It 'appened just as I was askin' 'er wot the problem was. All of a sudden she fell against me, pinned me down, an'—an' kissed me, right on the lips. I pushed 'er away, told 'er not ter be so bloody silly. But she did it again, and kept tryin' it on.

Next fing I knew, she slung 'er bloody 'ook an' left me like a lemon stretched out there. I fawt wot a silly little cow she was, goin' after a bloke over twice 'er age, an' I decided there an' then that I'd give 'er the boot, get 'er out of the act, out of my life fer good.' The smoke lingering in his throat made him cough, and it took him a moment or so to recover. 'Wot I din't know was while she was performin' 'er little act, she'd got one of 'er mates 'idin' be'ind a tree, takin' a few juicy snaps of us.' He finally summoned up enough courage to look directly at her. 'I was set up, Nell,' he said. 'Ange's a go-getter. She was only ever after all she could get from me. I knew that from the start.'

Nellie was unconvinced. 'Then why din't yer get rid of 'er?'

Monsieur drew hard on his fag and exhaled. It took him a moment to answer, and when he did, it was with difficulty. 'Nell, it's easy fer a man my age ter be flattered. I was a fool, a stupid, blind fool. I 'ad the gall ter fink that this gel, this good-lookin' gel really fancied me. By the time I knew the facts of life, it was too late. I was a fool, Nell. I admit it. I was a bloody fool!'

Nellie hesitated for a moment. 'Dad, I want ter ask yer a question. But please tell me the truth. I've seen yer kissin' Ange, back at Drury Lane. Was it fer real?'

Monsieur had a pained look. 'It weren't fer real, Nell,' he replied. 'But I was chuffed enough ter go along wiv it.'

Nellie sighed. 'Don't yer care about Mum any more?'

'Care?' Monsieur looked up, stubbed out his fag in a tin ashtray, and exhaled the last few remains of smoke. 'Let me tell yer somefin', Nell,' he said passionately. 'I care fer Doris more than anyone else in the 'ole wide world. I'd be lost wiv out 'er.'

Nellie came back at him like a shot. 'Then why din't yer tell 'er about all this? If yer love Mum as much as yer say yer do, why couldn't yer 'ave trusted 'er enough ter tell 'er?'

Monsieur shook his head. 'She wouldn't believe me, Nell.'

Nellie was exasperated. 'Dad! 'Ow d'yer know if yer don't try?'

''Cos she's always bin the same. Every gel I've ever bin in contact wiv, she's always got it into her 'ead that I've bin after 'em.'

''Ave yer, Dad?' Nellie asked.

Nellie's cool response upset him. 'No, Nell,' he said with quiet emotion but avoiding her look. 'Wot 'appened wiv Ange was the first time. I swear ter God I'll never let it 'appen again.' He covered his face with his hands and broke down. It was an extraordinary and quite unexpected moment, Monsieur so rarely showed any emotion at all, Nellie had thought him incapable of crying.

''Ave yer any idea 'ow I felt, seein' that boy of mine lyin' in that 'ospital bed ternight?' he sobbed. 'I don't care about the bloody Great Pierre, Nell. I don't care if I never tread the boards again as long as I live.' He looked up at her, and with tears streaming down his face added, 'I'd sooner lose me arms an' legs than let one of my own go through anyfin' like that!'

Nellie knelt down in front of him, threw her arms round his neck, and held him. 'I believe yer, Dad,' she said reassuringly. 'An' so will Mum, you'll see.' A determined, defiant look came to Nellie's face as she added, 'An' don't yer worry a fing about Ange. As a matter of fact, I know exactly 'ow ter take care of *'er.'*

Chapter 22

Sid Beckwith sat on the edge of his bed without saying a word. It wasn't his usual bed, for ever since his young brother had been taken ill, he couldn't bear being alone in the room that he shared with him so he slept in a small box room next to his mum and dad's bedroom on the first floor, where he spent most of his time after getting home from school in the evenings. Nellie did her best to be with him as much as she could; she had noticed the close bond between the two brothers, despite the fact that they often argued and quarrelled with each other. 'Is Len going to die, Nell?' was a question he frequently asked, and it revealed a great deal of the despair he was feeling.

Although young Lenny's condition had stablised, he was still seriously ill. It was now almost a week since he had been rushed to hospital, but despite rest, medication, and constant supervision, his temperature remained stubbornly high, and his dry cough was also troubling him. He lacked all energy, and the only time he showed any interest at all was when Monsieur and Madame took Sid to visit him. This did not go unnoticed by Lenny's doctor, who was of the mind that the brothers' closeness was the younger boy's best means of recovery.

Lenny's illness had at least brought the crisis between Monsieur and Madame to a head. With Nellie's encouragement, Monsieur told his wife everything about his association with Ange, including the reason she had been blackmailing him. Although this cleared the air, it still left the problem of the snapshots. If Ange showed them to a newspaper, it would put his marriage to Madame under the public spotlight and also cause intense embarrassment in his career. However, Nellie had one or two ideas of her own.

'How d'yer find a soldier?' retorted Ruby Catmonk, in reply to Nellie's question. She let rip with a great chesty laugh. 'Go an' stand outside any army barracks and grab the first one that comes out!'

Nellie laughed with her. 'No, Rube,' she said, 'I din't say 'ow d'yer find a soldier. I asked 'ow d'yer find out about a soldier. I wanna find out about this feller I met. 'E's in the army—a photographer.'

Ruby scratched her head. Her dyed ginger hair was getting a bit thin on top. 'A photographer in the army? 'Aven't the foggiest! Why? Wot's all this about then?'

'I'm curious, that's all. I've got a 'unch about 'im.'

Ruby took a fag end from her lips and pressed it into her ashtray. Then she immediately lit up again. They were sitting in her sewing room at the Finsbury Park Empire, and they could hear the sound of the first house performance.

''Ave yer tried the War Office?' she asked, as she picked up a pair of scissors and started trimming her heavily painted fingernails.

''Aven't tried anywhere,' replied Nellie, who was leaning on Ruby's table, looking at her, arms crossed. 'I fawt you might know. You know everyfin', Rube. You're a genius.'

'Yes, I know I am,' agreed the old lady. 'That's why I'm sewin' costumes in the bleedin' Finsbury Park Empire.' She took off her specs and flung them down carelessly on the table. 'As a matter of fact, I do know someone. 'Aven't seen 'im fer a while though. I once 'ad a bit of a ding-dong wiv 'is old man.' Without removing her cigarette, she blew smoke out of the side of her mouth. 'If yer want ter know about this photographer, you'll 'ave ter tell me more about 'im, gel.'

Nellie thought a moment. ''E's got a tattoo,' she said.

'A tattoo?'

'One on each arm.'

Ruby looked across the table at Nellie, then actually took the fag out of her mouth. 'Piece of cake!' she said, taking the mickey. 'We should 'ave no trouble at all findin' a soldier in the British Army who 'as a tattoo on each arm!'

'Stop takin' the piss, Rube,' Nellie replied. 'It's all I've got—well, at the moment. But 'e's a photographer, remember. That narrows it down a bit, don't it?'

Ruby sighed and shook her head. 'Why, Nell?' she asked. 'Why d'yer want ter know about this bloke?'

Nellie lowered her eyes uneasily. 'Can't tell yer, Rube,' she said apologetically.

Ruby briefly put her hands in front of her, palms facing Nellie. 'Ask no questions, 'ear no lies,' she said. 'But I still need ter know *somefin'* about 'im.' She cleared the bits of sewing material from her table and found a pencil and piece of paper. 'Right,' she said. 'Where der we start?'

A week later, Monsieur and Madame were asked to call in to see Lenny's specialist. He was a man they hadn't seen before, and when they arrived at the hospital they found him waiting for them in the ward sister's office. His name was Mr Timothy Whetstone, and to Monsieur and Madame he looked old enough to be near retirement. But he had a pleasant face, even if, like so many other people in his profession, he found it difficult to offer anything more than the suggestion of a comforting smile.

'I wanted to talk to you personally,' he said, once Monsieur and Madame had sat down, 'mainly because there are one or two things about your son's condition that you ought to know.'

'Is 'e any worse?' asked Madame anxiously.

Mr Whetstone sighed and took off his reading spectacles. 'I can't be absolutely certain about that at the moment, I'm afraid, Mrs Beckwith,' he said, again trying a smile. 'We still have one or two more tests to do.'

'Does pneumonia usually take as long as this ter clear up?' asked Monsieur, the knuckles of his hands white as they rested on his walking cane.

'That's just the trouble, Mr Beckwith,' replied the specialist, sitting back in his chair. 'Your son's condition is not as we first thought. It's not pneumonia. It's primary tuberculosis.'

Madame gasped, and put her hand against her mouth.

Monsieur went visibly white. 'Tuberculosis? Yer mean TB?' he asked, in a state of shock.

'It's not as bad as it sounds,' continued Mr Whetstone. 'Not for the time being anyway.'

'But don't people die wiv that?' asked Monsieur, his voice cracking with anxiety.

'People die of all sorts of things, Mr Beckwith. And I won't disguise the fact that this disease can be a killer. But young Lenny does have a fighting chance. As I said, what he's suffering from is the primary stage. We weren't absolutely sure until we took some X-rays.'

Mr Whetstone stood up to switch on a screen on the wall showing Lenny's X-rays.

'If you'd like to come over here,' he said, 'I'll show you what I mean.'

Monsieur helped Madame up from her chair, and they both joined the specialist at the screen.

'As you can see,' said Mr Whetstone, using the tip of a pencil to point out the affected areas on Lenny's X-rays, 'there's a dark patch at the base of his left lung, here. And there's a smaller one just here. That's why he's been coughing so badly, and spitting up blood and pus-filled sputum. What has happened is that the bacteria has attacked his lungs, which is the usual case.'

'Is there anyfin' yer can do ter get rid of it?' asked Monsieur.

Mr Whetstone sighed, and continued staring into the bright light of the X-ray screen. 'Well,' he said, 'this phase of the disease usually lasts for several months. Hopefully, the body will resist it by using its own natural defences. But there's always the chance that the bacteria may spread into the bloodstream.'

Madame seemed to shrivel up in despair.

'However, that's not always the case,' continued Mr Whetstone as they went back to their chairs. 'In our experience, the disease quite often never develops beyond this primary stage. Especially in youngsters of your son's age.' He looked at his notes. 'But sometimes natural resistance cannot subdue the bacteria, and although the initial outbreak can be overcome, it could flare up again after a lapse of several years.' He looked up from his notes. This time he didn't even attempt a smile. 'This phase is much more serious.'

'What are Lenny's chances, sir?' asked Monsieur sombrely.

Mr Whetstone paused briefly before answering. 'I'll be perfectly frank with you, Mr

Beckwith,' he replied. 'In someone whose natural resistance is abnormally low, primary tuberculosis spreads so quickly that it can be fatal unless it's treated very early. Your son, I'm afraid, has very low resistance.'

Madame felt the inside of her stomach collapse. 'But there must be somefin' yer can do,' she said, staring into the man's eyes, looking for just one ray of hope. 'There must be some kind of treatment yer can give 'im.'

'There are drugs, Mrs Beckwith,' replied Mr Whetstone. 'But they're not a cure, only a relief. The only effective treatment is the right kind of food and a prolonged period of rest. I'm afraid that, with this condition, it would be out of the question for Lenny to go back to school. We'll do all we can, but once we've got him on his feet again, it'll be up to you and your family to give him as much attention as you possibly can.'

While Monsieur and Madame were with the specialist, Nellie sat with Lenny in his room at the end of the ward. Although his breathing had improved enough for the oxygen mask to be removed, he was still lacking all energy and was too weak to engage in much conversation. Nellie couldn't bear to see her young brother like this, his face as white as the sheets covering him, and his eyes bulging out of their sockets. It was heartbreaking. It was so unfair.

'Yer better get out of 'ere soon, Len,' Nellie said in a soft, over-hearty voice. 'The Tigers've got quite a few big matches comin' up in yer school 'olidays. They need all the support they can get.' She knew that she sounded utterly false but she had to keep up the boy's morale somehow.

Lenny smiled, and Nellie detected just a trace of that old fanatical support for his team in his tired eyes.

Nellie moved her chair closer so that her legs were under the bed and she could talk to Lenny just a few inches from his face. 'Sid says when 'e comes in ter see yer on Sat'day afternoon, 'e's goin' ter bring yer that new Football Annual—you know, the one 'e got fer 'is birfday.'

Although he continued to stare at her, Lenny's reaction was silent and blank. He seemed so drugged, he was unable to focus. But at least the awful hacking cough had stopped, for the time being anyway.

Suddenly, Nellie noticed that he was trying to say something, so she leaned as close to him as she possibly could. 'Yes, Len?' she said eagerly. 'Wot d'yer say, mate?'

Lenny's voice was slow and precise, but it was clearly an effort to speak. 'Could yer ...' he wheezed.

'Yes, Len,' Nellie replied, quickly. 'Tell me, mate.'

'Could yer ... show me ... 'ow ter do boxin' ... like Sid?'

Nellie wanted to cry. She was so upset, and yet so happy that Lenny was showing interest in something. 'You bet yer life I'll show yer,' she said firmly, squeezing his hand.

The door opened quietly behind her and the ward sister came up to her. 'Could you come outside for a moment, please? Your mum would like to see you.'

In the corridor outside, Madame was in tears. 'It's TB,' was all she could say over and over again. ''Ow could 'e catch such a fing, Nell?' she asked, between sobs. 'We've never 'ad nuffin' like that on our side of the family, nor yer dad's.'

Nellie didn't know what to say. She had no idea what TB was, and when her mum told her about tuberculosis, she thought a disease like that was only ever connected to things like cows. But it sounded bad, and the whole business gave her a sinking feeling.

'I've got ter take care of 'im, Nell,' said Madame. 'I'm goin' ter give up the act, give up the 'alls. I'm never ever goin' ter leave that boy alone as long as I live!'

'*We'll* take care of 'im, Mum,' Nellie replied. 'I'm part of the family now, an' Len's me bruvver. We'll all stick tergevver, an' 'e'll pull fru, just yer wait an' see.'

Monsieur left the hospital in a daze. In fact, he was so shocked that he left his overcoat behind in the ward sister's office. But it didn't matter that it was freezing cold outside. Nothing mattered. What he had just heard from Mr Whetstone the specialist was, in Monsieur's opinion, more than anyone should have to bear. Tuberculosis? Damn the disease! Where did it come from? Who gave it to him? In a fit of illogical rage, Monsieur slammed his walking cane against a lamppost and it snapped in half.

But he hardly noticed and kept on walking.

He had left the hospital alone. Sid would be getting back from school fairly soon and he would think that something was wrong if he arrived home and found no one there. But the walk back to Tufnell Park Road turned into a faltering crawl. It was only a short distance home from the Royal Northern Hospital in Manor Gardens but by the time Monsieur had got as far as the Gaumont Cinema, his body felt quite numb. He put his hands in his jacket pocket. Without realising it, he had come to a halt and was staring aimlessly along the street he had lived in for so many years with his darling Doris and the two boys. For some reason, it all looked so different, as though he hardly knew the place. And then he thought about what Doris had said to him. Yes, she was right, he hadn't cared enough about her and the boys. It was one thing to think in your mind how much you cared for someone, but it was quite another thing to tell them so, and to show it. He was tormented by so many thoughts. He was beginning to believe that he had wasted his life on trivia, acting the fool on a music hall stage. Real life was outside the theatre, in the street, in the home, in the lives of ordinary people like his own family. Yes, his life was nothing more than a make-believe world, and he deeply regretted what he had turned into. Oh God, he thought, if only I could live my life all over again.

'Dad.'

Monsieur came out of his trance to find Nellie at his side. 'Nell?' he spluttered, almost as though he didn't know her.

'It's not as bad as yer fink,' she said firmly. 'Yer've got ter take 'old of yerself.'

''E's goin' ter die, Nell,' Monsieur said, distraught. 'My boy's goin' ter die.'

Nellie grabbed hold of his arm and squeezed it. 'No, Dad! That's not goin' ter 'appen, an' yer musn't carry on as if it is! Yes, Lenny's ill, 'e's very ill. But if 'e's looked after, 'e's goin' ter pull fru an' 'ave a perfectly normal life.'

Monsieur was shaking his head. He didn't believe her.

'Dad, listen ter me!' Nellie persisted. 'Please don't bury someone before they're dead! Lenny's only a kid. 'E's got plenty of fight in 'im, you'll see. But if 'e's goin' ter make it, 'e's goin' ter need all the love an' support yer can give 'im. So does Mum. Sid too. An' that means bein' strong, Dad, strong ter face up ter anyfin' that comes along.'

A queue was forming outside the Holloway Road side of the cinema; the current film was clearly very popular. Aware that she and her dad were attracting attention, Nellie took him gently by the arm and led him off slowly along the other side of the cinema, which was their own road. Daffodils, tulips, and other spring flowers in people's front gardens were dying off and gradually giving way to the pink and white blossom of cherry trees. Nellie was aware of this, and had often thought how touching it was that, despite the war, people in the city streets still tended their small gardens with such loving care.

'You're right, Nell,' said Monsieur, staring down at the pavement as he walked. 'I 'ave bin neglectin' my family. They need me as much as I need them.' He suddenly came to a halt and turned to look at her. 'I've made up me mind. I'm goin' ter give up the 'alls and spend more time at 'ome.'

'Dad!' protested Nellie. 'Yer've got it all wrong. That's not wot I'm sayin'. Yer don't 'ave ter give up everyfin' yer've ever worked for ter stay wiv yer family. The music 'all's yer life!'

'So are me wife an' kids,' insisted Monsieur. 'From now on, they come first.'

Nellie was frustrated that she wasn't getting through to him, so, without thinking, she propped herself up on the narrow coping stone of a front garden wall. 'Let me ask yer somefin', Dad,' she said. 'If yer give up the act, give up all the good work yer've ever done on the 'alls, wot would yer do then?'

Monsieur shrugged his shoulders. 'I'd find somefin',' he replied.

Nellie looked up at him. He towered over her, so she grabbed his arm and forced him to sit down beside her. 'Would yer, Dad?' she asked. 'Would yer really be able to find somefin' ter replace wot yer 'ave in yer blood, the one fing that drives yer along every day of yer life?'

Monsieur's only response was to shrug his shoulders again.

'There's nuffin' wrong wiv the music 'all,' Nellie continued. 'It's a wonderful fing ter be a part of, givin' so much pleasure ter everyone.

An' the people who tread the boards are pretty special people too. They're your friends, they're warm-'earted, they stick tergevver when you're in trouble, an' as long as there's someone ter come an' watch 'em, they'll keep on goin' till they drop. Wot der yer call 'em, Dad—troupers? Well, that's wot *you* are. You're a trouper, an' yer must never ferget it. You're one of the pillars of the music 'all. If everyone like you gave it all up, it'd all come crumbling down. An' fer wot?'

Monsieur was staring down at the pavement as he listened to her.

'Doin' wot you're doin' ain't responsible fer wot's 'appened ter Len, Dad,' Nellie continued, voice low. 'I din't know much about family life till I met you an' Mum. But wot I 'ave learnt since then is that bad times can come when yer least expect 'em. Yer can be up one day, an' down the next. Bein' ill is no one's fault. It just comes when it comes, an' yer just 'ave ter cope wiv it any way yer can.'

'Oy! You two!'

The shrill, angry yell coming from the house behind them caused Nellie and Monsieur to get up with a start.

A middle-aged woman with hair in curlers was leaning right out of her window, waving her hand and shouting at them. 'Who the bleedin' 'ell d'yer fink yer are?' she rasped. 'Ain't yer got no wall of yer own ter sit down on? Push off!'

Monsieur looked over the top of the hedge, took off his hat, and waved it at the woman.

'Sorry, Mrs Hoddle!' he called. 'We're just on our way.'

Mrs Hoddle looked horrified. 'Oh! It's you, Mr Beckwith,' she called, her voice immediately transformed into genteel sweetness and charm. 'I din't see it was you. You stay there as long as yer want, dear!'

Monsieur waved his hat once more then put it back on.

Nellie was grinning. 'See wot I mean?' she said, with a wry chuckle. 'Yer never know from one minute ter the next 'ow life's goin' ter treat yer.'

Monsieur's face lit up with a faint smile for the first time that day. Then he held out his arm for Nellie.

They moved on up the road and made for home. As they went, Monsieur was surprised to notice how tall his adopted daughter was. In fact, as far as he was concerned, she was much taller than he was.

Chapter 23

Summer was in full bloom, and during the first heat wave of the year, the streets were filled with people in their brightest summer clothes. In fact it was so hot that one or two teenagers tried frying an egg on the steps of the Marlborough Cinema in Holloway, but with disastrous effect. There was, however, a general malaise in the streets, for after a long lull enemy raiders were making two or three attacks on London and the south-east each week, which were officially described as tit-for-tat reprisals for Allied air raids on targets deep inside Germany, including Berlin itself. The people around the Nag's Head, Holloway, were not complacent but they did not rush straight out to the air-raid shelter as soon as the siren was heard. The Allied successes in North Africa were giving them renewed hope that the end of the war was in sight, and that feeling was reflected in the atmosphere of relaxed calm.

Several weeks had passed since Nellie had asked Ruby Catmonk to get her the information she required on the soldier photographer. Fortunately, apart from one-night appearances at a few Masonic dinners, the Great Pierre had, for the time being, no music hall engagements to fulfil. This suited Nellie, for, apart from spending as much time as she could with young Lenny, who was being lovingly cared for at home by Madame, she had some important business of her own to attend to.

During recent weeks, Nellie had spent a lot of time, usually in the afternoons, in and around Harvest Road. She kept watch from a scruffy workmen's cafe in nearby Hornsey Road. The cafe was used by some of the local Civil Defence workers, such as Special Constables, ARP wardens, and firefighters from the fire station round the corner in Shelburne Road School, and after a while they regarded her as a regular. They gave her some useful but casual information about the young couple who lived in the house she was so interested in on the other side of Harvest Road. The cafe was a perfect place to keep out of sight, especially when either Ange or her army photographer boyfriend came out of the house, for at no time did they take even a passing glance at the window where Nellie sat slowly sipping her cup of tea.

Ruby's information was taking a long time to materialise because her contact in the War Office was away on a secret mission overseas, and until he returned there was no one else they could approach to sort out who Ange's boyfriend was. Nellie refused to give up hope, there was too much at stake. Moreover, she was sure she had seen the soldier with tattooed arms somewhere before. Her feeling was confirmed when Ruby came back with her startling information.

During her vigil inside the workmen's cafe and on the streets nearby, Nellie had discovered that Ange left the house every afternoon regularly at around three o'clock. This suggested that she had taken some kind of part-time job. Her mysterious boyfriend seemed to spend a lot of time in civvy street, for he rarely came out of the house except to tinker with his rather battered Hercules motorcycle. She never saw him in uniform, which seemed strange for a soldier during war—strange, that is, until Ruby provided her with the information she was looking for. It was on that basis that she set up her plan.

One Wednesday afternoon, she took the bold

step of returning to the house in Harvest Road. Ange had already left. Nellie approached the front gate as quickly as she could and opened it without closing it behind her. She went straight down the stone steps to the basement area and knocked on the door. She concealed herself as much as possible in the porch so that anyone peering out through the bay window would not be able to see who their visitor was. She had to knock three times before the door was finally opened, and then only a crack. 'She's out.' The tattooed soldier was only just visible.

'It's you I've come ter see, not 'er,' replied Nellie with a small but mischievous smile.

The soldier didn't move. 'Got nothin' ter say to yer,' he growled. 'Come back in the mornin'.'

Nellie put her hand against the door, preventing him from closing it. 'I said it was you I've come ter see—Sergeant Fowler.'

The soldier glared at her, then opened the door fully. He was angry, unshaven, and wearing a threadbare white singlet and baggy khaki shorts. 'Wot d'yer want?' he asked, scowling.

'A little chat, mate, that's all.' She was feeling very unsure of herself but she was determined not to let it show. 'I fink yer might be in'trested in wot I've got ter say.'

The man hesitated then stood back to let her enter. 'This'd better be worf it,' he said, closing the door behind her.

Nellie didn't wait to be invited into the sitting room; she just marched straight in. The place was in exactly the same state as the last time she had been here, untidy, and, in the middle of the heat wave, Ange's ironing board smelt even more disgusting than ever.

'Right.' The soldier was standing in the sitting-room doorway, hands in his shorts pockets. ''Ow'd yer know me name?'

'I've come about the snapshots,' said Nellie, ignoring his question.

The soldier grinned. Nellie had to admit to herself that he was a handsome young bloke; it was a seductive grin and he had eyes that seemed to see straight into her. 'Wot snapshots?' he asked.

'The snapshots of Ange and my dad,' she said firmly, refusing to be intimidated.

'Oh, *those* snapshots,' replied the soldier, apparently amused. He came into the room, retrieving a half-finished fag from behind his right ear. 'Wot about 'em?'

'I want 'em back. Every one of 'em. Includin' the negatives.'

The soldier turned to look at her. 'Do yer now?' he replied, playing the game with her. 'Well, I'm not sure Ange can 'elp yer wiv that. They're worf quite a bit, yer know.'

'It's you I'm talkin' to, mate, not Ange.'

The soldier moistened the end of his cigarette with his lips, then lit up. 'You're wastin' yer time.'

Nellie went and stood right in front of him. 'An' you're in danger of ruinin' a man's life,' she growled.

''E should've fawt 'bout that when 'e tried to lay a gel 'alf 'is age, dirty ol' sod!'

389

Nellie wasn't taking any of it. 'You set 'im up,' she snapped.

'I beg yer pardon?' replied the soldier indignantly.

'You set 'im up,' insisted Nellie. 'You an' that bitch. It was a real con job.'

'Nice gels don't say fings like that, *Miss* Beckwiff.'

'An' army deserters don't burn their fingers blackmailin' people,' retorted Nellie, adding, 'Do they, *Sergeant?*'

The lit match the soldier was still holding burnt his fingers and he quickly threw it into the empty fireplace. 'You better start talkin', darlin',' he rasped menacingly.

Nellie stood her ground. 'On the run, ain't yer, Sergeant? Yer've bin on the run since before Christmas—so my contacts tell me. Somefin' about nickin' cash from the NAAFI at some army camp up norf. My contact says you're AWOL. Apparently, in the army that means absent wivout leave. Is that right, Sarge?'

The soldier's face was like thunder.

'Stroke of luck, really,' continued Nellie, moving away from him and aimlessly picking up and looking at some of the clothes that were waiting to be ironed. 'Y'see, me an' my dad we get ter tour round the army camps doin' shows fer ENSA from time ter time. Well, one day, we was just checkin' in at the main gates of some barracks or somefin', which 'appened ter be in the guard 'ouse.' She paused and turned to look briefly at him. 'You know wot a guard 'ouse is, don't yer, Sarge? Sort of gaol or somefin', ain't it—'

The soldier did not respond. In the stifling atmosphere of the small room, his forehead and chest were saturated with sweat.

Nellie smiled at him, then continued, 'Well, while I was standin' there waitin' ter sign in, I suddenly caught a butchers of this noticeboard—sheer chance, really. Anyway, guess wot?' She walked up to him. 'Lo an' be'old, your picture was there.' She was eyeball to eyeball with him. 'It was your picture, wasn't it, Sarge? The one that said WANTED ...'

The soldier flicked his fag butt into the fireplace and moved away from her.

Nellie's eyes followed him. 'Shows yer wot a good memory I've got fer faces, don't it, Sarge? It's a funny fing, but the moment I saw yer flittin' down that passage the last time I come 'ere, I knew I'd seen yer somewhere. I just 'ad ter put two an' two tergevver, an' get a little bit of 'elp from this pal of mine.'

'Wot d'yer want?' the soldier suddenly snarled.

'Yer know wot I want, Sarge,' Nellie shot back, utterly fearless. 'I want them snapshots, every single one of 'em.'

'An' if I don't give 'em to yer?'

Nellie chortled. 'As yer can see, Sarge, I've got friends in 'igh places.'

The soldier paused a moment, sizing her up. His lip curled up on one side in a slight suggestion of a smile. 'You're a real little firecracker, ain't yer?' he said.

Nellie smiled back at him. 'That's right, mate. Yer better watch out I don't blow up on yer.'

The sergeant waited a moment, then turned to look at himself in the mirror. Nellie watched him, fascinated, as he used his hand to rub the sweat from his chest. What a vain piece of shit, she thought. But she was only too aware that this lout had enough muscle power to make mincemeat of her.

Abruptly the sergeant stopped looking at himself in the mirror, went straight to the cupboard beside the fireplace, took out the snapshots, and held them out to her. 'Take the bloody fings!' he growled.

'No! Don't give 'em to 'er!'

Nellie swung round to find Ange standing in the doorway. She had not expected this, for only a short while ago she had seen Ange leave the house.

Ange rushed in and grabbed the photos from the sergeant. 'Don't listen to a word she says! It's bluff, all bluff!'

'It's your bloody fault!' the sergeant shouted at Ange. 'I told yer it wouldn't work! If she lets on, I'll 'ave that guard 'ouse brigade down on me like a ton of 'ot bricks!'

'It's your bloody fault,' Ange yelled back. 'I told yer ter keep out of sight when this little bitch was around!'

This was just what Nellie wanted, a real slanging match between them.

'Give 'er the bloody pictures!' rasped the sergeant.

'No!' shouted Ange, pulling the photographs

out of his reach. 'There's nuffin' she can do, nuffin'!'

'Oh, I wouldn't be so sure, Ange,' interrupted Nellie. 'My pal assures me that blackmail ain't looked on too kindly by the law. 'Specially when yer've done it before—several times.'

The sergeant darted a rapid glance at Ange. 'Wot's this?'

'Don't bloody listen to 'er! She's makin' it up!' she said, her forehead streaked with sweat. 'She's makin' up the 'ole bloody fing!'

Ange was right, Nellie was making it all up, but it was a good way of getting Ange and her boyfriend at each other's throats. 'Oh, I can assure yer my contact knows a lot about you, Ange,' she said mischievously. 'All them poor ol' geezers yer've bin knockin' around wiv, tryin' ter squeeze every penny yer can out of 'em. My contact says the rozzers've got a file on you six books 'igh. Just wait till they hear 'bout you aidin' an' abettin' a deserter.'

The sergeant immediately turned on Ange. 'Yer silly little cow! Give 'er the pictures!' he shouted, trying to grab the snapshots out of her hand.

'No!' barked Ange, pulling away from him. 'She's tellin' an 'ole pack of lies!'

'I said give 'er the pictures!' The sergeant gripped Ange's wrist and prised the photographs out of her hand. ''Ere!' he yelled to Nellie, throwing them at her. 'Take the bloody fings an' get out of 'ere!'

Nellie was about to leave when there was a loud banging on the front door, followed by men's voices shouting, 'Open up! Police! Get this door open!'

The sergeant, in a cold panic, rushed to the window and peered out through the blackout curtains. Pushing against the front door were two uniformed military policemen. 'MPs!' he gasped as he made a dash out into the passage.

'Sorry,' Nellie said as he pushed her out of the way, 'I forgot ter mention they was comin'.'

The two MPs outside were getting impatient; they were thumping and pushing hard against the front door. 'Open up! If you don't open this door, we'll break it down!'

'Wait, Mick!' Ange bawled as she, too, tried to push Nellie out of the way. 'I'm comin' wiv yer!'

But Nellie momentarily blocked her path. Although she was nearly three inches shorter than Ange, she grabbed hold of her chin and held on to it with a vice-like grip. 'If I ever see this poxy face near my dad again,' she said icily, 'I won't be quite so fergivin'.'

Now that young Lenny Beckwith was being looked after at home, 147A Tufnell Park Road had acquired a lived-in appearance that it had never really enjoyed before. The room that the two brothers had shared on the top floor was now occupied solely by Sid, for Madame thought it safer to keep Lenny in the small room next to her and Monsieur's own bedroom.

Madame had kept her word. She had given up her place in the Great Pierre's act, and was now devoting her life to looking after her family, which meant cooking the right kind of nourishing food for Lenny to help him rebuild his sadly depleted constitution. Fortunately, special food ration coupons were available for someone with his condition; black market food was becoming difficult to obtain owing to the many recent prosecutions of the dealers involved. But no matter how hard she tried, Madame could not escape the fact that Lenny was still a chronically ill child, and looking after him at home was difficult.

By September, the hospital was suggesting that the boy would stand a better chance of recovery if he were to be placed in a sanatorium, where the right treatment and conditions would be available twenty-four hours a day. 'Never in a million years!' was Madame's adamant reply to that. 'My boy stays at 'ome, where 'e belongs!' Although her reasoning was well intentioned, it was a selfish attitude to take, for Lenny's hacking cough could be heard throughout the night, every night, and there was no doubt that professional help was the obvious solution.

After the return of Ange's revealing snapshots, Monsieur had taken on a new lease of life. With the withdrawal of Madame from the act, he set about reshaping the form and style of the show so that whatever orchestra they were working with at the time could provide the accompanying mood music.

Despite the glamour and excitement of the twice nightly shows, Nellie had never really taken to the bright lights of the music hall stage. For her, there was something embarrassing and superficial about keeping a huge smile on her face night after night, and once Madame had gone, 'Miss Nellie' as she was billed, was becoming something of a name in her own right. Nellie didn't like all the attention she was getting, especially the wolf whistles and suggestive remarks that were yelled at her from the gods. But when she tried to express her concerns to Monsieur, he urged her to try and enjoy the admiration audiences clearly had for her, for if she played her cards right, one day she might become a star. Nellie told him that she didn't want to be a star. To her there was absolutely no point if she couldn't sing, dance, tell jokes, play a musical instrument, or walk a high wire. And even if she could have done any of those things, it still wouldn't have appealed to her. No. Being on stage turned her into something larger than life, the kind of person she just didn't want to be. All she wanted to be was plain Nell Beckwith, daughter of Mr and Mrs Albert Beckwith, of 147A Tufnell Park Road. But she assured Monsieur that as long as he needed her in the act, she would not fail him.

Fate had other ideas for Nellie, and they came in the shape of Monsieur's agent manager, Eddie Buxton. Nellie had met him many times backstage at various theatres, and once or twice when he came to the house to discuss business with Monsieur. Eddie was a jovial little man, who always seemed to wear rather loud three-piece checked suits. But he was a shrewd negotiator and in many ways he had been the driving force behind the career of the

Great Pierre. Right from the first time Nellie had joined the act, he had been impressed by the way the audience reacted to her. He finally made his feelings known one evening after a one-night performance during the Billy Cotton variety show at the majestic Astoria Cinema, Finsbury Park. The show played every Friday night between the supporting film and the main feature film. It was billed as a gala night, and audiences loved it so much that hours before the evening performance began queues would form outside the theatre, stretching right down Seven Sisters Road and Isledon Road on both sides of the massive white tiled cinema. When Nellie first stepped on to the stage and saw the three thousand faces of the audience staring at her, she felt as though her legs would collapse beneath her, but the shouts of approval from the male contingent in the audience soon dispelled her fears. By the time she had survived being levitated, climbed the Indian rope, and re-emerged in the audience after disappearing from the mystery cabinet, she got almost as big a round of applause as the star performers of the show, Billy Cotton and his band and singers, and Terry's Juveniles, a superb line-up of singing and dancing local youngsters.

'I won't mince my words, Nell,' said Eddie in Monsieur's dressing room after the show. 'You're dynamite out there. We've got to find you a piece of the action.'

Nellie hadn't the faintest idea what 'a piece of the action' meant. But she was worried about the suggestion all the same.

'They're crackers for you, Nell,' insisted Eddie, joining Monsieur in a glass of best brown ale. 'It's obvious they want to see more of you.'

Nellie sighed. She knew that Monsieur had been talking to him. 'Please, Mr Buxton,' she replied. 'I can't do nuffin' 'cept stand out there. I don't want ter do anyfin' else.'

Eddie was not listening to her. 'We're talkin' about big money here, Nell,' he said. 'Those audiences out there, they have an instinct. They know when someone takes their fancy. It's a kind of love affair. They want you to be there with them all the time.'

'But I can't *do* nuffin', Mr Buxton!' Nellie repeated.

'How d'yer know?' Eddie replied quick as a flash.

Nellie shrugged her shoulders. 'I just know, that's all.'

'Can you sing?' Eddie persisted.

Nellie roared with laughter. ''Ave yer 'eard me?' she spluttered.

'I've 'eard yer.' The voice was young Sid's. He had sat in the audience that evening with Grandma and Grandad Beckwith, who were also in the room, listening intently to the conversation. 'I 'eard yer the uvver day,' continued Sid, 'when yer was trying' ter get Lenny ter join in wiv yer.'

'Don't be a twerp, Sid!' Nellie retorted. 'That was diff'rent. Lenny's ill. I was only tryin' ter cheer 'im up.'

'She *can* sing, Mr Buxton,' Sid insisted.

398

'Yer should listen ter Eddie,' Monsieur told Nellie. ''E's bin in the business a long time. 'E knows wot 'e's talkin' about.'

With both hands, Eddie pulled Nellie up from the chair she was sitting on, placed her directly in front of him, then sat in the chair himself. 'Come on then. Sing something for me.'

'Oh no,' gasped Nellie. 'This is ridiculous.'

'Anything,' persisted Eddie. 'Anything you like.'

'I know, Nell,' suggested Monsieur eagerly. 'Wot about "Auld Lang Syne"?'

Nellie started to panic and tried to move away. 'I can't sing that.'

Eddie immediately got up and placed her back in position again. As he did so, Monsieur started to sing the song. 'Should auld acquaintance be fergot ...'

Nellie was acutely embarrassed, but not wishing to hurt her dad's feelings, she reluctantly joined in with the song.

As soon as Nellie began to sing, everyone in the room stopped to listen. Lack of confidence made her sound amateurish and faltering, but her voice was clear and pleasant, and as she stood there, staring at the floor self-consciously, her singing was strangely poignant.

When she had finished, everyone, with the exception of Eddie Buxton, applauded. Nellie was relieved that it was over and Monsieur's agent could now forget about her as a music hall performer.

Everyone watched the agent closely as he got up from his chair, put his hands in his jacket pockets, and went to Monsieur's dressing table to collect his half-finished glass of brown ale. After taking a quick gulp, he turned to Nellie and said, 'You've got a voice there, all right, Nell. All we need now is someone to train it.'

Over the following few weeks, Nellie was sent to a retired singing teacher, a Mr Pikestaff, who specialised in coaxing popular songs out of even the most mundane voices. Nellie was against the idea, for she saw no point in it at all. But both Eddie Buxton and her dad had talked her into the notion that if the public wanted something, then they should have it. And if they were willing to pay for it, so much the better. What she found hard to believe was Eddie's insistence that it wasn't just her legs and sex appeal that the audiences were going for, it was her personality that endeared her to them. Reluctantly, Nellie went along with the idea. firmly convinced that sooner or later it would all end in disaster. Nonetheless, if this was what it needed to breathe new life into her dad's act, then she would go along with whatever they asked her to do.

And so Mr Pikestaff set about turning Nellie Beckwith into a music hall songstress. It wasn't an easy task, for Nellie couldn't read a note of music, which meant that she had to memorise each song she was being taught. And time and time again she got the giggles when she was asked to do some rather animated breathing exercises, which usually resulted in her exploding a lungful of air straight into Mr

Pikestaff's face. It didn't help that the man who was teaching her had some very eccentric habits, such as sipping black tea and gargling with a mouthful before swallowing it. He always wore a Spanish troubadour's shirt, and while Nellie was struggling to sing 'As Time Goes By', he flounced around the room conducting every note she warbled. But after she had been working with him for less than six weeks, even she was surprised to realise how much she had learnt about volume and tone, rhythm and balance and, above all, pace and timing.

Ruby Catmonk was tickled pink by this new development in Nellie's life, and every time Nellie came to visit her, they roared with laughter at the antics that Nellie got up to with the prissy Mr Pikestaff. But Ruby did not go along with Nellie's dismissive assessment of her own potential.

'Go for it, gel,' said the old pro, as Nellie put some more coke on to the fire in the tiny fireplace in Ruby's flat. 'Yer know wot 'Etty King used ter say, Gawd bless 'er: take what's comin' to yer, an' get straight off.'

Like most of the artistes Ruby talked about, Nellie hadn't the faintest idea who Hetty King was, even though her act as a singing male impersonator was for years the sensation of music halls all over the country.

Since Ruby had helped her nail Ange and her army sergeant boyfriend, Nellie had grown more attached to the old woman than ever. Whenever the two of them got together, a lot of gossip passed between them about people they knew.

Ruby was an astute old dear, and during her long life in the music hall, she had learnt a lot about human nature. 'I'll tell yer this much about some of 'em though,' she said, her usual Capstan cigarette dangling from her lips while she sat at the table painting her ancient fingernails bright red. 'There are those who fink they've got it, and those who fink they ain't. I know the ones I'd go fer.' She blew smoke out of the side of her mouth and peered at Nellie over the top of her specs. 'I reckon you could get anyfin' yer set out fer,' she said with a twinkle in the eye, 'if yer really want it.'

'That's the trouble, Rube,' said Nellie. 'I *don't* want it. In fact, I don't really know wot I want at all.'

'*I* do,' replied the old girl.

Nellie swung a look at her.

Ruby had a sly grin on her face. 'When's that bit of Air Force blue comin' 'ome on leave again? The Jewish one.'

Nellie couldn't help smiling at Ruby's shrewdness. But then she sighed. 'No idea,' she replied. ''E writes me plenty of letters, but they're usually censored. I don't know why, but I've got an uncomfortable feelin' inside. Somefin's goin' on at these camps that we don't know about.' She finished putting the last pieces of coke on the fire and went across to join Ruby at the table. 'The papers keep goin' on about all these dog fights wiv Jerry over the south coast of England,' she said anxiously. 'It scares the daylights out of me. I never know from one day ter the next if Toff's alive or dead.'

Ruby put the brush back into its bottle, then blew on her nails to dry them. 'I shouldn't worry too much about that if I was you. In my experience, they soon let yer know if anyfin' like that's 'appened.'

This was little comfort to Nellie. Toff's absence only made her yearn for him even more. 'I know it's stupid,' she said, 'but even though I've only known him properly these past few months, I don't fink I could cope if—'

'Oh, don't worry,' interrupted Ruby, 'you'd cope all right. We all do. I know *I* 'ad to.'

Nellie looked at her inquiringly.

'It 'appens to most of us at least once in a lifetime, Nell. I 'ad this stupid geezer once. Years ago—the last war. 'E was younger than me, bright-eyed, bright-arsed little sod. But I loved 'im—oh yes, all that. Loved me, too. When we got married, 'e said it was fer life.' She finished blowing on her nails, then took off her specs, put them on the table in front of her, and squinted at Nellie. 'Trouble is, 'e didn't tell me 'ow long that life was goin' ter be.' She paused only briefly. 'Got blown up by a shell on the Somme.'

Without her specs on, Nellie could see that the old lady's eyes had faded from their original dark brown. 'I didn't know yer was ever married,' Nellie said. 'I'm sorry, Rube.'

'No need ter be,' replied Ruby, rubbing her eyes before putting her specs back on again. 'I only tell yer 'cos we all 'ave ter make the best of fings whiles we've got 'em. But I want ter meet this lover boy of yours. 'E don't get *my* seal of approval till I know 'e's goin' ter be the right geezer fer me best pal.'

Nellie's face lit up. 'Hey, Rube,' she said brightly. '*Am* I yer best pal then?'

'Don't push yer luck, mate!' Ruby replied. 'As my ol' mate Charlie Chaplin said ter me when we was in the same show at the 'Olloway Empire, back in 1907 it must've bin, 'e said, "There's only one person that's better than a good mate, an' that's a lover!"'

Both of them roared with laughter.

'Did yer really know Charlie Chaplin, Rube?' Nellie asked.

'Don't be daft,' replied the old girl. 'Ruby Catmonk knows *everyone*.'

The two of them continued to laugh together.

Nellie hadn't noticed that where her elbow was resting on the table, Ruby had dreamily dropped some small blobs of red nail varnish on to the clean yellow tablecloth.

Chapter 24

The deafening barrage of ack-ack guns was the fiercest London had heard for many months. From twenty miles outside the city, the constant flashes of bursting shells could be seen lighting up the sky as ground artillery did their best to bring down the small party of raiding enemy aircraft that had broken through the tight ring of coastal defences. The attack was as sudden as it was unexpected, and as usual Islington did not escape the onslaught, which seemed to be part of a renewed campaign by the Luftwaffe since the start of the new year.

At 147A Tufnell Park Road, Madame, Sid, Lenny, and Nellie were all taking shelter in a large, empty cupboard under the stairs. Since Madame had got it into her head that the damp conditions inside the Anderson shelter were responsible for Lenny's illness, she had decided that the family should take its chances inside the house. The old cupboard was a tight squeeze, and did nothing to insulate them from the deafening sound of the ack-ack fire outside which was rocking the very foundations of the house.

'Who was it said nineteen forty-four's goin' ter be the last year of the war?' groaned Madame, who was cradling Lenny protectively on her lap. 'Listen ter all that up there,' she sighed, looking up at the roof of the cupboard. ''Itler's not finished yet, not by a long way. An' the war's bin on fer over four years!'

'It's 'is last fling, Mum,' said Nellie, trying to sound reassuring. 'Once the invasion starts, there won't be any more of this.'

'Invasion, invasion!' replied Madame tetchily. 'That's all yer ever 'ear these days. If this General Eisen'ower bloke's s'posed ter be in charge, why don't 'e just get on wiv it?'

Nellie chuckled. ''E's only just got 'ere, Mum,' she said. 'Give 'im a chance.'

Another outburst of heavy gunfire caused

405

Lenny to whimper and snuggle up tightly to his mum.

'It's all right, son, it's all right,' she said, smoothing his hair comfortingly with her hand. 'We're all 'ere. We won't let nuffin' 'appen to yer.'

'Mum,' whinged Sid, who was cramped up in a tiny space on the floor, covered with his own eiderdown, 'I want ter go back ter bed.'

'Don't be so silly, Sid,' Madame snapped. 'Just listen ter all that rumpus outside. It's not safe ter stay in bed.'

'Then why don't Dad come down?' Sid moaned.

Madame had no real answer to that. Ever since the war began, Monsieur had solidly refused to abandon his own bed for an air-raid shelter, and he certainly wasn't going to start now. 'You know as well as I do, Sid,' said Madame, 'if the 'ouse came down on top of yer dad, 'e still wouldn't give up 'is kip!'

Nellie laughed, and adjusted the blanket covering Lenny on Madame's lap.

'I don't like air raids,' said Lenny, whose voice was so much weaker since his illness. 'The noise scares me.'

'Nuffin' ter be scared of, Len,' Nellie said brightly. 'It's just a few stupid ol' Jerry planes tryin' ter scare us. But they ain't goin' to, so there!'

'I wanna go back ter bed.' Sid was grizzling again.

'Tell yer wot,' said Nellie, all perky. 'Why don't we all 'ave a sing-song? By the time we've finished, I bet yer we'll 'ear the All Clear. What d'yer say, Len?'

By the dim light of the torch propped up on the cupboard ledge, Nellie could just see Lenny nodding his head wearily.

'Right then,' she said, sitting up straight on the stool she was perched on. 'What'll it be? Any suggestions?'

'You're the singer in the family now, Nell,' replied Madame. 'Choose somefin'.'

Nellie's stomach turned over as she was reminded that within the next few days she would be singing a song in public for the first time, a song which Monsieur was going to incorporate into the act. But the mood in the cupboard under the stairs called for something quite different, so she launched straight into a rousing version of 'Don't Fence Me In' which was currently a great favourite, made popular on a gramophone record by Bing Crosby and the Andrews Sisters.

It took a moment or so for the others to join in, but when they did, their voices did much to drown the sound of the guns belting away outside. And what an inspiring sound the Beckwith family made—Madame, with her high-pitched soprano voice, Sid, wide awake now and bellowing his lungs out, and Nellie with her newly trained crooner's delivery. Frail as he was, even young Lenny raised enough energy to join in the chorus.

When the song was over, Nellie applauded loudly, even more so when she realised that the ack-ack guns had actually gone silent. 'See!

Wot'd I tell yer?' she announced triumphantly. 'It's all over!'

No sooner had she spoken than the barrage of gunfire broke out once more.

Lenny quickly hugged up to Madame again, and Sid covered himself with his eiderdown. Undaunted, Nellie burst forth with a defiant rendition of 'Rule Britannia'. The others joined in with gusto, and the competition between the Beckwith family and the ack-ack outside became a battle of wills. But the singing became less and less vigorous as they turned their eyes towards the ceiling and listened to the drone of airplanes zooming down towards the rooftops overhead. Everyone tried very hard not to show how scared they were but gradually the singing stopped altogether and they just listened.

Out of the cacophony dominating the skies above them, there came a much more deadly sound, whistling down from the night clouds.

'Down! Down!' yelled Nellie.

The explosion rocked the house. Madame and Sid screamed out loud, glass shattered, plaster fell from the ceilings, and dogs barked in panic along the back gardens outside.

It seemed to take for ever before the terrifying sounds settled down, and when they did, Lenny was crying and nestling up as tight as he could against his mother's body. Everyone was covered in dust.

'Doris! Are yer all right!' Monsieur was hurrying down the stairs as fast as he could. 'Oh, Christ, Doris!' he called frantically. 'Are any of yer hurt?'

By the time he reached them, Nellie was already helping Madame and Lenny out of the cupboard. Then she pulled the dust-covered eiderdown off Sid and yanked him up on to his feet. 'Are yer OK, Sid?' she asked quickly, anxiously. 'Are yer?'

Sid's striped pyjamas were also covered in dust, but he seemed unhurt and calmly nodded his head.

'Are we 'it?' Madame spluttered, trying to spit out some of the dust. ''As it 'it the 'ouse?'

'No, fank Gawd,' replied Monsieur. taking Lenny from Madame's arms. 'We got the blast, that's all. It must 'ave come down up Junction Road somewhere.' Lenny was shaking, crying, and coughing in his arms. 'It's all right, son, it's all right,' he said, hugging the boy. 'The worst's over now.'

But the house was still being shaken by the gunfire outside. They stood there helplessly, not knowing which way to turn.

'Wot're we goin' ter do, Dad?' said Nellie, rubbing the dust out of her eyes with the backs of her hands.

'It can't last much longer,' he replied, making for the kitchen door. 'Better get down the shelter.'

'No, Bert!' Madame rushed to pull Lenny out of her husband's arms. 'This boy's not goin' down that shelter. It'll kill 'im!'

Monsieur held on to the boy. 'Don't be ridiculous, Doris,' he said angrily. 'The raid's gettin' worse. We can't take no chances!'

Again Madame tried to pull Lenny out of

Monsieur's arms, but he resisted, and it looked as though a tug-of-war was about to ensue. 'Leave 'im ter me, Albert?' she pleaded. 'There's nuffin' wrong wiv 'im. 'E'll be perfectly all right wiv me.'

Monsieur turned on her. 'Wot do you mean, there's nuffin' wrong wiv 'im? Just look at 'im, Doris. Go on, take a good look at 'im.' Lenny was deathly white and thin, and crying pitifully in between fits of coughing. 'Does this boy look as though 'e'll be all right, Doris? Does 'e?' Monsieur's face was stiff with tension and he had to shout to be heard above the barrage of ack-ack gunfire. 'When're you goin' ter listen to uvver people, Doris, when? Lenny shouldn't be 'ere in this ouse, any sensible person can see that. 'E should be where 'e can be taken care of, somewhere safe, away from all this, away from the bombs, the noise, the stress. Can't yer see 'e needs care an' attention? Attention that none of us 'ere can give 'im!'

He turned to go into the kitchen and Madame followed him. 'No, Bert,' she pleaded. 'I beg yer. For the love of God, please don't take 'im down that shelter!'

Monsieur stopped at the kitchen door and turned briefly. 'I'm sorry, gel. yer've got ter learn—we've boaf got ter learn—it's Lenny we 'ave ter fink of, not ourselves.'

With that, he turned away, kicked the kitchen door open with his foot, and made his way to the back garden door.

Nellie immediately went to comfort her mum who was in tears.

Neither of them noticed young Sid making his way back upstairs to his own room.

The trail of havoc and destruction caused by the previous night's lightning air raid galvanised the communities in and around the Nag's Head. The extensive blast damage to number 147A and other properties along Tuffnell Park Road had been caused by a high-explosive bomb on a chemist's shop in Junction Road, as Monsieur had guessed, less than a mile away. Fortunately, there were no casualties, which was more than could be said for other parts of London, but the aftermath of the raid left people in a deep state of shock.

The immediate problem was getting the place cleared up. Tiles had been blown off roofs, windows shattered, and plaster dislodged from walls and ceilings in houses within a two-mile radius stretching from the Archway to Kentish Town. There was an immediate rush to find carpenters, glaziers, plasterers, and anyone who knew anything about building repair work. Monsieur, however, was no mean hand when it came to do-it-yourself jobs, and so, with Nellie and Sid to help him, he set about replacing the glass in his windows himself. The only trouble was that putty was in short supply, so he had to use his standing as a local celebrity to prise some out of Smith's the builders' merchant in Upper Holloway Road. Plastering was not his strong point but he made a good stab at it and by the end of the day he had managed to patch up holes in three of the top floor ceilings.

Last night's tense exchange between Madame and Monsieur about young Lenny worried Nellie. She understood both their points of view, although in her heart of hearts she did think that Madame was being a little too possessive in keeping Lenny at home. He quite clearly needed the peace and tranquillity of care in some kind of convalescent home. But this was one area in which she could not interfere; Lenny's welfare could only be decided by reasonable discussion and mutual agreement between the boy's mum and dad. Nonetheless, as she swept up broken glass from the shattered stained-glass panels in the front door, she couldn't help feeling a bit depressed that things at the moment were not all they should be for the Beckwith family. She yearned for something nice to happen.

'Hello, Nell.'

Nellie's face lit up. 'Toff!'

They rushed into each other's arms and kissed passionately halfway along the garden path. It was several moments before they came up for air, during which time the neighbours not only had their money's worth, but also a timely distraction from their painful task of clearing up after the air raid.

'Why din't yer let me know yer was comin'?' Nellie said, her hands linked behind his neck. ''Ow long 'ave yer got?'

'Only a thirty-six hour, I'm afraid,' said Toff. He had come straight from Charing Cross Station, and was still in uniform, a rucksack over his shoulder. 'I have to be back by twenty-three hundred tomorrow night.'

Nellie hadn't the faintest idea what twenty-three hundred meant, but it sounded lousy. 'Yer should've let me know,' she said. 'I've missed yer, Toff.'

'I've missed you too, Nell.'

They both spent a full minute just staring into each other's eyes.

Alexandra Palace nestled majestically on top of a steep hill overlooking the wide open spaces of Alexandra Park below. It was a glorious building, much loved by the residents of Wood Green on one side and Muswell Hill on the other. The present palace, built in 1873, had never had any royal residents, for it had been built mainly to stage national exhibitions and symphony concerts, which set off the grandiose interior to perfection. The Ally Pally, as it was affectionately known, contained the very best of Victorian design, with marble floors, huge crystal chandeliers, and a glass dome which before the war had been magically lit up from inside and could be seen for miles around. The vast main hall, where many concerts had been held over the years, contained one of the largest and most beautiful pipe organs in England. The view from the main entrance steps outside the good old 'Ally Pally' had always been a favourite of Toff's. Whenever he wanted to get away from home in nearby Highgate, this was where he came.

'Before the war, I remember coming up here one Guy Fawkes night. There was a terrific fireworks display—bangers, Catherine wheels, sparklers, and rockets shooting right up into the sky over the park. You could see the rooftops over Hornsey and Crouch End in the distance changing colour every few minutes. It was magical.'

Toff was doing his best to pass on his enthusiasm to Nellie, but it wasn't easy. From where they were sitting now, the January evening view consisted of nothing more than total darkness, not a light to be seen in the bleak wilderness of the wartime blackout.

They crossed the road in front of the palace and made their way down into the park. 'Pity we can't turn back the clock,' she said. 'Everyfin' seemed ter be so much better.'

'If we turned back the clock,' replied Toff, 'we'd have to go through this whole damn war again. No. It's the future I want. A new start.'

They picked their way in the dark by the dim light of Nellie's pocket torch. It was slippery under foot in the wet grass, and bitterly cold. And yet, as they strolled along with their arms around each other's waists, it seemed to make no difference at all that Toff towered above Nellie. In their own world, tall or small played no part at all.

Stretched out before them in the dark were the strange, twisting shapes of trees, and although they could hear the far distant rumbling sounds of traffic, they were surrounded by an eerie silence. They came to a halt and for a moment, neither said anything. Then Nellie felt Toff moving round in front of her and both his

414

arms sliding round her waist. Almost at once, his lips searched for hers. When he found them, he kissed her hard and long.

'It's funny, isn't it?' he said softly. 'What a snotty-nosed little brat you were when we first met.'

'I beg yer pardon!' growled Nellie in mock indignation.

'It's true,' he said, teasing her. 'Brash, opinionated, full of yourself ...'

'An' wot 'bout you?' she countered. 'Mister Smoothie of all time. Why d'yer fink the gang called yer Toff?'

Toff was silent for a while. When he spoke again, it was with some difficulty. 'They called me Toff because I was the only one who seemed to offer them some kind of hope. I was someone they could look up to, to follow, and make the decisions. They were wrong. I was no better than any of them.'

Not far away, they could hear young voices whispering to each other in the dark. This was a popular area for courting couples.

Toff leaned down and hugged Nellie, so that her head was resting against the rough serge of his Air Force greatcoat. 'I blame myself for what happened to Rats and Bonkers,' he said with quiet anguish. 'When the police and the ambulance turned up to collect them that night, me and the others just split up and got away as fast as we could. I've never seen any of them again from that day to this.'

'It wasn't your fault, Toff,' Nellie replied. 'Yer told them not ter go after that kitten, but they did. It wasn't your fault.'

He shook his head. 'I was the oldest one among them. I should have been a leader, a *real* leader. I should have told them to go home, to go back to their families. I blame myself. I'm not a leader. I could never be one.' He squeezed her tight. 'I don't want to be Toff any more, Nell,' he begged. 'I want to be me. I want to be Martin. I want to be just like anyone else.'

Nellie listened to him in silence. Pressed hard against his heavy coat, her mind began to dwell again on the events of that horrible night outside the old furniture store. It reminded her of how wrong she had been at the time to blame Toff for trying to prevent Rats and Bonkers from taking their life in their hands. Whatever he had just said, she firmly believed that if anyone had displayed qualities as a leader that night, it had been him.

She could hear Toff's heart beating. It was a firm, decisive beat, and it made her feel warm and secure. But what a strange, complicated boy he was. Since she had got to know him, she had discovered that if there was a right or a wrong way to work out a situation, then Toff would invariably choose the wrong one. And the way he constantly tore himself apart for no reason was absurd, and totally different to her own way of thinking. And yet she was drawn to him. At this moment she felt so deeply for him, she wanted him to throw caution to the wind and make love to her. But every time that idea came into her mind, she thought about Patrick Duvall, and how she would never be able to trust a man again. Nevertheless, all she knew now was that she wanted Toff, she wanted him so much, and try as she may, she just couldn't understand why he always held back from that one ultimate, inevitable act of true love.

'Martin.'

Toff was taken by surprise. Without moving he whispered, 'Nell? What did you say?'

Nellie looked up and whispered back. 'I said Martin.'

Martin reached down in the dark, found her lips again, and kissed her passionately. 'I love you, Nell,' he said, softly.

'Don't be stupid,' she replied. 'Yer don't even know me.'

'Oh, I *know* you, Nellie Beckwith,' he said with an affectionate smile in his voice. 'I know you very well indeed.' He kissed her again, longer this time. 'I want us to move in together,' he said quite unexpectedly.

Nellie looked up at him in surprise. 'Wot d'yer mean?'

'I love you, Nell,' he repeated. 'I want us to be together.'

Nellie took a moment to think this one out. 'But we're both under age. We'd 'ave ter 'ave permission ter get married.'

'I wasn't talking about getting married,' Martin replied. 'Not yet, anyway.'

Nellie gently pulled away from him. 'We can't live tergevver, Martin,' she said awkwardly.

'Why not?'

''Cos—'cos it's not right fer people ter live

tergevver unless they get married. Nobody does fings like that.'

'Listen to me, Nell,' he said, drawing her close and lowering his voice again. 'We can do *anything* if we really want to. I love you. Stupid though it may sound, I really do love you.'

Nellie sighed. 'I love yer too, Martin,' she said, without a suggestion of doubt in her voice. 'But let's do it the right way. We've got plenty of time.'

'No, Nell, we don't have plenty of time. You see, I won't be seeing you for quite a bit. Something's happening, something important—I can't tell you what. But when I come back, I want to know that you'll be there. I want to know that we'll be together, that we can make love, and that nobody can ever part us again.'

Nellie hated opening nights. To her, there were always hidden terrors in appearing for the first time in front of an audience that she had never worked before. Collins' Music Hall on Islington Green was considered in the business to be a number two hall, which meant that it rarely attracted star names, and audiences there, particularly in the gods, had the reputation of being rowdy. Monsieur had turned down a six-week booking on the number two tour, but he wanted to try out the new act and Collins seemed to be the ideal place to do it in.

The act was already beginning to cause some controversy; Monsieur had decided to change its staging completely and to cut down the length of the performance from sixteen to twelve minutes.

Eddie Buxton had a hard time selling the new Great Pierre to potential managements, despite the fact that Nellie would make her debut as a singer during the act. 'Customers like what they're used to,' said one rather sceptical entrepreneur. 'Muck around with the goods and you've lost your profits.' In a sense, he was right, for during the past year there had been definite signs that variety on the halls was beginning to wane. During the war years, the music hall had done so much to boost people's morale, but despite the air raids of the previous few weeks, everyday talk now was of an impending Allied invasion in Europe, which was giving people the impression that the war was all but over.

'We've got ter face up ter the fact, Nell,' said Monsieur gloomily. 'Fings're never goin' ter be wot they used ter be, not as long as people've got the pictures ter go to an' the wireless ter listen to.'

'You're right,' agreed Eddie. The three of them were mulling things over in Monsieur's dressing room after the morning rehearsal. 'An' I'll tell yer something else. When the war's over, there's going to be quite a lot of competition when they start up television again.'

'Television!' spluttered Monsieur dismissively. 'Television can't compete wiv the wireless and live stage shows. It's nuffin' but a box wiv a flickerin' light.'

'Mark my words, mate,' warned Eddie ominously. 'Just mark my words.'

Nellie listened to all this with calm detachment. She didn't care one bit if people stopped going to the music hall or stopped listening to the wireless. She didn't even care if they stopped going to the pictures. But she did care about the effect it would have on all the people like Monsieur, whose whole life had been dedicated to the bright lights.

'Anyway,' continued Eddie, 'tonight's going to be a turning point for the act. I think you've got some great new ideas, Bert. And as for Nell's song,' he gave her a huge smile, 'touch of genius!'

Nellie smiled back at him, weakly. She knew he was only saying that because it had been his suggestion.

Eddie got up and went to the door. 'Whatever happens,' he said, 'it's now or never. See you at first house, boys and girls.'

After he had gone, Monsieur sat deep in thought. 'Mustn't take too much notice of Ed,' he said to Nellie, trying to put a brave face on it. ''E's just nervous to know 'ow the new routines'll go ternight.'

'So am I,' replied Nellie. 'I just 'ope I don't let yer down, Dad.'

Monsieur, who was sitting at his minute dressing table, swung round on his stool to look at her. 'You could never do that, Nell,' he said with a warm smile. 'Just be yerself, an' we can't fail.'

With the minutes ticking by before she went on stage, Nellie felt her mouth going as dry as a bone. She had already drunk two glasses of water, but there was not enough water in the whole world to quench her nerves. It was bad enough to be stuck in a dressing room that was no bigger than a broom cupboard, but to have to go halfway down the passage every time she wanted to go to the ladies made life even more difficult. And to make things worse, the girl she had to share the room with, who was part of an acrobatic dog act, could speak very little English and smelt a bit like some of the furry artistes she worked with.

The first house curtain was due up at six twenty-five, and for the final hour before the performance, Nellie must have looked at the wristwatch her mum and dad had given her at least a dozen times. She had plenty of reasons for doing so, for apart from the show itself, she knew that Martin was already well on his way back to camp. And the more she thought about that, the more depressed she became. Her only consolation was that she had at least been with him for those few last precious hours, and that, despite his complicated moods, she felt closer to him than ever. For Martin, meeting Monsieur and Madame had been a far more relaxing experience than he had anticipated, for music hall people had a reputation for being outgoing and demonstrative, which was something he had been dreading. But Nellie's mum and dad had been nothing but a joy to be with, and both Sid and young Lenny quickly treated him as one of the family. As she sat at her tiny dressing table, putting on her Five and Nine, Nellie mulled this over in her mind, and for one short moment it even brought a smile to her face.

Shortly after seven o'clock, Nellie joined Monsieur behind the flats at the back of the stage. The acrobatic dog act was in full swing, much to the approval of a full but fairly vocal audience. It had not escaped Nellie's notice that the Great Pierre act had lost its place as the climax at the end of the show's first half. Although Monseiur would never show his disappointment at such a decision, she knew it hurt him. 'Sign of the times, Nell,' he had said wistfully during the morning's rehearsals. 'That's life.'

At exactly five minutes past seven, the Great Pierre finally took the stage. But this time everything was different. There was no loudspeaker introduction, and the clash of the cymbal had been replaced by a far more formal opening, with the orchestra playing a selection of mood music specially chosen and arranged by Madame. Monsieur made his entrance quite simply, from behind a door cut into the black backcloth. Even his appearance was different. He was still dressed in black from head to foot, but to complement his white gloves he had used white make-up on his face, which gave him a droll, poignant look. His entrance provoked a few coarse whistles and remarks from some of the customers up in the gods but he was astute and professional enough to acknowledge them with a graceful bow, a flick of the wrist, and a silent snap of the fingers. This was to be the hallmark of the new Great Pierre.

As for the act itself, there was no longer any 'Sawing the Lady in Half' routine—Monsieur had decided that he would leave this trick to the traditional stage magicians. There was no climbing the rope either—this had been in the act since Monsieur first introduced it many years before. What he was now offering was a programme of *real* illusions, in which his audience would be offered deceptive impressions of the real thing. This he duly set out to do by skilfully mesmerising his audience into a state of unconscious *belief:* what they saw was not what they saw at all. Monsieur was, in every sense, a hypnotist, but he worked silently, using his hands and not his voice to speak the words. And as he worked, he spun round the stage with movements that were as light as a cat's; his eyes darted from the stalls up to the gods with lightning speed, he was never still for a single moment. His whole act was, in fact, an illusion in itself. And there to help him manifest it all was Nellie, getting the usual wolf whistles as soon as she appeared and still lusted after by every red-blooded male in the audience. But this time her sex appeal gave Monsieur's illusions the dream-like quality he was trying to project. Instead of posing endlessly to draw out the audience's applause, she was placed in a single spotlight at the side of the stage where, at the given time, she gracefully sang, unaccompanied, the poignant words of 'When I Grow Too Old to Dream'. Her voice, although not strong, was sweet and innocent, and helped to enhance the extraordinary atmosphere in the house. The audience were, quite simply, transported into an uplifting, trouble-free world of beauty.

When the curtains finally closed on the new act, it was for several moments greeted with total silence. But when Monsieur and Nellie came up front and joined hands to take their bow, the audience burst into life and applauded and cheered as they had never done before. Some people were so overwhelmed they had tears in their eyes. Even Monsieur's cynical agent, Eddie Buxton, couldn't believe that he was seeing the same artiste that he had represented for so many years. Shorter the act might be, but it was a sensation!

During the first and second house shows, the air-raid siren sounded the alert. But this did not deter the next house audience from filing into the theatre, for the management had immediately given a categorical assurance that the show would go on. And so it did, despite the fact that heavy ack-ack gunfire was heard from time to time, which caused the overhead chandelier to rock and sway in time to the carefully orchestrated songs everyone was invited to sing along with the top of the bill crooner Sam Browne. But shortly before the show finished there was consternation when the whole theatre vibrated to the sound of two heavy bomb explosions. They were a little too close for comfort.

In his dressing room after the show, Monsieur received the congratulations of endless visitors. Everyone was of the opinion that the the Great Pierre had taken on a new lease of life and was, quite simply, a supreme artiste. But a great deal of the praise was reserved for Nellie, for it was obvious that her beautiful singing of that one song had enhanced the act to perfection. Madame hugged Nellie for all she had done to help restore Monsieur's confidence; she couldn't wait to get back to tell Lenny and Grandma and Grandad Beckwith all about it. But Sid couldn't see what all the fuss was about. He boasted that he still knew how all the tricks were done. The only person who seemed to be missing from the celebrations was Monsieur's agent, Eddie Buxton, who had not been seen since the final curtain came down nearly an hour earlier.

As Nellie, Monsieur, Madame, and Sid left the stage door, the air raid was gathering momentum. Ack-ack shells burst constantly in the sky above them, and fire-engine bells clanged all the way along Upper Street. There was no sign of any buses running and apart from a few people hurrying to the nearest shelters, the streets were practically deserted.

'Better get down the Tube,' called Monsieur. 'Let it calm down a bit before we try ter get 'ome. We can't take any risks wiv all this shrapnel comin' down!'

Madame was at first unwilling; this was the first time she had left young Lenny in the charge of Grandma and Grandad Beckwith since he had left hospital. But with pieces of sharp, jagged shrapnel from the ack-ack shells raining down on to the pavements all around them, she had no choice. Nellie put her arm round her waist and led her on quickly behind

Monsieur, who was clutching Sid's hand and setting the pace towards the Angel Tube just down the road.

They had gone only a few yards when they heard someone calling to them.

'Bert! Doris! Wait!'

They turned to find Eddie Buxton hurrying out of a taxi.

'Thank God I've caught you,' he said, rushing to them where they were sheltering in a shop doorway.

'Wot is it?' asked Monsieur.

'Something terrible's happened, Bert,' Eddie replied. Even in the blacked-out street, they could see how distraught he was. 'There's a bomb come down. It's terrible! Just terrible!'

'Oh Christ!' gasped Madame. 'Not *our* place! Please don't say it's *our* place!'

'No, no,' replied Eddie, shaking his head vigorously. 'It's up Finsbury Park way. Just round the corner from the Empire. People killed. The whole place—terrible, terrible!'

Nellie felt a rush of panic. '*Where*, Mr Buxton?' she asked frantically. 'Where exactly 'as it come down?'

'Blackstock Road,' Eddie replied in utter despair. 'I went straight down there from the show. I've got friends there ... they told me ... they told me it was a direct hit on the Gas Board.'

'The Gas Board!' Nellie gasped, desperate with shock. 'That's next door ter the funeral parlour!' She was half-crazed with fear and anxiety. 'Oh Christ! Tell me, Mr Buxton, fer

426

God's sake, tell me, wot's 'appened ter the funeral parlour?'

Eddie shook his head. He could hardly bring himself to answer her. 'It's gone, Nell,' he said painfully. 'The whole bloody lot's gone.'

Nellie felt the blood drain from her body. All she could think about was the person who lived in the small flat above that funeral parlour, the best pal she had ever had in the whole wide world—that cunning, ginger-haired old cow Ruby Catmonk.

Chapter 25

The Finsbury Park Empire rarely offered matinee performances. But today was different. The fauteuils and stalls might not have been full to overflowing, but the people who were there had a very important part to play in these particular proceedings.

Ruby Catmonk's long association with the music hall, not just with Finsbury Park but with many of the other halls in London, had earned her a special place in the hearts of everyone who had ever had anything to do with live variety theatre. Ruby went back a long way, starting as a chorus girl in pantomime at the tender age of sixteen, but it was for her latter years that she would be remembered, for she had gained a reputation among artistes everywhere as 'the best needle and cotton in the business'.

A special matinee tribute had been arranged for her, and a lot of her old friends, famous and not so famous, turned up to pay their last respects. It was what Ruby would have wanted most of all, for, although she was Jewish by birth, she had lived her life as an atheist, leaving instructions that on her death there should be no religious service at her funeral. Her wishes were duly carried out, and she was cremated with the minimum of fuss at Golders Green crematorium on a bright and sunny winter's afternoon at the beginning of February. Few people attended the event. Those who did included Monsieur, Madame, and Nellie. It was all over very quickly, and there were no flowers. 'Bleedin' waste of money,' Ruby often said. 'Wot's the use of leavin' a bunch of beautiful flowers to rot on top of a grave, or bein' chucked in a fire on top of a coffin!'

Ruby's death devastated Nellie. The night the bomb destroyed the old girl's tiny flat, Nellie had wanted to rush up there straight away to help the emergency services dig her out. But Monsieur absolutely forbade her to go, saying that the last thing Ruby would have wanted is for anyone to put themselves in danger because of her. Nellie couldn't understand his attitude. 'Ruby's my pal!' she bawled, tears streaming down her face. 'Ever since I've known 'er, she's 'elped me. I can't let 'er down now, I can't!' But Monsieur had his way, and it was not until the following morning that Nellie finally saw what was left of those two small rooms she had visited so many times. By then, Ruby's body had been recovered and removed from the pile of rubble which contained the remnants of the few possessions she had owned.

At the matinee tribute, Ruby's old mates Gert and Daisy performed a few minutes of Ruby's favourite double act, and then shared their memories of a 'dear and trusted friend'. The wonderful crooner, Anne Shelton, invited everyone to join her in a chorus of 'You Are My Lucky Star', a song Ruby had adored. This brought a few tears to the stalls, which, said Monsieur at the conclusion of the matinee, 'would have tickled the old girl no end'. Everyone had something to contribute, including the manager and the theatre orchestra. The box office staff came too, as did usherettes and backstage staff from several other London music halls. Ruby had been one of them, and her death in such tragic circumstances had touched the entire profession. And on the stage itself, artistes lined up to contribute either a bit of their own act, or a few words about incidents involving 'that shrewd old bag who never let any of us down'. Ruby was held in such high esteem that the much-loved Lancashire comedian, Frank Randle, had come down all the way from Manchester to do a 'bit of a laugh for the old girl', and also to add his own poignant farewell. And to make this memorial performance even more personal, many of the artistes who were appearing wore costumes that Ruby had either made or repaired on her battered old Singer sewing machine.

During the extraordinary hour-long performance, Nellie was too distressed to sit with the
rest of the audience downstairs, preferring to
spend the time watching from the front row
of the gods, whose customers were, in Ruby's
own words, 'the real bread an' butter of the
'alls'. It was a sad and desolate feeling to be
sitting all alone in such a vast empty space, for
the music hall was all about togetherness and
having a good time. This was what Ruby had
loved about it all, and the reason why she had
wanted to be a part of it in some way or another
for the whole of her life. What an extraordinary,
sentimental lot of old softies they were down
there, Nellie thought. Just look at them, sobbing
their hearts out, when old Rube was probably
watching from somewhere, coughing her lungs
out on a Capstan and laughing her head off at
the jokes. But then Nellie thought to herself,
why shouldn't they be softies? After all, music
hall folk had feelings just like anyone else. The
only difference was that they found it difficult
not to show how they felt.

At the conclusion of the show, a huge laugh
went up when the stage manager asked everyone
to stand and sing the song that Ruby was often
heard lah-de-dahing to herself as she toiled away
at her sewing machine. It was a good old
Cockney song called 'Boiled Beef and Carrots'.
Nellie stood up too, but while she joined in
with the rest of the audience, her mind was
on something quite different—the hand-written
letter she had received two weeks before from
the son of Ruby's old flame who worked at

the War Office, the same officer who had provided the information about Ange's soldier boyfriend:

Dear Miss Beckwith,

I am a friend of the late Miss Ruby Catmonk.

Some weeks ago she asked me, in the event of her passing, to let you have the enclosed.

As you are probably aware, Miss Ruby possessed few personal belongings, and I fear that those that did survive are somewhat beyond repair. However, she asked me to pass on to you the warm feelings she had for you, and hoped that you would accept the modest gift, enclosed, as a token of her love and affection.

In the absence of any legal representation, I am duly carrying out Miss Ruby's wishes as she instructed.

Yours sincerely,

Richard Jeffreys, Captn.   Enclosed: £5.

The raucous climax of 'Boiled Beef and Carrots' brought Ruby's tribute show to a conclusion, with everyone cheering and applauding wildly. They all hoped that the old girl had been able to hear them, and that if she did, she had joined in. But up in the gods Nellie profoundly hoped that her old mate couldn't see her, for tears were streaming down her face.

The taxi arrived dead on time at 147A Tufnell Park Road. Sid was the first to see it as it approached from the Holloway end of the road, but when he ran into the house with an excited yell of 'It's 'ere! It's 'ere!' he was greeted with little enthusiasm. Especially from Madame.

'Go an' get yer coat on,' was all she could say as she solemnly put on her own hat and fixed it with a pin.

Monsieur came up behind her and put his arms round her waist. 'It's fer the best, Doris. It 'as ter be.'

Madame didn't know how to respond, for she had exhausted all the arguments she had had for trying to keep young Lenny at home. Over the past few weeks, his condition had clearly deteriorated. This had been obvious even before the blast from the Junction Road bomb had covered him with dust and ceiling plaster, which had got into his lungs and made him much worse. The boy was now too weak to be carried up and down the stairs, and Madame's excessive cleaning of the house to keep down the dust simply did not help his condition. The plain fact of the matter was that Lenny needed the sort of expert medical attention that he couldn't get at home. And so it was decided to send him to a sanatorium for tubercular patients near the sea, just outside Bristol in the West Country.

Nellie had been dreading this day ever since Monsieur had convinced Madame how necessary it was. From the moment it had been decided, Nellie spent a great deal of her time trying to excite Lenny about the wonderful place he was going to. She kept telling him to think of it as one long glorious holiday where he would be spoilt rotten by all sorts of people. But the greatest advantage, she insisted, was the certainty that he would fully recover there and be back home before he even realised that he had gone. Deep down inside, Nellie had as many misgivings as everyone else in the family, and it was not easy to stop an endlessly tearful Grandma Beckwith from conveying her fears to her grandson.

As usual, however, it was Sid who made his young brother's departure more easy to cope with. 'If yer want, yer can take some of my comics wiv yer,' he said as he watched his dad carry the frail boy in his arms down the stairs. 'I'll bring yer some of the uvvers when I come up ter visit yer.'

'Fanks,' replied Lenny weakly.

'Yer can't 'ave this week's *Film Fun* though,' Sid added. 'I 'aven't finished wiv it yet.'

'I din't ask for it, did I?' protested Lenny tetchily.

'I just fawt I'd mention it, that's all,' sniffed Sid.

This exchange between the two brothers made Nellie feel so much better; she was impressed that Sid had deliberately rejected any show of emotion in order to diminish the poignancy of the occasion.

'Better get in the taxi, son,' said Monsieur to his eldest boy. 'Don't wanna miss the train.'

Sid collected his school cap, wound his long

433

woollen scarf round his neck, and hurried outside to the taxi.

For a last brief moment, Madame fussed over Lenny in Monsieur's arms, making sure that he was tucked up snugly beneath his blanket. Then she and Nellie followed them out.

'God fergive us if we're not doin' the right fing,' said Madame as she came out of the front door arm in arm with Nellie.

'You *are* doin' the right fing, Mum,' Nellie reassured her. 'It's the only fing ter do. When Lenny comes back 'ome all fit 'an strong again, you'll kick yerself fer not doin' this sooner.'

Madame turned briefly to her with an appreciative smile. 'I 'ope so, Nell,' she said. 'I 'ope so.'

Sid had already claimed his place on one of the pull-out seats in the taxi. As soon as Monsieur reached the vehicle with Lenny held firmly in his arms, the taxi driver hurried round to meet them.

Nellie left Madame for a moment to give Lenny a mock boxer's jab towards his chin. 'Gels don't kiss boxers,' she said with a mischievous grin. 'At least, not till they win.' Then she made another light jab at his nose. 'So 'urry up an' win, mate!'

Lenny managed to smile back at her. ''Bye, Nell.'

The taxi driver made sure that Monsieur and Lenny were comfortable in the back seat, then turned to help Madame get in.

'See you later, dear,' said Madame after kissing Nellie on the cheek. 'An' don't wait up fer us,' she added. 'We shan't be back till the last train. If yer need us, yer've got the telephone number. I've left it on the kitchen table.'

''Bye, Nell!' called Monsieur and Sid.

''Bye!' Nellie called back. 'Safe journey!'

She closed the taxi door and waited for the driver to get in. As the taxi moved off, the last thing she saw was young Sid waving madly and pulling rude faces at her through the window. She waved back.

And then they were gone.

Back inside the house, she closed the front door and paused a moment to look around. Suddenly, everything seemed so quiet, so lost and empty. She slowly made her way upstairs towards her room, but when she reached the first-floor landing, she saw that the door of Lenny's bedroom had been left open. She went across to close it. Before doing so, however, she peered inside. The room was pretty untidy, mainly because Sid had got up early in the morning to play a last game of Snakes and Ladders on the bed with his young brother. Nellie decided to go in and clear up.

Her spirits were too low to do much, so she merely picked up pieces from an unfinished Spitfire model aircraft that Sid had been working on with his brother right up to the previous evening. Then she collected a pillow that had been dumped on the floor and she tossed it on to the bed. Her attention was suddenly drawn to the walls of the room, which were crammed with newspaper pictures of footballers. Nellie hadn't any idea who most of them were, but she knew that Lenny did. In fact there was hardly a footballer in the country that he didn't know about. Talk about football mania. But a huge grin came to her face when she caught a glimpse of a very different type of photo, pinned to the wall right in the middle of a poster of the previous year's Cup Final winners team. It was a pin-up of a very sexy, very glamorous film star called Betty Grable, posing in a dazzling yellow one-piece bathing suit and high-heeled shoes. And scrawled right across it in black crayon in Lenny's hand-writing were the words: 'Yes, please!'

Nellie suddenly felt uplifted, and she laughed out loud. ''Fanks a lot, Betty!' she said, giving the pin-up a salute. 'I couldn't agree more!'

Yes. Lenny *was* going to survive. Of that, Nellie now had no doubt whatsoever.

For the next few weeks, Monsieur refused to take on any more music hall bookings. He and Madame had carefully worked out a plan which enabled them to visit Lenny at the sanatorium twice a week, on Wednesday and Saturday afternoons, and until they were confident enough that he was being looked after properly, work took a very second place. It was an expensive arrangement; it involved taking a train on the Great Western Line from Paddington Station to Bristol, and then a taxi to the sanatorium, which was nearly two miles away. The sanatorium itself was also very expensive, but Monsieur had saved well over the years, and where his son was concerned, money was no object. Occasionally Nellie went along too.

By the end of May, Lenny's condition was showing such improvement that Monsieur and Eddie Buxton felt confident enough to start planning the next tour for the new Great Pierre act. The first booking to be arranged was for a season in pantomime later that year at the Ilford Hippodrome, which was a popular theatre on the fringes of London, in Essex. The panto was *Robinson Crusoe,* and the offer was for Monsieur to appear as a wizard, with Nellie as his assistant, which would give them ample opportunity to use some of their regular Great Pierre material. Although the booking was still a few months off, pantos had to be cast well in advance. Monsieur was cheered by the prospect of being in the same show as the Scottish star comedienne, Renee Houston, and her American husband, Donald Stewart, with whom he had worked several times before. Until then, Monsieur signed up to take the new act on a six-week tour of the Stoll Theatres circuit in and around London.

Before the tour commenced, worrying rumours were circulating in the newspapers of a new 'secret weapon' being developed by the Germans, who claimed that it was so powerful it would not only entirely destroy London, it would also bring a glorious victory to the German nation.

'Pilotless planes!' scoffed Monsieur after listening to Eddie Buxton reading out the latest newspaper speculation. 'Bloody lot of ol' rubbish! Wot der they fink they're goin' ter do wiv planes an' no pilots?'

'They say they can carry high-explosive bombs, Bert,' replied Eddie pessimistically. 'All they have to do is to head them our way, then use radio control to crash them anywhere they like.'

Nellie shuddered at the thought of it. 'That's wicked,' she said gloomily. ''Ow can they even fink of killin' innocent people fer no reason at all?'

'Oh, Jerry's got plenty of reasons, all right, Nell,' replied Eddie. 'Just think of the Jews. Hitler hates their guts. I tell you, if the Nazis ever got a hold on this country, they'd do the same to the Jews here as they've done all over Europe.'

Nellie immediately feared for Martin. She knew, because he had told her, that his own family had originally come to this country as refugees from Germany. If the Allies lost the war, there was no doubt that Martin and his entire family would be in grave danger. Deep in thought, she stared out anxiously through the conservatory window.

'Well, there's no way Jerry's goin' ter win this war now,' insisted Monsieur, quite unconcerned. 'Once the invasion comes, it'll all be over—pilotless planes or anyfin' else!'

Nellie didn't really hear what her dad had said. She was too busy thinking about Jews, and what made them, in the Germans' eyes, so different from anyone else. Was it the way

438

they looked, or the way they spoke? And then it suddenly came to her how some of the kids back at the orphanage used to pick on a small bunch of Jewish kids. 'Big nose!' was the usual jibe, and it was a kind of teasing that Nellie had always hated. Martin didn't have a big nose, and even if he did, what difference would it make? And what about all the Jewish people in the music hall? There were plenty of them, and they were no different from Roman Catholics or tall people or short people or thin people or fat people. Nobody had the right to single anyone out because of who or what they were, because prejudice, even at the most simple level, could lead to what was happening in Hitler's Germany. It was all so nasty and vicious—and mindless. Oh God, Nellie begged in her own silent way, please start the invasion soon.

The Allied invasion of continental Europe began on Tuesday, 6 June. Nellie was standing in a queue at Liptons general food store at the time, desperate to get to the front before the latest arrival of fresh Cheddar cheese disappeared in the scramble.

'It's started!' yelled an excited woman from the open doorway. 'They've landed on the French coast!'

A great cheer went up, and suddenly the whole place burst into excited chatter, with everyone in a state of euphoria. Nellie cheered with them, although she didn't share some people's view that 'it'd all be over in a week'.

The general excitement was so great that by the time she reached the front of the queue and handed over the family's four ration books, she got more than the one ounce of cheese per person per week everyone was allowed. In fact, the girl behind the counter was so emotional, she forgot to take any coupons from Nellie at all.

In Seven Sisters Road outside, news of the invasion spread like wildfire, and small groups of people started to gather everywhere. This was the news they had been waiting for, praying for. This was the beginning of the end for Hitler, a real sock in the eye! One rather large middle-aged woman was so overwhelmed with excitement that she started singing and dancing all by herself, shopping bags bulging with vegetables, and the curlers in her hair popping out one by one. The atmosphere was infectious, with cars, motorcycles, trucks, and bicycles stopping at the kerbside to find out what was going on. It was the culmination of years of frustration. Now, the tide had turned, and it couldn't be that long before the boys who had been taken away from home would return. But as Nellie listened to all the opinions, the hopes and dreams, and the speculation, she wondered how soon that return would be.

And then she remembered that she hadn't heard from Martin for over two months.

On the Monday evening following the Anglo-American invasion, the new Great Pierre act made its debut at the Wood Green Empire. For both Monsieur and Nellie it was a significant return engagement, for it was at this same theatre that Ange had had her serious washbasin accident, and where Monsieur had first tried out the dangerous Biting the Bullet sequence. Mercifully for Nellie, Monsieur had now dropped that idea and replaced it with an act that was altogether more classy. But even as she took her place in the solo spotlight, twice nightly from Monday to Saturday, singing her song like an angel, she often mulled over why it was that Monsieur had ever decided to change the act so radically.

In many ways, this new act was a complete change of direction for Monsieur, for in place of a traditional, rather tricksy music hall act, to Nellie's way of thinking, he had devised something that was really quite beautiful, almost surreal, with a wonderful use of mime, light, and shadows. But then in some ways Monsieur himself was also changing. Young Lenny's illness had affected him far more deeply than he would admit; it had made him take a closer look at himself, and to question what his life was really all about. Since then, he had felt that the Great Pierre act had become tired, shallow, and pointless, and when the management of a number two music hall like Collins relegated him to a minor spot during the first half of the show, he knew it was time to change direction.

It had now been a week since the Allied invasion, and each day the wireless and newspapers reported on the stiff enemy opposition Allied ground troops were up against. Consequently, the wave of D-Day euphoria had been replaced by a more cautious air of hope and prayers, and this was clearly reflected in the audience at Wood Green, who greeted Monsieur's new act with dignified enthusiasm.

With no chorus girls, jugglers, or dog acts on the bill this week, Nellie was relieved to find that she had the luxury of her own dressing room. But it was an odd experience to be using the same room that Ange had shared with the Sisters Tapp. The shattered washbasin had been replaced and a new, bolder warning notice stuck to the wall above it.

After the first house on Wednesday evening, Nellie usually went into Monsieur's dressing room where she shared some sandwiches which Madame always brought along. But to her surprise a knock on her door brought her two unexpected visitors tonight.

'Hello, Nellie.'

Nellie looked at the tall, middle-aged woman, with dark brown hair, dark brown eyes, and a complexion like porcelain. She hadn't the faintest idea who she was. 'I'm sorry,' was all she could utter.

'I'm Marion Hecht,' said the woman with just the faint suggestion of an accent. 'And this is my husband, Jacob.'

The woman stood back so that Nellie could see the man at her side. He, too, was tall, with jet-black hair, a bushy moustache, and slanting dark eyes. 'Hello, Nellie,' he said, his voice also revealing a slight accent.

Nellie was confused. 'I'm very sorry,' she said. 'Do I know yer?'

The woman, elegant in a plain black dress with a single piece of jewellery pinned above her left breast, answered for both of them. 'We're Martin's parents,' she said.

'Oh my—!' Nellie spluttered. 'I'm so sorry! Come in! Come in!' She opened the door wide to let them enter. Still wearing her skimpy stage costume, she suddenly felt coarse and awkward. 'Yer'll 'ave ter fergive me,' she said, rushing to put on her dressing gown. 'They didn't tell me I 'ad visitors. Please, sit down.'

'No, no, my dear,' said Marion. 'We only came for a few moments. We saw your show tonight. Congratulations. It was so very beautiful.'

'Really?' Nellie was astounded, particularly as Martin had always given her the impression that his parents wouldn't take too kindly to seeing his girlfriend half-naked on a music hall stage. 'Fanks very much.'

'So different to what we expected,' Jacob said, nervously fingering the rim of a dark trilby hat he was rolling around in his hands. He looked very smart in a long, grey overcoat. 'We think you have a most delightful voice.'

Nellie blushed. It was something she rarely did, but the compliment sounded so genuine, she couldn't help it. 'Oh, by the way,' she put her hand out to shake hands with Marion. ''Ow d'yer do. Pleased ter meet yer!'

Both visitors smiled warmly at her, then

Marion took Nellie by surprise and gently kissed her on both cheeks. Jacob shook her hand.

'We've heard so much about you,' said Marion.

Again Nellie was surprised. 'Yer 'ave?'

'Martin left out the most important part though,' said Jacob. 'He didn't tell us how pretty you are.'

Nellie was determined that if they carried on like this, she'd make them her friends for life. ''E never tells me nuffin' eivver,' she said. ''Ave yer 'eard from 'im lately?' she asked, trying to sound as casual as possible.

There was a difficult pause, during which their expression's changed from warm smiles to concern.

'No, Nellie,' said Jacob exchanging an uneasy glance with his wife. 'We were wondering if you had heard from him.'

Nellie shrugged her shoulders. 'Not a word for over two months.' She looked from one face to the other, and as she looked at Jacob, she could see the resemblance between him and Martin, the same jet-black hair and dark slanting eyes. 'Is there anyfin' wrong?' she asked.

There was another moment of hesitation.

'There's been a lot of—trouble on the south coast, Nellie,' said Marion with some difficulty. 'Jacob knows a journalist—he's a war correspondent on the *News Chronicle*. You mustn't repeat this, but he says that just before the invasion last week, two enemy fighter planes attacked one of the Air Force stations in Kent.

444

He didn't say which one—precisely.'

'Nellie,' said Jacob, taking over where his wife left off. 'There was an—incident—with an Air Force truck. It was on its way from the base to Folkestone. There was a huge build-up of troops all along the coast.'

'The truck was full of ammunition,' Marion said. 'It was hit by gunfire from an enemy fighter. There was an—an explosion. It—blew up.'

Nellie clasped her hand to her mouth, horrified. 'Oh Gawd, no,' she gasped. 'Yer don't mean—'

'At the moment, we know nothing, Nellie,' Jacob said. 'Absolutely nothing.'

Nellie didn't know what to say, or what to think. 'But 'e didn't 'ave anyfin' ter do wiv trucks. When I was down there that time, 'e told me 'e worked in this office.'

Marion was shaking her head.

'They were short of men, Nellie,' said Jacob, with a despondent sigh. 'They needed drivers urgently. With the invasion so close, there was pandemonium. Everyone had to do any job that was necessary.'

'But 'ow der we know that Martin ...'

Marion took hold of Nellie's hands and held them tightly. 'Our friend told us that there are quite a few men unaccounted for,' she said anxiously. 'He says the authorities have refused to release the names of casualties until the invasion is well on its way.'

'Until then, Nellie,' said Jacob grave-faced, 'we shan't know if Martin is one of them.'

Chapter 26

The war was entering a decisive stage. In North Africa and Italy, the Allies were pushing forward on all fronts, and now that the Anglo-American invasion had secured a foothold on the Normandy beaches in France, there was a feeling throughout the country that the German war machine had at last been halted. But, once again, Prime Minister Winston Churchill warned the nation not to be complacent. The Luftwaffe were still capable of launching reprisals for the massive Anglo-American air raids on Berlin and other German cities, and these could come at any moment, without warning.

In the early hours of the morning following the second house show at the Wood Green Empire, two pilotless planes exploded within about ten minutes of each other. One came down on a vegetable allotment in Gravesend, Kent, and the other destroyed a railway bridge in Grove Road, Bow. Most of the Beckwith family were in bed and fast asleep at the time, but Nellie woke up immediately and rushed to her window. There had been no air-raid alert, so she assumed it was either a hit-and-run attack by a stray enemy aircraft or an explosion caused by something other than an air raid. However, whatever it was seemed to be some way away, and after scanning the sky for several minutes,

Nellie thought no more about it and went back to bed.

It was a somewhat different story a couple of evenings later when Monsieur, Madame, and Nellie were in Monsieur's dressing room, tucking into the dried egg and sausage flan that Madame had made for supper. The final turn of the first house show was still on stage, and over the loudspeaker in their room they could hear the audience rocking with laughter at the comic aristocratic capers of 'Britain's premier radio personality', Mr Gillie Potter. The Squire of Hogsnorton, as he called himself, was no more than five minutes into his witty tales of country life when the entire theatre suddenly became aware of a loud, piercing, shuddering noise. Everyone backstage, on stage, and in the audience turned their eyes up towards the ceiling, as though the noise was somehow being manipulated from the roof. But then there was relief as the sound went as quickly as it had come. But before the star performer had managed to improvise a gag about what they had all just heard, a tremendous explosion rocked the theatre.

The stage manager rushed on to the stage, and with Mr Potter staring on in disbelief called through the microphone: 'Ladies and gentlemen, please stay calm. The performance will continue.'

But the performance did not continue, for the audience rose almost as one and filed out in orderly procession through every exit.

In Monsieur's dressing room, as in the

auditorium itself, small pieces of plaster fluttered down from walls and ceilings, and the contents of the dressing table either toppled over or went crashing to the floor.

'Outside!' barked Monsieur, rushing to open the door for Madame and Nellie. 'Quick as yer can, gels!'

In the back alley outside, a group of stagehands had gathered. Most of them were staring up at the sky, for it was a fine summer's evening and the air was crystal clear. By the time Monsieur, Madame, and Nellie got there, they were quickly joined by other turns from the show, including Gillie Potter himself.

'What is it?' asked the star performer. 'I didn't hear the alert.'

'There wasn't one,' replied one of the backstage electricians.

'Looks like it's over Stoke Newington way,' added the stage manager who was drawing everyone's attention to a great cloud of thick black smoke in the distance.

Nellie put a comforting arm round her mum who was shaking like a leaf. 'Must've bin a one-off,' she said, having to shout above the clanging of fire engine and ambulance bells, and the sound of general mayhem echoing out from the High Road nearby.

While the group was standing there, bewildered and confused, someone shouted, 'Look out! Anuvver one!'

'Oh my God!' gasped Madame as she, Nellie, and Monsieur flicked their eyes up towards the sky.

They could hear the sinister drone of what had already been described in one newspaper as a 'robot' plane approaching at high speed, drowning every other sound in the vicinity. It was a terrifying, menacing sound as it chugged and spluttered across the sky, and when it finally came into sight, it looked like a small black rocket, with clipped wings, a light in the nose, and a fierce red flame burning from the tail.

'What the hell is *that* thing?' asked Gillie Potter, his assumed upper-class voice thoroughly outraged and indignant.

'Looks like its arse is on fire,' called one of the stagehands.

Nobody laughed. They were all mesmerised by this extraordinary new weapon.

As the pilotless plane sped across the sky, leaving a trail of thick black smoke in its wake, fascination turned to fear when the sound of the machine cut out and the flame from its tail disappeared.

'It's diving!' yelled the stage door keeper.

Somebody else yelled, 'Take cover!'

Automatically, everyone crowding around the stage door threw themselves to the ground. Monsieur did his best to cover Madame and Nellie with his own body.

The eerie silence from the robot machine seemed to last for ever. When the explosion finally came, it was deafening, and closely followed by the sound of glass shattering. Someone on the corner of the road nearby shouted, 'Christ Almighty!' In a shop doorway, a woman was stretched out on the ground, desperately trying to shield her two young children.

For the next few moments, nobody moved. But as the second robot plane seemed to be the last, eventually everyone felt confident enough to get up on their feet again.

'It's all over, dear,' said Monsieur, cool as a cucumber as he helped his wife up. 'That's the last one.'

Frantic with worry, Madame said, 'Bert, I've got ter get back ter Sid. Oh God, I shouldn't've left 'im on 'is own. Ternight of all nights!'

'Don't be silly, Mum,' said Nellie, holding on to her. 'Sid's perfectly all right wiv Grandma and Grandad. They're probably all tucked up nice and safe in their Morrison shelter.'

'Damn 'em!' shouted Madame, angrily shaking her fist up at the trail of black smoke that still streaked the sky. 'Who was it said this bloody war was all over?'

'So wot 'appens about second 'ouse, everyone?' called the harassed stage manager from the back of the group. 'Do we pull it fer the night?'

'Pull it?' Gillie Potter was outraged by the suggestion. 'The customers have paid good money to see this show. For God's sake, don't let's hand it on a plate to Herr Hitler. Let's get back on stage and get on with it.'

Everyone stood aside to let the star performer get back into the theatre, then they followed him in, including Monsieur, Madame, and Nellie.

During the course of the second house show, three more robot planes droned mercilessly across the darkening evening sky.

Then they cut out, dived into the middle of whatever populated area they happened to be above, and exploded with a devastating roar. Fortunately, the Wood Green Empire did not sustain any damage, and although the theatre rattled and shook, the show continued without interruption.

There was no doubt that the customers on this extraordinary night certainly got their money's worth.

Nellie thought that Marion Hecht was one of the most beautiful women she had ever seen. She had almost classical features, a delicate complexion, and wore just a suggestion of lipstick, no other make-up; it was hard to believe that she was old enough to be Martin's mother. Even the way she brushed her dark wavy hair, so that it was held behind her ears with brown oyster-shell combs, had such style, Nellie thought she was glamorous enough to be in the pictures. Her husband, Jacob, was a wonderful match for her, for he had distinguished features, kindly eyes, and a full moustache, which exactly complemented the slightly greying hair above his ears. They both towered above Nellie, but as all three of them sat together over tea in the Hechts' ornate lounge, Nellie didn't feel at all ill at ease, especially after Jacob made a light-hearted joke about how he, his wife, and his son were often compared to a family of lamp-posts.

After all the bitter things Martin had said about his parents, Nellie had had many preconceptions of what they would be like. But when they had so unexpectedly turned up in her dressing room at Wood Green just a couple of weeks before, they couldn't have been more different from what she had imagined. There was still no news about Martin's fate after the enemy attack on the RAF lorry he might have been driving, and sitting here in his home in Highgate with his parents, Nellie was all too conscious of the fact that Martin, for some reason, had not wanted her to meet his family.

'Isn't it strange,' said Marion, sitting alongside Nellie on a large velour settee, 'we've only known each other for a short time, and yet I feel as though I've known you for years.' She looked across at her husband who was in one of the chairs of the matching suite. 'Isn't that so, Jacob?'

He shrugged his shoulders. 'Absolutely,' he replied, putting down his fine bone china teacup and saucer on the coffee table.

Nellie, who was wearing her Sunday best, a pastel yellow cotton dress she had bought on the clothes ration while she was working at Beales Restaurant, nodded her head in agreement. 'I feel the same way about you,' she replied. 'I don't understand why Martin always kept so cagey about 'is 'ome life.'

Marion exchanged a pointed look with her husband. 'When you've known Martin as long as we have, my dear,' she said with a sad frown, 'you'll know what a complicated boy he is.'

Jacob Hecht leaned forward in his chair. 'I

452

can assure you, Nellie,' he said, 'he talks an awful lot about you. I think he wants to make us jealous.'

'Oh, that's not fair, Jacob,' scolded his wife. 'Martin's just like any boy of his age. When he has somebody he cares for, he wants to boast a little.' She turned to Nellie, smiled, and briefly clutched her hand. 'And I don't blame him one little bit!'

Nellie's eyes were discreetly scanning the room. It was much bigger than she was used to, even in Tufnell Park Road. Behind the blackout blinds, there were expensive floor to ceiling brocade curtains, antique furniture, a Persian carpet covering most of the floor, and a lamb's wool rug in front of a big, open fireplace with a brass fender and companion set. Surrounded by so much comfort and style, she found it difficult to understand why Martin had once chosen to roam the war-torn streets of North London.

As if knowing what was going through Nellie's mind, Marion got up from the settee and picked up one of the large collection of framed family photographs on the mantelpiece. 'This is Martin soon after his Bar Mitzvah,' she said, handing Nellie the photograph. 'He was thirteen when that was taken.'

Nellie smiled, at the picture. It showed Martin in a smart navy-blue suit with short trousers, an open neck white shirt, and a plain black yarmulke skullcap trimmed with white brocade on his head.

'Bar Mitzvah marks a Jewish boy's assumption

of his religious obligations,' Marion said, watching Nellie closely as she looked at the photograph. 'You did know Martin is a Jewish boy?' she asked carefully, her face a little taut.

'Oh yes,' replied Nellie, nodding her head.

'It doesn't concern you?'

Nellie was puzzled to be asked such a question. 'Course not. Why should it?'

Marion relaxed. 'To some people it does,' she replied. 'Especially Martin.'

Nellie was confused. 'Wot d'yer mean?'

Marion took the photograph back from Nellie and replaced it on the mantelpiece. 'You know, Nellie. Martin's father and I have never tried to force religion down his throat. For reasons that only Martin himself understands, he has problems with being—what he is.'

Nellie shrugged her shoulders. 'Yer can't 'elp wot yer come from.'

'I know, I know,' Marion replied. 'But Martin has always felt that fingers point at him. He feels that he can be pinpointed in a crowd, wherever he goes. And it repulses him.' She sat back in the settee, crossed her arms, and stared out aimlessly through the large windows on the other side of the room. 'I think it had something to do with his grandmother's Yahrzeit, the anniversary of her death. He was very fond of her. They used to play card games together, and laugh a lot. But when he went to light a candle in her memory, he just couldn't bring himself to recite the holy Kaddish—our prayer of mourning. We said it didn't matter, but in his strange mixed-up way, he blamed us—Jacob and me. He said she

454

would never have died if we had looked after her more.'

'It was rubbish, of course,' said Jacob bitterly. 'I loved my mother just as much as he did, but she was old, she was at the end of her time.'

'What I'm trying to say, Nellie, is that although Jacob and I actively pursue our own religious faith, we have never expected Martin to do the same. We love him. He's our son. If anything has happened to him ...' Her face began to crumple. 'But we don't want to own him,' she insisted, fighting back her distress. 'He will be alive long after we are gone. He must make his own decisions.' She took out a small, lace handkerchief and dabbed her nose with it. 'The only thing that we find hard to accept is that he should be ashamed of who and what he is. When he was an evacuee, it took him a long time to come back to us after he had run away. It hurt us. It hurt us deeply.'

'It's because he's an only child,' added Jacob. 'I blame myself. We should have had more.'

Marion immediately swung him an anxious glance. 'Please, Jacob, one guilt complex is enough for any family.'

Nellie listened in silence. Remembering all the odd things Martin had said about his parents, about their not wanting him to go into the services without a commission, and about his father not wanting to be anything but a Jew, she was fascinated to hear the other side of the story. But who to believe? Who to trust?

'You know, Nellie,' Marion continued, 'when Martin first started talking about you, I felt so good. I felt that, for the first time in his life, he was not taking everything so seriously, that he had found someone who could love him, and be his equal.' She looked directly into Nellie's eyes. 'You do love him, don't you, Nellie?'

Nellie suddenly felt that a great weight had been placed on her shoulders. But then she thought about the possibility that none of them might ever see Martin alive again. And although there was something inside her which slightly resented being asked so personal a question, a question that concerned only Martin and herself, her heart told her that there was only one reply she could give.

'Oh yes. I love 'im all right.'

Towards the end of July, Monsieur and Madame took a momentous decision. Despite the Allied advance on all fronts in Europe, hordes of robot planes, now nicknamed buzz bombs or doodlebugs, were streaming over London day and night. The destruction caused by these terrifying machines was awesome, and the loss of life was mounting relentlessly. Everyone somewhere had a relative or friend whose house had been either hit or caught in the blast; there seemed to be no escape from the rain of terror pelting down on the rooftops of thousands of innocent civilians. The military came under increasing pressure to shoot down the buzz bombs before they had the chance to reach London, and this they did with a certain amount of success but there were still far too many of the deadly bug-like machines getting through, and the last straw for Monsieur and Madame came during the second week of August when a flying bomb smashed through the roof of the huge Gaumont Cinema on the corner of Tufnell Park and Holloway Roads.

Now temporarily recovered from the primary stage of his tuberculosis, young Lenny had only been home for a couple of weeks when his father decided to evacuate Madame and both their sons to the safety of Aunt Ethel's house in Somerset. Madame was reluctant to agree to her husband's wishes, but the danger posed by the flying bombs and the talk of an even more deadly rocket weapon being tested by the Germans forced her to comply. Nellie was asked to go too, but as she and Monsieur were still on the road with the Great Pierre act, she insisted that she stay behind and continue to support him.

After the family had gone, the house in Tufnell Park Road seemed like a mausoleum. On the few nights that Monsieur and Nellie were there, there was little hope of any sleep, for the air was constantly fractured by the thunderous sounds of ack-ack gunfire trying to bring down the pilotless raiders over the least populated areas. After a hazardous week of appearances at the few music halls in and around London that had remained open, Nellie persuaded her dad that it would be safer to spend at least part of the nights in the Anderson shelter. In the event, this was only possible once Nellie had helped Monsieur with the back-breaking job of pumping out three feet of rainwater, using an officially provide stirrup pump. Even then the place was n habitable, for it needed at least fourteen hou to dry out.

With the family away, Monsieur's morale w; very low. 'I just don't see the point in carryir on wiv a show when the 'ouse is only 'alf full he said to Nellie as they endured yet anoth grim night in the Anderson.

It was true, of course. The 'new Blitz', as th V-1 was being called, was driving people out London in their thousands, and this inevitab had an effect on audience numbers in theatr and cinemas all over London, most of whic were playing to no more than a handful sturdy regulars. Even business in the pubs w; down, and the streets looked empty.

'I don't see wot else they can do, Dad replied Nellie, propped up in a wicker chai wrapped in a blanket, only half awake. 'The 'ave ter keep the 'alls open somehow,'

'Why?' snapped Monsieur. 'Why should w risk our lives just fer the sake of uvver people D'yer realise that one night you an' me coul be up there on that stage and—boom! All a sudden we could cop our lot. These blood buzz bombs don't tell yer they're comin', ye know.'

'Come on now, Dad, this isn't like you. Ou chances of bein' 'it are no more than if we wa down the Tube.'

'At least down the Tube we'd 'ave a coupl a tons of earth ter protect us.' By the dim ligh of the hurricane lamp, Nellie could see hir shaking his head. 'No. Nell,' he said gloomily. 'I can't take much more of this. I don't like bein' parted from my family. It's not natural.'

Nellie leaned across and tried to calm him. 'Don't give in, Dad,' she said. 'It won't be long now. The war's nearly over. Just yer wait an' see, we'll soon 'ave Mum and the boys back 'ome wiv us.'

Monsieur was not convinced. He leaned his head back in the chair and tried to settle down. But his eyes remained wide open, staring up despondently at the curved, cold steel roof of the tiny shelter. This was not what life was all about. This was life in hell.

'Try an' get some sleep, Dad,' Nellie said, yawning and closing her eyes. 'It'll all be over soon ...'

Even as she spoke, the night was pierced by the sound of yet another flying bomb as it ground its way across the sky above. Nellie's eyes sprang open. Eventually, but quite suddenly, that most feared of all wartime sounds cut out. It was almost as though a switch had been turned off.

In the heart-stopping silence that followed, Nellie and Monsieur waited tensely.

'Please, dear God,' she prayed silently. 'Don't let it be us.'

Mercifully, Nellie's prayer was answered.

By the end of August, most of the launching sites for the V-1 flying bombs at the Pas de Calais on the French coast had been overrun by Allied forces. The number of raids gradually diminished, and those people who had fled from London at the height of the new Blitz, including thousands of children, started to return. The music halls that had closed reopened but Monsieur and his fellow artistes were still playing to half-empty houses.

Madame, Sid, and young Lenny returned home from their evacuation in Somerset to a rapturous welcome from both Monsieur and Nellie. It had been the first time Monsieur and Madame had been apart for so long, and their reunion was very emotional. On their first evening at home, Nellie surprised them all by cooking the evening meal, which she had carefully planned all week. When she first came to live with the family, she had no idea about cooking, but having watched Madame so many times, she had picked up quite a few ideas. For her welcome home meal she gave them sausage meat with fresh breadcrumbs and chopped fresh parsley, well-seasoned, shaped into patties, and fried. With this she served mashed potatoes, fresh beans and carrots which she had bought that morning at Hicks the greengrocers in Seven Sisters Road. The trifle that followed was delicious, and was a particular favourite with both Sid and Lenny, for it was full of tinned fruit, topped with strawberry jelly, and finished off with a strawberry blancmange made with dried milk. Everyone made short work of the meal. Nellie was thrilled to see Lenny looking so much more like his former self, with colour in his cheeks and a little more flesh on his bony limbs. The family reunion was a joy. All that was wanting now was the end of the war.

But in the early hours of the morning, a new type of rocket bomb came down on a populated area in Chiswick, West London.

Nellie's hopes of seeing Martin alive again were fading fast. It had been over two months since his parents had told her about the attack on the RAF lorry in Kent, and since then there had been a security clampdown. The Allied invasion was now being consolidated, and the last thing the Government wanted at this delicate stage in the campaign was for the general public to feel that there had been any kind of setbacks. But for those who lived in hope for even the barest minimum of news, it was a heartbreaking ordeal.

Life, however, had to go on, and two weeks after the first rocket bomb fell on Chiswick, Monsieur accepted an invitation to take part in an all-star benefit show at the Chiswick Empire, which was being held to raise funds for the victims of the devastating tragedy. Nellie was thrilled to be there, for it gave her the chance to be among some of the greatest names in the music hall. The turn she was most excited to see was by the famous stage and radio comic Rob Wilton. His sketch, 'The Day War Broke Out', had boosted the morale of so many of his radio listeners and audiences since the darkest days of the Blitz. But despite the fact that there were so many great names on the bill, including the Western Brothers, Jeanne de Casalis ('Mrs Feather'), Wilson, Keppel and Betty, Arthur

461

Askey and Richard 'Stinker' Murdoch, Will Fyffe, Flanagan and Allen, Gertie Gitana, and G.H. Elliott ('The Chocolate-Coloured Coon'), Monsieur and Nellie more than held their own. In fact, while Nellie was singing her 'When I Grow Too Old to Dream' number, the entire celebrity-packed audience joined in.

For this once only performance, Nellie had to share a dressing room with some of the Tiller Girls who were just about the best line-up of chorus dancers in the business. But during the interval, she joined her dad and mum in the dressing room Monsieur was sharing with Arthur Askey and 'Stinker' Murdoch. The laughs came fast and furious, but although Nellie adored being with the man whose catchphrase 'I thank you!' was a national favourite, she found that he, like so many comedians, was far more quiet and serious than she had imagined.

The finale of the show had been arranged as a patriotic sing-song for the company and audience combined. Nellie was placed right at the end of the line, nearest to the wings. During the first song, 'Two Lovely Black Eyes', Nellie noticed one of the young stagehands signalling to her. She edged her way discreetly towards him.

'Telephone call! Urgent!'

'Don't be daft,' spluttered Nellie in disbelief. 'Not now, yer idiot! Tell 'em ter phone back!'

'It's urgent!' insisted the stagehand. 'She must speak to yer *now!*'

Nellie thought the young bloke had gone stark, staring mad. 'Who is it?'

'She says she's Martin's muvver!'

Nellie left the stage running and pelted down the small passage that led to the stage door where the keeper was holding out the telephone receiver to her.

'Mrs 'Echt!' she said breathlessly. 'It's me, Nellie.'

The following morning, Nellie could hardly get up to Highgate fast enough. It wasn't easy, for although there were normally plenty of trolley buses running up to the Archway, for the past two weeks there had been regular V-2 rocket attacks and transport was even more unreliable than usual. Eventually she managed to get a bus which dropped her outside the Tube station. From there she had quite a walk up the hill to Highgate Village.

On the way, she felt as if she'd been born all over again. The telephone call from Martin's mother had left her feeling exhilarated. Martin's home! He's alive! All through the night, she hadn't had a wink of sleep, and every fifteen minutes or so, she had switched on the light to look at the time. It was too wonderful for words. Martin's home! He's alive! The only thing was why hadn't he called her himself? His mother had explained how he was still recovering from his injuries, but surely, surely he could have come to the phone to talk to her, somehow.

The Hechts' double-fronted house was set well back from the leafy lane where it snuggled comfortably between other similar grand houses. The driveway was paved with York stone, which was badly cracked and in need of replacing. But as she rushed up to the front door of the large imitation Tudor house, the only thing she could see in her mind's eye was Martin.

Marion Hecht was already opening the front door before Nellie reached it. As usual, she looked as immaculate as ever, except that she seemed somewhat drained and tired. 'Thank you for coming, Nellie,' she said wearily. 'I'm so grateful.'

Nellie's expression changed immediately. She found Marion's greeting curious. 'Thank you for coming, Nellie.' Why was she thanking her?

Marion took her into the farmhouse-style kitchen where Jacob was sitting at the kitchen table, his head buried in his hands. As Nellie entered the room, he got up to greet her. His face was pale and drawn. 'Nellie, my dear,' he said, trying to smile. 'Thank you for coming.'

Nellie was taken aback. What was wrong with them both? 'Thank you for coming, thank you for coming.' What were they going on about?

'Martin's in the garden,' Marion said softly, nodding her head towards the window.

Nellie briefly looked out through the small leaded glass windows; she could just see Martin at the far end of the lawn, sitting in a wheelchair with his back to her. 'Is he—all right?' she asked tentatively.

Marion exchanged a brief, strained glance with her husband. 'There's something you should know, Nellie,' she said, with obvious difficulty. 'Martin doesn't know you're here. He didn't want me to tell you that he's home.'

Nellie was devastated. 'Why not?'

Marion took hold of Nellie's hands and held them tightly. 'His injuries were—far more serious than I told you on the telephone last night. You see ...' It was too much. She had to stop.

Jacob took over. 'There was a fire, Nellie. The lorry he was driving ... it was a bad fire ...'

Nellie wanted to hear no more. She pulled her hands from Marion's grasp and made for the door.

'Nellie!' Marion called.

Nellie stopped and turned to look at her.

Marion wanted to say something to her, but she found it impossible. So she merely shook her head and turned away.

It had been a beautiful sunny September so far. As Nellie hurried out into the garden, she felt the warmth on her face, and smelt the faint, sweet scent of late-flowering roses. The garden was so big, Martin appeared quite lost in it, such a tiny figure in the distance, sitting at the side of an ornamental pond.

She decided not to rush. She slowly paced her way along the narrow stone path that led first to a central round flowerbed, then on to the pond at the far end of the garden. As she drew closer, she could see more clearly the wheelchair Martin was sitting in, and even though his back was turned towards her, she could see that he was still in his dressing gown. She also saw that he had a large bandage round his head.

Martin didn't hear her approach, and for a moment or two she just stood there, looking down at him from behind.

Finally, she plucked up enough courage to say quietly, 'Martin.'

Martin stiffened but didn't turn.

'Oh, Martin,' she said, putting her arms gently round his shoulders, and kissing the top of his head. 'You're alive. Fank God you're alive.'

Martin still didn't respond. So she calmly moved round in front of him. As she did so, she saw that his head was bent forward. 'Martin?' she said, with growing concern.

Martin slowly raised his head to look at her. His face was white and drawn, and his eyes stared straight through her.

Chapter 27

It had been a harrowing experience. Nellie spent almost an hour and a half with Martin, crouched on the grass beside him, holding his hand, talking to him quietly, just letting him know that she was there, that she cared for him, and that she loved him. Martin was in deep shock; he'd been like that ever since the RAF lorry he was driving came under attack from two enemy fighters just before D-Day. It had left him in a serious condition: a broken left ankle, and second-degree burns down the left side of his body. Some of his black hair had been burnt off, and if it hadn't been for the quick action of his mates, his scalp would have been in one hell of a mess. On top of that, the choking smoke from the fire had practically asphyxiated him. The shock had been so great, he found it difficult to use his vocal chords. Mercifully, his hair was now growing again, and every so often he would say a few words. Martin had been one of the lucky ones. Three of his mates travelling with him in the lorry at the time had been killed outright. It was a miracle that Martin had survived.

Nellie didn't unwind until she got back home to Tufnell Park Road. By then, the shock of seeing Martin in such a condition caught up with her, and the moment she reached her own bedroom, she threw herself down on to the bed and bawled her eyes out. When her mum came in to find out what was wrong, Nellie found it difficult to hold back all the pent-up emotions she had felt inside since her first sight of Martin sitting in his wheelchair at the end of the Hechts' garden.

'At least 'e's alive, fank Gawd,' said Madame, holding Nellie in her arms and trying to comfort her. 'It could've been worse, Nell. Don't ever ferget that.'

'Oh, I know, Mum,' Nellie sobbed. 'But it's so unfair. Martin 'ad so much goin' for 'im. 'E was such a good-lookin' feller, an' 'e 'ad so many brains ...'

'You're talkin' about 'im as though 'e's dead, Nell. 'E's not dead. 'E's alive, an' there's no reason why in a few munffs' time 'e shouldn't be back on 'is feet again, doin' all the fings you

an' 'im want ter do. Now listen ter me, child,'
Madame continued, stroking Nellie's hair as she
talked. 'If you love your boy as much as I fink
yer do, then you can be the one ter get 'im back
on 'is feet again. D'you know wot I'm sayin'?'

Nellie nodded, and used her knuckles to wipe
the tears from her eyes.

'I know yer, Nell,' Madame said. 'I know
wot you can do fer people, 'cos yer've done it
fer me and yer dad, yer've done it fer Sid and
Lenny. You 'ave so much love in yer, you'll
never fail in anyfin' yer want ter do. An' d'yer
know why?' She leaned down closer. 'Because
yer know what it's like ter survive, Nell. Yer've
'ad ter do it, since the day yer was born.'

Nellie thought carefully about what Madame
was saying to her. In fact it made her think back
over her entire life—those early years without
a mum or dad to call her own, her time in
Barratts' Orphanage with Miss Ackroyd, the
bomb and the debris of the orphanage all piled
up on top of her. And yet she had survived it
all. But how? Why was she singled out to be
the one who crawled out of all that carnage,
to walk the streets without name or direction?
Her life could have ended right there and then,
but it didn't. But most of all she thought about
Toff and the vacs gang, Shortso, and Nutty,
and Rats and Bonkers. In her mind's eye, she
could see them all as if they were standing
in front of her right now. Yes, Madame was
right, she *was* a survivor. Her whole life was a
testament to it.

'Let me ask yer somefin', Nell.'

Nellie blinked, to find Madame still holding her.

'When yer dad an' I first saw yer waitin' on tables in Beales wiv yer neat little cap an' apron—remember? Yer told us about all that time when yer lost yer memory. Yer couldn't remember one single fing, right? Not even yer name.'

Nellie nodded.

'Wot did it feel like, Nell, not knowin' who yer were, or where yer came from?'

Nellie thought for a moment. 'It's 'ard ter tell,' she replied. 'All I can remember is that everyfin' was blank, as though a big wall was shutting me out from who I really was.'

'An' yet it never stopped yer from gettin' on wiv a new kind of life.'

Nellie shook her head. 'No,' she replied. 'When you an' dad asked me ter come an' live wiv yer, it was like bein' born all over again.'

Madame smiled. 'Well, 'as it occurred ter you that perhaps it's the same wiv Martin? P'r'aps 'e needs some 'elp ter do exactly the same fing.'

Nellie turned and looked up at her.

Madame nodded. 'Yes, Nell,' she said. 'An' you're probably the one person who can 'elp 'im do it.'

During October, the V-2 rocket bomb attacks increased, and at the beginning of November one of them came down in Upper Holloway, almost completely destroying a whole street of working-class terraced houses. The number of casualties ran into hundreds, including many deaths, and the blast was felt up to two miles away.

At the time of the explosion, Nellie and Martin were having Sunday tea with the Beckwith family in Tufnell Park Road, which was less than a mile away from where the rocket had come down. The blast ripped off quite a lot of tiles from the roof, and the chimney pot, like many others in the area, tilted at a dangerous angle. A few minutes earlier, the family had been out in the back yard letting off fireworks. It was, after all, 5 November 1944, Guy Fawkes night.

In the six weeks since he had come home on indefinite sick leave, Martin, with Nellie's help, had made slow but significant progress. Within ten days or so, Nellie had revived his confidence so much that he had discarded his wheelchair, which she had insisted was totally unnecessary for the injury he had sustained to his ankle. Her first task was to get him mobile again, and with the initial aid of a pair of crutches, he was soon getting around without the help of either Nellie or his parents. Every week he had to go to the burns unit at the Charing Cross Hospital in the West End of London. The burns all down the left-hand side of his upper body, thigh and leg were kept under strict supervision, and treated with the most up-to-date lotions, creams, and drugs that were available. Ignoring his protests, Nellie always accompanied him to the hospital, and waited in the corridor outside until he was allowed to go home again. Her presence helped his morale, for the burns took longer to heal than he had anticipated. Eventually even they started to improve, and when the prospect of some skin grafts for the worst areas was suggested, his full recovery was in sight.

Martin's psychological scars were quite a different matter, however, and despite Nellie's sensitive and loving care, he found it difficult to readjust. This was never made more obvious than the few moments immediately following the Guy Fawkes V-2 explosion, which left him shaking from head to foot and unable to speak coherently for nearly an hour.

Towards the end of the month, Nellie took a bold decision. She had thought about it for some time, in fact every time she accompanied Martin to the hospital. The burns he had received on his body had left him highly sensitive to anyone, other than the hospital staff, seeing his scars. Especially Nellie. Whenever they met, he made quite sure he was wearing a polo-neck pullover that covered his neck, and he never took the risk of letting her see him without a shirt. It was a tragic situation, and Nellie knew that unless Martin could be persuaded to overcome this traumatic revulsion for his own body, their relationship would never flourish.

Her opportunity came one afternoon late in November. Martin's injured foot, which had been in plaster for so many weeks, was now fully healed, and he was able to walk a little more each day. Usually Nellie would go up to Highgate to collect him and they would take a slow stroll together around the quiet back lanes where many of the rich and famous of pre-war days had bought opulent houses overlooking smart golf courses. Hampstead Heath was only a few minutes' walk away. Nellie loved the heath best in winter, for it seemed to have a peace and tranquillity that was often lacking during the summer months, when a huge fairground was the centrepiece of most Bank Holidays.

The sky was heavy with dark grey clouds as they wound their way along Hampstead Lane, past the old Spaniards Inn and into Spains Road where two mobile anti-aircraft gun units mounted on army lorries were parked. At Jack Straw's Castle pub, they paused to buy two cups of tea from a stall, joining several soldiers and Civil Defence workers who were discussing the number of V-1s and V-2s they had brought down during the previous twenty-four hours.

The grass on the West Heath was long and damp, and Nellie and Martin were both glad that they were wearing wellington boots. It was hard going, for over the past few days it had snowed quite a lot, and in places it was five or six inches deep. On the way, they passed children tobogganing on boards down a steep slope. Their shouts and laughter echoed around the leafless trees whose dark branches were highlighted with snow. When they reached the Leg of Mutton pond, they found it covered with a thin layer of ice and snow. A notice warned: 'DANGEROUS. KEEP OFF.' For several minutes they stood at the edge of the pond, just staring down at it. The clouds permitted a thin ray of sun to break through, and its narrow beam settled on the surface of the pond, transforming it into a dazzling array of tiny snow crystals. But no sooner had the ray of sunlight come than it disappeared back behind the grey clouds.

Nellie slipped her arm round Martin's waist and leaned her head against him. 'D'yer know wot I was finkin' about last night?' she said.

Martin shook his head. 'No,' he replied, putting his arm round her shoulders.

'That church. D'yer remember it? That Catholic place you, Rats and Bonkers found me in.' She looked up at him. 'It was the first time I set eyes on yer.'

'You looked half dead when I saw you,' he said, still struggling to regain his normal pace of speech.

'I *was* 'alf dead. If it hadn't been fer you, I'd never've survived.'

Martin grinned down at her. 'Don't you believe it. You're tougher than you think.'

Nellie paused a moment, then asked him a question. 'Martin, wot did yer fink when yer first saw me?'

'I thought, if she was a couple of years older, I could go for her.'

Quick as a flash, Nellie retorted, 'Well, I *am* a coupla years older. So wot d'yer fink now?'

He didn't answer. She could feel him stiffen.

'Martin?' she asked uncertainly.

He broke away from her and moved a few paces closer to the pond.

Nellie joined him. 'Did I say somefin' wrong?'

'It's not going to work, Nell,' Martin said, staring aimlessly down into the pond. 'Not now.

Everything's changed.'

'Yer mean yer don't go for me any more?'

Martin swung round. 'No, Nell,' he said firmly. 'That's not what I mean. I've never met anybody in my whole life like you. When I was lying in that hospital bed back at the base, it was your face I could see, night after night. It kept me going, Nell. It was the only thing that kept me going. But I'm not the same person I was. What happened in that lorry has changed my whole life, changed the way I think, changed the way I *feel*.'

'An' it's the same wiv me, is that it, Martin? Yer just don't feel the same way terwards me any more.'

'Please don't say things like that to me, Nell. It isn't true. I'll always feel that way towards you. What I'm trying to say is ...' He was talking with such difficulty, he turned away from her again. 'I can't expect you to spend the rest of your life with me.'

'A few munffs ago yer was sayin' yer'd never let me go,' she reminded him. 'Yer said yer wanted us ter live tergevver fer the rest of our lives.'

'That was before, Nell,' he replied, his back still turned towards her. 'Not now. Not the way I am now. I don't have the right.'

Nellie took a pace towards him and used both her hands to turn him round to face her. 'I 'ave a few rights too, yer know, Martin,' she said. 'Don't *I* get a say in the matter?'

For a brief moment, he looked her in the eyes. It was the first time he had done so for a long time. 'Nell,' he said, raising his voice above the sound of some ducks having a heated argument on the other side of the pond, 'would you really want to spend the rest of your life with someone who's been through what I've been through? Would you?'

Nellie decided that she would no longer listen to him feeling sorry for himself. 'You're not the only one in the 'ole world that's suffered, Martin. As a matter of fact, I've 'ad my share too. So 'ave a lot of people.'

It did the trick, for Martin immediately leaned down and hugged her. 'Oh, Nell,' he said guiltily. 'What's wrong with me? What the hell is wrong with me? It's not what I meant. You've been so good to me. I couldn't have got through these past few weeks without you. What I'm trying to tell you is that I can't bear the thought of your seeing me like this. I'm just not the same person I was when we first met inside that church.'

'Neiver am I, Martin,' Nellie replied, her voice muffled against his thick duffel coat. But when she looked up at him again, he heard her loud and clear. 'But it don't make no difference, mate,' she said with a cheeky look. '''Cos I still fancy yer!'

Behind them, two ducks swooped down from the sky and skidded boisterously across the surface of the pond. High in the sky above, a long, thin vapour trail cut in and out of the dark clouds, indicating that another V-2 was on its way to yet another target.

And then it started to snow.

By the time Nellie and Martin got back to Highgate, the snow flurries had turned into a blizzard. The snow was drifting heavily in the biting wind, making it difficult to struggle against.

When they got into the house, Martin told Nellie that he felt a bit like Scott of the Antarctic, and he was glad he had built up the fire in the drawing room before they set off on their walk. A few minutes later, his mother telephoned to say that she and his father had been caught in the blizzard at his grandmother's home in Hertfordshire, where they had spent the day, and wouldn't attempt to get home until it had cleared.

Once Martin had got the fire going, they sat for a few moments warming themselves in front of it. Then he suggested that if she would like to have a hot bath, she could use his mother's bathroom upstairs, and he would have one in his own bathroom. Nellie was impressed. Two bathrooms in one house! So this was how rich people lived. No signs of water rationing here, she thought to herself. But she was grateful for Martin's suggestion. He laid out one of his mother's dressing gowns for her, then he left her for his own bedroom upstairs.

Nellie enjoyed the luxury of her bath, and it certainly warmed her up as she lay there, soaking in the maximum amount of hot water permitted under Home Office war regulations. The wooden ledges round the bath were covered with Marion's cosmetics, and there were also two soft cotton flannels in different colours. Jacob's toiletries were more modest, and included a shaving stick and brush in a small bowl, and on the ledge above the sink, a lethal looking safety razor which looked anything but safe. Outside, the gale-force wind was blasting the windows with snow, which gave the bathroom a bright white glow.

When she had finished her bath, Nellie dried herself on what was definitely the largest bath towel she had ever seen, let alone used. She wrapped herself up in Marion's dressing gown, which almost touched the floor, and left the bathroom.

Martin had suggested that when she finished her bath, she might like to make them both a cup of tea, so she started to make her way to the kitchen which was on the other side of the stairs. She could hear Martin splashing about in his bath upstairs. She stopped and listened for a moment. In a carefully considered change of mind, she turned round and slowly made her way up the stairs.

Despite the fact that his injuries were now virtually healed, Martin still had to be careful as he got out of the bath. As he began to dry himself, he took a long, lingering look at his reflection in the full-length mirror. He hated what he saw, for although his black, wavy hair was now full and thick again, the burn marks down the side of his body still looked red and patchy, and no matter how hard he tried, he just couldn't dismiss his feelings of despair. As he averted his eyes from the sight, he was shocked to see someone else's reflection in the mirror, standing in the open doorway. It was Nellie.

'No, Nell!' he gasped, quickly covering himself with his towel.

Nellie didn't respond. After staring at him for a moment, she closed the door behind her and moved slowly across to him.

Martin backed away, agonised, shaking his head, trying to cover himself. 'No, Nell, please, I beg you, there's no way ...'

Nellie ignored his protests, loosened the cord round her dressing gown, and let it fall to the floor.

Feeling traumatised and threatened, his face crumpled in anguish, Martin shook his head. But gradually his eyes could no longer resist the delicate white curves of Nellie's smooth, naked body.

She slowly moved forward and stood directly in front of him. Then she stretched out and with one hand removed his towel.

For one brief moment, they just stood there, staring into each other's eyes. Nellie took hold of both his hands and kissed them. Martin watched her, as if in a daze. Then Nellie moved to the side of his body that had been burnt. And in one, gentle, touching movement, she started to kiss the scars delicately, one at a time, until she had tenderly caressed and kissed every one of them she could find. When she had finished, she looked up into Martin's eyes. They looked angry. But then Nellie smiled. Slowly, he smiled back.

He threw his arms round her, embraced her

tightly, and kissed her passionately.

For the rest of the afternoon, they made love.

Monsieur and Madame were aware that Nellie was at last beginning to find the happiness that had eluded her for so long. She didn't have to tell them anything. They could see it in her eyes, in the way she got up in the mornings, and in the way she talked and looked. It was wonderful to see, for they knew how hard she had worked to help Martin regain his confidence and self-respect.

With young Lenny now on the road to recovery and back at school, times were at last improving at 147A Tufnell Park Road. Both Monsieur and Madame had put behind them the ugly events surrounding Ange and her so-called revealing snapshots, and they were now closer in their married life than they had been for many years. Nellie made quite sure that whenever there was an opportunity, her mum and dad should spend time together on their own. After all the years they had worked as a stage partnership, they needed to rebuild their life as husband and wife. Times were also changing for Sid. As he approached his seventeenth birthday, he acquired his first girlfriend; he was becoming more independent, and spent a lot of time with his friends.

At the beginning of December, Monsieur and Nellie started rehearsals for their panto season at the Ilford Hippodrome in Essex. Although the theatre was only just outside London, the journey there and back each day proved to be more of a hardship than they had expected, for it was already turning out to be one of the most severe winters for several years. The other problem was the V-1s and V-2s. Although the number of attacks was now considerably down from the height of the campaign a few weeks before, the Germans, in a last desperate attempt to stem the tide of the war against them, were launching V-1 flying bombs from regular heavy bomber planes. A considerable number, however, were caught in the lethal barrage balloon wires, and many more were shot down by the determined efforts of anti-aircraft gun crews. Much more sinister and worrying were the V-2 rocket bombs which came without warning, leaving the most horrific devastation in their wake.

Before the first read-through of *Robinson Crusoe* at Ilford, Monsieur had more or less decided to pull out of the show, insisting that he hadn't the right to put Nellie's life at risk by taking her into what he considered a danger zone. It was true that the eastern side of London was, at this time, more susceptible than anywhere else because the launching sites for the V-2s were based in Holland, but Nellie wouldn't hear of him pulling them out of the show. 'This is 'Itler's last fling,' she said. 'We mustn't let 'im ruin the kids' enjoyment. Not now, not after all we've bin fru.' Monsieur reluctantly agreed to go ahead with the show, but in order to prevent a hazardous journey by train to and from Ilford each day, he booked them into bed and breakfast digs just behind the theatre.

When Nellie arrived at the Ilford Hippodrome, she fell in love with the old music hall at first sight. Situated right on the main Ilford Broadway facing the clock tower, she thought it looked just like a large house, with three tall windows above the foyer entrance, a red and grey brick facing wall, and a tiled roof. Just beneath the huge words ILFORD HIPPODROME were four small sculptures in stone, like cupid's faces, and the impressive entrance below had no less than six polished timber doors. To Nellie, this was the ideal music hall, the perfect setting for a pantomime.

The theatre was equally impressive inside. The auditorium was a delight, with fauteuils, stalls, a grand circle and an upper circle, all in gilt and red plush like so many other music hall theatres. The orchestra pit seemed to be so small, however, that Nellie wondered if there was enough room down there for any musicians.

Meeting the cast was an extraordinary event because there were so many of them. Apart from the featured artistes, there were hordes of young teenagers in the singing and dancing chorus, some of them as young as thirteen and fourteen. Nellie wondered how all of them were going to fit into the few available dressing rooms.

The moment the cast got together, it was as though they had known each other all their lives. When Monsieur introduced Nellie to the stars of the show, Renee Houston and Donald Stewart, she knew at once that this was going to be a panto season that she would not forget. 'I tell ye,' muttered Miss Houston in her broad Scottish brogue, 'if I can squeeze into that sailor's costume, it'll be a downright miracle!' It was easy to see why she was not entirely comfortable playing the leading boy, for she was a lady of fairly ample proportions. Her American husband, Donald Stewart, who seemed to tower over her, just smiled affectionately at everything she said. He was clearly madly in love with her.

The first day's get-together was not entirely successful as far as Monsieur was concerned. It started soon after the read-through of the script, when the panto's energetic manager, Rex Mervyn, told Monsieur that, owing to the fact that the show was playing to three houses daily, Monsieur's regular Great Pierre act would have to be reduced to no more than a few minutes, which meant that both he and Nellie would have to concentrate more on ensemble work within the company. Monsieur was not at all pleased, but Nellie reminded him that it was, after all, only panto, so perhaps the best thing they could do was to just get on with the show and enjoy themselves.

Three days before Christmas, Martin told Nellie that he had now been declared fit enough to return to his unit.

On their final day together, Nellie asked him if he would marry her.

Chapter 28

'*You* asked '*im* ter marry yer!'

'Yes.'

'You're round the loop! Gels don't ask fellers. Fellers ask gels.'

'Oh, don't be so old-fashioned, Sid. Why shouldn't a gel ask as much as a feller? It's the same fing.'

Nellie's exchange with Sid brought the Beckwiths' New Year's Eve party to an astonished halt. Even Madame was a bit taken aback. 'Yer 'ave ter admit, it is a bit unusual, dear,' she said tentatively.

'Oh, I don't know, Doris,' said Monsieur. 'I wouldn't't've minded if you'd proposed ter me.'

'Not a hope!' replied Madame to gales of laughter from the other guests. Grandma and Grandad Beckwith were there, Monsieur's brother Louis and sister-in-law Merle, Madame's mum, and quite a few of Monsieur and Madame's music hall chums.

'The important fing is,' said Grandad Beckwith, 'wot answer did 'e give?'

Nellie was thoroughly enjoying the excitement she was causing, so she delayed her reply while she scanned the expectant faces of the party guests. ''E said—yes.'

There was a roar of approval, delight, cheers, and applause.

Madame threw her arms round Nellie and hugged her. 'Oh, Nell!' she said, quite overcome. 'I'm so 'appy for yer.'

'Not so fast, Mum,' said Nellie, taking a good, hard look at her. 'I'm still under age, remember. As your legally adopted daughter, I 'ave ter get yer permission first.' Then she turned to Monsieur. 'Yours—an' Dad's.'

Monsieur had a broad, happy grin on his face. 'Well the answer's—no!'

There were groans and protests all round.

'Yer've only bin our daughter fer five minutes. an' you're goin' ter let some young bloke take yer away from us.' Then, after exchanging a mischievous look with Nellie, he opened his arms wide for her. 'Come 'ere, you!'

Nellie left her mum and went straight to her dad for a hug.

''E'd better treat yer right,' said Monsieur quietly into Nellie's ear. 'Or 'e'll 'ave me ter deal wiv.'

With the final hour of 1944 ticking away, Monsieur and Madame's party now had even more to celebrate. In many ways, it had been a grim Christmas, for not only was the winter turning out to be the worst many people could ever remember, with temperatures consistently below freezing, there was also a shortage of just about everything—fuel, turkeys, meat, vegetables, dairy products, sugar, basic toiletries such as soap, toothpaste, and corn pads, and even Christmas trees and paper decorations. Despite all these hardships, however, everyone at Monsieur and Madame's party had made up their minds that this was the last time they would have to celebrate the start of a New Year during wartime.

As most of Monsieur and Madame's pals were from the music hall, everyone, as usual, was expected to do their party piece. This meant a song or a stand-up comic routine or, once the sitting-room carpet had been rolled back, a soft shoe shuffle. There were plenty of old favourites, including ballads like 'I'll Get By', 'You'll Never Know', and 'The White Cliffs of Dover', and good old rousing knees-up songs such as 'Any Old Iron', 'She'll Be Coming Round the Mountain', and 'Daisy Belle'. There were lots of impersonations of great artistes like Marie Lloyd, Randolph Sutton, Vesta Tilley and, of course, George Formby. Perhaps the most poignant duet of the evening, however, came from Grandma and Grandad Beckwith who, accompanied by Madame on the piano, sang unfalteringly 'My Old Dutch'. Nonetheless, final honours went to Nellie who, to thunderous applause, gave a flawless and utterly charming rendition of the song that was now so closely associated with her, 'When I Grow Too Old to Dream'.

At about ten minutes to twelve, Monsieur said his few traditional words to round off the year. 'When it come ter December thirty-first,' he said, 'most of us 'ere are convinced that the New Year's goin' ter be different to any year we've ever 'ad, an' in our case that means a few good bookin's an' 'opefully a summer season that goes on right fru till winter!'

Although Monsieur's comment brought laughter and applause, it was tinged with a certain amount of foreboding, for there was no doubt in most of the guests' minds that once the war had ended, variety shows were going to have a hard struggle to survive.

'But I tell yer this much, me friends,' continued Monsieur, 'when Jerry's finally bin licked once an' fer all, you lot 'ere, an' all our mates up an' down the country, well, I reckon we can 'old our 'eads up 'igh.'

Murmurs of ''Ear, 'ear!' from the others.

'The war this time round 'asn't only bin wiv our boys out on the battlefields, it's also bin right 'ere, amongst ordinary people, in the back streets, the pubs, the factories—in every walk of life. An' where they've bin, our lot 'as bin too, keepin' up their spirits, no matter wot it took. Like everyone else, we've risked our lives over an' over again—yes, an' we'd do it again if we 'ad ter.'

Calls of 'Absolutely!' and 'We would!' from the others.

'Wot I'm sayin' to yer, mates, is that as we come ter the end of this bleedin' war, our lot 'ave got quite a lot ter be proud of. Oh yes, they can call us show-offs but when we tread those boards, we at least bring a smile ter people's faces. It may not be much, but it's done its bit ter end this war.'

Nellie joined in enthusiastically with the chorus of approval.

'The uvver day,' continued Monsieur, 'I 'eard someone on the wireless say that 'e fawt music 'all folk've got 'earts of gold. Well, maybe 'e's right, I dunno. But one fing I do know is that in years ter come, wherever you and me an' all our mates may be, I 'ope people won't ferget us, ferget wot we done in this war, an' not only in the war. 'Cos it's the good old music 'alls themselves that's given us our 'earts of gold. Make 'em sing, make 'em laugh, make 'em 'appy. That's our motto, it's always bin our motto. Whatever nineteen forty-five brings, no one can say that we didn't try. Gawd bless, an' 'Appy New Year to yer all!'

Everyone responded with a combined, ''Appy New Year, Bert! 'Appy New Year, Doris!'

'It's time!' yelled Lenny as he turned up the volume on the wireless.

The solemn chimes of Big Ben ushered in the New Year, and everyone joined hands to sing 'Auld Lang Syne'.

By one o'clock in the morning, Monsieur had drunk so much brown ale that he was packed off to bed. It was left to Madame and Nellie to see the remaining guests off at the front gate. It was bitingly cold outside, and the two or three inches of snow that had fallen during the previous few days had turned to ice. There wasn't a cloud in the sky, and Nellie thought that the moon was so bright, it looked like a huge theatre spotlight picking her and Madame out on a vast white stage. Despite the cold, for a moment or so the two of them stood at the gate, staring up at the magnificent sky with its great universe of stars flickering down at them.

Nuffin' seems to 'ave changed, does it?' said

Madame, her arms crossed to keep warm. 'Them stars up there. They don't look any different ter last year. An' that was only an 'our ago.'

Nellie put her arm round her mum's waist and leaned her head against her. 'They look just as beautiful,' she said, the warmth from her breath mixing with the cold night air and quickly disappearing into the stark white moonlight.

For a moment, they said nothing, their faces bathed in the incandescant glow.

'Goin' ter be quite a change fer all of us though, this year,' said Madame, soft and reflective. 'The end of the war. You married.' She sighed wistfully. 'We're goin' ter miss yer, Nell. In yer own way, yer've changed all our lives.'

Nellie hugged her tight. 'Yer won't get rid of me that fast, Mum. In fact, yer'll *never* get rid of me.' She raised her head and looked up at Madame. 'I'm a Beckwiff, remember. Us Beckwiffs 'ave got a rosy future ahead of us.'

High above them, a shooting star shot across the cold dark sky. It reflected in both women's eyes.

Nellie didn't say what was in her mind. That the shooting star reminded her a bit of a V-2 rocket.

Robinson Crusoe opened at the Ilford Hippodrome on Monday, 8 January. Once again it was freezing cold outside, but the first house three o'clock matinee was a resounding success. Nellie loved the way everyone mucked in with each other. Even the stars of the show, Renee Houston and Donald Stewart, moved scenery around when something didn't go quite right, and there were an awful lot of giggles among the cast. Monsieur soon got over his resentment at being given so little to do in the panto, and during the long periods that he was not required on stage, he either put his feet up in the dressing room he shared with some other male members of the cast or took the opportunity to pop out and have a quick half-pint at the nearby Black Horse pub.

Nellie found being in a panto three times a day quite hard work. But the atmosphere, both in front and behind the footlights, was quite unlike anything she had ever experienced. It was mainly because of the excitement generated by the audience themselves, and especially the kids. The look of awe on their small faces as they saw Robinson Crusoe come to the edge of the stage to talk directly to them was a sight to behold. The excitement was infectious, so much so that the cast forgot how exhausted they were after two or three weeks of rehearsals. Nellie herself was astonished at the things she had learnt to do. For this show, she was joining in the popular songs of the day, dancing, and at one point even taking part in a fantasy scene involving Kirby's famous flying ballet. But she didn't mind what she was asked to do, and by the time she and Monsieur launched into a condensed version of the Great Pierre act, she felt like an all-round trouper.

Between those Monday first night shows,

Nellie decided to write a letter to Martin. To her delight, he had already written one to her, even though it had been less than a fortnight since she last saw him. She had no idea where the letter had been posted, and it had clearly been heavily censored, but as she read the words she had been allowed to read, she felt a warm glow, as though she was snuggled up right there in his arms:

New Year's Day   Somewhere
                                (Can't tell you where!)

My Dearest Nell,
  It's the first day of 1945, and here I am in XXXXX where it's so cold, I can't even feel my toes! Worst of all, I miss you like hell. Every time I get depressed, I look at that snapshot you gave me, and I suddenly remember that I'm the luckiest bloke alive. I love you, Nell. If you don't know that by now, then you're just as crazy as I am. I want to marry you. I want us to have a place of our own. I want us to have kids. I want us to have more kids. I want us to have even more kids. Oh, and by the way, I'm not going to put you through the ordeal of being converted (to a Jew!). I think you already know my feelings on that matter. In fact, I've told my mother and father that when you and me get married *(soon!!!)*, we can do it in a registry office, no problems, no worries, no upsetting anyone. I hope you agree? Yes?
  Sorry. Got to go. Please keep away from

490

V-1s, V-2s, anything that Jerry can still send over. Oh, and by the way, keep away from any other bloke, because if you don't, I might commit murder.

I love you, Nell. Oh God, I can't tell you how much I do love you.

Your Toff (Martin to you!) X X X

Although she had only received the letter two days before, Nellie had read it so many times, it was getting Five and Nine make-up all over it. The problem was, how to reply to a letter like that, so full of love and determination? Nellie had sighed to herself many times since she first read it. If only she had Martin's brains and was capable of telling him all the things she wanted to tell him.

With three performances of the panto each day, Nellie was relieved that Monsieur had booked them into a lodgings just behind the theatre. The digs, in a terrace of small cottages, were fairly modest, but at least they were clean and, thankfully, quiet. Nellie particularly loved the breakfasts, which were cooked by the elderly landlady and her husband. She never bothered to ask where they managed to get the fresh farm eggs from, nor what seemed to be an endless supply of bacon, tomatoes, and even baked beans.

When Nellie and Monsieur returned to the cottage after the third house show on the fourth day of what was to be a two-week season, Nellie was surprised to find Monsieur going into the tiny downstairs sitting room instead of straight to his own room, as he usually did. 'Got somefin' ter tell yer, Nell,' he said, kicking off his shoes and flopping down into a comfortable easy chair. Nellie knew something was brewing; she had sensed it ever since opening night a few days before. She curled up on the settee opposite him. 'Wot's wrong, Dad?' she asked.

'Nuffin' wrong,' replied Monsieur. 'In fact, I feel better than I've felt fer a long time. Can see fings straight,' he said, lighting up a Woodbine fag without using the holder. Nellie had noticed that he had stopped smoking his Abdullahs. 'Now I've made me decision, I feel marvellous.'

Nellie was puzzled. 'Decision?'

'I'm callin' it a day, Nell,' he said. 'I'm turnin' it in.'

'Wot d'yer mean?'

'I've 'ad enough treadin' the boards. It's time ter move on.'

'Dad!'

'It's nuffin' ter worry about, Nell,' he insisted. 'Me an' Doris've bin talkin' it over fer a long time. I just feel I've done all I can wiv this act. I don't want ter go on till the customers start peltin' me wiv tomarters or somefink. Every pro knows when it's time ter call it a day. We can't go on ferever.'

'That's not true, Dad!' Upset, Nellie sat up straight on the settee. 'Yer mustn't give up just because they 'aven't given yer full time in the panto.'

Monsieur was shaking his head. 'It's got nuffin' ter do wiv the panto, Nell,' he said.

'I've bin wantin' ter do this fer a long time. I want ter live the rest of me life wiv me family. I want ter be part of 'em. I want them ter be a part of me.' He leaned forward in his chair. 'In a few years' time, Nell, there won't be such a fing as music 'all any more. When the war's over, we'll be on the scrap 'eap, just like anyone who's bin around fer too long.'

Nellie stared at him with incredulity. 'But the 'alls've bin your 'ole life, Dad. Wot're yer goin' ter do wivout 'em?'

'I'm goin' inter partnership with Eddie, my agent. We're goin' ter set up an office down the West End, bookin' acts for revues and clubs, that sorta fing. Believe me, Nell, it's goin' ter be big business.'

Nellie slumped back onto the settee again.

Monsieur could see Nellie's concern, and immediately sought to reassure her. 'Don't you worry about a fing, Nell,' he said eagerly. 'Eddie and me've got big ideas fer you. We reckon we could get you into the new revue at the London 'Ippodrome wiv no trouble at all. They say Vic Oliver's goin' ter do somefin' really big there, and—'

'Dad. I don't want ter be in the feater. Not wivout you. Not wivout the people I care for most. I joined the Great Pierre by accident, remember. If it 'adn't bin fer Ange an' all that, I'd still be sewin' away backstage, just like Ruby taught me.'

'But, Nell,' protested Monsieur, 'you're a natural. The customers love yer. Yer can really go to the top if yer set yer mind to it.'

'I don't want ter go ter the top, Dad,' replied Nellie, taking his hands and holding them. 'I told yer once before, the bright lights ain't fer me. When you've frown yer 'at in, the only fing I want ter do is ter get married ter Martin.'

Monsieur paused a moment, looking deep into Nellie's eyes. 'D'yer mean that, Nell?' he asked. 'D'yer *really* mean it?'

Nellie took a deep breath. 'I've never meant anyfin' so much in me 'ole life.'

'It's a big decision ter take, Nell,' he replied, after another pause. 'Marriage is fer life. Yer 'ave ter work 'ard at it. You're still only young, gel. Yer 'ave ter be sure you're makin' the right decision.'

Nellie had a resolute look on her face. 'I *am* makin' the right decision, Dad. Believe me.'

'It won't be easy 'itchin' up ter someone from a strict religious upbringin'. A lot of me mates 'round the 'alls are Jews, Nell. They don't all take kindly to their kids gettin' mixed up wiv people from uvver religions.'

'Dad,' said Nellie, 'Martin and me ain't marryin' our mums an' dads. We ain't marryin' our diff'rent religions. We're marryin' each uvver. Trust me.'

Monsieur squeezed her hands. 'I trust yer, Nell,' he replied, moved by her candour. 'I trust yer more than anyone else in the 'ole wide world.'

The matinee performance on Friday was a real pig. It had something to do with the kids being too overawed by the occasion. Some of them cried when the pirates threatened Robinson Crusoe, and for some reason or another they just wouldn't join in with the traditional sing-song at the end. It was hard going for most of the cast, and good-natured as she was about the young panto customers, even Renee Houston was so exhausted she was heard to exclaim as she came off stage, 'Aye. Well, I know what I'd like to do with *that* little lot!'

Fortunately, the second house customers were totally different. From the gods to the fauteuils, they filed to their seats laughing and joking, calling excitedly to each other, and staring hard at the front of house curtains as though they couldn't wait for them to open to reveal a whole world of fun, mystery, and magic. Which was exactly what they were about to do.

Backstage in the dressing room that Nellie was sharing with some of the younger chorus girls in the show, the call boy had already called the 'five', which meant that the overture would be starting in five minutes, and that opening performers should be ready to go on stage. Monsieur had nothing to do in the show for twenty-five minutes or so, but Nellie was already togged up in her sailor costume to take part in the opening ensemble number.

The audience was now in its usual high state of excitement and anticipation, and by the time the orchestra had finished playing a medley of popular tunes for the overture, the cast was in position for the opening number.

Exactly on cue, up went the main front curtain to the strains of 'The Fleet's In', to reveal the entire stage filled with pantomime sailors in white uniforms. Within a few moments, Robinson Crusoe, in the person of Renee Houston, came strutting on to the stage in true nautical style. It was a typical star entrance, and the star played it up for all she was worth. As she launched into the song, the whole stage, with its backcloth of a sailing ship, came to life, with singers and dancers, including Nellie, and all the show's supporting artistes, swaying in time to the music. It was a glorious, colourful spectacle, which thrilled the family audience who joined in with the song, waved, and clapped their hands and tapped their feet in time to the music. This second house audience could not have been more different from the dour matinee crowd. Even the leading man, Donald Stewart, who was waiting to go on, told the stage manager that this was the sort of audience that all performers loved playing to.

During the opening number of each show, Renee Houston would stop the music, lean over the footlights, and talk to the children who were nearest the stage. This was the part of the show that Nellie liked best, for the faces of the small children were an absolute picture as they watched Robinson Crusoe actually talking to them. Tonight, the theatre was packed to the rafters, and when the music stopped, Nellie was certain that she could hear every little heart in the theatre pounding with excitement.

'Hello, children!' called Robinson Crusoe to all his young crew out there in the audience. But before there was time for their response, the show came to a dramatic halt as a loud explosion suddenly shook the entire building. There were screams from all parts of the house as scenery came crashing down on to the performers, with the star of the show knocked off balance and thrown heavily into the orchestra pit. In the wings, the leading man was struck hard on the head by a falling beam, and soon everything and everybody was covered in dust and masonry from the collapsing walls round the stage. Nellie was blown off her feet by the force of the explosion, and before she had the chance to recover, the huge sailing ship backcloth came hurtling down on top of her. The orchestra had immediately stopped playing, and the sound of young teenage chorus girls screaming out in terror seemed louder than ever. Meanwhile, the audience, who were so far unhurt, looked on in horrified astonishment as the entire stage area seemed to disintegrate before their very eyes.

Dazed, and covered in dust and plaster, the stage manager struggled on to the stage and grabbed hold of the microphone in a desperate appeal to the audience, 'Keep calm, everyone,' he called. 'Please, keep calm.'

The audience made their way in an orderly retreat to the nearest exits. Cut, bruised, and in a state of shock, Renee Houston was helped back on to the stage, where she immediately joined in the rescue operation. Whilst this was going on, the orchestra's conductor, who had himself been cut by falling debris, raised his baton, and got his musicians to start playing again. The departing audience were astonished to hear music booming out from the orchestra pit, and turned back to applaud and cheer this amazing display of courage.

On stage, there was pandemonium, with everyone searching for friends and fellow artistes buried beneath the rubble.

'Sylve! Where are yer, Sylve?'

'Over here! Please, somebody, over here!'

'Give us a hand, someone!'

'Watch that beam!'

'Get back! Get back!'

The frenzied calls for help were in danger of being overwhelmed by the sound of 'Daisy Belle' belting out from the orchestra pit. Scenery and masonry was still crashing down everywhere, and it seemed as though the whole stage would cave in at any moment.

Adding to all the mayhem, a special effects machine high above the stage started to spray everyone with water. 'Bloody thing!' shouted one of the backstage staff who was desperately trying to remove a steel girder which had pinned one of the chorus girls under a heap of rubble. Then several girls started to scream as sections of one of the upper stage boxes came crashing down. Someone else was yelling out hysterically after a large pane of glass had dropped straight down on to her foot, almost severing it, and one of the stage electricians was struggling to free himself from some lighting equipment which had toppled over, sending huge blue sparks across the mass of smoking cables. Cut and bleeding, Renee Houston finally reached her husband, Donald Stewart, who had been injured by falling timber and masonry and was being helped off stage by the stage manager.

Mercifully, Nellie had missed the worst of the falling debris. All around her, young teenage chorus girls were wandering about, dazed and sobbing, trying to come to terms with the chaos around them. The smell of gunpowder was everywhere, giving the only real clue to the source of the blast.

Struggling through the wreckage backstage, Nellie finally managed to reach the stairs leading up to the dressing rooms, where she found scenes of horror. As most of the lighting system had been demolished, the place was in darkness and she had to pick her way carefully over the debris. There were shouts of panic and confusion everywhere, and by the light of the few available torch beams, Nellie could see that some walls were bulging dangerously, others had simply collapsed, and inside the dressing rooms window frames had been blown out completely, glass shattered, and dressing table mirrors and electric light bulbs fragmented. In her own dressing room, she immediately set about helping some of the stagehands who were using their bare hands to try and free two teenage chorus girls who were trapped under a pile of rubble, screaming their heads off. The young girls' injuries were terrible, including severe cuts and facial injuries. One of them had an eye that was bleeding profusely, and another had lost several front teeth. 'It's all right,' Nellie said, over and over again, trying to comfort and reassure both girls who were sobbing hysterically. 'They'll soon 'ave yer out. It's all right. Just 'old on.' The look of terror on their innocent young faces upset Nellie deeply. It was something she would remember for the rest of her life.

Once the girls had been freed from the rubble, Nellie went off to find her dad. 'Bert Beckwiff!' she yelled at every person who passed her in the dark. 'The Great Pierre! 'Ave yer seen 'im?' There was too much going on all around for anyone to help her very much. She picked her way over the rubble to the dressing room her dad had been sharing with three other performers. When she got there, she was horrified to find that all that was left of the room was a pile of rubble.

'Nellie? Nellie Beckwiff? Is that you?'

Nellie turned with a start to find someone pointing a torch beam directly into her face. 'Yes!' she answered, unable to see who was talking to her. 'Me dad. Wot's 'appened ter me dad?'

''E went back ter the cottage, Nellie,' replied the shadowy figure. ''E said 'e was goin' ter wait there till 'e was due on before the show started.'

Nellie gasped and clenched her hands together in relief. 'Oh, fank God!' she said. 'Fank God!' But as she started to rush off, the shadowy figure called out to her.

'Nellie!'

Nellie stopped and turned. The torch was shining into her face again.

'The cottages, Nellie. The rocket, the V-2. It

came down on the cottages at the back of the theatre. It was a direct hit.'

Nellie had to fight her way through the audience hurrying out of the theatre. Everyone was in a state of shock and seemed too dazed to get out of the way to allow the Civil Defence and other emergency services to get through. The street itself was nothing less than sheer chaos, for hardly a building had escaped the V-2 explosion. Shops, houses, a cinema and various pubs, including Monsieur's favourite, the Black Horse, looked as though they had taken a tremendous hammering. Windows were blown, chimney pots and roofs were down, and customers were wandering about in a daze, blood streaming from face and hand wounds. Nearby, a trolley bus had clearly had a miraculous escape, despite the fact that all its windows had been blown in. Its poles had become detached from the overhead electric cables and were producing dangerous blue flashes as they dangled about perilously. The noise was indescribable, for apart from the constant clanging of fire, police and ambulance bells, every person in the entire street seemed to be shouting in desperation.

For Nellie, the worst part of the nightmare was still to come, for when she finally reached the cottage where she and her dad had been lodging, she found that, like other houses in the same terrace, there was nothing left but a heap of rubble. As the Civil Defence started to move in searchlights to begin rescue operations, Nellie's mind was torn by images of her own escape from Barratts' Orphanage just a few years before. 'Dad!' she yelled at the rubble, her hands tearing through her hair in despair and tears welling up in her eyes. 'Don't do this ter me, Dad! Don't do it!'

The searchlights were turned on and the whole area was immediately transformed into a sea of glaring white. Within seconds, special sniffer dogs arrived and were soon scrambling all over the debris, in a race against time to find survivors.

Nellie stood there, her face still covered in stage make-up but now smeared with dust and soot and blood from a gash on her forehead. Her carefully permed hair was full of small particles of glass and plaster dust, and her white sailor's costume and stockings were grey and torn. For one brief moment as she stood there, with the glare of the searchlights on her agonised face, she felt as though she was back on stage again with her dad, facing those bright lights with the Great Pierre. With tears now streaming down her face, and the noise of the frenzied, desperate rescue operation going on all around her, she slowly started to sing to herself, 'When I Grow Too Old to Dream'. Until finally she sank down on to her knees, covered her face with her hands, and dissolved into tears.

'Nell.'

At first she didn't hear who was talking to her. Then she felt a pair of arms round her shoulders. Her eyes glistening with tears, she slowly looked up. 'Dad!' She leapt to her feet and hugged him. 'Oh Dad!' she sobbed. 'I fawt yer was gone. I fawt yer was gone!'

Monsieur held on to her tightly. 'No, Nell, not me,' he replied, his own voice cracking with emotion. 'They don't call me the Great Pierre fer nuffin', yer know.'

Chapter 29

Nellie was becoming a little worried about her eldest daughter, Vicky. It wasn't that she was a bad girl, far from it. In fact, she often did things that surprised both her mum and her dad, like clearing the table after a meal or taking the dog for a walk, and occasionally helping to bath her newly arrived little sister Esther. The trouble was that Vicky was at a difficult age, when kids sometimes start getting a bit cheeky and independent, like her mum had been at the same age. Nellie and Martin, however, had begun to notice that Vicky, at eleven years old, and the eldest child, was beginning to show some resentment of the way her parents were, in her mind, showing too much attention to the younger members of the family, her brother Abraham, who was four years old, and baby Esther. That was the main reason why Nellie had suggested a day out, for it gave all the family a chance to be together and to show that there were no favourites.

Of course, it helped that Grandma and Grandad Beckwith were with them. After all, a day at the seaside wouldn't be the same without them, especially as the old folk would be able to keep an eye on the kids if Nellie and Martin should want to go off and spend a little time on their own. There was certainly enough room in the car, for now that Martin had a secure job as a senior floor manager at Woolworth's department store in Holloway Road, he had been able to put enough money aside to rent a decent two up, two down semi in a quiet back street up near the Archway. He also had a good enough credit rating to put a down payment on a second-hand Ford Anglia car which Nellie washed and polished so regularly, it was a wonder any of its green paint was left intact.

'I wouldn't mind an 'alf-crown fer every time we've done this journey, eh, gel?' Monsieur said to his wife who was sitting at his side in the back seat, with young Vicky squeezed up by the window and Abraham perched on his grandad's lap.

Madame sighed, then turned and gave him a wistful smile.

'I must say, I was amazed yer wanted ter go ter Soufend again, Dad,' said Nellie from the front seat, cradling little Esther in her arms. 'I fawt yer'd be bored stiff wiv the place by now.'

'Bored stiff?' spluttered Monsieur indignantly. 'Me bored stiff wiv Soufend? Yer got ter be jokin'! Soufend can knock spots off the French Riviera any time!'

'We've 'ad some of our 'appiest days there,

that's fer sure,' said Madame. ''Specially wiv you, Nell. An' Sid—an' our dear young Len.'

Nellie didn't have to see her mum's face to know how she was feeling. Young Lenny's death from secondary TB a couple of years after the war had devastated the whole family. It was a loss that none of them had ever really got over. In her mind's eye, she could see his face before her now, reflected in the windscreen in front of her, so lively, so cheeky, so curious about life, and living. Lenny's death at such a young age was a tragedy. He had so much to live for.

Madame leaned forward slightly so that Nellie could hear her. 'Remember that first outing you ever came wiv us?' she asked. 'We went ter Clacton, that Easter Monday, 'bout forty-two it must've bin.'

Nellie half turned and said over her shoulder, 'Don't be silly, Mum. Course I remember!'

Oh, Nellie remembered all right. She remembered every single day she had ever spent with her family, not only the trips to the seaside. She remembered every Christmas and New Year, the parties with Monsieur and Madame's music hall pals, and the chin-wags with her mum every time they went out shopping down Seven Sisters Road together. She remembered those days when she first met her future mum and dad, when she waited on them at Beales Restaurant, and Monsieur relished the fact that some of the other customers recognised him. And she remembered her brother Sid, oh, long before he got married, then divorced, then married for a second time. What a lot of water had passed under the bridge since those days when she taught him how to box and to stand up for his rights against Alfie Clipper, the school bully. Fifteen years ago! It hardly seemed possible. But most of all, Nellie remembered what it had felt like to be part of a family, a real family, with all its ups and downs, all the bad things as well as the good, the crises, the disagreements, the sulks, the moods, the tensions. On the day God was dishing out luck, she thought to herself, she must have been in His good books.

'Are you sure you want to go via Ilford?'

Martin's voice snapped Nellie out of her thoughts. 'Sorry, love,' she said. 'Wot did yer say?'

'Ilford. We have to turn off at the next junction if you want to stop off there.'

'All right, Dad? Shall we do it?'

'All right wiv me,' replied Monsieur. Even as he said it, he wasn't sure that it was all right. But it was something that had to be done. He knew that.

In fact, both he and Nellie knew that this was their last chance to do something they should have done a long time ago.

Martin drew the car to a halt outside a chemist's shop at the far end of Ilford Broadway. Everything looked very different from how it was during that traumatic time in the last year of the war. A lot more people were around, building was going on everywhere, there was more traffic, and a lot more in the shop windows than there ever was during the war. But this was, after all, 1957, and the world had moved on. Not necessarily for the better, Nellie often thought, with the Russians invading Hungary, and the British and French seizing the Suez Canal. It seemed as though no one had learnt anything from all the horrors of the last war.

Once everyone had got out of the car, Martin retrieved little Esther's pushchair from the car boot and helped Nellie to strap her into it.

'Where's the sea, Grandad?' asked Abraham as he held firmly on to Monsieur's hand.

'Don't be so stupid, Abe!' snapped Vicky. 'Ilford's not by the sea. Everyone knows that!'

Madame was the only one who really understood why her granddaughter was always so spiky towards her kid brother, so she put a reassuring arm round her and walked along with her.

Nellie and Martin moved off first, with Martin pushing little Esther, and Grandma and Grandad following on behind with Vicky and Abraham. 'Are you sure you're going to be able to cope with this?' Martin asked Nellie as they went.

Nellie turned a brief, weak smile towards him and nodded her head. 'I want ter see it just this once before they start pullin' it down,' she said. 'Then I can put it all be'ind me. It's best fer Dad too.'

Martin put his arm round her waist and pushed Esther's chair with one hand. As they slowly wandered along the Broadway, she leaned her head against him, and if it hadn't been for

Esther in her pushchair, passers-by would have taken them for any young lovers. To Nellie, however, her Toff had been so much more than a lover. Ever since the V-2 explosion had nearly killed her and her dad on that cold January evening twelve years before, Martin had been a tower of love and support, not only to her but to the entire Beckwith family. The thought that he might have lost her for ever had been too much for him, and as soon as he was told what had happened, the only thing he wanted was to take Nellie and hold on to her for the rest of his life. That time came on a rainswept morning in August, soon after Martin was demobbed from the RAF and just a month before Nellie's twenty-first birthday, when they got themselves, in her brother Sid's words, 'well and truly hitched' at the registry office at Islington Town Hall. And despite Martin's concerns about his parents' religious objections to the marriage, they and other members of his family turned up in force on the day, and got on like a house on fire with everyone on Nellie's side.

It was only a short stroll to the old Hippodrome, and when they heard the sound of pneumatic drills, they knew they were drawing close. The old music hall, or what was left of it, was due for demolition. Nellie knew it was bound to happen one day, but she still felt a sense of loss and grief that it was actually going to disappear for ever.

The whole family was now standing on the pavement which had at one time been the entrance to the theatre. All they could see now was a mass of fallen, twisted steel girders, the shell of a once beautiful auditorium, and mountains of rubble over what had once been the stage. It was a sad and poignant sight.

'Is *this* a music 'all, Mum?' asked Vicky, who was clearly not going to grow any taller than Nellie had been at her age.

'It was, darlin',' Nellie replied. 'A long time ago.'

'Don't you believe it,' said Monsieur. 'It's still a music 'all. Can't yer 'ear it?'

A blank, quizzical look came over Vicky's face. She was trying to listen really hard. 'I can't 'ear nuffin',' she said.

'It's there,' insisted her grandad, putting his arm round her. 'Listen to 'em, Vicks, listen! People laughin', singin'.' He drew close to her and lowered his voice. 'Now they're tap-dancin'. Can yer 'ear 'em tap-dancin'? An' the band. Can yer 'ear the band?'

Again, the child listened carefully, then shook her head. All she could hear was the sound of building workers with their pneumatic drills.

'Yer 'ave ter listen real 'ard, Vicks,' said Grandad. 'You ask yer mum.'

Nellie exchanged a knowing, affectionate smile with her dad. She didn't have to listen hard, for she could hear everything. She could see it too. In fact, in the middle of all that rubble, the dust, and burning timbers, she could see not only the beautiful old Ilford Hippodrome but every one of those magnificent music halls she had ever been inside. Empires, Hippodromes,

509

Metropolitans, Grands, Alhambras—they were all there. Wood Green, Chiswick, Shepherd's Bush, all those wonderful boards up and down the country, and of course her beloved Finsbury Park Empire. And as she raised her eyes to look up at what had once been the old Hippodrome gods, the sun on her face felt just like a bright spotlight, picking her out on stage. But there were no bright lights for Nellie now, and there never would be again. The only lights she wanted, had ever wanted, were her own family, and all those she would never stop loving—the brightest lights of all.

'Not much point in 'angin' 'round 'ere, eh, Dad?' said Nellie, linking arms with him. 'Bit too noisy fer me.'

It wasn't too noisy for Monsieur. He wasn't aware of the sound of pneumatic drills or falling masonry and steel girders. No. As he and his small family group slowly turned and moved off, the only sound the Great Pierre could hear was that of a girl's pure young voice singing 'When I Grow Too Old to Dream'.

This Large Print Book for the Partially sighted, who cannot read normal print, is published under the auspices of

THE ULVERSCROFT FOUNDATION